Cap'n Jonathon Bourke

& The Tear of the Eclipse

Craig Godfrey

Black Rose Writing | Texas

ISBN: 978-1-68513-228-6
PUBLISHED BY BLACK ROSE WRITING
www.blackrosewriting.com

Printed in the United States of America
Suggested Retail Price (SRP) $22.95

Cap'n Jonathon Bourke is printed in Book Antiqua

*As a planet-friendly publisher, Black Rose Writing does its best to eliminate unnecessary waste to reduce paper usage and energy costs, while never compromising the reading experience. As a result, the final word count vs. page count may not meet common expectations.

For Bourkie
1955 -

Cap'n Jonathon Bourke

& The Tear of the Eclipse

PROLOGUE

The wet season, 1897, Cooktown, Northern Queensland

Five-foot-ten, mid-thirties, athletic and slim, blonde beauty Miss Samoa Plum disembarked the passenger steamer *Cassowary* with five hundred bibles in four trunks. She was in search of her older brother Rennison, whom she had last heard was stationed with Lutheran missionaries on Mist Island in the South Pacific. Arriving in Cooktown, Samoa sought out Tatsuo Gaston, skipper and owner of the *Mystery*, a local pearling lugger. Tatsuo, a few years Samoa's senior and a handsome chap – the result of a liaison between a French woman and a Japanese pearl diver – was short of cash, and accepted Samoa's charter to take her to her brother.

However, an unexpected stopover on Thursday Island in the Torres Strait attracted the wrath of Captain Gerald Rafferty Reynolds of the Royal Navy, stationed at Green Hill Fort. Reynolds had always seen his old adversary Tatsuo as competition for the affections of his fiancée, the most attractive, slightly foolish, twenty-four-year-old Briana Pledge, the daughter of no other than General Christian Pledge, of Her Majesty's Army. Not to mention the fact he suspected Tatsuo was running guns to Pacific Islanders to aid their threat from the German Navy in the area.

For this reason, the *Mystery* had cause to leave Thursday Island rather urgently, after a warning shot was fired across the bow ordering him to return. Tatsuo, Samoa and his crew headed for Mist Island near Malaita two weeks sail away, only to encounter a fierce cyclone, dangerous saltwater crocodiles, a conniving Chinese bêche-de-mer fisher and cannibals in remote Coral Sea islands. Tatsuo had also attracted the attention of a seafaring rival, Captain Bligh, of the pearl lugger *Beacon*, a rogue at the best of the times, and always on the hunt for a quick guinea or German mark.

• • •

At Mist Island they discovered Rennison had moved on. It appeared he wasn't the missionary type after all. But what Rennison had discovered were answers to a twenty-year-old mystery, the loss of the *Coral Moon*, a Chinese junk that sailed from Cooktown with millions of dollars in gold dug from North Queensland goldfields. With taxes owed to the Australian Government the Chinese owners, avoiding the Royal Navy, sailed the junk east via New Guinea and through the Solomon Islands before sailing north-west for Canton. Unfortunately, a cyclone had other plans. The ship was wrecked on Half Moon Reef and disappeared without trace, with all those on board lost.

The *Mystery's* pursuit followed a trail of clues, while they closed in on Rennison's whereabouts, only to find out Rennison was in cahoots with the Germans, and in particular Kapitan Schtumph and Admiral Stosch of the SS *Prinzessin* of the German Imperial Navy, steaming about the Pacific in search of islands to add to Germany's Protectorate.

All the while Captain Gerald Rafferty Reynolds from Green Fort Hill pursued the *Mystery* aboard his Royal Navy gunship HMS *Pride*. This pursuit came to a head at Wakanai Bay, Bougainville, where the Germans were attempting to take possession of the island, only to encounter an army of people under the rule of Maori Chieftain Hatsie Raven, a determined foe.

Rival gunships, HMS *Pride*, under the captaincy of Captain Jonathon Bourke, a no-nonsense old-school sea captain, and the SS *Prinzessin*, finally met and a battle in the bay ensued. The damaged German ship steamed away. The Royal Navy pursued them while Hatsie Raven celebrated her victory, waving farewell to the German ship whilst wearing a souvenired officer's pickelhaube helmet, left behind on the beach when the Germans abandoned the island in haste.

Meanwhile, Samoa's brother Rennison was finally located, abandoned by the Germans for reasons then unknown, on a desolate rock in the middle of the ocean called the Shoal of Ghosts – 7 a terrifying coral reef barely above high tide mark and home to every conceivable nasty in the region, especially large tiger sharks.

With Rennison's reunion with younger sister Samoa, the *Mystery* sailed for Half Moon Reef where a recent tsunami had temporarily uncovered what remained of the lost junk, the *Coral Moon*. Tatsuo wasted no time. The wreck was in relatively shallow water. Wearing a hard hat diving suit, he managed to salvage ninety per cent of the gold, only to be robbed at gunpoint by Captain Bligh on the *Beacon*. Bligh sailed away with the treasure. But his sailing lugger was caught in the doldrums and in turn encountered the SS *Prinzessin*. The Germans, naturally, were only too pleased to relieve Bligh and his crew of the bullion. They sank *Beacon*, allowing Bligh's crew the use of *Beacon's* lifeboat.

Days later Bligh ended up marooned himself, on the Shoal of Ghosts. In his search for the *Beacon*, Tatsuo discovered Bligh on the reef and Bligh, shady as ever, told Tatsuo he would only tell him where the gold was if Tatsuo took him on board the *Mystery*. Against his better judgement, Tatsuo agreed.

Once Tatsuo heard the truth he went in search of the German ship, guessing correctly, that the damaged ship would head for repairs at the nearby Santa Isabel Island, a German Protectorate. Tatsuo put Bligh ashore, effectively making him a prisoner of the Germans, before going in search of the SS *Prinzessin*. But once again things didn't go to plan. Whilst searching the island, they were captured by the Germans. To make matters worse, Rennison showed his true colours. He was lauded by the Germans and lead away, with his furious sister, Samoa, as prisoner. Believing Tatsuo's explanation that he was just a fisherman, the Germans ordered Tatsuo to leave the island immediately.

. . .

A week later Captain Jonathon Bourke, spoiling for a fight and determined to avenge the Germans for firing on his ship in Wakanai Bay, caught up with the repaired *Prinzessin* sailing north, off the Solomon Islands. However, the *Mystery* had also been in the area, planning to follow the German ship and rescue Samoa.

Captain Jonathon Bourke, whose intention was to board the *Prinzessin*, accidentally collided with her stern and HMS *Pride's* bow ram sent the German ship to the seabed along with the bullion. The *Mystery's* crew watched in shock as the German lifeboats ferried survivors to the shore only three kilometres away.

There was no option but to return to Thursday Island. Tatsuo had lost the gold and the woman he had grown so fond of, if not fallen in love with. Sometime during their sail back to Australia, Rennison's bibles, once destined for the missionaries, were to be jettisoned when it was discovered each book was hollowed out and filled with pounds sterling. Against his crew's recommendation, Tatsuo insisted on sailing to Thursday Island before home to Cooktown, in the vain hope Samoa may have made it there. Knowing the Royal Navy would search his vessel, Tatsuo left the cash from the bibles temporarily on Horn Island off Cape York with an old hermit friend, Rambling Jack.

But word leaked out and Rambling Jack was murdered and the cash stolen.

Defeated, angry, the crew of the *Mystery*: Selma the cook, Horace the Aboriginal first mate, William the young deckhand (who suffered from Tourette's and bouts of bad language) and Captain Tatsuo ended up back in Cooktown where the story had begun.

Weeks passed, then Tatsuo happened to hear of the good fortunes of a local bêche-de-mer fisher, a Taiwanese, Benjamin Chen. Convinced Chen had murdered Rambling Jack and stolen the money, Tatsuo crept aboard his boat, only to encounter Chen's disgruntled wife in the process of leaving her drunkard, violent husband. Under duress and herself searching for the cash, she told Tatsuo that Chen was preparing to sail to the Solomons to dive on a German gunboat that sank in shallow water, loaded with gold. The SS *Prinzessin* and Tatsuo's gold, no less.

Chen arrived back early from a drinking session to find Tatsuo and his wife. They fought and in the struggle a lantern was smashed and Chen's boat went up in flames. Chen dived overboard only to be killed by crocodiles.

Once again, all seemed lost, when the passenger steamer *Cassowary* docked once more in Cooktown. To Tatsuo's delight Samoa had finally found him. They reunited at the White Horse Hotel where Samoa explained that her brother Rennison worked for Whitehall and was a double agent. The German's thought he spied for Germany. Tatsuo now told the others that the *Prinzessin* was not in deep water like they initially thought, but as Chen had known, it was in fact in shallow water and accessible. The hundreds of thousands of pounds in gold bullion were in fact, now within their reach, once more.

That was in 1897. Time passed. Rumours became obscure Chinese whispers.

Tatsuo developed an incurable ear infection and would never dive again. Samoa Plum became Mrs Samoa Gaston and the two had four children and eventually nine grandchildren. They lived the comfortable lifestyle that was attainable for most hard-working Australians. There was no outward sign of wealth, or mansion. There was no luxury yacht. Just a timber house on stilts amongst tropical trees overlooking the ocean.

On the other hand …

•　•　•

When Captain Jonathon Bourke heard of the gold stowed aboard the SS *Prinzessin*, the ship that he accidentally rammed and sank, he could never forgive himself. He often dreamt of how rich he might have been. He grew old, retired to Darwin and repeatedly told stories of his adventures to his first born, a handsome young fellow he named after himself – Jonathon Bourke. Jonathon the younger was ten years old at the time of the incident. Jonathon matured and went to sea at fifteen. Seafaring was in his blood. In 1915 he joined the Australian Navy at the age of twenty-eight, saw action in the English Channel, the Dardanelles, and the Mediterranean, returning home in 1919, a wiser and savvy seaman. In 1920 he purchased an eleven-year-old, ninety-foot, fifty-ton steel hull steamship with his inheritance from his old man, renaming her *Drifter*. Two years later he won a small rundown cannery north of Cooktown, in a poker game.

Jonathon Bourke managed to turn business around. The cannery turned a profit, but it was hard work and never enough. It was time to dabble outside the law.

And his old man's stories of lost gold off the Solomon Islands had always been on his mind.

CHAPTER ONE

Hotel Marigold, Papeete, Tahiti Nui 1924

Cap'n Jonathon Bourke woke groggily, his head a fug of sozzled memories. It felt like a squashed crab. But the pounding in his head was nothing compared to the angry pounding on the hotel room door. He sat bolt upright and wished to hell he hadn't. His blood pressure plunged; the room spun. His stomach churned.

A woman's voice lying next to him rasped, 'Mon amour.' She had sounded softer than silk last night.

Last night! Oh Christ!

'Qu'est-ce qui se passe?'

What is happening?

With her rouge blotched, her lipstick smudged, her mascara smeared and any sign of last night's sophistication deserting her, the sailor's lover appeared to have fared worse than him. The forty-something miscreant wife of the French diplomat, Monsieur Felix Du Bellay, certainly had the figure of a leopard with an appetite in the boudoir to match, but right at this moment she looked more like something the cat dragged in. Cap'n Bourke swung his legs over the side of the bed skittling an empty Armagnac bottle.

Armagnac! Jesus, why do I do it?

The fist pounded harder. 'Vignetta! Je sais que tu es là-dedans!'

I know you are in there!

'Your husband?' Bourke twisted about to face the woman. Her terrified eyes, smeared with mascara confirmed the affirmative. 'Jesus!'

'Vignetta!' the male voice shouted. 'Ouvre cette porte.'

The thirty-three-year-old seafaring *Don Juan* stumbled into his britches, hopping one leg to the other.

My belt, my belt! If the cap'n had had time to look, his belt was under the bed. Bourke dived into his shirt and rushed to the window, holding his britches aloft with one hand. He was on the second floor. He would have to jump. On the positive side, there was a vegetable garden below.

'Jon-a-thon, my love,' Vignetta's voice was urgent. 'You promised.'

The pounding grew more desperate. Bourke looked back at the woman. It was agreed in a state of intoxication, jokingly of course, that they would stage an assault scenario. Should they be sprung that is; and they were sprung. The captain hurried back to the bed. He took a deep breath. Sighed. 'Are you certain?'

'Oui … yes … quickly my love.'

'I … I can't.'

'You must.'

'Jesus Vignetta … I … I can't do this …'

'Do it!' she ordered, her voice immediately deep with nervous anger. 'Now!'

'Christ!' With open hand, he struck the woman a decent blow on the cheek.

'Again,' Vignetta hissed.

Christ! The woman's a sadist.

Cap'n Jonathon Bourke, who saw himself as a lover not a fighter, closed his fist, then his eyes. 'I can't do it I tell yer,' he said anxiously.

Vignetta bunched her own knuckles, punching her lover in the cheek. 'Do it,' she taunted through clenched teeth, desperate. Motivated for the wrong reasons, Bourke punched the woman in the eye. Bruising was instant. The red patch around her eye would turn black in no time. Dazed, Madame Vignetta Du Bellay must have been thinking, *not that hard!* She staggered to her frock slung over the back of a chair. But Bourke reached it first; taking the neckline in both hands he ripped the dress almost in half.

There, you've been molested.

A door panel splintered.

'Au revoir my love,' Bourke said in a whisper. He hurried to the window. His unsecured britches slid to his knees. He stumbled, tripped and fell out the window chasing his shoes and hat. The pomegranate tree was rich with ripe fruit. Every large piece plum ripe and red. But the branches broke Bourke's fall. He lay on his back, dazed, staring back up at the open window. He heard voices. Shouting. Vignetta screamed back.

Get it together man, a voice shouted inside his head. With head pounding and bones aching he sat up abruptly for the second time in as many minutes.

Jesus Christ!

His wounds were horrific. Jonathon Bourke looked as though he had been gutted by an apprentice slaughterman. Blood ran down his face, down his arms. His britches were shredded, and his legs smothered in blood. Yet he felt no pain.

Am I dead?

Immediately the lothario saw his torn flesh, shredded from his body, scattered about, dotted with black …

Seeds!

Pomegranate!

'Oh, thank you lord!'

'You!' the heavily accented male voice hollered down at him from the second-floor window. The husband was no other than Monsieur Felix Du Bellay, French Consul, and a large man at that, as in large portion, not stature. He filled the window, eyeballed Bourke, shouted something in French and disappeared. Clearly, the husband was on his way down.

Bourke stood dazed. Looking about he realised he had gathered an audience – passing onlookers congregated for the imminent altercation.

'Captain … Captain Jonathon sir.'

The seafarer heard his name called. Music to his ears.

The Model T Ford braked at the roadside a dozen feet away. 'All aboard Captain sir.' And in case the captain hadn't noticed, the driver squeezed the klaxon.

Loud enough to wake the dead. *Awooga!*

'Arsala!' Captain Bourke's Ghurkha first officer, leant across the car seat. He unhitched the passenger door.

'Golly gosh captain sir. What you do now huh? You been bad mans?'

The front door to the Hotel Marigold crashed open.

And the French diplomat burst onto the street like a raging bull seal. 'Enfoiré! You bas-tard!'

Jonathon Bourke limped to the car. The fat Frenchman waddled after him. The driver tugged at Bourke's shirt, hauling his captain aboard. Arsala increased the throttle, engaged gear, and released the clutch pedal with his prosthetic foot. The Ford pulled away. Bourke looked over his shoulder. The Frenchman was actually gaining. 'Faster man, faster!'

'She's going to go faster sir, god promise.'

As the skipper's luck ran with him this early morning, so did the downhill slope to Papeete's Harbour. The Ford picked up pace. The speedometer oscillated around thirty miles an hour. Too fast for a bull seal.

'Ah, lookee now,' the driver cheered. 'Bastard Frenchman too fat. Yes sir. Too fat for Arsala, yes?'

Bourke looked at his saviour's smiling black face and slapped the man on his back. 'You're a sight for sore eyes.'

'Yes. I know these things.' Arsala had a moment to recognise pomegranate pulp and not the flesh of his revered captain. 'Are you alright captain sir?'

'Fine Arsala,' Bourke said, brushing pomegranate seeds off his arm like they were flies. 'But I fear we will have company at the docks sooner rather than later. Has Bill got the fire stoked?'

'Yes, yes of course. I know you want these things.'

Jonathon Bourke grinned at his first mate, his right-hand man and good friend Arsala Singh, and wondered what he would do without the Ghurkha. 'You're a good man Arsala. A good man indeed.'

'Yes yes. I know this.'

Dockside was a bustle of industry. Although it had been ten years since the German warships SMS *Scharnhorst* and *Gneisenau* had bombarded Papeete back in 1914, many buildings were still in a state of disrepair. Arsala rushed the Ford to the garage where he had rented the vehicle on business the day before, and the two men hurried to the docks.

The ninety-foot, steel-hulled steamship *Drifter* was tied up at the quay. Smoke clouding about the smokestack was whisked away in an early morning easterly. Built in 1913 in Fraserburgh, Scotland, the once commercial fishing vessel maintained a mizzen sail, to help steady the boat when the nets were out, with the modern advantage of a steam capstan for hauling in the loaded nets. Although now-a-days, *Drifter* was more a merchant with a large wheelhouse and comfortable quarters below deck.

· · ·

'Christ skip!' Old Bill the silver tongue stoker had a decent chuckle. 'Where yer been, fighting in a jam factory?'

'Long story. Get steam up.'

'Aye aye cap'n.'

Harry Pickles, the head deckhand met Bourke at the gangway. 'Custom's been sniffin' 'bout.'

Bourke bristled. 'Now what?'

'Said somethin' 'bout a cable from Hawaii and smugglin' grog to the Yankees.'

'Don't they know there's a prohibition on grog in America?'

'That's wha' I told the bloke,' Harry winked. 'But you know what them frogs are like. An' yer can't understand the bastards when they don't speak the King's English.'

Truth be known, the *Drifter* had departed Honolulu post haste a fortnight earlier.

Bourke twisted to Bill. 'How much coal was delivered?'

'Five tons.'

'That'll have to do.' It would be enough to get them some distance up the coast.

'Harry screwed up his face. '*Have* to do?'

'We're leaving.'

'Right away, Cap'n?'

'Yes man, we're leaving, *now!*'

'Ah ... but ...' Harry looked worried.

'But what Harry?'

'Some o' the lads are still at the Minou Rose.' Minou Rose, or the Pink Pussycat, being Papeete's swankiest whorehouse with the prettiest Tahitian beauties on the island. 'With that generous bonus you paid 'em, they treated themselves to some horizontal refreshment.'

'Christ. Harry, get yer arse over there, round 'em up. Quickly now.' Bourke headed for the companionway. 'Whorehouse ... Jesus!' he cursed.

Bill and Arsala watched their captain descend below deck. 'Where'd yer find him anyhow?' Bill asked the Ghurkha.

'Hotel Marigold.'

Bill's face bunched. 'What's he doin' there?'

'I'm thinking, do you remember Frenchmans, Monsieur Du Bellay?'

'Frog ambassador or somethin' ain't he?'

'Important diplomat, yes, yes. Well, the captain, he … um … he spend the night with Madame Du Bellay.'

'Fare dinkum?'

'God's promise.'

'Oh shit.'

'Yes. Me thinking same same. *Oh shit.* Now Frenchmans, he look for captain. He find. He kill, I am thinking, yes?'

.   .   .

Harry tripped through the whorehouse door with the urgency of a womanising sailor twelve months at sea. Deckhand Salty was already in the foyer, pulling on his boots while starting the new day with a cold beer. 'Mornin' Harry,' Salty grinned. The cute doxy sitting on the couch with him scarpered. 'In for a quickie for the road, eh?' Salty was a six foot four, thirty-one-year-old Aussie from Wollongong, given the sobriquet Salty after he saved a mate from a crocodile attack at Cape York several years back by stabbing the eighteen-footer in the eye with his hunting knife. He was also the man you wanted on your side in a bar brawl. A man whose opponents avoided, with his *shoebox* jaw and teeth to bite through a leather saddle.

'Where's the others?' Harry barked. 'We have to leave. It's urgent.'

'Urgent?'

'Yes. Quickly man.'

'Well Hank's in Sasha's room … I think … an' … ah, I last seen Flash with Jeanette …'

'Oh Christ, round 'em up Salty, hurry.'

.   .   .

Seven minutes later Harry Pickles was first up the gangway followed by five deckhands in various stages of dress, or undress depending on how you looked at it. It wasn't a pretty sight. Sponged down and changed, including a pair of britches fastened at the waist with a spare belt, Captain Bourke watched his crew return. He stepped from the wheelhouse where Arsala had positioned himself at the helm, complete with his artificial leg of wood, leather and metal. 'Is that everyone?' Bourke called to Harry.

'Aye. All present and accounted for.'

'Good. Cast off.'

There was a strong current Arsala telegraphed the engine room, *slow ahead*. The twin cylinder Sunderland steam engine coughed into life. Dark coal-fired smoke clouded from the funnel and *Drifter* steamed out of Nanuu Bay, between the reefs and into the deeper waters of the South Pacific.

'Where to captain sir?' Arsala asked.

'Hitiaa O Te Ra.'

Arsala pointed the bow north-east where he knew they would find a coaling station a few hours distance along the coast at the small village. Immediately activity on the docks drew their attention.

'Oh … lookee captain sir,' Arsala said. Although they were now some distance offshore Captain Bourke recognised diplomatic vehicles and the gendarmes assembling where *Drifter* had been berthed. Standing, ranting and waving his arms like a madman, Monsieur Du Bellay led the fray in an impressive display of anger. Bourke focussed his binoculars. Du Bellay filled the lens like a balloon on chopsticks with a tiny round, fat face. He snatched the pistol from a gendarme's holster and managed to fire three shots into the air before the firearm was wrestled from him.

Arsala looked on philosophically. 'One angry mans, isn't it?'

Bourke replaced the binoculars and studied the horizon. They weren't out of the woods yet, as his father would have said, and they desperately needed coal to return west across the vast

Pacific to reach home in North Queensland. And if that angry frog asked around, he would discover *Drifter's* dilemma and could drive overland to Hitiaa O Te Ra to rendezvous with him. But, everything considered, it had been a successful night.

Madame Du Bellay, Bourke grinned through the wheelhouse window at the shrinking docks. *The little frog minx.*

· · ·

No man on the high seas looked more Caucasian than Jonathon Bourke. Born back in '87 the six-foot-two, ruggedly handsome thirty-seven-year-old, was bred from toughened seafaring stock. He had a pencil-thin moustache in the style of new Hollywood heart throb Clark Gable, while his chiselled jaw was clean shaven. His shoulder length hair, pulled back in a ponytail, exposed his high forehead and dark striking eyes. Rarely seen without his leather flying jacket – a gift from a British airman whose life he saved in the English Channel in 1917 – and his denim jeans, Bourke walked with a confident gait, turning heads wherever he travelled. And he was blessed with the gift of the gab, especially around women, as men close to him noted with envy.

Bourke's father, born at sea near Singapore on their voyage out from England to Sydney in 1839, had joined the Royal Navy in the '50s and was a midshipman at the Siege of Sevastopol in '54. Wounded by a rogue bullet, he grew a moustache the size of a fat slug to hide the scar on his left cheek. His wife Clarabelle, mother of his eleven children hated *the slug*. But as the old seadog was at sea most of his life she had little say in the matter. Captain Jonathon Bourke Senior – yes, he named his youngest son Jonathon – skippered HMS *Pride* – a Royal Navy gunboat – for many years in the 1890s, retired in Darwin and passed away at the ripe old age of eighty-one in 1910.

So, the sea truly ran through the veins of his son, Cap'n Jonathon Bourke.

. . .

An hour later Cap'n Bourke took up his cook's offer of breakfast, realising just how hungry he was. *Drifter's* cook, Penang, born Juvita binti Musa was raised in Malaya's north-west. Juvita was a middle-aged Oriental beauty, with exotic dark-chocolate eyes and smooth skin the colour of coconut husk. The cook kept herself in good shape. Working in a galley day in day out with fire, she wore tight fitting, Teluk Belanga style clothing; no collar with a sarong wrap-around and occasionally, outside the galley, she wore a shawl. Juvita placed a breakfast bowl on the table in front of Bourke, sitting in the crew mess. Fragrant rice with coconut milk, fried anchovies, spicy shrimp paste, peanuts and a boiled egg.

Jonathon looked at his breakfast and wondered how his groaning belly would handle such a breakfast with his hangover.

'Juvita.'

'Yes captain?'

'That painting.' Bourke pointed to a rather interesting rectangular painting, thirty inches by eighteen hanging on the far wall of the crew saloon. It hung next to the captains' precious books, shelved behind a thin rail so as not to dislodge in bad weather. The painting was of a small-breasted, large-bottomed native woman, bathing naked under a waterfall. Clearly, she was Tahitian. 'Where did that come from? It wasn't there yesterday.'

'Flash stole from whorehouse,' Juvita said in her sultry voice.

'From the Minou Rose?'

Juvita grunted a nod.

The captain took a closer look. *'Woman bathing,'* he read out loud. *'Paul Gauguin. 1891.* I wonder who he was, some local artist I guess.'

'You like?'

'Not really, she's got a big backside and looks a bit lumpy.'

'Hmm.' Juvita tried to look reflective. 'Flash like picture.'

'I'm sure he does. Gauguin huh, I trust he did this as a leisurely pursuit only. I doubt if he sold any.'

·   ·   ·

Arsala Singh and Juvita binti Musa.

Breakfast restored a semblance of good health and Bourke joined Arsala standing at the helm in the wheelhouse where he checked the compass heading. 'How long 'til Hitiaa O Te Ra do yer reckon?' he asked Arsala.

'Six hours I am thinking captain sir.'

'Okay … sounds good.' Bourke looked at his right-hand man. Today he had certainly acted above his duty. 'Thanks for this morning,' he said, and meant it.

'Was lucky, I am thinking, I still have automobile at my service to come pick you up,' Arsala said. Bourke agreed. Arsala looked at his skipper a moment before speaking his mind, something he always did and something that Jonathon Bourke respected from the older man. 'Tell me captain sir, why you not take whore like the other mans?'

Bourke grinned. The familiar salacious grin of an addicted ladies' man.

Arsala studied Bourke's face. 'God's promise. I know this answer,' Arsala tutted.

Bourke changed the subject. 'How's the leg this morning?'

'All good captain sir, I can't feel a thing,' he laughed, slapping his prosthetic limb. 'But thanking you for asking.'

Arsala Singh may have only been five foot seven, but the nuggetty Ghurkha had the strength of four soldiers. Arsala was with the 6th Battalion Ghurkhas who landed at Cape Helles at Gallipoli in 1915. He went on to fight in France. Came home unscathed. After the war he was wounded back in India at the Jallianwallah Bagh massacre in April 1919. The Jallianwallah Bagh massacre, Arsala explained to Bourke, occurred when the British Government passed the Rowlatt Act, giving the Indian Viceroy power to quell sedition by censoring the press. Arsala was wounded, shot in the leg, which he lost to amputation due to gangrene. Arsala escaped to Australia, ending up in Cooktown where he met Bourke in the White Horse Hotel. At the time Bourke was hiring crew for his recently purchased steamer, *Drifter*. With some training from the captain, it was discovered Arsala was a natural at the helm.

'You've got the navigation skills of a shearwater,' Bourke had told him. That had been two years ago now, and the two men had become good mates.

And as for Arsala's amputated limb, Arsala told anyone who asked that he lost his leg to

Turkish artillery fighting with Lawrence of Arabia in Palestine in 1918.

Arsala had been immediately attracted to Juvita the cook, bonded by their faith, Hinduism. Juvita was several years the Ghurkha's senior, but he was enamoured by her stories of descending from Malayan royal blood line, apparently. Juvita liked to tell new acquaintances she was a distant princess of the Perak monarchy.

However, Bourke knew better. Juvita was raised in a palace, yes, but truth be known she was found as an abandoned baby by palace servants and raised in the palace kitchens. Bourke first met Juvita in Papeete, Tahiti, where she had married a Tahitian French businessman. But their marriage failed, and she worked as a cook in a wealthy household. Wanting to return to Malaya she offered to work her passage on *Drifter*. But she enjoyed the company so much she changed her mind and stayed on as crew. That was also two years ago and, Malay princess or not, she shared Arsala's cabin.

• • •

'I hope French womans was worth it,' Arsala said to Bourke sagely, gazing for'd out the bridge window.

'Who?'

'You know of who I speak, captain.'

'Madame Du Bellay?'

'Yes! Madame Du Bellay.'

Captain Bourke smiled knowingly. 'As you all know, I have told you before, my old man was captain of the Royal Navy's HMS *Pride* out of Thursday Island.'

'Yes, yes. You tell me this things before. He in Royal Navy?'

'Well not exactly. He captained the ship on several occasions because he knew the Coral Seas like the back of his hand. But he was a civilian captain, a rarity, but for the British, a necessity.'

'He was captain when *Pride* ram German warship you say to me once.'

'Yes … the SS *Prinzessin*.'

'Yes.'

'But *Prinzessin* was built as a 120 cabin passenger steamer originally, but later converted into a gunboat to service the German Protectorates in the Coral Sea. My old man said she was a magnificent ship with her tall slim funnels amidships, rounded stern and richly decorated clipper bow featuring a figure head of a German princess.'

'*Prinzessin* … German's meanings Princess, yes?'

'Exactly.'

'So,' Arsala asked, looking suitably matter of fact, 'what does thees things have to do with the price of bacon?'

'Price of eggs you mean.'

The Ghurkha frowned. 'Don't eat my head. I say bacon, you say eggs.'

'Alright then, bacon.'

Arsala smiled at his small victory.

'Well, I'm glad you asked that question Arsala,' Bourke said, 'because when the crew were chasing women at the Pink Pussycat ...'

Harry Pickles opened the bridge door, catching the tail of the conversation. 'It's the *Minou Rose* cap'n,' he said with a straight face. 'Sounds more eloquent don't you agree?'

'The Minou Rose then,' Bourke conceded, and was about to elaborate on the virtues of whoring when Juvita joined them.

'Juvita, I'm glad you have joined us, because I have a proposition for you all.'

'Proposition?' Harry frowned, wary of his captain's mad schemes.

'Yes. When you were all preoccupied, at the Minou Rose, I was studying another problem.'

'Studying French Captain?' Harry grinned.

'Cheeky sod. No. I happened upon a Madame Vignette Du Bellay, the wife of Monsieur Du Bellay, a diplomat ...'

Arsala shook his head. 'We know these things.'

'Let me finish. We got talking, me and Madame Du Bellay, and I happened to mention my father, Captain Jonathon Bourke was with the Royal Navy back in the '90s and she said, *You mean your father was the infamous sea captain that attacked and sank that German gunboat in the Coral Seas in 1897? Yes*, says I. *The very same man.* And she says, *It caused some difficult diplomacy for the British, so I heard. How did you know about this?* I asked. *Well, my husband was only talking about it recently*, she says. *You see we were at a dinner at the consulate in Noumea in New Caledonia, about a month ago*, she told me, *and the dinner conversation got around to Germans in the Pacific and how they had fallen from grace since the war. Then the* Prinzessin *was mentioned, and its sinking at the hand of the British and the rumours of gold lost with the ship, supposedly in shallow waters. Gold? The men at the table asked. Yes,* the consul said. *The* Prinzessin *had a ton of gold bullion on board, so they said. Then he says, quite out of the blue, we have a German prisoner on the Isle of Pines here, who was on that ship when it sank. He knows exactly where, and he said the hull was damaged right where the gold was stored. Really?* says I. *Did you perchance hear his name? Yes,* says she. *I remember because it was unusual, Herr Kohl, which is the German word for cabbage by the way. Mr Cabbage, she giggled.'* Bourke looked at his audience on the bridge. 'And what a cute giggle it was, too, I must say.'

'Where this Isle of Pines,' Juvita asked.

'It's a small island south-east, off the coast of New Caledonia. It's a penal colony, a prison for French criminals, mainly political.'

'So why is Herr Cabbage imprisoned there?' Harry Pickles asked.

'I asked Madame Du Bellay and she told me he was captured with other German sailors after the grounding of the *Emden* in 1915.'

'*Emden*?' Arsala's eyes widened. 'The SMS *Emden* destroyed by HMAS *Sydney*?'

'That's the one.'

'I know this … this Australian Navy proudest adventure, isn't it?' Arsala beamed.

'Sure was.'

Juvita looked puzzled.

Bourke explained. 'The *Emden* was causing mayhem in the Indian Ocean during the war and the Aussie ship hunted her down and completely destroyed the German warship.'

'An' Herr Cabbage was one of the prisoners taken, eh?' Harry said.

'Well yes … and no.'

'Pardon?'

'Well, he wasn't taken prisoner by the Australians. You see thirteen survivors managed to evade being captured during that night and escaped in a lifeboat where they commandeered a schooner off Coco Islands. They were picked up by a French ship in the Timor Sea a week later, headed to Java we think, and the French took them as prisoners and sailed to New Caledonia where Herr Cabbage, that is Herr Kohl, remains to this day.'

'So, why's this Herr Cabbage still there?' Harry wanted to know.

'Glad you asked, Harry,' Bourke said. 'Somehow, Monsieur Du Bellay got wind of the fact Herr Kohl was on board the *Prinzessin* when she sank back in '98. Kohl was twenty at the time. Then, apparently Kohl told other prisoners at Isle of Pines his story that he knew the location of the German ship. It seemed he wanted to use it as a bargaining chip to escape. So, when the war ended six years ago the other Germans were allowed to return to Germany, but Herr Kohl has been held on other charges. Madame Du Bellay didn't know what charges or wouldn't say, but she hinted that he is being interrogated by the frog gaolers, keen on finding the gold.'

'For six years?'

'Aye, but he's a stubborn bastard apparently and remains silent.'

'How do we know this gold isn't just another wild rumour?'

'Because my old man talked about the missing gold a lot before he passed,' Bourke said. 'He even drew a sketch of one of the ingots, stamped with Chinese writing. Yes my friends, it's real alright. He was there, remember.'

'So,' Arsala asked, 'why you telling us this things captain sir?'

'I'm suggesting we go looking for it.'

'Alright.' Harry looked particularly philosophical. He turned to Arsala and Juvita for support. 'Clearly you have a plan cap'n, I think.'

Bourke grinned, and they had all seen that face before.

'So,' Harry persisted, 'what are you suggesting cap'n?'

'As this prisoner is possibly the only man alive who knows where the wreck lies, we sail to New Caledonia and break the poor devil out of prison, that's what we do. I swear, he will be desperate to be free and there's plenty of gold for everyone.'

'And how, may I ask, do you plan to break the man out of a French prison?' Harry said.

'Not certain,' Bourke had that contemplative look that often bothered his crew. 'But I'm working on it.' He shot Harry a wink.

Harry smiled. If the cap'n said he was working on it, then, the cap'n *was* working on it.

Bourke had a lot of respect for Harry Pickles who had been a devoted friend for five years now. At fifty-two he was his oldest crew member for starters. So back in 1915 he was old for a soldier on the Western Front, at forty-three, fighting Germans, surviving horrific battles along the River Somme. Nowadays Harry hated Germans and loved guns.

•   •   •

Six hours later.

Hitiaa O Te Ra was a small fishing village on the north coast of Tahiti with a coaling station for passing steamers.

If the French diplomat Monsieur Du Bellay hadn't sought information on *Drifter's* destination, the Tahitian Customs had. Monsieur Pierre Aubert watched the Australian fishing steamer dock, with an element of anticipation.

Bourke watched the man approach *Drifter*. He wore white jodhpurs tucked into long black boots, khaki safari suit, pith helmet and carried a switch as if he was an army colonel in the foreign legion.

Harry Pickles fed out the gangway and Aubert strutted aboard with two minions at his heels.

'Can I help yer mate?' Pickles stood firm, blocking the man's path.

'I wish to see the Cap-itan, oui,' the Frenchman demanded in good English. 'Bourke, I believe ees his name,'

'Well, have yer got an appointment?'

Bourke stepped from the wheelhouse. 'It's alright Harry.' The captain looked to the Frenchman. 'I'm guessing you are customs?'

'Yes. You are Cap-itan Bourke, oui?'

'Oui …ah, yes.'

'I am Monsieur Aubert. I have driven here from Papeete. I wish to see your ship log and your inventory.'

'Sure mate, come to my cabin.' Bourke had a thought. 'Ah, Monsieur Aubert.'

'Oui.'

'We need to fill our bunkers with coal.'

'Very well. Tell your men to go ahead.'

Bourke turned to Bill Brown the fireman. 'Get to it Bill.' He turned his back to the Frenchman and said quietly, 'And tell the store clerk there's an extra hundred francs in it for him and ten each for his lumpers if they pull their finger out, savvy.'

'Savvy.'

But Bill knew even with the gratuity and co-operation of the coal lumpers – the shovelers, winch drivers, plank men and trimmers – it would take most of the afternoon.

Monsieur Pierre Aubert proved to be an officious little public servant with an appetite for authority above his station. With the two accompanying officers ordered to keep an eye on the crew, Bourke entertained the thought that the man was possibly angling towards accepting a bribe, being alone with him in his stern cabin.

'Your papers Cap-itan Bourke, if you please.'

'Call me Jonathon,' Jonathon said passing a deeds tin from a cabin cupboard containing all his legal paperwork. 'We're all friends here, are we not?'

Aubert avoided the last comment, scratched about in the tin and spread the inventory onto the table first. He studied the paperwork in detail. 'Hmm … tell me Cap-itan, why were you delivering sixty thousand cans of mullet to Honolulu.'

'Well as you must well know, monsieur, I have my own cannery back in Australia.'

'Well yes, but why do you travel all the way to Hawaii to make a personal delivery?'

'To cut out the middleman of course.'

'What is this middleman?'

'The bloke in the middle. The merchant that pays me bugger all and sells at a high profit. I decided to make the delivery myself. The Yanks are busting to get my mullet, it's a bloody top product. Tell yer what, I've got a spare carton you can take with yer if yer like. Assuming you like tinned mullet.'

'That won't be necessary.'

'No, I insist.'

'Why did you travel south to Tahiti, instead of sailing to, say Suva on your journey back to Australia?'

'You will see bills of sale from Papeete for ten tons of copra and five hundred pounds of dried vanilla bean. All fine products of this island.'

'I see. What will you do with this vanilla?'

'I will extract and bottle the essence back at my cannery. Vanilla is plentiful here and therefore cheaper than most places.' Jonathon didn't mention the ten dozen black pearls he was buying on the black market. Contraband he had laid out a deposit for in Papeete and to be collected, here in Hitiaa O Te Ra, for which there was no paper trail. 'Then there are the beautiful women here monsieur,' Bourke winked at the Frenchman. 'I'm certain you have noticed. And like Captain Bligh's crew all those years ago, my men needed R&R.'

'R&R?'

'Rest and Recreation. They've been working hard you must understand.'

'Hmm,' the Frenchman stroked his moustache, firstly pinching the right side between forefinger and thumb, securing its waxed configuration like the tine of a carving fork, before coiffuring the other. 'There is one more thing. Our authority in Papeete, customs that is, had a request from our counterparts in Honolulu. They were concerned that you sold alcohol, that it was unloaded during the night.'

'In Honolulu?'

'Oui.'

'Now why would I do that?' Bourke feigned shock. 'There's a prohibition against alcohol in America. Why would I do something as stupid as that?'

'It is true, I do not understand these Americans and their prohibition. But I am under orders to search your hold for traces of any contraband.'

'Fill yer boots mate. I'll lead the way.'

●　　●　　●

The self-important official took his time. He and his two minions searched the hold and crew quarters, comparing the manifest with the cargo. They found no discrepancies. Captain Bourke was as meticulous in that department as the customs officials. From the wheelhouse Bourke and Arsala shared a quiet chuckle watching Monsieur Aubert's attempt to wipe coal dust from his white jodhpurs, only to make the smears worse. Fireman Bill had encouraged the coal shovelers not to hold back when customs were in the coal hold. The ensuing black dust was attracted to white cotton, like seamen to a whorehouse. Eventually Monsieur Aubert packed his carton of mullet into a travelling trunk fixed to the rear of the government's 1915 Alva automobile and chugged off back in the direction of Papeete.

'We should get a favourable report,' Bourke said.

'God promise captain sir, that we should. Now move along captain sir,' Arsala told his captain. 'Let us get the hell out of this place.'

'Certainty. Prepare to cast off by all means my friend,' Bourke said. 'But give me fifteen minutes, I have one last job before we leave Tahiti.'

Arsala looked immediately bothered. 'Where you travel to now captain sir?'

'To see a man about a dog.'

'What you say? See man about dog? You have dog?'

'It's just a saying Arsala.'

'Saying?'

'Like *get the show on the road.*' Clearly Arsala struggled to make the connection. He pulled one of his disturbed faces. 'Just keep the fires burning,' Bourke ordered. 'I'll be back in a jiffy.'

Arsala watched his captain hurry down the wobbling gangway and cross the dock into the village when Harry joined him in the wheelhouse. 'What's happenin'?' the chief deckhand asked Arsala.

'He see man 'bout dog.'

Harry Pickle knew instinctively their skipper was up to something. 'Did 'e now. I better keep an eye on 'im then.'

'I am thinking also. Good thinking Harry.'

Moments later Harry Pickle and two deckhands, Salty and Flash, hurried ashore. Salty was always good for a scrap. Flash was a short, dark and handsome Irishman from Melbourne who earned his nick-name from his mates because he was a snappy dresser, on shore leave that is. He loved nothing more than the chance to dress up for a night in a jazz club, wearing his one and only black open front jacket with its cream trim lapels, gold waistcoat, white shirt, and gold bow tie. From straw hat to white spats, Flash represented the complete gentleman, preferring the verbal approach to a situation rather than bare knuckles, and being of Irish descent, he could talk his way out of most altercations. His favourite saying being, *I'll bury the bastards in an avalanche of bullshit.*

$$\bullet \quad \bullet \quad \bullet$$

Monsieur Felix Du Bellay

'Excusé moi monsieur … ah …,' Bourke asked the wiry old fisherman mending nets on a tropical beach under a coconut palm. He looked like the cliché photographic postcard. 'Benjamin Chevrolet … ah … Où vit-il?'

The old man pointed to a cluster of grass huts on an embankment well above the high tide mark, amongst a copse of coconut palms. Although Bourke's French was limited, he recognised the word rouge, and sure enough there was one hut standing out with a red sailcloth hanging over the entrance. 'Merci.'

Bourke stepped onto a shallow *porch*, rapping his knuckles on the cane door frame. He called out. 'Benjamin. Benjamin, it's Jonathon Bourke. Are you there?'

No answer. But Bourke sensed someone inside. The wife maybe, afraid to reveal herself. After all Benjamin Chevrolet dealt in the black market, avoiding taxes to the French authority. One could never be too careful. Bourke looked over his shoulder, back towards *Drifter* two hundred yards away. Fresh smoke was escaping from the funnel. Time was paramount. 'Benjamin … Monsieur Chevrolet … es tu là? Are you there monsieur?'

Silence.

'Monsieur?'

Finally. 'Entrez.'

Lanky Bourke was forced to bow low to enter. Inside was dark, making the interior even more difficult to distinguish, after stepping into the shadows from the bright tropical sun. At first Bourke thought he was hearing things. There was no sign of the owner. He took in his surroundings. The bamboo framed hut was thatched with palm leaves, the floor was compacted dirt. Lingering smoke filled the air from a cooking fire smouldering in a central hearth where the smoke lazily spiralled clear through an opening in the roof. An iron pot camp oven was pulled to one side of the coals, where Bourke thought he could smell something like damper. Strips of pig meat preserved in the smoke, hung on long twine, and fishing equipment hung from the walls. Children had left the roost years ago, so bedding now was just the two hammocks hanging to one side.

Stored beneath the hammocks were crates that once held European products, now packed with jars of pickles, preserves, spices, herbs and oils.

'Monsieur Chevrolet … Benjamin … hello …'

'Jonathon,' the occupant's voice sounded anxious. Chevrolet stepped into his hut from a low rear exit, also slung with a red coloured sail cloth. 'I … I thought maybe … you forget me captain,' the older Tahitian said. The man's face was lost in darkness, silhouetted against what little light penetrated the hut. He shifted nervously foot to foot. He was alone and looked uncomfortable. The curtain hadn't closed fully, and Bourke caught a glimpse of the wife outside. It appeared they had company.

'Well, have you got the pearls?' Bourke asked. He was growing impatient. Benjamin Chevrolet looked forlorn, lost for words. He floundered, stalling to answer.

'Monsieur Chevrolet, I haven't much time, do you have my …'

Instantly Monsieur Du Bellay squeezed through the opening. He shoved Chevrolet aside, who instantly scarpered.

'Well, well, well. Monsieur Bourke.' The fat man was short of breath. 'You were easier to catch than I expected.'

Catch?

Jonathon didn't wait for confrontation. He spun on his heels diving through the main entrance and into the firing line of a gendarme. The policeman raised pistol aimed directly at Bourke's face. He was inches away. Du Bellay doddered after him out onto the front porch.

'Such theatrics Monsieur Bourke,' he wheezed. 'Do you fancy yourself as a swashbuckler?'

'What do you want Bellay?' Bourke said sourly.

'I want you monsieur. And now I have you.'

'Well, I'm sorry matey, but I'm not available.'

'You think you are funny, Bourke. But you are really pathetic.' Du Bellay dropped the smile. He scowled. 'Arrest him.'

'What?'

'You are under arrest for the …' Du Bellay's voice became theatrically emotional, 'for the assault of Madame Du Bellay in Papeete this morning.' He was not a great actor.

'Arrest!'

'Yes. You are under arrest.'

The policeman waved the pistol inches from Bourke's forehead. 'Les mains en l'air!'

'He said put your hands in the air.'

Bourke read enough body language to grasp the situation. 'Tell your guard dog to go easy with that gun will yer.' Bourke raised his hands slowly. The gendarme shouted something, spittle hitting Bourke's face. 'Alright, alright, go easy tiger.'

The policeman unclipped handcuffs from his belt, reaching for Bourke with his free hand.

Harry Pickle appeared behind the gendarme. 'I don't think so matey.' He poked the point of his seaman's knife into the nape of the lawman's neck. The Frenchman's eyes widened. Du Bellay stepped backwards. Immediately Salty and Flash also appeared. They covered Harry from both sides. Salty armed with his own blade, Flash wielding a lead-weighted cosh. Both spoiled for a fight. If there was anything that rocked their boat, it was an arrogant frog, and a fat one at that.

'You okay cap'n,' Harry asked.

'Never been better,'

Bourke's audacious confidence returned. He managed a smile. 'What were you saying Monsieur Du Bellay?'

Harry Pickle pressed the point of his blade into the gendarme that little bit harder. His intention was clear. 'Drop – the – pistol.' The policeman hesitated.

'You heard the man,' Bourke said. 'Drop the gun.'

The policeman allowed his pistol to swing by its trigger guard. The muzzle aimed loosely towards the ground. He eyed Bourke a moment, holding his gaze with angry disdain. Bourke reached out, about to disarm the man when …

Another four gendarmes appeared. They were surrounded, each man armed with a La Belle rifle with fixed bayonet.

'Shit!'

Monsieur Du Bellay smiled weakly. 'Yes. Merde! And you, monsieur, are in it up to your neck. Drop your weapon,' Du Bellay ordered Harry. Harry looked at the cap'n. Bourke pinched his lips, breathing out his nose. They were defeated. Harry let his knife fall. Du Bellay wasn't in the mood for shenanigans or gentleman rivalry. *Drifter's* three crew were forced back at gunpoint.

'Arrest this man,' Du Bellay ordered. He stabbed a chubby digit at Bourke. The police pounced. Bourke was immediately secured in ankle irons, fastened by chain to a waist strap and his wrists locked in handcuffs. Cap'n Jonathon Bourke felt his misdeeds flash before him.

Salty started forward, fists balled, white knuckled. But it was a foolish decision. He was felled by a blow to the back of his head from a rifle butt. The most senior of the French police asked the diplomat of his plans for the *Drifter* deckhands. 'Et les marins, monsieur?'

Monsieur Du Bellay stepped up to the shackled Bourke staring him face to face now that he was restrained. His breath pungent from digested garlic. 'You think you are so smart don't you. You don't know half of it. You have messed with the wrong man, Capitaine Jonathon Bourke.'

'You been eating snails?' Bourke said. Harry, Salty and Flash laughed out loud. Du Bellay pounded Bourke in the stomach. The blow was unexpected. Winded, Bourke dropped to his knees. Du Bellay added insult to injury by kicking his prisoner in the side while he was down. Harry Pickle and Flash leapt forward, taking an arm each, they lifted their captain to his feet. 'You bastard,' Harry spat. 'Hit a man in chains. Coward!'

The French diplomat wanted retribution from Bourke only. 'It is this man who is arrested,' Du Bellay said to Harry. He allowed a moment pause. 'So, unless you and your comrades are looking for a fight with the French authorities, I suggest you return to your ship, immediately.'

Du Bellay stepped to within inches of Bourke's face once more. 'Your ship is seized, and your cargo impounded. And I will deal with your crew in good time. Now ...' Bellay was savouring his victory. 'Get this scum out of my face.'

Cap'n Jonathon Bourke was defeated and deflated. He watched as two gendarmes paraded his three crewmen back to the *Drifter*, and his heart sank.

Shackled, Bourke was marched to a prison van, now parked in the village, where he was forced into the back like a trussed boar. For the first time in his thirty three years Bourke thought maybe, just maybe, he had gone too far with Madame Vignetta Du Bellay.

• • •

Arsala, Juvita and Bill Brown the fireman watched their captain's fate unfold from the bridge. They were devastated. Helpless, they watched the police van trundle out of the village and head slowly up the steep dirt track leading into the mountains for the cross-country trip back to Papeete. Harry, Flash and Salty were led back to the ship at gunpoint, where they were allowed to join the others on the bridge. Salty nursed a lump on the back of his head for his trouble. All were cursing.

At the gangway four assigned gendarmes gathered, looking rather confused. However, their orders were to maintain *boat arrest* for the crew and await further orders.

Arsala paced the bridge, angry. 'I tell him true, stupid bastard Casanova. I tell him over and over and over. Woman's, I say, will be the death of you Captain Bourke sir.'

'What the bloody hell are we gonna do?' Bill said.

'What can we do?' Flash glared down at the guards, gripping the rail like he was ringing necks. 'Nothing.'

'That Du Bellay bloke,' Harry said, 'is talking about confiscating the cargo.'

'That must not happen,' Juvita's eyes narrowed. She watched the guards light cigarettes. They seemed uncomfortable with the situation, which set her mind to work.

'There is more to this I am thinking,' Arsala said. 'You do not imprison a man, take him away by armed guard just for infidelity.'

'You do if yer a powerful public servant, and it's *your* wife he was infid … infi … infidel … ah, shit, fiddlin' with,' Flash said.

Harry stared after the police van half a mile distant. It disappeared behind trees high up the slope. 'Well, cap'n, I hope she was worth it.' He massaged his forehead.

Juvita turned to Arsala. 'If you want me, I'll be in the galley.'

Harry Pickles faced Arsala. 'Any ideas?'

'I am thinking goddam it,' the Ghurkha ground his teeth.

'Because we can't 'elp the captain if they take *Drifter* too,' Harry added.

'Cap'n Bourke sir, always say, Arsala, he say, Arsala you are first mate. If anything go arse up, or if I get very very sick, then it is you Arsala who is skipper.'

'I know that Arsala,' Harry agreed. 'An' the lads know it. You take the helm mate. But I'll organise the lads, right.' Secretly Arsala was pleased with this arrangement. The crew needed someone like digger Harry. Harry stepped onto the bridge wing staring down at the guards who looked away smartly. 'We just need a damned plan.' He spat over the side. 'Thart's all.'

CHAPTER TWO

Some time prior to the above events. Pacific Ocean. December 1922
The shipbuilder's brass plaque riveted to the funnel of the freight steamer read:

Caledonia
J.C. Higgins – Maine - 1897

Mountainous waves built their momentum and the 2456-ton tramp steamer en route to California rolled like a well-fed hog in mud. The sea boiled. In the cargo hold – crammed with merino wool, hides and copper – restraints were tested as the tired old steamer dipped and twisted. Seventy-three-year-old Captain Thomas Cosgrove and his twelve-man crew looked forward to the return voyage, bringing back motor cars, radios, telephones, and household appliances such as electric kettles. It was supposed to be a prosperous round trip. But destiny had other plans.

Ship's cook Arthur J Money watched the storm loom on the horizon and muttered a silent prayer. It looked bad. Really bad. Sheet lightning strobed the horizon. And as if being in the middle of the vast Pacific Ocean during a violent storm wasn't bad luck enough, night approached. Arthur felt his guts knot.

Blackness swamped the *Caledonia*. Walls of water endlessly assaulted them from all directions. Twenty minutes later the thunder pounded from directly overhead. Lightning arced on the waves all around the ship. White water frothed and boiled forty feet above the funnel.

It was terrifying. It was enough to bring the most courageous to their knees.

For two days and two nights the *Caledonia* tossed on the ocean like some toy boat washed down a fast-flowing storm drain. The captain tried to mark their course, dividers in hand, gripping his cabin table for support, poring over charts. But if truth be known, he feared he was off course by many leagues. As for the crew, they were beyond exhaustion, and with Arthur's galley fire dampened, they had barely eaten. No one remembered it was Christmas Eve. Not until the storm passed to the west. The sky cleared. And all aboard sighed with relief.

· · ·

About 5PM, December 24th, 1922.
Christmas Eve was surely upon them. 'Merry Christmas lads,' no one was more relieved than Captain Cosgrove. The old veteran had been through many a storm in his fifty-four years a seafarer, and this last storm was the worst yet, but now the sea was calm. Actually, it was eerily calm, but the captain had ordered Arthur rustle up a Christmas feast. As far as the crew were concerned, it could remain a millpond. Meanwhile the Stephenson's engine throbbed below the saloon deck driving the single screw, while ten of the crew attacked a turkey dinner, especially thawed for the occasion. The helmsman, Johnno, ate his on the bridge and Baz the stoker would be relieved by the engineer, to join the others, in half an hour. The captain ordered Arthur open a crate of dark ale.

It wasn't long after the plum pudding, which by the way was made by the first mate's mother and had been dangling on a string in the galley for the past month, was smothered with hot vanilla custard, when the helmsman's voice rasped through the speaking horn.

'Better come top-side cap'n, we got more weather afoot.'

The moment Captain Cosgrove stepped out onto the main deck he saw the problem. He climbed the steep steps to the bridge, forward of the funnel. 'It don't look good cap'n.'

The fog hovered towards them, inches above the surface of the sea like a spectral dragon. It was thick as cotton wool and barely translucent. The wind had dropped completely.

'It'll be dark again in a coupla hours.'

The captain looked on the positive side. 'At least it's not another storm. Keep her on the nor-east course and if it persists cut back to five knots. And sound the foghorn every minute.'

'Aye cap'n.'

'Oh, and Johnno …'

'Cap'n.'

'Soon as the lads finish their Christmas dinner get one of the boys up the forward mast.'

Johnno knew the captain wanted a lookout. The *Caledonia* had two masts to assist loading and unloading cargo at ports without cranes.

By the time the captain returned to the dining table the fog had surrounded the ship. The muggy air was replaced with a chill and electric lights were switched on. Unperturbed, Captain Cosgrove ordered more ale opened and Walter, a deckie, sang Christmas Carols with Sam Bull on the fiddle. By ten most of the crew had retired to their bunks.

Just before 2AM Walter, was woken for his watch, which, at the first mate's orders, were four-hours long. Walter pulled on his oil-skin jacket and climbed up the forward mast and made himself as comfortable as was possible under the circumstances, in the makeshift crow's nest.

· · ·

Nearly four hours later.
A good hot meal, ale and the rhythmic foghorn afforded Captain Cosgrove several peaceful hour's rest, when …

'Land … land ahead port bow!'

Walter's warning echoed through the soupy mist and emptiness of the still ocean. Captain Cosgrove woke from a deep sleep and sat up, disorientated at first. He looked to his compass, fixed above his bed, *N, Nor-east.* 'Land. Port bow!' The cry sounded urgent. Cosgrove slipped his arms into his oilskin and rushed to the bridge.

The sea fog seemed to have thickened. So thick in fact the captain could barely make out *Caledonia's* bow, even though dawn was breaking on the horizon. 'Land cap'n!' 'Hear that?'

Breakers crashing against cliffs.

'Aye.'

The foghorn's mournful wail echoed back. Captain Cosgrove knew this warned of danger. He focussed through the fog. His first mate Dickie Sutton joined him, fetching binoculars from the drawer. He passed them to the captain. 'You've got better eyes than me Dickie.' The mate stepped out onto the bridge wing. 'Where?' he called out to Walter, their voices echoing like they were in a cave, worrying all those on board. Sutton focussed awkwardly as a rolling sea had picked up and the old freighter lifted and dipped on an increasing, undulating swell. Arthur left the warmth of his cabin close to the galley, to venture on deck to see what all the fuss was about.

'Walter!' Dickie Sutton shouted again. 'Land … Where?'

'Port bow.' Sutton studied the wall of dense fog surrounding them and thought it couldn't possibly become any thicker. Pulling on oilskins, Arthur joined the captain on the bridge. Fifty-year-old Arthur and the captain went back a-ways. Cosgrove as the captain on two other ships and Arthur as his ship's cook. 'How bad?' Arthur asked.

'Bad.'

Both men fixed worried stares through the bridge window. The cliffs drew closer. Cosgrove turned to face Arthur; the look of fear scrawled across his face in ever deepening furrows. Reaching in through his waterproofs he pulled a silver fob watch and chain from his waistcoat pocket and unbuttoning it, he passed it to Arthur. 'Here.'

'What's this?'

'If I don't make it you must get this to my son.'

'What are talking about Thomas?'

'The watch man! Take it.' The captain dropped the watch into Arthur's open palm, the chain spiralled after it and he closed the cook's hand securely around it. 'You must never lose it. Look after it and get it to my son Daniel.'

'Jesus cap'n, what are yer on about? Here,' Arthur made to pass it back. 'Give it to him yourself.'

Cosgrove ignored the protests. 'He lives with his mother at Williamstown in Melbourne,' he persisted. 'We're the only Cosgroves in the area. It is paramount, you hear me, paramount, that my boy gets that watch. My wife will understand.'

'Understand what captain?'

'Jesus Arthur. Just do it man.'

Arthur pinched his lips in frustration, pushing the watch deep into his own trouser pocket, wedging it safe with his handkerchief. Cosgrove leant in close to his cook, aware that his words must not be heard by any of the crew. 'Arthur,' he said softly, suddenly strangely calm.

'Thomas?'

'I have dreamt of my end, my day of passing. And this is it.'

'Jesus Thomas.' Arthur was about to make one last protest when Cosgrove pushed past him to the helmsman.

'What's our bearing?' he studied the binnacle. 'This doesn't make any …'

'Jesus Christ!' Sutton cut the old man short. Suddenly the foghorn sounded more urgent.

'What?'

'There!' Sutton passed Cosgrove the binoculars. The aging seafarer's eyes took a moment to focus, and then register … there was the slightest hint of land. 'What the …'

'That's Slag Island!'

'Jesus no! Can't be …' but Cosgrove's words trailed off; he knew he was well off course. The four-hundred-foot volcanic rock, named for its flesh lacerating slag-like surface and shaped like a rock pile with forty-five-degree slopes on all sides was uninhabitable, in the middle of nowhere and terrifying to behold. Even seals avoided it. Its presence was every mariner's nightmare. The gargantuan rock rose from the seabed like a murderous assassin. And at its centre the seamen recognised Satan's Yawn – a cave eighty-feet high, hundred and fifty feet wide and, some guessed, three hundred feet in depth.

Where the island penetrated the surface, Cosgrove watched white water breaking. The peaceful night was now interrupted by crashing surf as the *Caledonia* drifted closer, each ten-foot swell gathering speed towards the cliff face, exploding into foam like fireworks.

The fog thinned.

The cliff face towered overhead.

'Full astern! Full astern!' the captain screamed. The helmsman snatched the telegraph handle. He cranked the message to the engine room.

Full astern.

The propeller change juddered through the ship. It was too little too late. The *Caledonia* appeared disobedient.

'Hard to starboard,' Cosgrove yelled at the helmsman. 'Hard to starboard.' But Sutton pre-empted the order. Shouldering Johnno aside he spun the wheel clockwise. Over and over and over. Satan's Yawn awaited victory while the *Caledonian* seemed to have resigned herself to her own fate. The steamer drifted helplessly, port side, into the jaws of the cave. At first the bow crashed against the cliff. She ground to a halt. It all felt in slow motion. The rising swell swung the stern about …

Now the portside scraped the jagged rock face while the bow itself nosed further into the giant cavern. An ugly sound resonated. Metal hull plates popped rivets while steel plate crumbled like cardboard. The ship squealed, a painful metallic squeal of defeat. The impact threw all off their feet. Above them the mastheads loosened stone from the sheer cliff face. Huge rocks pummelled the deck and the masts collapsed, maiming one deckhand and killing another instantly. Another seamen's head was crushed under a falling rigging block and Cosgrove watched helplessly as four others were thrown overboard, followed by the aft mast and all its rigging.

Arthur J Money was catapulted into the water. Tangled in rigging he was dragged into the depths. Arthur had no idea how deep he had sunk, but if nothing else he was fit for his age, and in some ways, fearless. Self-preservation manifested. Arthur jettisoned his oilskins. He groped for his knife sheathed at his side. He hacked at the ropes. Dawn's faint light cast shadows of mayhem underwater. Arthur realised he was knotted amongst a dozen signal flags connected to a lanyard. He tugged at the flags, severing each one, but still he sank … deeper and deeper.

Captain Cosgrove rushed to the ship rail, port side. The four men lost overboard had disappeared. There was no sign of Arthur. There was no time to lament his decision about the watch.

'Cap'n!' Sutton screamed. Cosgrove turned to his first mate as the *Caledonia* listed sharply to starboard. Sutton gripped a fireman's axe. He hacked furiously at the starboard lifeboat swinging on its davits. 'Cap'n … we'll have to abandon ship.'

Cosgrove was frozen to the rail. He had seen his destiny. But now it was a reality he was terrified. Paralysed. The swaying lifeboat hit the water as the ship tilted. Sutton struggled but managed to secure the bow line. Two seamen jumped for the boat. One managed to land squarely but the other landed in the sea. The ship's second officer, Jack, appeared, staggering awkwardly along the sloping deck, his arms burdened with tinned food and a keg of water. 'Here!' he heaved his load into the lifeboat and jumped in after it. Sutton was losing his grip. 'Cap'n, in the boat man.'

Cosgrove stared back with ashen face. His bloodshot eyes beacons of fear. His mouth opening and closing like a suffocating cod.

'Jesus Christ man,' Sutton yelled. 'Hurry.'

Another seaman rose from below decks. But seawater filled the companionway to claim him. He was closely followed by the stoker. *Caledonia* listed to a perilous fifty degrees. The water swelled up over the first man, washing him back down the companionway. But the stoker broke free. He struggled to balance and made a dive for the lifeboat, but luck deserted him. His head smashed into the guardrail knocking him unconscious and he too slid into the sea.

Panicked, Captain Cosgrove positioned himself over the rail. Terrified the ship was about to capsize, he manoeuvred himself along the exposed port hull. Sutton didn't wait any longer. He *couldn't* wait any longer. He leapt onto the stern sheets of the lifeboat and cast away from the sinking ship with the use of an oar. Another seaman joined him, and together they managed to drift to a safe distance.

The *Caledonia* groaned in her death throes, rolling onto her superstructure. Compressed air and steam hissed from the ship. Captain Cosgrove screamed out for help. He slid from the hull, tumbled over the keel plunging into the dark waters where his heavy oilskins soaked up the ocean … dragging him below.

Three fathoms deep Arthur's lungs screamed for air. He kicked off for the surface.

Close by a large body sank quickly.

The captain!

Arthur reached out, grabbing the man's collar. Cosgrove rewarded Arthur's valour by snatching at Arthur's shirt. He thrashed about, desperate to return to the surface, slamming his foot into Arthur's face. Arthur felt himself sinking once more, burdened by the threshing, hysterical captain. Arthur's cheeks blew out. His chest was about to explode. He stared at the drowning captain, his clenched fist holding Arthur down by his shirt. There was nothing more Arthur could do. He wriggled free from his shirt and made a final lunge for the surface.

Air was never so sweet.

Arthur gasped, coughed and spluttered, greedily gulping precious fresh air. Fifty feet away the *Caledonia*, keel upwards, was filling rapidly with water, sinking stern first where she filled with water through the damaged panels at the bow. Instinctively Arthur ducked below the surface. Desperate to save the captain, but the man was disappearing into the depths. Arthur barely recognised his old friend sinking fast, eyes wide open, looking up towards the dawn light. The fear had gone from Cosgrove's face. His oilskins dragging him deeper and deeper to the seabed two hundred feet below. He was dead well before he hit the bottom.

Immediately Arthur felt hands snatching at his naked arms, tugging at the back of his britches. Two, maybe three sets of hands landing him in the bottom of the lifeboat.

'What's yer doin' matey?' one said.

'The captain … he's …'

'We know Arthur,' Hutton said. 'He's gone mate. There's nought yer can do.'

•   •   •

Minutes later the survivors watched the *Caledonia* in her final moments. For fear of being sucked into a watery vacuum, Sutton ordered they row a hundred yards offshore. Moaning in defeat, the steamer eventually disappeared below the surface beneath a gushing geyser of spray, sinking into two hundred feet of water, following her captain to the seabed. The survivor's position was dire. It would be impossible to land and even if it were possible, Slag Island was one of the world's most desolate islands.

Sutton was a natural leader. He was disappointed and angry at their captain's behaviour. But there was no point dwelling on it. He stood at the stern tiller and cast a wary eye over his charge.

Sutton watched Arthur shivering, sitting behind the two oarsmen, amazed at the cook's survival. Sutton liked Arthur. He never argued, kept out of trouble and he was smart too. Jack the second officer was a strong character, but at this moment he was in shock. He had watched his best mate the stoker washed helplessly back below deck and now questioned himself. *Could I have saved him?* More importantly, Sutton noted, Jack sat on a crate of tinned bully beef and a two-gallon keg of water sat at his feet. There were only three others in the boat, all deckhands.

'Nugget'. As the captain had told him when he signed up, 'I need more nuggetty bastards like you.' Nugget – no one knew his real name and it seemed he liked it that way – was in his early thirties. Then there was Old Fitz. Full name Roy Fitzgerald. He was only forty, but he always complained about aches and pains and in general carried on like an old man, hence 'Old Fitz'. The fifth survivor was an Aboriginal deckhand, Kevin. Kevin was twenty-four, had been for several years Sutton thought. Truth be known no one knew his real age, including Kevin.

'Row back,' Sutton ordered, speaking of where the ship had foundered. He was hoping for other survivors amongst the wreckage floating on the surface.

The two-oarsman rowed and Sutton at the tiller steered for Satan's Yawn where an eternal swell smashed against the rocks.

No one said another word. Nothing of any value rose from the wreck. There were no survivors in the water. 'There,' someone called out, pointing to a body floating face down, buoyed by air pockets in his oilskins. They all recognised Frank, one of the deckhands, his head stove in by a rock. The two-foot dorsal of the great shark brushed by the lifeboat as it dived for the attack. The survivors watched in shock and terror as the beast twisted about, jaws open and surfaced again beneath the body. Frank's mangled head was bitten away instantly while other sharks, attracted by the blood, joined in the feast. Immediately the castaways were aware there were several sharks surrounding them.

'Jesus Christ!' Sutton gripped the tiller to steady himself. 'Row … row for Christ's sake. Let's get outa here.'

Suddenly Slag Island took on an even more fearful presence. Beside the circling sharks, it seemed the spirits of their mates and ghosts of shipwrecks past were watching from another dimension. A malice hung in the air. Dawn was now upon them, the day appeared to brighten, the sun shone and all aboard the lifeboat agreed, they wanted to sail away as soon as possible.

• • •

By midday the sun directly overhead was fierce. Sutton had set the jib stored in the lifeboat sail locker, but there was little breeze and the cool of the breaking dawn was but a memory.

Days passed.

1922 passed onto 1923. There was no celebration.

They were alone. Lost. And Sutton fought hard to keep up morale. Fortunately, the night skies were clear, and Sutton navigated by the stars. By studying the Southern Cross, the first mate drew an imaginary line from the top of the cross to its *foot*. He managed to keep the celestial south behind them and figuring if they sailed nor-nor-east they would hopefully encounter Fiji or the Samoan Islands.

On the ninth day the last can of the bully beef was passed around. The next day the rationed water was down to a mouthful each. Sutton notched the gunwale, each long and lonely day recorded by a nick in the timber.

On the twelfth day the wind picked up considerably and the small lifeboat made considerable distance. But that night a storm hit. They were forced to bail, using the empty bully beef tins. On a positive note, they were able to catch a little water off the jib and half re-fill the keg.

Two days later the keg was dry once more.

On the fifteenth day a school of flying fish swam passed, two miraculously landing in the boat. They were immediately clubbed, portioned and eaten, innards and all.

•   •   •

Sutton studied his fellow sufferers with sunken dark eyes. He didn't know what was worse, the hunger or the thirst. The men were starving. Cannibalism crossed his mind, but he kept his thoughts to himself.

On the seventeenth day Sutton grew violently ill. It was possibly sunstroke, although he vomited bile. Arthur took over the tiller and kept a vigil all night, but by sunup it was clear the first mate was dead. The Lord's Prayer was recited, and after Arthur removed Sutton's shirt to cover his own blistered body, the man was hoisted over the side. His cadaver was instantly taken by a lone shark that had followed them for days.

The following day the lifeboat was hit by a sudden a gale. Again, they bailed. And once again they managed to collect a little water.

Day nineteen and day twenty they received little wind. The castaways drifted at the mercy of the elements.

By the twenty-first day they again ran out of water. The last food they had eaten had been the flying fish. Keven and Nugget grew delusional, calling out for mother in the night. Feeble from malnutrition, exposure and chafed by seawater they developed huge open sores.

On the twenty-second day Nugget drank sea water. The others were too debilitated to argue, let alone stop him. The following day, the twenty-third day drifting at sea since the wreck, Nugget screamed for water. By evening he had fallen into a coma.

Jack the second mate saw his opportunity. He didn't hesitate. He stabbed Nugget in the throat and placing a bully beef tin to the cut he caught the warm flow. Instantly Fitz and Kevin joined him and the three drank greedily. Arthur watched on in horror, too afraid to do anything but watch. But the blood proved a restorative, and his three companions were soon in better spirits. Jack passed Arthur the can full of blood. Reluctantly he took a drink himself and the thick warm metallic soup on his knotted empty stomach tasted delicious. But the very thought saw him vomit the first mouthful. Arthur's accomplices groaned at the waste. He disconnected himself, unburdened his mind of the image of his dead shipmate, and took another drink before the tin was snatched from him to be shared.

For two days and nights the weather deteriorated. A huge swell hampered them, threatening to capsize the boat. Bailing frantically, they managed to stay afloat.

On the twenty-ninth day a sail appeared on the horizon. Five miles distant. Four maybe. But no amount of waving, screaming or shouting could attract their attention.

Physically they had improved marginally, due to Jack portioning Nugget's flesh into strips, hanging them over the jib rig to dry in the sun.

Mentally they fought their demons.

'It's the custom of the sea,' Jack assured the others. But cannibalism was cannibalism in Arthur J Money's book, no matter how much you sugar-coated it. He had read of such rare events in the past. The authorities, especially those of the church, struggled to approve the immoral practice. They attempted to prosecute shipwreck survivors who admitted to the abhorrent act. Murder, they screamed.

But public opinion was often sympathetic to these perpetrators, and convictions were rare.

All the same, the human jerky tasted *so* good.

Day thirty-three.

Arthur lay slouched at the tiller. He was asleep. Fitz and Kevin slept head to shoulder amidships. Suddenly Jack leapt to his feet. 'Land!' he cried out, his throat parched, his voice croaky. 'L-land ...'

Arthur opened his eyes into a blaring sun. His face blistered red; his lips cracked. Jack held the jib mast and swung wildly gazing off into the distance. 'Land. Quick wake up yer bastards and row.'

Arthur stood. He was weak. He could feel his ribs beneath his taut weathered skin. He felt lightheaded but gripped that tiller and steered for the shore.

'Land ... bloody land ...' they all shouted.

About five miles away the low island could be seen through a heavy mist.

Fitz and Kevin rowed hard and then the breeze picked up and Jack set the jib. The hours passed and the island grew steadily closer. However, by late afternoon it was clear the island was surrounded by breaking water. Evening approached and they realised there was nowhere safe to land. They were close enough to hear the roar of thunderous waves.

They could see the jagged reef.

So close yet so far.

Would the reef be a death sentence?

They would have to circumnavigate the island. All that night the castaways held their position off the coast. By morning they were exhausted. No one had slept for fear of drifting back out to sea. Again, they searched for a safe place to row ashore … but in vain.

They had no choice. They would have to risk surfing in over the reef. In desperation, late that following afternoon they rowed for the reef, praying they would be thrown up on the beach. Their luck held. The lifeboat barely cleared the coral reef. An eight-foot wave rose beneath the craft, heaving them over rocks that would surely shred them. But the moment they were safely over the reef good fortune deserted the castaways. The lifeboat spun sharply to port. It dipped into a trough. The next huge wave built momentum. It towered over the boat before smashing into them. The swamped vessel reared on the next wave's crest … and flipped.

Arthur was jettisoned the moment he snatched an oar. He was hurled free but the vessel splintered against submerged rocks. Wave after wave pounded Arthur. But he held the oar firmly. He was washed ashore on the next big wave and flung onto a stone ledge. The wave detonated against a cliff face before rolling back, threatening to drag Arthur back into the boiling sea. Arthur clawed at the ledge. The wave subsided and he crawled to high ground.

At last, after more than a month adrift at sea, Arthur was on terra firma.

. . .

On board Drifter.
Hitiaa O Te Ra fishing village and coal station north Tahiti. 1924
As it transpired, the French gendarmes guarding the *Drifter* and
Cap'n Jonathon Bourke's crew were a pushover. Juvita knew
enough about French men to know they loved pretty women
and good food. And although the Malaysian princess was
considered middle-aged she cut a fine figure of a woman and
knew how to manipulate them.

The curried goat she prepared them, with grilled naan bread
and accompaniments, dhal and her own spiced mango chutney
were to die for. Well, dying wasn't an option, but drugging them
was. The hot and spicy curry was the perfect host for the opium
Juvita liberally laced through the sauce. The goat and the whisky
took an hour to take effect, but by early evening the four men
were carried ashore like regular patrons of a Canton opium den,
and placed in a nearby hut to sleep it off. By the time their
superiors came for them, *Drifter* was on the horizon.

CHAPTER THREE

On board La Belle Dame. Papeete Harbour. Tahiti.

French diplomat Monsieur Felix Du Bellay heard the news of *Drifter's* escape during breakfast. He was dining alone on chocolate hazelnut croissants and thick Turkish coffee at the sheltered breakfast alcove on the sundeck aboard a colleague's 120-foot luxury motor yacht, *La Belle Dame. La Belle Dame* was an extravagance Du Bellay could ill afford, an opulent *toy*, but a distraction none the less. This was the lifestyle he so desperately wanted, and at any risk. For the moment; the owner and colleague was on business back in France and left his yacht at Du Bellay's disposal to island hop the Pacific.

'Escaped!' He shot at the messenger. 'What do you mean escaped?' Pastry flakes speckled the starched linen.

'It appears the guards were drugged monsieur.' The gendarme stood to attention like a palace guard. He knew of Du Bellay's temper and shuffled nervously fumbling with his neat white pith helmet held firmly under his arm.

'What of the Australian prisoner Jonathon Bourke?'

'He left in irons for New Caledonia aboard the *Patria* at first light monsieur.'

'Are you certain?'

'Oui monsieur. I saw him being boarded under guard myself.'

Du Bellay sighed with some relief. At least he knew this bastard Bourke could not escape the French Navy on board the SS *Patria,* an ex-troop ship from the recent war in Europe now servicing the Pacific for France.

To his credit Du Bellay heard the man out, before dismissing him and calling for his head steward. 'Fetch the capitaine immediately and prepare to sail. This instant!'

• • •

La Belle Dame was built in Dunkirk at the Ateliers et Chantiers de France shipyards in 1921.

Decorated in the Art Deco style, so popular now in the *Roaring Twenties* – as many called this decade with its surging economy, mass consumerism and flapping jazz. The vessel displayed mahogany panelled walls, Art Deco furniture and brass fittings that shone like a soldier's boots on parade. She boasted a card room on the main deck with pearwood detailing. Varnished timber predominated, with a chic Parisian bench curving around the stern, with each guest cabin enjoying its own telephone.

La Belle Dame steamed between the channel markers out through the reefs and into deep water at a comfortable fifteen knots. Captain Marcel Badeaux welcomed Du Bellay on the bridge. 'They've had a good eight hours start Monsieur Du Bellay. Do you have in mind a course to maybe intercept them?'

'I know these rogues. Bastard pirates all of them. They will be following the *Patria* for certain. I would bet my money on it. So full speed ahead for Noumea, s'il vous plait.'

• • •

Suva. Fiji.
Ten days after Drifter slipped away from Tahiti. 1924
Arsala was on a mission. The only way he thought he could possibly help his friend and mentor, Cap'n Bourke, was with

legal action. And he hoped his cousin Aalok Khatri, a lawyer in Fiji's capital, Suva, would be able to help.

Drifter steamed into Suva Harbour amidst a tropical downpour while fruit vending natives sailing lateen rigged canoes vied for business with the new arrival. Juvita prepared to accompany Arsala ashore, having met his cousin once before a year earlier. It would look good, she thought, and not attract unwelcome attention, if they appeared as a married couple. Harry, insisted on joining them. He slipped a sailor's lead headed cosh into his trouser pocket. He knew there had been political unrest lately, with the Indian population clashing with the indigenous Fijians and the English landowners.

'What's their bloody problem anyway?' Harry asked as they tied up at a finger jetty adjacent to a long wooden wharf built on tall log piers to accommodate high tides.

'For fifty year now,' Arsala said. 'Plantation owner indenture many many labourers from Mother India. They indentured …'

'You mean contracted?' Harry said.

'Yes. And when contract finish Indians stay in Fiji. The natives no like this. Too many Indians they say. But Arsala say, Indians good workers. Indians stay in Fiji. Make life in Fiji. Have many babies. Now we have troubles. Also, Indians in politics and Englishman don't like it. That's why cousin Aalok, he lawyer, he make much much money here.'

But the political situation was fickler than the weather. The three made a dash through the wet. Fiji was like that; Arsala knew it rained most days of the year here, with its tropical rainforest climate. Because of the trade winds it had occasional cyclones also.

Hurrying along the pier chasing cover beneath the veranda of the Union Steamship Company of New Zealand offices, Harry felt Suva reminded him of home. Similar to the pioneer towns in North Queensland – like Cooktown or Townsville. Being the capital, Suva was on the south coast of the largest island in the Fijian group, the island of Viti Levu. Streets of neat white timber buildings with iron roofs were skirted with coconut palms, banyans and frangipanni. There were, of course, more natives here in Fiji Harry noted, the Indians wearing Jodhpurs and the bare-chested indigenous people wearing sarongs.

A final downpour kept the group under the awning of the Bank of New South Wales before a last-minute scramble across the mud to the offices of cousin Aalok Khatri.

'You wait, yes,' Arsala told Harry. Harry ground his teeth. 'If'n yer insist.' Harry looked through the window into the cramped office where a pretty young Indian secretary busied herself with paperwork. The only other occupant was clearly the lawyer, an obese Sikh Indian wearing a turquoise turban, with a snowy Saint Nicholas beard from his ears to the top of his sternum, and the happy jolly face of a fat man who enjoys life, no matter what the cost.

'Go on then,' Harry told Arsala. 'Make it snappy eh.'

Arsala and Juvita entered what, it seemed, was a fug of broken wind, until Arsala noted the jar of pickled eggs on the desk that he remembered his cousin adored. It was only mid-morning but Khatri had attacked his lunch a few hours early. The office was airless and humid with one wicker fan turning lazily overhead, barely doing its job.

'Arsala!' The overweight cousin who was much older than Arsala stood unsteadily to cross the room on thin legs one would not believe capable of supporting the man. 'My dear cousin, how it is so nice to be seeing you.'

Juvita reluctantly closed the door behind her, tempted as she was to stand in the fresh air. 'And you have brought me Juvita. How lovely this is.' The lawyer took Juvita's hand in both of his, cupping them warmly in greeting. Juvita smiled, although his chubby sweaty palms and essence of pickled egg made her want to pull away.

'And how nice it is to see you cousin Aalok,' Arsala said. 'So nice indeed.'

'Sit, sit,' Aalok insisted and pulled two flimsy wicker chairs up to his desk before resuming his own sturdy seat. Aware his brow was damp, the lawyer wiped sweat from his face with a handkerchief, and Juvita noted the dye in his hair was running. 'As much as I love you little cousin, I know you are here on business, isn't it?'

'How well you know me big cousin.' Arsala caught a slight twitch in his big cousin's eye and regretted the title. 'How well indeed.'

'Sabita,' Khatri turned to his petite secretary who looked positively doll-like next to her employer. 'Have a break,' he said in Hindi before asking Arsala, also in his native tongue, 'So, what can I do for you?'

Arsala and Juvita took it in turns to explain the situation. Aalok Khatri listened in silence. He had met Cap'n Jonathon Bourke on several occasions and liked the rough and ready Australian seaman. And besides, he was good to his little cousin.

'But the Isle of Pines is a French Prison. It has a bad reputation,' Aalok started. 'If a powerful French diplomat has seen fit to have him incarcerated there, it would be near impossible to have him released. Maybe we could apply through diplomatic circles to have him extradited. I'm certain France and Australia have a treaty for such things. But ...' his voice trailed away. 'Isle of Pines?'

Finally, it was agreed Aalok Khatri would contact a colleague in Noumea by cable telegraph. He would make enquiries about the Australian prisoner Jonathon Bourke.

'I really cannot guarantee a positive outcome little cousin, but I will try, yes.'

Arsala and Juvita felt helpless. 'We can but try.'

'Then I should have some information by end of business today.'

.   .   .

6PM.

Aalok Khatri face said it all. 'Bad news I am afraid,' the corpulent man of law shook his head as Arsala and Juvita entered. Aalok spoke Hindi. Harry read the man's face through the window. He pushed his way into the office. 'What is it?' he demanded.

Aalok Khatri stiffened.

'Sorry Aalok,' Arsala said. 'This is Harry.'

'Harry,' Aalok switched to English, trying to be cheerful. 'Mr Bourke, he talk of you sometimes, yes?'

'I said what news do you have of our cap'n?'

'Ah, not good I am afraid.'

'Yes. Yes. And?'

Aalok Khatri sighed deeply. 'I have returned telegram here. You read.' He passed Harry the communication.

Prisoner Bourke to be sent to Devil's Island ... stop ... currently in solitary ... stop ... prison awaits transport to Guiana ... stop ... maybe two weeks ... stop.

'Devil's Island!' Harry exploded. 'Guiana! Guiana in South America!' He thrust the paper at Arsala. 'They can't do that.'

'They can I'm afraid,' Khatri said, keeping his distance from the angry Irishman. 'And they will. The man you say, the French diplomat of whom you speak ... Monsieur Du ... Du ...'

'Du Bellay,' Harry spat. 'A proper bastard if'n I ever heard o' one.'

'Yes, Bellay. He is a powerful mans, a what you say ... ah ... tyrant. Yes, tyrant I am told. I hear things before, he is not a good man.'

Harry stepped closer to the lawyer. Directly in his face. 'You've gotta stop this. Devil's Island my arse.'

'But ...'

'But nothing. I want you to start legal action to slow down the transfer. What do yer call it, extradition? Yeh. Sue for an extradition, if that fails, we'll break him outa gaol ourselves.'

Arsala pinched his lips, frowning in embarrassment but Juvita agreed.

'Harry is right,' she said. 'We can seek to extradite him to Australia can we not?'

Khatri's chest rose and deflated in a sigh. 'I will see what I can do. I like this man Bourke also, but I promise you nothing.'

CHAPTER FOUR

Sometime earlier. Late January 1923.

Arthur J Money lay in the fine dry sand well above the high tide mark. He hadn't a clue how long he slept but guessed it was well over an hour, lying in the warm sun, exhausted. Nearby seabirds surrounded Arthur, circling, wary to peck at what they thought was a possible meal. Arthur stirred. Panicked, the birds rose in a raucous, loud enough to wake the dead. Arthur sat weakly. His bones ached. His head thumped but a nagging thirst saw him on his feet. His immediate thoughts went to his companions.

Jack the first mate lay on his back where the retreating tide had deserted his body. His eyes already empty bloodied black orbs, where the birds had started to feast. Arthur retched, but there was little in his stomach to lose. Roy Fitzgerald, Fitz, rolled about like a rag doll in shallow water a hundred yards away. He too was dead. There was no sign of Kevin or the shattered lifeboat, but the oar that saved Arthur's life was nearby, trapped in a wreath of stubborn seaweed.

• • •

Urgency took hold. Arthur was certain from their surveillance the day before, that he was a castaway on a lonely island. No other land had been sighted. The realisation of his dire situation sunk in. Panic clouded his thoughts. The thought of dying of thirst and starvation now terrified him.

Water was a priority. The island was certainly barren. There were no trees and little vegetation of note. Arthur climbed to the highest point, maybe two hundred feet above sea-level and his heart sank. He was doomed to die a terrible slow death. From his lookout Arthur could see the island was no more than half a mile long and quarter of a mile wide. Everything was desolate and there was no sign of a spring or any source of fresh water. Fate had dealt Arthur J Money a cruel blow. A month drifting aimlessly on the South Pacific in an open lifeboat and now this.

And he was alone.

Anxiety overcame the young seaman. Arthur J Money wished he could die here and now.

Self-pity suffocated him and as his parched throat choked him, tears welled up and Arthur collapsed to the ground weeping.

· · ·

A sudden wind whipped across the rocky landscape. The sky darkened and briefly, a squall swept over the island. Arthur rolled onto his back, his mouth wide open, and gulped at the rainwater as it lashed about him. But as fast as it appeared, it disappeared. Arthur lay in a puddle, drenched. The ground around him momentarily soaked. Depressions in the craggy high ground around him filled with water and Arthur had the foresight to find flat stones to cover as many as possible, to prevent the sun evaporating the precious commodity, or worse, the sea polluting it.

The squall had been a tonic. The aches subsided, the head cleared, and the tiniest measure of hope gave Arthur encouragement. A shelter became a priority. Arthur returned to the shoreline. He stripped his shipmates of their clothing and, after an apology and a short prayer, he buried each man in a shallow sandy grave.

Finding a crevice between huge boulders, Arthur made a bed of bracken and dead seaweed. With some kind of shelter for the approaching night, he wandered the island in search of food and water. At the northern end of the islet, he found several small shellfish. Prising the meat from the snail-sized shell with his knife – thankfully still sheathed at his side – Arthur found the meat almost inedible, however they moistened his throat and offered some sustenance. That night Arthur slept soundly on his cold and damp bed. He dreamt of home, his parents, brothers and sisters. His dreams were gay and positive. Then dawn arrived offering a still, warm sunny day and the realisation, that his pleasant dreams, were just that … dreams. The days passed ...

•   •   •

Arthur worked on his shelter, building walls of rock and a rudimentary cover with seaweed. Arthur's water supply was drying fast, and the shellfish barely kept him alive. Starved, his legs began to swell, his belly bloated, and he now realised just how malnourished his body had become.

Wishing to acknowledge the Sabbath, Arthur remembered Sutton's notches carved into the lifeboat gunwale, the tally record to keep track of the calendar. He knew he had landed on the island on a Monday. Today was Friday. Using his knife to nick the salvaged oar, Arthur kept record of the days. All he had eaten were the shellfish and the odd dead fish washed ashore. His belly groaned for sustenance. Starvation threatened, when he came across the carcass of a dead seal rotting between rocks on the eastern shore.

Eat or you will surely perish.

The voice in his head was persistent. If he didn't eat, he would surely die. Taking small slices from the belly Arthur persevered with the decaying meat. The first mouthful he brought back up. But with a tenacious will to live Arthur forced himself to eat enough protein to live another day. The following day his water supply dried up. Depression set in once more. Arthur spent the day in his shelter, silently praying.

The Sabbath arrived. Seven days since the landing. The sky darkened, the seas grew angry, massive waves pounded ashore and thunder crashed overhead. The skies opened up and the rains pelted down. It seemed Arthur's prayers were answered. Hollows filled up with rainwater all over the island. Ecstatic, Arthur secured dozens of pools and puddles with rocks. The tempest also delivered large quantities of seaweed washed-up onto the rocks, which Arthur dried and used as extra lining for his bed.

There was reason to rejoice.

The following day Arthur forced himself to eat more decomposing seal meat, washing it down with plenty of fresh water. But the carcass was beyond putrid, and he doubted he could pick at it much more.

Another notch in the oar.

Arthur retired as the night fell upon the island and slept soundly. If nothing else, he was rested and many of his ailments were improving. The next morning, he woke to a raucous noise. What sounded like barking had him springing from his bed.

Seals. Thousands of seals had swum ashore to mate. Arthur didn't hesitate. Using his oar as a weapon he clubbed several to death in a delirious frenzy before they realised what was happening. He must have slaughtered a dozen before he realised what carnage he had created. A sudden guilt descended upon him. He could never eat all the kill. Arthur spent the remainder of the day slicing the meat and hanging it over rocks to dry in the sun.

The guilts deserted him along with starvation. But so did the surviving seals.

CHAPTER FIVE

Isle of Pines, prison island to the south of New Caledonia.
Little over two weeks since Bourke's arrest. 1924

If Bourke had to answer the question, what do you miss most in incarceration, he'd have to say Scotch and female company. More than anything right now though, he would love access to his books, his personal library aboard *Drifter*. It numbered over fifty books the last time he counted, and that didn't include his set of 1911 Encyclopedia Britannica, the American revision with the simplified articles for a broader readership. But it was the loss of freedom that really haunted him.

Approaching from across the water the Isle of Pines, surrounded by the New Caledonia barrier reef, was a low-lying crop of land. Because of its forests of tall pines it could be best described as a scrubbing brush floating on its back. It was 9.3 miles long and 8.1 miles wide lying just south-east of Grande Terre, New Caledonia's main island. The capital, Noumea, was sixty-two miles off to the north-west.

Escape? Near impossible.

And swimmers beware. Offal and scraps were fed daily into the channel between the mainland and the island, attracting giant tiger sharks.

Captain Bourke knew the French took possession the Isle of Pines, only a small part of what was now French Polynesia, in 1853, and built the penal colony back in '72. Fifty years on, the buildings were tired. Imprisoned here were at least three thousand lost souls, mostly political deportees from the Paris Commune. However other criminals, including Captain Jonathon Bourke, arguably under false arrest, were incarcerated here, cut off from the civilised world, unable to communicate or seek legal aid. They were nothing but ghosts.

Bourke paced the high-walled exercise yard like a caged lion, where twenty men at a time were allowed one hour of physical activity a day. There was only one entrance at the far end of the twenty-five-foot rectangular space. It was, maybe, twelve foot wide. Open to the elements, the smooth rendered cement brick walls were thirty feet high with buttresses at the top angled inwards, and capped with barbed wire. At one end an armed guard stood sentry on a walkway, crossing wall to wall twenty-foot overhead, well out of reach of the wretched prisoners.

Talking was prohibited. Touching was prohibited. For one hour they were to walk around and around and around, within the perimeter of the human cage.

Jonathon could not understand what had gone so terribly wrong. Arsala had warned him over and over and now Bourke heard the Ghurkha's voice clearly. 'Your pecker captain sir is going to be your ruination. Yes, you listen to me good captain sir. You keep this up and your pecker will fuck you up. Just like that.'

If nothing else the memory of Arsala put a brief smile on Bourke's face. The smile brought hope and with hope came thoughts of escape. But how?

•　•　•

The home of the French High Commissioner. Noumea. 1924.
Monsieur Du Bellay found the breast of the roasted waterfowl a little dry and congratulated himself for the fact he had his own teeth and not dentures to tackle the chewy meat. But he had to

concede the gamey meat married well with the orange sauce. And that the creamed yams prepared *a la Parisienne* were an acquired taste. But this *was* New Caledonia, not Paris. Besides he'd had an upset stomach the past few days. All this foreign food was affecting his digestion. Thoughts of his younger wife, Madame Vignetta Du Bellay, back in Tahiti, plagued him and Du Bellay was starting to question his own naivety regarding the fidelity of his insatiable spouse.

Sharing the dinner table of Monsieur Olivier Martinez – the commissioner, and wife Catherine – with Du Bellay, were a dozen colleagues, diplomats and high-ranking public servants. Most were accompanied by their wives, all quaffing French wines like they'd heard a whisper that the cellar was running low on supplies. Immediately Monsieur Du Bellay's reverie was disturbed by the brusque baritone voice of Monsieur Maxence Paquet, the new superintendent of the Isle of Pines Prison. The aging public servant had consumed enough wine to drop all formalities, addressing Du Bellay by his given name.

'Ah … Felix.'

Du Bellay turned his whole body to face the warden, as he had woken this day with a stiff neck that was causing him some aggravation. 'Yes, Monsieur Paquet.'

'Please, call me Maxence, Felix, we are all friends here after all.'

Friends?

Du Bellay had only met the newly appointed warden this very evening and had taken a disliking to the overweight man immediately, although the two had one thing in common – greed. And they were both grossly overweight. Felix Du Bellay had conspired with the previous Warden, Monsieur Noir, to keep the German survivor Herr Kohl, from the *Emden* debacle back in '15, as a guest of the French Republic. That is at least, until he told them the exact co-ordinates of the sunken German gunboat, SS *Prinzessin*. After all Kohl had boasted to fellow prisoners that he had been on board that fateful day when she was sunk by a Royal Navy ship and knew its whereabouts on a reef off the coast of Solomon Islands.

'*Friends!*' Du Bellay lingered on the word. 'Yes of course Maxence.'

'Tell me, what are your plans for the Australian prisoner Bourke?' the warden asked, red wine spittle landing on his starched serviette tucked into his collar and draped over his corpulent gut. 'I mean, the Australians are our allies are they not? They have made enquiries about opening a consulate here in Noumea I have been informed.'

'That is correct. I am in fact due in Melbourne to speak in Parliament about the matter.'

'Oh, really.'

'Yes, in one month's time.'

'Well,' Monsieur Paquet looked slightly confused. 'Should the Australians get wind that we are holding one of their citizens without a trial it may cause a rift between the two countries.'

'Fear not warden.' The warden noticeably flinched. Du Bellay went on. 'Don't worry yourself Maxence. I have found the criminal a permanent home far away.'

'Oh. Well, that is news to me. And where is this said, new home?'

Anticipating the reaction, Du Bellay answered audaciously, 'Devil's Island.'

The prison superintendent reeled back. Of course – he knew Devil's Island only too well. Opened in 1852 in French Guiana off the coast of Cayenne the penal colony was the most feared of the French colony prisons. Men were imprisoned in solitary confinement for up to five years. Healthy strong-willed men went insane. It was nothing less than inhumane.

'Devil's Island you say. But the man has not been sentenced.'

'Monsieur,' Du Bellay's eyes narrowed. He ground his teeth. Vengeance was sweet and he was savouring every minute of it.

'That … that filthy maggot. That scum seaman assaulted my wife. He deserves to rot in hell.'

If there had been even one ounce of humanity in the warden's nature, the wine had now extinguished it. 'Well, you got that bit right monsieur … Felix.' He raised his glass. 'Here's to rotting in hell.'

'Excellent Maxence,' Du Bellay said. Noticing the waiter heading his way with the decanter, Du Bellay drained his glass, returning it to the table ready for a refill, before facing the warden once more.

'I heard,' Maxence said, 'that this Bourke fellow's crew escaped Papeete after you arrested them and impounded their vessel.' The warden hid a slight smirk behind his raised glass.

'You are well informed, *friend*,' Du Bellay could hardly conceal his anger. 'But I will find them sooner or later.' His stomach rumbled.

'What if they have returned to Australia?'

'I think not. Something tells me they are skulking around the Pacific somewhere.' Du Bellay was keen to change subjects. He ordered a bowl of sorbet, maybe that would ease the problem, because gut ache or not, he wasn't going to miss out on the next course – cheese.

'So, how are you enjoying your new position at the prison?' Du Bellay asked. 'Do you miss *the Bastille*? Madame Guillotine maybe?' Du Bellay joked, knowing Monsieur Paquet's last position was deputy warden at La Sante Prison in Paris.

'It's fine, just fine, thank you for asking.' Maxence stuffed a large piece of bird skewered on his fork with a piece of courgette, a load that barely fitted sideways into his slobbering mouth. 'But I need to assess some of the prisoners,' he spat in the diplomat's direction. 'The prison is overcrowded you must understand. Some, I am led to believe, can be rehabilitated earlier than their original sentence.'

'Oh really.'

'Yes. There's a German war prisoner here for god's sake. Been here since 1915. I have been told he is a repeat offender. I'll be looking at his file tomorrow.'

Du Bellay felt a hot and cold shiver. 'You can't do that,' he said without thinking.

'Why on earth not?'

'I … ah … you said he's a repeat offender. You can't allow him wander the islands a free man.' Du Bellay knew released prisoners were not allowed to return to France. They were expected to work the land and populate the French Colonies in the Pacific.

'And why not, pray tell?' Maxence said.

'He might escape the island, for one thing.'

'Well, he would be a fool to try,' the warden said. 'He would only end up back in prison.'

Bellay had heard enough. He needed fresh air before the course of French cheeses was served with its traditional accompaniment and dessert wines. Excusing himself he stepped out onto portico. The night was balmy and still, with only a quarter moon to cast a subtle light amongst the coconut palms surrounding the commissioner's homestead. Du Bellay stepped onto the manicured lawn and walked into the shadows where he was not observed. Noisy crickets fell silent on his approach. Hidden by the night, Felix Du Bellay took out his silver cigarette case using it as a platform to empty a neat line of cocaine from a glass phial, before snorting a generous portion. The effect was instant. Energised, Du Bellay smoked a Gauloise and savoured the strong distinctive taste of Mother France.

•   •   •

Somewhere in the South Pacific on a lonely small island. March 1923
Over five weeks had passed since castaway Arthur J Money saw his first ship on the horizon. He ran to the highest peak on the

island waving frantically, but the ship was a good ten miles away. All Arthur could do was watch it cross the horizon and vanish.

But if nothing else, this encounter warned him, he needed to be more vigilant. It also gave him hope. He would spend most of his days looking out for a ship. Arthur moved camp, building himself a larger, more solid and more comfortable shelter on the highest peak. Shaped like a sugarloaf, it had two rooms, one for sleeping and one for storing food. The walls were three feet thick, and the sealskin roof secured with rafters of driftwood. Hanging on its chain from a driftwood hook was Arthur's most precious possession, the silver pocket watch bestowed upon him by Captain Thomas Cosgrove. The watch gave him hope, along with determination that one day he would hand it over to the captain's son, like he promised. Soaring from his shelter was the trusty oar, with a white flag made from Fitz's weathered shirt.

Weeks turned to months.

1923 made way for 1924. Again, there was no celebration. Arthur fought depression. Over the past year he had sighted a dozen vessels, all distant. None had any purpose to visit the island marked on their charts, *uninhabitable*.

Arthur muttered to himself constantly. He craved company, even a dog or a pet rat. Sometime during the changing of summer to autumn, a storm like no other appeared. Gigantic waves washed over the island. Arthur cowered in his shelter. It held. Just. All his hard work paid off. With first light came calm and Arthur was ecstatic to discover flying fish flapping urgently on the shore. As he had not the means of making fire, Arthur ate the fish raw, as he done everything else.

Another lonely month passed when one morning Arthur woke with an acute belly ache. Giving up all hope of rescue he lay in his shelter feeling sorry for himself ...

When he heard a gunshot.

Arthur sat up so sharply his blood pressure dropped dramatically and he nearly fainted. *Was the gunshot a part of a cruel dream?* He dragged his weary body out onto the rocky peak and searched the coast …

A ship!

• • •

Isle of Pines exercise yard. Noon. 1924
After two and a half weeks in solitary Jonathon Bourke treasured his hour exercise more than anything. It allowed him to take his mind of his desperate situation. He couldn't for the life of him work out exactly how or why he ended up here. He could die here.

No! He chastised himself for his negative thoughts. *You must escape. There's gotta be a way.*

He remembered his conversation with Arsala, Harry and Juvita and how he told them about Herr Kohl and the SS *Prinzessin* gold lost on the reef. And how Kohl was now a prisoner on the Isle of Pines. *'As this prisoner is possibly the only man alive who knows where the wreck lies, we sail to Noumea and break the poor devil out of prison, that's what we do,'* Bourke had told his crew. *'I swear, he will be desperate to be free and there's plenty of gold for everyone.'*

'And how, may I ask, do you plan to break the man out of a French prison?' Harry had asked Bourke. *'Not certain,'* Bourke had answered. *'But I'm working on it.'*

Working on it. Yeh right. Now *here he was in more shit than the early settlers*, as his old man would have said.

• • •

Herr Adolf Kohl

For twenty-three hours a day Bourke was held in a cell six foot by eight foot. His ankles were shackled at night. The cell was humid, hot, and plagued by rodent-sized insects – cockroaches – and spiders.

For those prisoners not in solitary, fights were common, and murders went uninvestigated. Physical abuse of a guard was punishable by death – death by guillotine; a macabre rectangular framed structure fitted with a sharp steel blade designed for beheading. It looked more like a portal with a cane bucket at the bottom to collect the severed head. Like a portal to the afterlife. The guillotine stood in the quadrangle within the prison walls. If a prisoner avoided the guillotine there was a good chance disease, hunger or mistreatment would finish him. And as if that was not humiliating enough, the dead were wheeled in barrows to the water's edge and fed to the ever-present sharks.

Bourke lost all sense of time. He feared he was losing his sanity.

•   •   •

Asmodeus Boucher was a sadistic bastard, a guard with a fierce reputation. The twenty-eight-year-old had spent his war years on the Somme back in France and had seen it all, from bodies shredded by artillery to the cold-blooded murder of captured enemy soldiers. He entered the war an eighteen-year-old innocent and was discharged a cold-hearted murderer. Boucher had no respect for his fellow humans. He had killed many Germans on the battlefield, some with his bare hands. Human life meant nothing to him. In fact he harboured a dark secret. Deep down he knew if he was not here on the Isle of Pines, he would be stalking the streets of Paris at night, killing vagrants, or prostitutes – or anyone to rid mankind of what he considered vermin. To Boucher, being a prison guard on this godforsaken island was a natural promotion after his war years. That's why he volunteered five years ago. It was a picnic. Life on a tropical island. What more could he ask for?

The short but powerfully built warder with the chiselled body, short cropped hair accentuating his block-shaped head and cold dark eyes, unlocked Bourke's cell door and scowled.

'Sors ton cul ici, vite!' He spat at Bourke. *Get your arse out of there, quickly.*

Bourke saw the truncheon and hesitated, only to infuriate Boucher further. Today he avoided a belting but the poke in the ribs had him seething with anger.

One day …

But a chain of events changed everything.

With several exercise yards in use Bourke was herded into *Cour d'Exercice C* with nineteen other miserable souls. The one-hour circling of the yard perimeter commenced, and the continuous, monotonous, yet rhythmic, rattling of leg irons followed Bourke in his wake.

'You … hey you,' the whispered voice startled Bourke. The man directly behind him was risking a beating if caught talking. Bourke ignored the man whose accent didn't sound French. 'You from Australia … ja?'

Bourke longed for company. He hadn't had a conversation for six weeks. 'Yes. Why do you ask?' he said in a barely audible voice, keeping his head down, facing the man in front of him.

'I hear Australian prisoner here for assaulting French whore?'

'Hardly. I … I didn't assault her. Ah … it's a long story.'

'Ja. I am thinking the French bitch, she ask for it, ja?'

'No, not exactly. It was a misunderstanding. Say …' Bourke had a thought. 'You're German are you not?'

'Ja. Come here as prisoner of war but bloody war end years ago. Still here! I have enough, I kill some bastard and escape I'm thinking.'

Bourke turned. 'Herr Kohl?'

Herr Kohl had aged. He was now forty-eight, imprisoned when he was thirty-eight. He looked sixty-eight and felt eighty-eight. 'How you know my name?'

'I …'

There was no recourse to answer. Asmodeus Boucher descended from the gantry screaming and cursing. The prisoners froze. The iron door at the end of the yard slammed open and four guards bulldozed their way through the miserable bodies between them and the two conversing prisoners. Boucher flew into Kohl with his truncheon, beating the man mercilessly about the arms, head, shoulders and legs.

'Leave him!' Bourke shouted over the commotion and tried to pull the German away, but he was beaten about the legs with a truncheon for his trouble. Bourke fell to his knees, while Kohl punched into Boucher the best he could with shackles and chained wrists, his pent-up anger from years of abuse rising to the boil. Unprepared for the assault Boucher slipped and fell.

Kohl pounced.

He rammed a knee into the guard's throat and used secured fists to pummel the man's face. Boucher screamed for help. Kohl had overstepped the line. He was relentless. Ruthless. And Boucher's face split where Kohl's shackles pounded his head.

But it was futile. Kohl's five seconds of rage was his death sentence. The other guards pummelled him with truncheons relentlessly, their clubs a frenzy of retribution until another guard detail took charge. The other prisoners cheered but were smartly silenced and herded prematurely back to their cells, but not before witnessing Boucher's beating. The guard had lost face, cowering beneath the large German, as weak and old as the prisoner appeared. Kohl's adrenalin had matched his hatred. Now Kohl was the beaten man. Bruised and battered, unconscious, he was dragged away to the infirmary.

The next day Bourke learned he had earned a measure of respect from his fellow prisoners. In the brief moment it took for the prisoner on duty to slip his only meal for the day through the cell door, Bourke was told that as soon as Kohl was of reasonable health, he would be taken to the courtyard and executed.

'La guillotine,' the man whispered to Bourke and ran a finger across his throat in a gesture of decapitation. 'La guillotine Monsieur Australien.'

CHAPTER SIX

Somewhere in the South Pacific on a lonely small island. March 1924
A single funnel steel-hull steamship anchored off the reef.
Arthur waved feverishly. He yelled. He screamed. He hoisted
the oar and flag from its foundation wielding it like a madman.
He could barely make out the crew, but another gunshot told
him they had seen him. Arthur rubbed at his eyes. Was this some
sadistic mind torture? His imagination? Immediately a boat was
launched, and men rowed towards the shore. Arthur snatched
the watch and rushed to the shoreline where he had been
washed ashore a year and a half earlier.

The boat crew searched desperately for a safe landing. But
there wasn't one. Arthur watched, in desperation. The men
rowed up and down the outer reef. Finally, in frustration they
made signals that they could not land. Arthur watched the
longboat start to row back towards their vessel, which he now
recognised as a Japanese commercial fishing boat. They were
unable to find a safe landing to rescue him.

Arthur panicked. So close yet so far. Suddenly life was not
worth living without salvation. With oar in hand Arthur J
Money rushed into the surf and, using his oar once again for
buoyancy, he swam for the reef.

The boat crew cheered him on. They rowed as close as they
dared to the breaking surf where they threw him a glass fishing
buoy on a rope. Arthur managed to grab the buoy on the fifth

wave and was hauled over the reef. The lacerations encountered were nothing compared to the jubilation of being rescued.

The crew of the Japanese whaler *Tsukyo Maru* were as astounded at their rescue as Arthur was to be liberated. He wept as they carried him below, wrapped him in blankets, fed him hot soup and poured him sake. No one spoke English. He had no way of telling them his story. He simply cried, laughed, hugged and nodded his appreciation as the ship sailed north with a hold full of whale meat destined for Osaka.

The days passed. Arthur slept, ate and drank. His health restored, eventually he was able to stand with the captain looking at charts. The captain, whose name he understood to be Toshiro Hayakawa, pointed to where they found him. Toshiro drew a rough sketch of the island with the oar and flag that Arthur had erected and Arthur now understood that it was his makeshift flagpole that had saved him. He understood their final destination to be Osaka, their home port, but eventually through sign language, he requested he be disembarked en route.

· · ·

Isle of Pines. Six weeks after Bourke's arrest in Papeete. 1924
Days later Bourke's luck changed. He was halfway through his sixth week of solitary. It was vanilla season on Lafou Island, the largest of the Loyalty Islands off the east coast of New Caledonia. The fact that the vanilla bean was so labour intensive to harvest – making it second only to saffron in price – meant good behaviour prisoners were ferried to Lafou to work as pickers. This left a shortage of workers back at the Isle of Pines. Men were required for labouring on the infrastructure and able-bodied men were in short supply. It was Bourke's lucky day. Along with sixty others in solitary he was herded into the mess hall at dawn, fed an unexpected breakfast of gruel and water and finally mustered in the quadrangle. Here, surrounded by cell blocks

with their plastered terracotta-coloured walls, the infamous guillotine stood proud at one end, its steel blade a threatening reminder to toe the line.

What cruel twist of fate was this? The men muttered. *Feed us a full belly and then force us to watch an execution.*

But it was not to be. Not directly. The prisoners' relief was palpable. Each man was unshackled and given a change of clothing; a striped long sleeve shirt with trousers, and to protect them against the tropical sun, wide brimmed hats of plaited straw. The leg irons were replaced, but their wrists kept free. Each man was given a number and equipped with a sledgehammer, to be carried over the right shoulder like a rifle. Finally, they were marched in two orderly, well-guarded lines out through the main gate and towards buildings under construction two miles away. The hard labour had commenced. For the next twelve hours, 6AM until 6PM, the men would crush rocks and cart heavy stones. But Captain Jonathon Bourke felt a freedom he hadn't thought possible in over six weeks.

The days passed. A positive energy returned – energy that had deserted him in 'solitary'. To Bourke's delight, at night he was locked in a dormitory with ten prisoners to a cell. He had company. He polished his French language. Being the only foreigner, he was ostracized by some. But these lost souls underestimated the resilience of Captain Jonathon Bourke and slowly he befriended most.

One barbarian, Ivan Toussaint, was a six foot six, two-hundred-and-forty-pound muscleman. A showman from a travelling theatre who took it upon himself to beat his employer almost to death's door for being accused of sleeping with the man's flirtatious wife. He and Bourke had something in common.

The toil continued, every day except the Sabbath.

•   •   •

The news from Arsala's lawyer cousin Aalok Khatri hadn't been good. An extradition wasn't worth thinking about. The Australian Government certainly were not going to interfere with French justice when they agree Captain J. Bourke of Cooktown was guilty of assaulting a diplomat's wife. A lady in fact!

'The Australian Consulate,' Aalok Khatri told Arsala, Juvita and Harry back in his office twenty-four hours after the telegram was read. 'They say they would monitor the sentence. They agreed he should do some time, maybe two years yes.'

'T-two years!' Harry detonated. 'Two bloody years ... not friggin' likely mate.' Harry twisted about to the other two. 'We gotta bust 'im outta there. No question.'

'I agree,' Arsala shook his head. He had felt squashed between a rock and a hard place. Juvita nodded silently. Her face pinched in concentration as scenarios and ideas flashed through her mind.

'I do have however ...' Khatri looked through the office window out onto the busy street before lowering his voice as if prying ears were pressed against the glass. 'I do however have friend in Noumea, yes. Old friend from Bombay.'

Harry looked hopeful. 'Yes, yes. What about him?'

'Her, actually.'

'Her? A she ... I mean a woman?'

'Yes of course. Well ... she doesn't exactly have much respect for law, yes.'

Harry managed a slight smile. 'You sayin' she's dodgy mate?'

'Dodgy! Yes, good word for her I'm thinking. Yes, dodgy.' Khatri went on to explain, albeit under the strictest confidence, how he had an acquaintance who ran a small bar and café in Noumea but her main bread and butter came from black-marketing. 'In fact, I tell you true, there is nothing this woman cannot procure ... for a price of course.'

Harry grinned. 'Guns?'

'Anything.'

Arsala shifted foot to foot. 'Now Harry, we won't be wanting guns.'

'Bullshit.' Harry saw the shock on both Arsala and Juvita's face. 'I ain't gonna shoot no one, just scare the bastards.'

'Can this woman be trusted?' Juvita asked.

'She is Muslim, of course she can be trusted … I think.'

Khatri explained Ghunwah Darwish was now in her fifties. She was born in Persia but grew up in Bombay, immigrating to Fiji with her Indian husband who was indentured to a sugar plantation, before the war in 1913. But when her husband died of the Spanish Flu in 1919, she moved to Noumea where, at forty-five-years of age she had to use her wits to survive. Darwish learnt French and opened a food stand before progressing to a small eatery, then upgraded to the Café Chez Moi three years ago. But along the way she found the black market far more lucrative. Now the café is a front for her nefarious activities.

'She dabbles in this and that,' Khatri had told the others. 'And I hear there is nothing she cannot source.'

•   •   •

Unfamiliar with the reefs and coastline Arsala waited for first light to sail *Drifter* into Mont-Dore Bay, a little over six miles south of New Caledonia's main town, Noumea, located on a peninsular in the south of New Caledonia's largest island of Grande Terre. Harry had sailed into this bay before of course, suggesting the deserted village a good place to anchor, row ashore and walk to Noumea. This way they could blend in with the mixed-race population of the island, with Europeans living side by side with Polynesians, Indonesians, Vietnamese, Melanesians, and the indigenous Kanaks. Like *Drifter's* mixed-race crew, the island was a cosmopolitan melting pot.

The village was home to a few families only. Originally settled as a small convict settlement to exploit the timber resources here for building materials for Noumea, it had been abandoned fifteen years earlier.

The anchor chain rattled through the hawsehole, reverberating about the stillness of the deep-water bay. Along the shore, well above high tide mark, smoke spiralled from several grass huts where local Kanaks cooked their staple breakfast of fish with fresh lime and yams. Behind the villagers steep-sided mountains rose sharply creating a magnificent vista.

•   •   •

Out at sea a tropical storm rolled across the horizon north to south like an angry serpent. Arsala's attention was drawn to the lightning, some ten miles distant he guessed. But there was a stillness on land than made him check the barometer. The reading was low and dropping. 'More storms coming,' he said. 'I'm thinking good time to be on land.'

The walk along the coastal road to the capital was tiring, the heat oppressive. It was early afternoon by the time Arsala, Juvita, Harry and Bill Brown made the township. Harry noted the buildings weren't unlike those of Suva. Noumea was very much a frontier town, a suitable site for a trading post with its deep-water harbour. Near the *centre du village* they found *la place du marche et le marche,* the marketplace where Khatri said they would find Café Chez Moi.

Ghunwah Darwish was easily recognisable from Khatri's description. A most attractive woman in her fifties, if she embraced Islam, there was no outward sign. She certainly did not wear a hijab. Arsala approached her first, squeezing amongst the crowded tables of happy alfresco diners. 'Bonjour madame,' he said, before switching to Hindi. 'Would you by chance be Ghunwah Darwish?'

The woman looked at Arsala with the eye of a soaring eagle over a field of mice. There followed a pause while she scrutinised Juvita, Harry and Bill waiting out on the street. 'Yes. Why do you ask?'

'Aalok Khatri sent us.'

'Aalok! I haven't heard from him for some time. Is he still taking lots of money from the rich in Suva?'

Arsala nodded with a chuckle. 'He's my cousin.'

'Poor you. What do want? You can see I am very busy.'

'Aalok said you could help us.'

'Did he now? How?'

'We have a dear friend on the Isle of Pines. He needs help.'

Darwish looked about at her noisy diners, fearful they might be overheard. She frowned and walked away towards the kitchen. If anything, Arsala thought he had upset the woman. Darwish spoke to another older waitress, a dark-skinned native woman with a large afro and the whitest of eyes. She nodded and went about her business. Darwish looked back to Arsala, tipping her head for him to follow. The others joined Arsala, and they were ushered through the busy kitchen where half a dozen cooks and kitchen hands wok fried, steamed and ladled curries with expertise and confidence that had Juvita's admiration.

Darwish showed them into her storeroom office at the rear of the property. She closed the door. 'Parle français ou anglaise,' she said in French. Harry was immediately smitten. This dark-skinned exotic beauty with the husky voice had a fine firm figure, with long legs for a Persian woman.

'Parle what?' Harry asked.

Darwish looked to Arsala. 'French or English?'

'English then,' Arsala said.

'Very well. I haven't got all day. What do you want?'

As spokesman for the group Arsala explained the situation. Their captain and good friend was in prison on the Isle of Pines for …

This is where Arsala lied.

'For having a liaison with a French diplomat's wife.'

'Come now,' Darwish smiled wryly. 'There's more to it than that, surely?'

'I speak true … ah … Mrs Darwish. The diplomat caused quite a kerfuffle.'

'Who is this diplomat?'

'Monsieur Felix Du Bellay.'

'Bellay!' Darwish's eyes narrowed with anger. 'That bastard!' Suddenly Harry found the woman positively striking. He wanted to say, *damn woman, you are so desirable when you're irked.* Instead, he laughed out loud. 'Bastard. Aye, yer got that bit right.'

'I know this man,' Darwish went on. 'He is a pig,' she spat on the dirt floor. 'So, what can I do to help?'

'Have you heard of Devil's Island?' Harry asked.

'Of course, off Guiana in the Atlantic. Another French catastrophe, worse than Isle of Pines, much, much worse.'

'Well, that's where this bastard Bellay is sending our skipper.'

'Are you serious? No one, and I mean no one, escapes Devil's Island.'

'That's why we must free him now,' Juvita said. 'It is most urgent.'

'He's in solitary,' Bill said. 'We know that much.'

'Solitary.' Darwish shook her head. 'That is high security. Very, very difficult.'

'Can you get a message to 'im like?' Harry said. 'Give the poor bugger hope to start with.'

'I have contacts, yes. One friend I have, she is housekeeper to Monsieur Paquet the new warden. She was housemaid to last warden also, three years now, and she knows many guards whose palms like to be crossed with silver.'

Bill looked confused. 'Palms? Silver?'

'Take a bribe.'

Harry looked to his colleagues. 'I'm not leavin' this island without the skipper, alright?'

Arsala and Juvita agreed. 'But it's going to be tough.'

'Tough,' Darwish scoffed aloud. 'It's near impossible.'

Harry swung back to Darwish. 'You dabble in contraband, yes?'

'Maybe,' she said warily.

'Guns, ammo?'

Darwish immediately had a renewed respect for this rough and ready Australian. Her face broke into a seductive smile that had Harry's heart racing. 'What did you have in mind sailor?'

Sailor. Was this woman flirting.

'What do I have in mind?' Harry wanted to say *throw you over that tea chest honey and party 'til there's no tomorrow.* 'What do I have in mind? Maybe small arms. Pistols?'

'P-pistols?' Arsala coughed, nearly choking on his words. 'Pistols? Small arms! Harry, we're not killers.'

'No, we ain't Arsala, but like I said, we can scare the bastards … bluff our way like.'

Fireman Bill Brown shifted from foot to foot and rubbed his hands together. 'I'm with you Harry,' he grinned, an infectious grin with one tooth missing.

Arsala said. 'Fine.'

Darwish checked the storeroom door was bolted. Fetching a carbide lamp from off the shelf she lit the wick and tweaked the light, before leading them through a narrow passageway a short distance. They came to a dead end. Darwish held the lamp to be certain all her visitors were behind her, then leant forward rolling a large secret panel aside, sitting on castors, like a sliding door.

'Open sesame,' she rasped in her bewitching voice, proud of her hidden cache. Hooking the lamp on a ceiling peg, the shifting light illuminated shelf after shelf of contraband - duty free booze, cigarettes, perfumes, and wines. But it was the guns that had Harry's attention. Harry entered first. He whistled. 'Maschinengewehr 08.'

'You know your guns,' Darwish smiled.

'I was in France love,' Harry spoke of the war a few years back.

'Oh.' Nearly every second Australian who Darwish met had served in Europe.

'Aye. And I've seen a few o' these in me time.' Harry walked over to stroke one of three machine guns on their tripods in the centre of the room. 'Twenty-eight-inch one-gallon water-cooled barrel jacket, 250 round fabric belt capable of firing 450 rounds of Mauser 7.92 by 57 millimetre bullets per minute with an effective range of over 2200 yards.' Harry lifted a heavy belt of live ammo from an open ammo crate on the floor and let the bullets drop back into place with a satisfying tinker. 'You know by 1917 the Huns were manufacturing nearly fourteen and a half thousand of these little mongrels per month.'

Darwish was mightily impressed.

'How much?' Harry asked, his face smiling like a kid in a sweet shop.

Darwish stood with her mouth open. She was incredulous. 'You *do* know your guns.' Her cheeky grin was positively seductive. This gave Harry confidence. There seemed a chemistry between them.

'Like I said lady, France 1916 to '18 and Turkey before that in '15. I was a gunner. Now, how much?'

'Hundred pounds each.'

'We'll take one. And the ammo?'

'Five pounds a belt.'

'We'll take one crate.'

Arsala swallowed hard. He knew there would be no compromise. 'Where did you acquire these?' Arsala asked. 'If you do not mind me asking the question.'

Darwish didn't mind at all. In fact, she was quite proud and considered their pedigree worth crowing about. 'Have you heard of the *Emden*?'

'The *Emden*,' Arsala said, his voice suddenly high in pitch. 'Of course, one of Australia Navy's biggest achievements.'

The others too, of course, knew Darwish spoke of the German light cruiser SMS *Emden* hunted and sunk by HMAS *Sydney* off the Cocos Islands in the Indian Ocean at the beginning of the war in 1914.

'There were several of these stored in the ship's hold and they were 'souvenired' by the local people. About a year ago six made their way to Noumea. I have sold three already.'

'Nice work,' Harry couldn't help himself, he shot Darwish a rakish wink. 'Any pistols?'

'Only Lugers.'

'Off *Emden* too huh?'

'No. They came from Bita Paka German-occupied New Guinea actually. In September 1914 Australian forces captured the German wireless station there.'

'How much?'

'Ten pounds each with hundred rounds.'

'We'll take two.' Harry looked to Arsala. 'Pay the lady.'

'Ah ... yes ... but there's the thing see.'

Harry asked, 'What thing?'

'I do not carry such moneys on my person. You know these things Harry.'

'But you have funds, right?' Darwish said. 'On your boat?'

'Yes, yes,' Arsala nodded vigorously. 'Of course, Mrs Darwish.'

'We're anchored at Mont-Dore Bay.' Harry said. 'You're gonna get a word to our skipper in prison, right?'

'That's my intention,' Darwish said. 'But I will need bribes also.'

'How much?'

Darwish though a moment. 'I think fifty pounds will be enough ... yes ... fifty pounds.'

Juvita looked at their host with distrust. 'Fifty!'

'Yes. Twenty each for two guards and ten for my friend at the warden's house.'

'Then I will return with the money,' Harry said.

'When you return, I will fetch you a donkey and cart to carry the machinegun and ammunition, once I have the money. But you will have to pay the owner another pound for the hire. He is a friend. I trust him.'

'I'll bring the money back myself,' Harry said.

'If that's what you so desire, Harry.'

Darwish tapped a cigarette from a packet of Camel, sliding it into the corner of her mouth before offering Harry the packet. *Harry.* Harry thought, there she goes again; she *is* flirting. He shook his head at the offer before taking a shagreen Dunhill table lighter he always kept in his pocket, and lit Darwish's cigarette.

'Nice lighter,' Darwish said, drawing in the smoke in a most satisfying breath. She was impressed.

'Yeh. A souvenir from an officers' club in Tahiti.'

'You mean you stole it,' Darwish craned her neck towards the ceiling and exhaled. The chemistry between them was real, Cupid had fired his damned arrow. Bullseye.

• • •

Outside, back amongst the hustle and bustle of the busy market the periphery of the storm edged towards land. It seemed the locals were preparing ahead, buying up supplies.

'We should buy vegetables while we are here,' Juvita suggested.

'Buy what we need in the village,' Arsala spoke of the fisherman's village where they had anchored. 'It is closer. May I suggest Harry, when you collect your gun and ammunition, that you buy more fresh supplies to hide your completely illegal purchase.'

'Aye, I will.'

'I think she likes you Harry,' Bill Brown said with a cheeky smile showing off his missing front tooth.

'Do yer think so Billy?'

'I know so Harry. And so do you, I'm thinkin'.'

Harry was adamant, he would return to Noumea alone. Bill was disappointed. Arsala was nervous. 'I should be back by midday tomorrow,' Harry told the others, folding the pound notes and stuffing them tightly into his right boot.

'I should be comin' with yer Harry,' Bill said.

'Nar Bill, I'll attract less attention on me own.'

•   •   •

Noumea waterfront. On board the Japanese whaler Tsukyo Maru.
Japanese sea captain Toshiro Hayakawa studied the weather with an experienced eye. The barometer was falling. He read the signs. But with a full cargo of whale meat he wasn't prepared to risk spoiling, and a pregnant wife expecting their fourth child in two weeks back in Osaka, he threw caution to the wind, literally. Besides, he reasoned, the storm was heading south-west and if they continued their north-west passage to Osaka, they should outrun the worst of it. Hayakawa watched the coal bunker being filled. They should be underway by midday.

Arthur J Money made his farewell to the captain, bowing the way Japanese bowed, not through any particular politeness. He just thought it proper. The captain had enjoyed the Australian's company the week they had been at sea together and returned the gesture. He said a few words in Japanese that Arthur would never understand, and Arthur thanked the man several times in return. They may have been worlds apart, but their feelings were mutual.

Arthur had no idea where he was headed, but he did not wish to be at sea in a storm anytime soon. He would take his chances in Noumea. It couldn't be that difficult he considered, finding a passage to Australia from New Caledonia. Arthur's only fear was being recognised by the law. But after his terrifying ordeal as a castaway, he was prepared to risk anything to return home to Australia. Arthur stepped onto the gangway when Captain Hayakawa caught up with him one last time.

'Ah … mizzer Arthur … Arthur Money san,' the captain bowed, and passed his cap upside down to Arthur. It was full of foreign banknotes and coins of all denominations. He gestured for Arthur to take the money. Clearly the captain had passed his hat around the crew for donations. Arthur felt tears well up. He gratefully accepted, and continued on down the gangway, humbled by the experience.

Arthur pocketed the money, secreting it with his only other possession, Captain Cosgrove's silver fob watch. There wasn't a great deal of cash, but enough to buy a meal or two. Arthur had visited Noumea before of course, but today there seemed to be more gendarmes around in their smart white uniforms and white pith helmets. Arthur had also passed counterfeit banknotes in Tahiti some time back. He was on the brink of being arrested but managed to leave before he was charged. Maybe it was paranoia or maybe there were extra policemen on duty with a possible cyclone imminent. So today was not the day to take risks. Either way Arthur felt uncomfortable. He decided to walk south out of the main township, where he could sit out the storm and then search for a passage home.

Fate is an interesting beast.

Arthur took shelter from the burning early afternoon sun amongst a copse of coconut palms near a village at Mont-Dore. He had walked six miles to an area he knew reasonably well. Prising the cork from a bottle of Burgundy, Arthur took a swig of wine, his first alcohol beside sake in eighteen long months. The effect was instant. He took another long drink before biting into a fresh baguette. He was in Heaven.

Immediately activity caught his attention. He studied the old steamer anchored in the bay. She could do with a paint job, but more importantly he saw the flag hoisted at the stern post. And it was the Union Jack with the Southern Cross. She was Australian. As he watched on, the tender was lowered, and crew started to row ashore.

CHAPTER SEVEN

Isle of Pines

Warder Asmodeus Boucher paid a visit to prisoner Herr Kohl in the prison infirmary daily. Whilst Kohl's bruises might fade and other wounds heal, he would have to be executed with the cracked ribs. Boucher let himself into the locked hospital ward and stood alone at the end of Kohl's bed. He said nothing, he never did. Kohl struggled, but he was shackled with handcuffs to the iron bed rail. Boucher poked the patient's ribs with the end of his warder's truncheon. Kohl winced, he tried to ignore the pain but unless he cried out in agony the bastard would simply continue until he did. Kohl groaned in pain. Boucher stared deep into his adversary's eyes, draining his soul like a vampire would suck the life blood from its victim. A minute passed when, for the first time in two weeks, Boucher spoke.

'Tomorrow my friend … tomorrow you die. But don't worry, it will be quick. I promise you.' Kohl struggled violently, rattling the bed with his restraints. The room was unbearably humid and beads of sweat soaked his brow. Boucher took up a swab and patted the prisoner's face.

'Just think of me as your head rolls into the basket,' the warder said in a mock, softly caring voice. 'Think of me, Monsieur Asmodeus Boucher, drinking your warm blood.' Boucher thought a moment. 'A doctor once told me that the brain lives on for a good minute or two after being severed from its pumping heart, its blood supply you see. He told me in that minute the victim is aware of all activity about him before death takes over.'

Kohl made to shout, to yell at his tormentor, but Boucher stuffed the swab into the wide yawning mouth before he had a chance. Kohl battled to breath, just managing enough air to survive. Fighting anxiety, he tried to slow his heartbeat.

Then, as a final act of humiliation, Boucher drew a finger across his own throat in the age-old pantomime of death and smiled – a heinous grin that would make Satan proud. The warder threw his head back and closed his eyes briefly, luxuriating in his evil thoughts. He took deep sharp breaths, as the very thought of watching a man lose his head to the guillotine aroused him. Finally, with a maniacal laugh, he relocked the infirmary ward and stepped out into the quadrangle.

Outside was sultry. The afternoon was hot, uncomfortably so. Asmodeus Boucher sniffed the air. The thug could smell trouble brewing in the darkening sky. Had he noted the barometer reading in the infirmary he would have been uneasy at its interpretation. The feel of the atmosphere was dense, heavy. The barometric pressure was dropping dramatically. Yes, a storm was imminent.

Boucher crossed the quadrangle to the administration buildings and sought out the warden in his office. Monsieur Paquet wasn't pleased with the interruption. He had freshly baked pastries and a pot of coffee delivered from the cookhouse, and it sat on his desk before him.

'What is it Boucher?'

'The prisoner Kohl monsieur.'

'What of him?'

'He's to be executed.'

'Yes.'

'When sir? I just came from the infirmary and in my opinion, he is well enough.'

'In your opinion huh?'

'Yes monsieur.'

'It is scheduled for tomorrow afternoon, but it appears that a decent size storm is approaching, if not a cyclone. I want all the prisoners to witness this punishment. We have to stay on top of the situation. It's been prison regulation since this colony was opened, assaulting a guard is punishable by death.'

'Yes monsieur. I agree absolutely. Tomorrow then. Good day to you sir.' If Boucher's sickening, departing smile worried the warden, he kept it to himself.

•   •   •

Noumea. Late that afternoon.

As Darwish had promised, she telegraphed the postal service on the Isle of Pines with a coded message for Rose Wajoka, the housekeeper at the warden's residence. This wasn't the first time information from the prison had been leaked in this fashion. Years earlier Darwish had taken Rose under her wing when she was destitute. She gave her work in her café kitchen and looked after her children when Rose's fisherman husband drowned. Three years earlier, it had been Darwish who secured the housekeeping position for Rose at the prison. Now Rose owed Darwish, and she was only too happy to help.

Clean shaven and sponged with perfumed soap, Harry returned to the Chez Moi with the cash and a spring in his step. It was early evening when he arrived on foot, wet from the fine rain that had been falling consistently all afternoon.

Darwish liked what she saw in Harry. He was rough and ready, grew up tough, called a spade a spade. They had a lot in common. However, business was business. She kept a straight face and if Harry was disappointed, she didn't seem to notice.

'You have the money?'

'Straight to business huh,' Harry said, pushing his cap to the back of his head.

'Well?' Darwish had been hoodwinked in the past. Taken in by other, less than honest men. She was sharp. Savvy. Harry looked about him. The weather had kept diners away this evening and only the tables under cover were occupied. Curious eyes looked in Harry's direction. He lowered his voice. 'Yes, I have the money. Can we go somewhere private?'

Darwish led the way back through the kitchen. If she had flirted with him earlier in the day, now she seemed at odds. Spirits dampened, Harry took a deep breath and followed.

With a carbide lamp lighting the store about them once more, Harry didn't hesitate. He pulled the wad of notes from his boot and started counting.

'Hundred quid for the Hun, twenty quid for the Lugers, fifty for bribes, and fifty quid for the crate ... that's ten belts of ammo at five quid a belt.' Harry was left with three single one-pound notes. 'And here's two quid for the donkey.'

Darwish took the money, stashing it down the front of her tight-fitting blouse. 'You have one pound over I see,' she said with the slightest smile.

'Aye.' Harry's lascivious thoughts returned. 'I thought I might buy yer a drink.'

'Oh, did you now?' Darwish made to pass Harry between the Maschinengewehr 08 and the crates of ammunition, when Harry caught her with both hands, turned her to face him, and, taking a buttock in each hand, pulled himself closer trying to steal a kiss.

'What the hell?' Darwish had the strength to match Harry. 'What do you think I am?'

Harry's mouth opened and closed like a landed mullet. At the same moment the dark-skinned woman with a large afro and the whitest of eyes walked into the store unannounced. She saw everything. Harry stepped back, floundering. 'I ... I ... ah .... I'm sorry, I thought ...'

'Thought what?'

'Me and you,' Harry stammered. 'I ... damn!'

'Well, I'm sorry soldier boy, but you got that bit all wrong.'

'I feel such a fool.'

The afro stepped closer. 'Everything alright in here?' she said in a strong South Carolina accent. 'Everything okey-dokey sweet pea?'

Sweet pea?

Harry wasn't certain he heard right, until Darwish joined the waitress and put an affectionate arm about her, her hand resting on her booty.

'Was this 'ere man tryin' you on babe?' Afro said, enjoying Harry's discomfort.

'It's all good Raven,' Darwish said. 'Old Harry here had a misunderstanding, didn't you Harry?'

'Ah ...' Harry knew he was blushing. His face was red-hot. 'Ah ... a misunderstanding. Yer, you could say that again.' He tried to reclaim some dignity.

'Here's the last telegram,' Afro said, passing Darwish the document. 'It just come in from the Post Office a moment ago.'

'Thank you. Close the door after you, I need to explain all this to Harry.'

'Sure, sweet pea.' Raven made to pull the door closed, leaving it ajar a moment, her bouffant afro-style hair filling the gap. 'You certain you want to be left alone with *Twenty-thousand Leagues under the sea* here,' she laughed.

Darwish dismissed Raven with a flick of the hand, leant against the ammunition crates and ran an eye over the latest telegram.

'Hmm ... your skipper, Jonathon Bourke, is out of solitary and doing hard labour with a road gang. You know what that means?'

Still hurting, Harry shrugged.

'It means it's good news. If you are serious about freeing the man, then this is more do-able. Now I can get a message to him, no problem. And for the twenty pounds you gave me we can buy the support of one guard, that is, this guard will turn his back and let Bourke escape. But we've got to be certain he is rostered on; the day Bourke makes his attempt.'

'How will we manage that?'

'You leave that to me. Bourke will be given instruction to make it to the south coast of the island. Nearly all escapees attempt to run north, trying to reach the New Caledonia mainland. But you and your friends will sail to Koroxu Bay and wait. You will have the tender ready, waiting at a rendezvous point here.' Darwish handed Harry a hand-drawn map. 'I must warn you; the authorities will throw everything at this. They will pursue. They are relentless. You will have to sail out to sea immediately.'

'Thank you. As you said this looks do-able. It's gotta work. The skipper's a good man.'

'I'm sure he is. You just be certain you aren't caught, otherwise you'll *all* end up on Devil's Island.'

'Don't worry, we won't be caught.'

'Good, I might have that drink with you now.' Darwish took a bottle of Scotch whisky off the shelf, peeling away the pewter seal, she prised the cork free. Although the store smelled of the mechanical scents of machine grease and cordite, Harry's sensitive nose caught the malty cereal undertones of the whisky's mash. *Bit like bread or maybe biscuits*, his old man would say whenever he cracked a bottle. Which was often. Darwish took a swig from the bottle and for the first time Harry sensed the *man* in the woman. She passed it to Harry. He drank for good luck, and a second deep tug to forget his embarrassment.

'Thanks, now if yer don't mind I'd appreciate yer fetching the cart and donkey and I'll be gettin' back to the lads.' Harry looked

Darwish in the eye for the first time since his mistaken identity. 'Hey,' he said, the whisky giving him courage. 'Sorry about … well, you know.'

'Forget about it … tiger.'

. . .

Ten bob – that's half of the remaining one quid note left in Harry's boot – purchased four bags of vegetables: one each of yams, potatoes, carrots and turnips. Besides the vegetables being much needed supplies, the sacks made the necessary camouflage for the German machine gun, its hefty tripod mount, water hose, tank and the crate of ammunition. The other ten bob bought Harry two bottles of whisky.

Under cover of darkness and increasing rain, at the rear of Café Chez Moi, Harry loaded the purchases onto a barrow-like cart pulled by a donkey. His companion, the donkey's owner, was a simple yet happy local, whom he only knew as Armand. Armand could not speak English. Fifty minutes after Harry's faux-pas with Darwish, he set off on the six-mile hike back to Mont-Dore Bay.

It was nearing midnight when Harry arrived at the bay. An Irishman, drunk on Scottish whisky, he'd sung sea shanties and poor renditions of Irish folk ballads for the last four miles through heavy rain and increasing winds. Both Armand and the donkey were glad to be rid of him.

Harry's best mate Bill Brown heard Harry singing badly well before he saw him, stumbling towards the shoreline in the dark, the wind and the mud. He was drunk. Bill climbed out from under his shelter aboard the tender. Harry sat heavily in the sand. The empty bottle slipped from his fingers. He was not in any condition to be of assistance. *I suppose he's done his bit,* Bill muttered to the donkey, and with the help of Armand he loaded the supplies into the boat. Minutes later Harry was manhandled aboard where he collapsed into the sheets and immediately fell asleep.

On board *Drifter*, Arsala smelt the whisky on Harry and realised what had taken him so long. 'He gave me these before he collapsed,' Bill said, handing Arsala the telegrams, a hand drawn map and instructions. 'And he mumbled something about the cap'n being messaged.' There's a copy of the message amongst that lot.' Bill, who couldn't read, nodded to the papers he had passed to Arsala.

Arsala read messages and for the first time in several weeks he felt a measure of hope.

'So, what's the plan skip?' Bill asked, noting Arsala who was fully rigged in oilskins and clearly preparing to sail.

'We head for Koroxu Bay.'

'That's near the Isle o' Pines in'it?'

'That is correct, yes.' Arsala was comfortable wearing the skipper's hat. 'Now I tell you true, you're needed below. Flash has got the fires up. We must sail before this weather gets worse.'

'I was afraid you'd say that.' Anchored in deep water *Drifter* rose and listed as heavy swell trundled beneath them before crashing ashore three hundred yards away. 'Koroxu Bay huh?'

'Yes, yes. Tell the others. It's going to be a long night.' Arsala was not happy sailing at night in such conditions. But with a pending storm or possibly worse brewing out at sea, the life of their beloved captain was at stake, and he was prepared to take the risk. They all were. Harry was hoisted aboard with the tender, now secured on its davits, and covered with canvas. He was dead weight. 'Leave him, I am thinking,' Arsala said. 'Let the drunken sod sleep it off, yes.'

•   •   •

With first light came the disturbing sight of white-capped peaking waves. Arsala was exhausted but fearing a rogue wave he and Juvita kept a sharp eye. They had sailed six hours through darkness, heading first for deeper seas. Arsala was familiar with these waters; he knew of Uo, Noe, Peumba, Ndo and other native-named reefs and rocks off the coast. From Ile Ouen he headed south-east for the Isle of Pines, his position comforted by the searching light of Amedee Lighthouse, far off to starboard, to the south-west.

It was early afternoon when *Drifter* steamed into Koroxu Bay. Earlier they had passed the lights of the prison settlement on the west coast of the isle. Because of the worsening weather, Arsala was confident they would not have attracted any attention from curious villagers. Sailing deep into the bay, he found a snug cove and prepared to batten down hatches. But there was no time for rest.

A cyclone was imminent.

•   •   •

As it eventuated, the warden's housekeeper, Rose Wajoka, found her most reliable ally at the prison was the native gardener, Benjamin Kakou. Kakou had been mistreated by the retired warden and the new warden Monsieur Paquet was shaping up to be no different from his predecessor. Certainly, the gardener was a little simple-minded, which made for good cover in reality. So what if he was caught in an area of the prison he was not authorised to enter. The warders tolerated him, and he humoured them with his simple actions.

Cap'n Jonathon Bourke was slipped the tiny scrunched up note by the clumsy gardener who bumped into him as they filed along to their work site outside the prison gate. Bourke, not expecting such contact was wary, until the man snatched his hand in passing, insisting in a hiss, 'Bourke, yes? Take … take paper.'

It simply read; *Drifter … Arsala … Koroxu Bay*, and in Hindu, of which Bourke had learnt a little from time to time गॉडस्पीड: God speed.

Whose god? Bourke muttered to himself.

．　　．　　．

Cap'n Jonathon Bourke and his road gang were in their second week working on the new road from the prison to the government wharf on the north of the island. For two days now the weather had worsened. The seas were choppy and the top of the palms waved like immigrants aboard a passenger ship embarking for a new life to the other side of the globe. Today the sky grew dark, darker than the devil's lair, and finally the rains came, turning the roadworks into a quagmire. The prisoners read the concern in the eyes of the few locals living in grass huts along the coast – locals who grew fruit and harvested coconuts for the authorities on the prison isle.

'A big storm is on its way,' one of the longer-term prisoners told Bourke, pleased with himself. He looked up into the fast-moving cloud overhead and grinned. 'They'll have to retire us early today.'

True to the man's prediction and to the joy of the road gang they were marched back to the prison and locked in their cells.

By late afternoon it was clear this was no ordinary storm approaching. Off the coast to the east a tropical cyclone was building strength and already reports of devastation from the Fijian Islands were reaching New Caledonia.

．　　．　　．

Warden Monsieur Paquet had planned a luncheon with a friend, Madame Ernestine Labourbe. The prison kitchens had prepared a fine picnic including cold roasted spatchcocks and coconut lime pie. Paquet had chilled two bottles of Laurent-Perrier vintage champagne. Now his plans had to be cancelled and the lonely widow ferried back to the mainland poste-haste. This had placed Paquet in a foul mood as he returned to the prison in his precious chauffeur driven Lorraine-Dietrich Torpedo. The twelve-horsepower, silver-enamelled 1920 Torpedo had been his pride and joy in Paris, a most expensive accessory and necessary for any French gentleman. He had had it shipped with him on his recent voyage from France. Paquet watched his driver reverse the automobile into the stables that had been converted to a garage for his treasured machine. On cue, a valet with an umbrella met the warden at the barn before the two hurried across the quadrangle to the administration block.

• • •

Paquet immediately ordered a muster of the warders and all prison personnel. The sixty-three staff on the payroll met in the canteen where the warden had to shout to be heard over the rattling windows, flapping roofing iron and the screeching of the wind rushing through the palms.

'Clearly we're in for a big blow. I've heard reports sent on the radio of extensive damage in Fiji, and we can expect the same here. I've been sent estimates that the cyclone is sixty miles off the east coast and travelling west at ten knots, so we are expected to be right in its path, under its eye, in about eight hours. That'll be three o'clock tomorrow morning. But as you can see, the preliminary winds are here and it will get progressively worse hour by hour. Now, I've ordered the prisoners to be fed immediately then it's a full lockdown, even privileged prisoners are to be held in total confinement. Have I made myself clear?'

'Yes monsieur.'

'Any questions?'

Asmodeus Boucher looked sullenly out the window, through the driving rain to the guillotine now battered with foliage and debris. 'The Hun,' Boucher said, his face displaying signs of unease. 'Herr Kohl, he is to be executed this afternoon.'

'Are you crazy man?' Paquet shouted.

'Are you saying, Monsieur Paquet, that the execution will be postponed?'

The warden was furious. 'Will someone kindly explain to Monsieur Boucher here why the execution of the German prisoner will be postponed until tomorrow, or maybe even the following day. Jesus Christ man. Now all of you, you have your orders. Get to it.'

. . .

Hour after hour the storm worsened. The vortex of terrifying winds edged closer and closer to the island. For once in their miserable sentences, those prisoners in solitary confinement felt reasonably safe trapped in their claustrophobic stone cells. Bourke was locked in with nineteen other men. With the penitentiary built from thick, heavy quarried stone they were safe enough, until they heard roofing iron lifting off the buildings close by.

Alone in his own room in the guardhouse Asmodeus Boucher sat on his bed shivering. He was scared. He pushed his empty brandy glass to one side and drank directly form the bottle. Boucher was angry, upset and now the cyclone terrified him. The noise, the shaking building all brought back recent memories of the war; artillery shells exploding and grenades detonating in his trench. The pandemonium of thunder, flashes of lightning and devastation had driven the man to the bottle.

. . .

Just after midnight the cyclone made landfall. The first reports of a death were being passed about from nervous warders. One of the ground staff, a gardener from the prison vegetable gardens, was killed instantly by flying corrugated iron as he helped other yardmen tend to chicken coops about to blow away. The unfortunate man was sliced in two. By now, on the coast, the native villages were being annihilated. Ten and twenty foot waves crashed ashore making short work of grass huts before retreating, taking the villagers' livelihoods with it, and leaving the lowlands flooded. Some villagers, too slow to make it inland, were swept out to sea.

All about the prison settlement coconut trees were stripped of foliage and uprooted. Sheets of iron were a major problem, like massive scythes slicing through the air at head height across the island. The more vulnerable buildings collapsed, walls caved in and their contents scattered. It was scene of devastation. Telegraph poles dropped like skittles while power lines arced in the darkness adding to the terror.

· · ·

At 2.45AM the Isle of Pines entered a period of surreal calm. Overhead clouds had cleared while a dreamlike blue light from the moon filtered down upon them. They were directly under the eye of the cyclone as it passed over the island. All about the prison grounds grew eerily quiet.

Instantly Bourke heard shouting, screaming from the quadrangle. With the aid of fellow prisoners, Bourke managed to peer out an air vent near the ceiling.

'No!'

'What's happening?' the men holding Bourke shouted.

Herr Kohl was being frogmarched in his irons from the infirmary towards the guillotine, and by no other than an angry Asmodeus Boucher. Restrained in irons and still in agony from his cracked ribs, Kohl was thrown to the muddy ground at the foot of the guillotine. Boucher started beating the man into submission. As Bourke watched on helplessly, Boucher hoisted the thirty-kilo guillotine blade into position, twelve feet above the stocks. Kohl shouted for mercy, but Boucher silenced him once more with a back-handed slap and a swab of cloth crammed into his mouth. Bourke couldn't believe what he was witnessing. He shouted through the vent. But his words went unheeded. Boucher was a loose cannon, an angry drunkard.

Where were the other guards for Christ's sake!

But Bourke was soon answered. The eye passed overhead. The vortex of wind changed direction. It approached once more and this time with twice the strength. Bourke watched roofing iron lift from the furthest buildings across the quadrangle. Trunks of palm trees uprooted, slamming into the penitentiary. Debris smashed Bourke's block, ramming the vent. He fell backwards, landing heavily on his back.

'It's returning!' he shouted at the cowering inmates as torrential rain peppered the opening. Everyone was on the floor, climbing under the bunks where possible.

There was no warning …

An uprooted coconut palm with a ton of wet soil ploughed into their ward. Brickwork crumbled, avalanching down on the inmates. Rafters were ripped up and roofing iron peeled back exposing the sky. Several men were injured. Bourke stood, mouth open, gaping at the turbulent blackness overhead. Foliage, timber, and detritus attacked the building. He couldn't believe his luck. Bourke didn't hesitate. Mounting the bunks, Bourke clambered to the opening, squeezed through crumbled brickwork and eased himself down to the corridor on the other side of the wall. A dozen men dared to follow. The pandemonium was their saviour. From the corridor the door leading to the quadrangle was damaged. Bourke kicked it off its hinges. He stepped into the open … and was immediately thrown to the ground.

Struggling to stand, Bourke turned to the guillotine fifty metres away. Through the blackness and potage of flying debris, flash lightning strobed Boucher. The maniacal warder was battling the elements to fulfil his demented plan to behead the Hun.

Kohl was now trapped in the stocks, his head locked in the lunette. The blade bolted within its assembly, hanging from the cross bar directly overhead.

This was madness!

The contraption wavered in the wind.

Bourke held his arms before his face. Little protection that it was. Stooped low he pushed into the wind, only to be immediately assaulted by a wayward barrow. Bourke dropped to the ground, summersaulting against the wall. Another strobe of lighting exposed Boucher. He reached for the guillotine lever, but the wind hampered his progress.

No!

Bourke's scream was stolen by the storm. Hail like shotgun pellets stung his face. Head down, he raised himself on hands and knees and crawled, pressing on into the cyclone. Bourke worked his way to the guillotine. Now he saw Boucher's dilemma. The ropes had tangled in the blade grooves. Boucher floundered about, tugging madly to unsnag the ropes. Suddenly Boucher turned. Through sheets of pelting rain, he caught sight of the escaped prisoner. He shouted, cursing pure hatred in his native tongue. With his words lost to the storm he attacked. But Bourke was fit and toned from weeks on the road gang.

The two men tackled each other. Struggling against the tempest. Boots sliding in mud, battered by debris. They fought for their lives. Boucher jerked his truncheon free, hammering Bourke. Bourke ducked and weaved. The club connected. Bourke over balanced, slipping in the mud. Boucher pounced, laying into Bourke with frenzied blows. Bourke rolled aside. He flipped onto his hands and knees … as Boucher pulled a knife … and lunged.

Bourke dodged aside. A large palm frond slapped the warder in the back. Boucher was thrown face down into the quagmire.

Lashed with foliage, Bourke rolled on top of Boucher and with a closed fist he delivered a powerful blow to the man's head. A second punch cracked the warder's nose. Blood spiralled off with the wind. Boucher answered with a string of vitriolic profanities. He threw wild punches, but Bourke was too fast – the stronger, younger of the two adversaries. Pinning Boucher to the ground Bourke delivered more blows, breaking Boucher's nose completely. Other prisoners arrived. Three restrained Boucher, hoisting him to his feet, while two others released Kohl … And … locked Boucher's head firmly into the guillotine stocks in the prisoner's place.

Overhead the cyclone raged. The escapees were bombarded with debris, whipped with palm fronds, their skin stippled by the horizontal rain. But they persevered. All the pent-up anger was released. Suddenly a cheer went up and a curdling scream from Boucher as the guillotine blade was released. The steel blade fell with a squealing of plummeting metal. There was a hollow thud as it sliced through Asmodeus Boucher's neck, severing his head in a silent scream and his blood gushed off into the storm.

The prisoners cheered.

Kohl watched the head roll across the yard. He punched the air in a victory salute, staggering to stand while rain whipped about him. A gust knocked the Hun to the ground, yet he dived after the head like a soccer goalie might chase the ball. The head wedged against the scaffold. Kohl clambered up to it on his hands and knees. He glared into its open eyes. He waited in macabre silence before whispering something into the dead man's ear.

· · ·

Even over the pandemonium the prisoners' commotion could only attract prison personnel. While one prisoner took keys from

Boucher's corpse, another unshackled a grateful Kohl. But immediately, somewhere over the tempest's din they all heard a whistle … and then the siren screamed.

All electrical power was down.

Lantern lights filled the windows of the administration buildings, followed by the guard house. They were sprung.

With the wind in Bourke's favour, he rushed the main gate, tripping and stumbling. But the arched gate was secured with a huge wooden bar locked with padlocks.

So close. So damned close.

A hundred metres away prison personnel gathered. But the cyclone slowed their progress. The other prisoners circled Bourke. Someone shouted. 'The gate's locked!'

'Now what?'

Bourke would never surrender. He spun on his heels. The stables. Although the roof had been destroyed the warden's Lorraine-Dietrich Torpedo was still parked within its walls. Ivan Toussaint, the circus strongman was closest. 'You, Ivan,' Bourke yelled over the din. 'Come with me.'

Ivan enjoyed a grasp on the English language. 'What's the plan boss?'

'I'm not too sure. Follow me.' Bourke made a dash for the stables. Although the storm was weakening, the wind was still fierce with blinding rain. Bourke made the shelter of the garage. Rain flooded in through the open roof. But the walls kept the direct gusts at bay. Bourke tossed Ivan the handle for the crankshaft. 'Ever started one of these before.'

'Of course,' the huge man laughed. 'I circus man remember.'

The Torpedo coughed to life. She was a sturdy strong beast but had seen better days.

'Get in,' Bourke shouted. Ivan grinned. There could be only one use for the warden's precious automobile. 'Ram the gate, huh?' Ivan's mouth was so wide with approval he could have swallowed a cantaloupe.

'You're a clever bastard Ivan. Hang on mate.' But Bourke saw a problem. Engaging gear he motored out into the screaming rain and turned *away* from the gate.

Ivan looked over his shoulder and yelled, 'The gate's that way boss.'

'Yes, I know.' Bourke also knew the hundred yards to the gate was not enough of a run-up. He drove across the football-field-sized quadrangle as far as possible, before turning for the charge. Off to their right figures appeared through the downpour. Guards were gathering but they seemed disorganised, hesitant. Bourke pressed the accelerator flat to the floor. The twelve horsepower Lorraine-Dietrich picked up momentum slowly but Bourke guessed, with so much weight, she would make a formidable ram against the gate.

'You really going to do this boss?'

'Yes Ivan, ready.'

'Merde!' Ivan's voice sounded broken over the storm. He pushed his back into the seat and gripped the side of his seat. The automobile trundled, gaining pace. Faster and faster. Ahead of them the other prisoners realised Bourke's plan and scattered either side of the main gate. Foot flat to the boards, gripping the juddering steering wheel, Bourke stole a glance at the speedometer ...

Twenty miles an hour ...

Thirty ...

Thirty-five miles an hour ...

The gate now approached at what seemed a terrifying speed. The prisoners started cheering. The storm gave them a tailwind ...

Forty-five miles an hour ...

Twenty feet from the gate Bourke checked the steering was true. 'Jump!' he shouted.

'What?'

'I said ...' Bourke opened the driver's door. 'Jump!'

Bourke rolled from the speeding roadster. Ivan spilled from the passenger side. The Speedometer had reached over fifty miles an hour …

And slammed into the gate. Overhead timbers crashed onto the car while a segment of the brick apex crushed what remained.

But the gate held fast.

Bourke stood disorientated, groggy from the somersault. He realised the gate was unscathed. Immediately whistles screeched through the pelting rain. Shapes of angry guards could be seen approaching though the haze.

'Look!' someone screamed out. Others pointed to the top of the pile of bricks which had collapsed onto the automobile. A small gap at the top of the pyramid. An opening showed in the wall.

Suddenly gunshots rang out.

Bullets ricocheted off the stonework followed by an immediate scramble. Bourke and Ivan were the last of twenty men to escape. Clambering up the brick pile Bourke took a final check back into the prison yard. Guards had gathered in numbers only thirty feet away. Now that they were armed, they were confident. More shots had Bourke ducking.

'Give us a hand.' Bourke yelled, tearing bricks loose. With Ivan's help they collapsed the wall even further, effectively closing the escape route.

'That'll hold the bastards for a few extra minutes.' Bourke dropped to the ground on the other side of the rubble pile. With the warden's automobile and twenty tons of brickwork blocking the main entrance to the prison, there was only a rear gate remaining. Ivan hadn't had so much fun since he was incarcerated. 'Now what boss?'

'Run mate,' Bourke yelled as dawn somewhere on the horizon heralded a new day. 'We run.'

CHAPTER EIGHT

Koroxu Bay, south of New Caledonia

The steamship *Drifter* was wedged bow first a dozen yards up the beach in a furrow of sand, like a dud torpedo run ashore. She was stuck fast. Listing to port on a rakish angle and covered in shredded vegetation, nature's debris and other flotsam – but she had survived the cyclone. There appeared to be no serious injury to the *old girl*, just superficial damage to the superstructure. The tender was nowhere to be seen.

The crew stood dumbfounded on the beach. 'We've been very very lucky,' Arsala said animated, in his undulating accented English 'Very lucky indeed. I tell you true, all we need is a good high tide, god's speed an' she'll re-float in a jiffy.'

'He's right,' Bill agreed. Salty nodded. 'It were a high tide that left us 'ere and it'll be another what'll see us afloat.'

'Aye, we got props in the water, a good tide and we can reverse 'er.'

'All very well,' Flash said, running a finger beneath his cravat. 'But the incoming tide's hours away.'

Juvita joined them on the sand, descending the rope ladder with the agility of a circus performer. She stood on the beach staring at the buckled davits that once held the tender. 'Please tell me Harry wasn't still in the tender asleep.'

'Jesus!' Bill shouted. 'Harry!' He ran along the side of the ship. 'Harry!' he shouted. 'Harry, fer Christ's sake where are yer? Haaaaaa-ree!'

'What?' Harry's red flushed face filled a port bow porthole, Harry's cabin. Clearly, he was aching from a thumping hangover. 'What yer shoutin' for Bill? Jesus!'

'Argh! Mate. I thought yer was still in the tender.'

'No, yer crazy bastard. The weather turned.'

'Turned, you can say that again.'

· · ·

There was only one cure. Only one way for Harry to escape the filthy hangover pounding his head. Whisky. He took a decent sip at his hip flask and shuddered, smacked his lips in satisfaction, and tipped his elbow once more for a second long swig. With his cabin on a ten degree lean he watched on out the porthole, while Juvita, Bill, Hank and Flash took up shovels and commenced digging a deep trench into the sand, each side of the ship's bow. Arsala, hampered by his wooden leg, supervised, and Salty busied himself tidying the deck and making repairs where necessary. The sea waited for no man. They could only standby and hope their plan worked.

Mid-morning the tide changed. By one o'clock the waters of Koroxu bay lapped about the bow. Arsala gave her full steam in reverse and thankfully she slowly backed into deep water. It had been eight hours since the cyclone had moved away. They steamed back out of the bay, into what was a sobering sight, clear to all those on board just how damaging the cyclone had been.

'I wonder how the prison fared?' someone asked.

'The road gangs would have been locked back in their cells with the cyclone approaching.'

'Maybe cap'n managed to escape before lockdown. Maybe he escaped the road gang early.'

'Maybe, maybe,' Salty said. 'It's just a damned guessing game.'

'The note said Koroxu Bay,' Juvita said. 'We must wait.'

'If he doesn't turn up,' Bill asked. 'What's plan B?'

'Plan B! There's no plan B. Maybe we can get another message to him.'

. . .

Bourke's plan of course was to escape overland to Koroxu Bay which he knew was part of Kotomo Island five or six miles southeast of the prison, as the crow flies that is. There was a narrow inlet that separated the island from the larger Isle of Pines, so he relied on borrowing a canoe. Well, steal a canoe, anyway. He had no money, and he was desperate.

The other prisoners had scattered. This pleased Bourke, he had a better chance of escaping alone. But this was not to be. He soon realised two men stubbornly saw Bourke as a natural leader and stuck by him. Ivan Toussaint and the Hun, Herr Kohl, none other than the German sailor from the SS *Prinzessin*. Fortuitous maybe, Bourke thought, but first they had to make good their escape.

All along the coast villages were destroyed. Fishing boats lay trashed hundreds of yards inland where giant waves had tossed them. All communications were down with telegraph wires tangled about felled poles. Drays, carriages, automobiles were thrown about like children's toys. Plantations of fruit trees and thousands of pine trees were flattened. As dawn attempted to deliver a warm sunny day *in paradise*, the Isle of Pines was covered in a fine wet mist. The cyclone had passed over.

'We need to head to the north coast,' Ivan told Bourke, stabbing his finger in the opposite direction. 'Get boat, sail to main island.'

'Fill your boots mate,' Bourke said. 'But I'm telling you that's the direction the others have gone and that's where the guards 'll go first. I'm heading this way.' Bourke knew they had a short window of opportunity. He knew the island was only nine miles long and eight miles wide with the highest point less than a thousand feet. The message from the native gardener had been specific.

Koroxu Bay.

And Bourke had made it a point to learn everything he could about the island, for exactly this reason.

Just over an hour later the three escapees reached the south coast of the island. The walk had been a hard slog, over and through difficult terrain. On the coast, formerly pristine tropical beaches were strewn with wreckage, flotsam and jetsam and Bourke prayed none of it belonged to the *Drifter*. The coast here was deserted. There was no sign of life. Bourke knew Koroxu Bay on Kotomo Island was over the inlet, but swimming was not an option. Already Bourke could make out several dorsal fins of large sharks feasting on animal carcasses taken by with the tide.

'Now what we do?' Ivan was snatching breath, but Herr Kohl was travelling far worse with his cracked ribs.

'We need to cross this inlet,' Bourke said. He stooped forward with his hands on his knees catching his own breath. Finally, he ran an experienced eye the length of the beach north-east to south-west.

Paradise! *Paradise in hell.*

Ivan immediately stood his full six foot four, shielding his eyes from the sun with his hand. 'Sacré bleu! Is that what I am thinking it is?' A kilometre along one end of the beach a knot of men rounded the headland. 'Please god, no!'

'Guards?' Bourke asked.

'It must be. Who else would it be?'

'I'm not going back to prison, nein, nein,' Herr Kohl face reddened with anger then fear.

Ivan focussed. 'Oui, oui, is guards. I number eight ... Oui, eight.'

Bourke looked across the inlet. If anything, the dorsal fins had doubled in number.

'Herr Kohl ran into the water. 'I am swimming. I never go back alive … never!'

Suddenly a steam whistle pierced the stillness of the calm after the storm. Three heads turned to the opposite headland south. The vessel was over half a mile away, but Bourke recognised the red funnel immediately.

'*Drifter!*' Bourke shouted, punching the air.

•   •   •

On the bridge Arsala held the spyglass tight to his eye. 'Yes, yes, god promise, it is our captain.' The Ghurkha was beside himself with excitement.

'Cap'n Bourke?'

'Is it really him?'

'Yes, yes … is him I say.'

'Huzzah!'

Salty, Harry and Flash rushed onto the bridge wing. 'It's him!' Salty shouted. 'It really is the skipper.'

'I never thought I'd see the day.'

'Yes, yes,' Arsala confirmed. 'I tell you true once, I tell you true once more. It is Captain Bourke sir.'

'They've got company,' Harry said. 'Look at the other end o' the beach.'

'Oh!' Arsala's jaw dropped, the spyglass raised to the eye once more. 'Golly gosh no.'

'Golly gosh yes mate, and they aren't happy.'

CRAIG GODFREY

'French?'

'Who else?'

Arsala didn't hesitate. He snatched the telegraph handle ...
Full steam ahead.

Harry took the spyglass off Arsala while the Ghurkha turned
the wheel to port, hoping to hug the shore without going
aground once more.

'Bloody prison guards,' Harry said out of the corner of his
mouth. 'Eight o' the bastards, and they're all armed.' Harry
ground his teeth. He uncapped his flask and took a swig of
whisky. 'It's not gonna happen I tell yer,' Harry shouted. 'Not
on my watch. Cap'n shouldn't 'a been arrested in the first bloody
place an' he sure as hell ain't goin' back now.'

'Hear, hear.'

Bourke and company ran towards the *Drifter,* but the guards
seemed to be closing the distance between them. Harry turned
on his heels to the remaining crew. He was in fight mode, wide
eyed, angry and unforgiving. 'Salty!'

'Harry!'

'I need a hand mate.'

'Got yer.'

Arsala imagined the worst. 'Harry Pickles. I ask you true sir,
what are you up to doing now?'

'Just keep 'ere steady as she goes skipper,' Harry yelled back
as he and Salty disappeared down the companionway.

•   •   •

The armed prison guards quick-marched in two files along the
beach, closing the distance fast. Too bloody fast! The three
escapees headed in the opposite direction. Shots were fired.
Warning shots plugged the clouds from the guards La Belle
rifles. But now they meant business. Bayonets were fixed.

They were close enough to be heard. 'Arrêtez! Arrêtez! ... Stop or we shoot.' More warning shots were fired.

At full speed *Drifter* steamed forward close to shore. Never before had Bourke felt so vulnerable. And never before had those on board been more determined. The distance closed between all parties. At two hundred yards it was clear the prisoners were not going to surrender. An order was shouted. The guards dropped to one knee and took aim.

Shoot to kill!

Harry watched the guards. They raised their rifles ... and aimed.

Harry squeezed the trigger. The German machine gun stuttered to life. Bullets ricocheted off the water. The sand, inches from the guards, exploded about them.

'Take that yer bastards!'

Salty fed a fresh belt of two hundred and fifty bullets into the Maschinengewehr 08, while Harry held his finger tight to the trigger. Lead peppered the beach.

The Frenchmen scattered.

The escapees were now in earshot.

Bourke shouted, 'For Christ's sake don't kill anyone Harry!' He raced into the water, wading deeper and deeper towards the fast approaching *Drifter*, cutting a fine picture slicing through the inlet so close to shore. Salty and Flash heaved lifebuoys over the side, tying them off at the rail. Bourke turned to his fellow prisoners.

'Are you ready? Hurry lads. Yer only get one go at this.'

As pained as he was, Herr Kohl forced himself into deep water. The steamer's bow wash threatened to send him under. Bourke grabbed the man's arm. The ship drew alongside. The first buoy skipped across the surface. Bourke snatched it. He forced it over his head the moment the rope tightened, and the two men skipped across the water. Ivan was strong, easily taking hold of the second buoy, he held on for the ride. Never had he felt so relieved. Running parallel to the beach *Drifter* made a sharp turn to starboard. But the guards regrouped. Once again, they dropped to one knee … and took careful aim.

A volley of .292 bullets splintered the woodwork. Others pinged off the metal hull. 'Bastards!' Harry screamed, lying belly down on the quarterdeck, the tripod legs spread wide and a thousand rounds of machinegun bullets draped in belts over his shoulder. 'Bastards, all o' yer!' Harry let them know he was the man with the big gun. He was boss. He was in charge. He squeezed off two hundred, three hundred rounds. Geysers of sand danced all about the Frenchmen who dropped their rifles and fled.

Drifter was soon well out of range.

'You bastards!' Harry waved a fist at the French while the escapees were hauled on board. 'Huzzah, huzzah. By Jesus,' Harry cried out, uncapping his whisky flask. 'That was the most fun since the trenches.' For a rare few, war had been an adventure.

• • •

Bourke lay on his back like a drowned rat. He was free. By Christ he had had his doubts on occasion, yet here he was, a free man again. Catching his breath, Bourke dragged himself onto the bridge where Arsala steered through the channel and out onto deep water.

'You made it. Arsala, you mad Ghurkha,' the skipper cheered. 'You pulled it off.'

Harry was over the moon. He joined them at the helm, an empty ammunition belt wrapped around his chest, his shirt sleeves torn, showing off powerful muscles, three-quarter britches and giant bare feet. He gave his cap'n a huge bear hug. 'Good ter see yer cap'n.'

'And you too, you crazy bastard,' Bourke said to Harry. 'That was bloody awesome.' The others crowded the bridge. After congratulations Arsala said. 'Here captain Bourke sir, you take the helm.'

'No mate. You keep it. Just get us out o' here.'

'Yes, yes. We best be skedaddling out to sea before the bloody French Navy, army and air force all come looking for us.' Arsala studied his captain and his two partners in the escape a moment. 'One more thing Captain Bourke sir.'

'What's that Arsala?'

'I'm thinking you best take off those prison clothes, they are not a good look Captain Bourke, sir.'

• • •

Noumea. Later that evening.

Consul Monsieur Felix Du Bellay ripped his starched serviette from his collar and rose as briskly from the table as his obese body would allow, heaving his high-backed chair across the dining room. His hosts, the aging high commissioner Monsieur Olivier Martinez and his wife Catherine, were horrified. With the cyclone causing so much damage around the gardens and environs, they did not expect such volatile behaviour indoors.

Madame Martinez spoke first, her diplomatic husband preferring to let the man cool off. 'Monsieur Du Bellay!' Catherine said. 'Control your temper. What on earth was in that message you just received could not be worse news than the devastation all around us?' Besides, Du Bellay was spoiling what should have been a perfect candlelit dinner. Candlelit because the electricity was down.

With all telegraph communications destroyed also, the full extent of the damage to the Isle of Pines wouldn't be known until the following day. Monsieur Felix Du Bellay, however, had received a radio message from on board *La Grenouille* in

Noumea's harbour, his official maritime transport on the vast Pacific Ocean.

And he was furious.

Du Bellay paced up and down the room, his pin-like legs supporting a rounded belly made even rounder by this recent feast. Angry with the note scrunched in his hand, angry with himself.

'Madame.' Du Bellay took a deep breath and brushed his unruly hair back into place. He uncrumpled the document, thrusting it into the woman's bosom. 'That scoundrel, that vile Australian who assaulted my wife ...'

'Yes?'

'That monster who struck my Vignetta ...'

'Yes?'

'That filthy creature who was to be sent to Devil's Island next week when *La Lorient* arrived in Noumea to take him away ... he ...'

'What monsieur?'

'He has escaped!'

'Escaped!' Commissioner Martinez saw this as his entrée into the situation. 'Escaped. How?'

Du Bellay turned on the High Commissioner like a pugilist smelling blood. 'It doesn't matter how he bloody escaped!' Du Bellay's face was the colour of beetroot. 'The bastard escaped!'

'Now listen here my man, I will not have you speaking like that in front of my ...'

'Bah!' Du Bellay shouted and stormed out in a lather of sweat and anger.

•   •   •

The consul managed two generous snorts of cocaine off the back of his hand before arriving at the docks where he demanded an immediate conference with the captain of *La Grenouille* and his officers.

If he was going to catch this bastard Australian, Du Bellay thought, *he needed a warship not a yacht.*

He was pacing the stateroom on board the converted minesweeper, when the crew arrived.

The first officer André Caron arrived before the captain. The second and third officers held back. If they were to sail, first officer Caron needed to have the VTE Belleville coal fuelled boiler attended to immediately, to get up steam. And he sensed the urgency. 'What are your orders monsieur?'

'Orders!' Du Bellay stood at the stateroom window grasping a balloon of Armagnac, gaping out at a moonlit harbour strewn with trash. 'Orders! You can get a path cleared through all this garbage blocking our path out of this godforsaken place to start with.'

The two officers at the doorway hurried away.

'Certainly monsieur,' Caron said. 'Immediately monsieur … ah … monsieur …'

'What?'

'We are to sail then?'

'Of course, you idiot,' Du Bellay yelled over his shoulder, his back to the officer. He guzzled the spirit.

'Sailing tonight monsieur?'

'Yes, yes. Now move it.'

Du Bellay watched the officer's reflection in the glass. Caron hurried away, passing by the ship's captain in the doorway, wearing his mandatory immaculate officer's uniform. Du Bellay wheeled about to face Capitaine Claude de Forbin, who immediately recognised the bloodshot eyes, irritated nose and jerky mannerisms of a man possessed by cocaine. But something more than cocaine agitated him.

'What is it Felix?' the Capitaine said, the only man on board to use the consul's Christian name.

'Jonathon Bourke escaped prison.' Du Bellay poured another even stiffer Armagnac from a cut-glass decanter on the stateroom bar.

'Yes, I was just informed?' de Forbin stole a glance at his sleeves and dusted himself with the flick of his fingers. 'How did the man escape?'

'Apparently the prison wall was damaged by the cyclone, and twenty men escaped.'

Claude de Forbin pinched at a loose cotton thread on his lapel. 'That man has a guardian angel watching over him.'

'What the bloody hell's that supposed to mean?'

'I mean he has the luck of the Irish, as the English would say. Well, he can't get far. He'll be hiding on the islands somewhere; we'll soon find him.'

'No! He had planned it somehow. He had a rendezvous arranged. His friends on that damned tub of his, *Drifter*, picked him up on a beach south of the prison.'

The Capitaine was dumbfounded. 'What? And sailed away?'

'It gets worse Claude,' Du Bellay sat heavily at the stateroom table. 'Don't ask me how, but he was kept in a lockup with Herr Kohl.'

'No!'

'Yes.'

The captain caught himself in the window, straightened to face his reflection, tugged at his jacket and straightened his tie. 'And he escaped too huh?'

Du Bellay nodded. 'He escaped on the *Drifter* also.'

'That's too much of a coincidence.'

'That's what I thought.'

Capitaine Claude de Forbin was well aware of the consul's less than legal activities. He knew only too well that Cap'n Jonathon Bourke had been falsely imprisoned because he knew about the *Prinzessin* gold. Forbin also knew that it was Du Bellay's less than faithful wife who had been hoodwinked by

Bourke into telling Bourke everything she knew, like the existence of prisoner Herr Kohl.

'So, what do you suggest we do?' Forbin said, finally turning to face Du Bellay and straightening like a palace guard.

'We leave for Malaita.'

'Tonight?'

'As you are aware Claude, I am due in Melbourne to speak on the behalf of France in the Australian Parliament in less than a fortnight. So, we must leave as soon as we can.'

· · ·

On deck the night was balmy and calm. Although a full moon lit the harbour like a stage, the minesweeper's massive bow floodlights were engaged, to be certain they didn't collide with a half-submerged vessel or anything else that could damage the ship. It had been 4AM before the crew ashore could be rounded up and they had enough steam up. Eventually, *La Grenouille* was maintaining fifteen knots courtesy of her 600-horsepower steam engine, heading north-east for the Solomons Islands.

CHAPTER NINE

On board Drifter. Twenty-four-hours earlier

Bourke savoured the very words. 'Curry fish with potatoes Singapore style.' Juvita put a huge bowl on the mess table for each of the two new crew members and her cap'n. They were starved and ate like boys at a boarding school. But the rich cuisine they had so missed would see them rushing to the heads for half the night.

'Herr Kohl,' Bourke said as his bowl neared empty and his belly full.

'Call me Adolf, Herr Bourke.'

'Adolf then. I've been meaning to ask you.'

'Ja?'

'When the guillotine dropped and that bastard Boucher lost his head, you chased after it. You dropped to your knees and … well … I don't quite know how to put this but … well you spoke to it … you spoke to the man's severed head!'

'Ja.'

'Why?'

'That bast-ard, he torment me. Relentless. Every day he relish my misery. And then, when he come to tell me I was to be executed the next day he tell me story how during French Revolution in old days, men of science believe the conscious thoughts still operates in the severed head for one or more minutes, until oxygen leaves the brain.'

'Okay, so what did you say.'

'I says to him, fuck you bast-ard. Who's the daddy now?'

• • •

Juvita was about to join Arsala on the bridge when Bourke noticed the time. It was Harry's watch, Harry's turn at the helm. 'Fetch Arsala here please,' Bourke told Juvita as he turned to Herr Kohl literally licking his spoon clean and wiped stale baguette inside the rim of his bowl. Kohl had been imprisoned ten years and never had anything been so flavoursome. 'You too Juvita,' Bourke said as the Malayan princess started up the companionway. 'We all need to talk.'

Arsala and Juvita joined the three escapees at the table. Flash and Salty, both off duty, joined them.

'Whisky please Flash,' Bourke ordered.

Flash looked at the two foreigners who he had taken a dislike to the moment they came on board. 'Ain't none left cap'n.'

'What do yer mean, none left?' If there was one thing Bourke missed in prison it was a tipple.

'No whisky,' and Flash scowled at Herr Kohl. 'Ain't no schnapps for Herr Cabbage 'ere neither.'

Arsala spoke, 'We had no time to buy supplies. We leave in hurry cap'n sir. There was some whisky but Harry ... well, Harry finish.'

'Harry what?'

'Harry finish. He had very very mortifying experience with womans in Noumea. Bad time. Humiliated by womans who like other womans, not man.'

Bourke cracked a smile. 'Oh, you must tell me more, later. But for now, I think you know what to do Flash.'

'Aye skip.'

'So, I'll not beat about the bush,' Bourke turned his chair to face Herr Kohl. 'Let's get down to business ... Herr Kohl.'

'Ja.' Kohl looked worried. Was his freedom jeopardised?

'You were a young sailor on board the SS *Prinzessin* when she collided with HMS *Pride* and sank off the Solomons in 1897, yes?'

'Ja. How you know thees things?'

'A little bird told me.'

'A little bird!' Herr Kohl looked completely confused.

'It doesn't matter how I know. The fact is you were there.' Herr Kohl nodded warily. The years in prison had made him distrustful. 'So, what would you say if I told you my old man was there also?'

'Old man? Dein Vater? Ja?'

'Yes.' Bourke cast an eye at his long-time crew. They knew what was coming next. 'What would you say if I told you my father was the captain of the *Pride*. He was the one who sank your ship.'

'Vot? For real?'

'Yes Kohl, for real. It was an accident. He meant to scare you, not sink you.'

'I hear stories. Many stories.' It took a moment for Kohl to analyse the information when Flash returned from the hold with a carton of canned mullet, sliding it onto the table with a huge grin. He tossed a can opener onto the carton.

'So, let's drink to the SS *Prinzessin* and HMS *Pride*.'

Drink? Herr Kohl looked even more confused, until Salty punctured a can and poured rum into the glasses Juvita spread before the gathering.

'Contraband my friend,' Bourke said. 'We smuggled sixty-thousand cans of this stuff into Hawaii a few weeks back.'

'Prohibition!' Ivan Toussaint laughed, reading the bright red and yellow label, *Lighthouse Brand fresh sea mullet, Cooktown.* 'You are smugglers, oui?'

'Well sort off.' Bourke raised his glass high. 'Up your bum!' he called out, and skulled the glass, slamming the empty on the table. They all followed suit. Everyone winced, Ivan punched his chest and Kohl smacked his lips. Bourke filled their glasses. 'This time we drink to *Prinzessin* gold,' he said, fixing eyes with Kohl. 'Ja?'

Kohl's eyes widened.

'Was war das ... ah ... what ees thees about gold?'

'The *Prinzessin* gold Herr Kohl. We all know the ship sank in shallow water with a ton of Chinese gold on board. And you, my friend, are going to show us where that reef is, exactly.'

'Nein, no ... ah, thees gold is lost. The *Prinzessin*, she was washed off the shallow reef the year after, in 1898, she sink into the abyss, they say.'

Salty stirred. 'Who says?'

'A German diving party went for thees gold, in 1899 I am certain. And the natives, they tell of a big storm, and how the ship, she ... shift off the reef and disappear, for ever and ever I'm thinking.'

• • •

Of course, Bourke had heard these rumours also. But he always suspected they were just that, rumours. Now hearing Herr Kohl's version of the story, it seemed to make sense. His own old man, Cap'n Jonathon Bourke Senior, had always said it was there for the taking but he suspected it was in extremely deep water.

Disilutioned, disappointed, Bourke joined Harry at the helm to give the order for a new heading for Cooktown and home. The *Prinzessin* gold was a lost cause, a pie in the sky, besides he knew the French would be looking for him.

Best to make ourselves scarce a while.

'Beautiful night huh,' Harry said, holding the wheel steady, rosewood pipe clenched in the side of his jaw.

'It is, indeed, Harry.' Bourke watched his fearless mate and good friend a moment. Harry sucked on the pipe and a fiery glow illuminated his whiskery cheek on the dark bridge. 'Thanks,' Bourke said, and meant it.

'Don't worry 'bout it,' Harry didn't handle compliments too well.

'No seriously Harry, I could 'ave died back there.'

'Arsala reckons yer should keep yer pecker in yer pants,' Harry laughed, using humour to slice through the gravity. Both men laughed.

'I did it to find out more about this gold rumour,' Bourke said in all honesty.

'Yer right.' Harry may as well have said *bullshit*, but both men were on the same page. 'So, you've definitely given up on the *Prinzessin* then?'

'For the moment. It's deep Harry. I always thought it was. But I'm getting Herr Kohl to draw up accurate charts and one day ... maybe ...'

* * *

Suddenly Arsala stumbled onto the bridge dragging a body with him. His dark-skinned face accentuating the whites of his wide eyes, his turban skew-whiff from the struggle.

Bourke stepped back. 'What the hell?'

Arsala had by the collar a total stranger looking like a deer in the crosshairs. 'Look what the cat drag in!' Arsala shouted, and with his powerful short arms he heaved the wretch to the deck. 'A stowaway!'

The cowering man made no attempt to stand. Arsala hooked one leg up onto the stowaway's chest, positioning himself like he was the conqueror of Everest. He may as well have held a flag; he was so proud. But Arsala was also as mad as a disturbed hornet.

'Wh-what on earth?' Bourke and Harry looked at the intruder, incredulous.

'I find this bastard thief in the hold Captain Bourke sir. I tell you true. Hiding amongst the mullet.' And Arsala narrowed his eyes and lowered his voice, staring at the captain, '*The mullet* … Captain Bourke sir. The bastard is drunk.'

'I'm not drunk,' the man slurred.

'Shut it!' Arsala yelled, incensed he should talk back. 'You speak when captain say speak, bastard!'

'I was hungry.'

Arsala kicked him in the ribs. 'I said …'

'Let the man speak.'

Arsala tutted.

'I saw the cartons of mullet and opened one with my knife and … well … well I found the rum …'

Clearly, this man knew it was contraband. And whilst the stowaway knew he had that information over his reluctant hosts – to barter with so to speak – it could also backfire on him. He could be thrown overboard, and that thought terrified him. 'I'm sorry sir, I won't say a word. Not a word to anyone.'

'I know yer won't,' Harry threatened.

Amazingly, as the crates stacked at the front were actually full of the real thing, fish, the stowaway had managed to open one of the crates labelled 'mullet,' Bourke realised.

'Where the bloody hell *did* he come from?' Harry asked Arsala.

'The hold.'

'No. Where … how …'

'He's a stowaway,' Bourke said to Harry, while not taking his eyes off the man. By now the entire crew heard of their intruder and crowded the bridge wing.

'How did you get aboard?' Bourke demanded.

'I've been hiding two days now … I think.'

Harry said. 'You think?'

'Well, I came aboard when you were anchored off Mont-Dore Bay. You were all ashore at that time.' Collective heads nodded. 'And I swam out. I've been in the hold the entire time …'

'Like a bilge rat,' Salty growled.

'You were down there during the storm?' Flash asked.

'Yes, throughout the cyclone. It was terrifying down there.' The stowaway looked at the faces all staring down at him. 'I thought we were all going to die and that no one would find my body.'

'And maybe they won't,' Bill said. 'Chuck 'im overboard.'

'Please,' the man squealed. 'I'll work my passage. Honest. I just want to get home.'

'We don't need no extra 'ands,' Bill said.

'I'm a cook. A good one too. I can cook anything …'

'What's yer name?' Bourke asked.

'Arthur … Arthur J Money.'

'Money?' Salty said. 'Is that yer real name?'

'Aye.'

Bourke leant over and offered his hand. 'Get up Arthur.' He hoisted Arthur to his feet. 'You were hungry you said.' Bourke caught a whiff of the man's breath. 'Jesus! So, what do yer think of our rum?'

Finally, a slight smile returned, where the fear had sobered Arthur. 'I've tasted better,' he said in all honesty.

'Cheeky bugger,' Harry said.

Arthur looked confused. 'We distil it ourselves,' Bourke said. The stowaway already knew they were smugglers so why not tell him the truth. 'Made from the purest rainforest water and Queensland sugar.'

'Oh,' Arthur cleared his throat. 'When I said, I've tasted better, I didn't mean yours was inferior or anything like that.'

'Of course not,' Salty said sarcastically.

'No. It was quite delicious actually if I can use the word delicious.'

'Juvita,' Bourke said, noting her standing quietly in the background. 'Why don't you take Arthur here down to the galley and give him a feed, show him the ropes too. You've got a new helper.'

Juvita wasn't impressed. 'I don't need helper.'

'Pot washer then.'

'Yes, yes. He wash pots. I burn special for him.' Juvita looked at Arthur. 'Come.'

Arthur followed obediently. 'And no more rum, got it?' Bourke called out.

'Aye cap'n.'

• • •

Jonathon Bourke finally joined Arthur J Money below decks when Arsala took the helm from Harry, needing rest before his next watch. Juvita had begrudgingly fed the man who was already rake-thin from his castaway experience, let alone another two days hiding in the hold.

'You like books I see,' Arthur said, replacing a copy of *Robbery Under Arms* on the shelf as the captain entered.

'Yes. Reading's a passion, one could say.'

'Mostly reference I notice.'

'Yes, there are a few novels. You're welcome to borrow any on the voyage home if yer like.'

'Thank you. And that Gauguin,' Arthur pointed with his chin to the painting of the woman bathing, the painting Flash misappropriated from the Minou Rose in Papeete.

'You've heard of this bloke Gauguin, huh?' Bourke said.

'Yes. He is becoming very popular these days I believe. Artists often do after they die.'

'He's dead?'

'Yes, twenty years at least.'

'Oh well, each to their own I say.'

Arthur had a rapport with Jonathon. The two men had been incarcerated recently, Bourke in prison and Arthur on his desolate island. And the stint in solitary had made him more compassionate. Arthur opened up and told Bourke everything, up to his stowing away aboard the *Drifter*.

They compared stories and spoke until the small hours of the morning.

'I have nothing now,' Arthur finally said. It was a fact, he wasn't seeking charity. 'I lost everything on the *Caledonia*, everything, including papers and identity.'

'Maybe you can work with us,' Bourke said. 'We have a humble business in Cooktown.'

'Distilling rum,' Arthur said all too readily and wished he hadn't. 'I mean, good for you. How do you move it?'

'Sell it?'

'Yes.'

'We have a ready market, especially in Honolulu.'

'Ah, the American prohibition huh?'

'Exactly.'

Juvita hovered about pretending to tidy. She didn't trust this stowaway and wanted to air her opinion.

'You know,' Bourke continued, 'With your skills as a cook you would be a natural at the distillery. Maybe we could diversify into flavoured liqueurs, there's a huge market there with women consumers.'

'Sounds wonderful. I'm certain I'd like that. Thank you. But first I must deliver this watch to a young man in Melbourne.' Arthur emptied his pocket and amongst a few scrunched banknotes and a few franc coins left from the Japanese captain's donation, was the silver fob watch.

'This belonged to Captain Cosgrove,' Arthur told Bourke the story, and how he promised to take the watch to Williamstown in Melbourne. 'It's an heirloom see and meant a lot to the captain. The family know nothing of the wreck, mine neither, for that matter. It's the least I can do.'

Bourke rolled the silver fob in his hand as Juvita joined them with a tin mug of hot tea for each of them. The timepiece was smooth and worn with a porcelain face, and not particularly imposing. 'Fusee de Paris. 1798,' Bourke read the inscription aloud. 'Heirloom huh?' He wasn't that impressed.

'There's other stuff engraved under the back lid,' Arthur said, as if it was important. The captain flipped the lid and concentrated on a bunch of words that meant nothing. In the centre was what appeared to be a finely engraved map and more writings. 'Hmm, strange.' Bourke's curiosity peaked. He opened a drawer in the mess dining table and took out a magnifying glass before tweaking the oil lamp to brighten the subject.

'te maueraa e o te iraa o te iraa,' he muttered, fogging the glass before cleaning it with his handkerchief. 'What the bloody hell does that mean?'

'Give me,' Juvita took the watch, stubbornly rejecting the magnifying glass. 'These are Tahitian words. It mean *tear of the eclipse*.'

'Tahitian?' Bourke remembered Juvita had lived in Tahiti for some years.

'You know these things,' Juvita said. 'Juvita, she smart lady.'

'Oh, I know you're smart Juvita binti Musa,' Bourke crowed, using her full name respectfully. 'So, what else does it say?'

'Ah, island call Kanantui.'

'Kanantui, huh?' Bourke knew of the remote island, however he had never visited it. There was no reason to. On the map, originally drawn by English explorer William Dampier in the year 1700, the island was a small volcanic island with a massive freshwater lake in its centre, resembling a donut, Bourke thought.

Arthur looked confused.

'It's off the east coast of Papua New Guinea, between the island of New Britain in the Bismarck Sea.' It was re-named after the German Protectorate no longer existed following the Great War.

Arthur looked none the wiser. 'So, what's this got to do with that watch?'

'I remember people, Tahiti people speak of stories,' Juvita said. 'They speak of a Princess who was killed, a hundred year ago, more even.' It all flooded back and Juvita became animated. 'Yes, yes. *Tear of the eclipse*. It was pearl. Big black pearl, worth much much moneys. It was taken and Princess, she was murdered.'

'Of course. I seem to remember this story,' Bourke jumped to his feet and started through his Encyclopedias. '*T ... T ...*' he muttered aloud. '*T* for Tahiti.' He speed-read the reference on Tahiti. 'Nothing. Pacific Islands ... blah, blah, blah ... nothing. Tahitian Royalty King Pomare ... blah, blah, blah ... No ... no mention of a murdered princess or a black pearl.'

'Look up pearls,' Arthur suggested.

'Papeete ... Peakrel ... Pear ... Pearl ...' Bourke ran an experienced reader's eye over the information. 'Ah, here ... historic pearls.' His finger slid down the column. 'Black pearls ...

Ah! Here we go ... *Tear of the Eclipse*.'

Arthur leant forward pushing his mug aside. 'Really?'

'Yes.' Bourke read aloud. '*Tear of the Eclipse*. An extremely scarce tear-shaped black pearl of extraordinary size, supposedly the size of a chicken egg, was so named as it was discovered on June 3rd, 1769, during the transit *eclipse* of Venus across the sun as observed by British navigator Captain James Cook, naturalist Joseph Banks and astronomer Charles Green in Tahiti. The discovery quite excited the European visitors to the island, who desperately tried to barter with the Tahitians for its acquisition. However, all offers were refused, and the pearl, considered sacred by the Tahitians, was set into a pearl shell ceremonial head piece with many other pearls, and given to the chieftain's queen ...'

'Fascinating,' Arthur said.

'On her death the legendary pearl was handed down to the next King of Tahiti, Pomare 11 who gave it to his daughter, Princess Tetuanui. Then in 1815 the princess was kidnapped, but a ransom never extracted ...' Bourke and Arthur fixed stares. Juvita interrupted. 'Yes, yes, read more.'

'Tetuanui disappeared and with her the fabled pearl also,' Bourke continued reading. 'At the time the Tahitians were fighting amongst themselves, and it was assumed she had been captured by Pomare 11's enemies. But later it was revealed there was a French Merchant ship anchored in the harbour of what is now Papeete. The Merchant ship *Africain* sailed shortly after the alleged kidnapping, and it was suspected its crew were responsible. Nothing has been heard of the pearl or the princess since. It has been rumoured throughout the years since, that the pearl is cursed.'

'What edition encyclopedia is that?' Arthur asked.

'1911.'

'Thirteen years ago.'

'This watch,' Juvita said. 'French.'

'Yes, but Tahiti has been a French Protectorate since the 1880s Juvita,' Bourke said. 'So is New Caledonia and dozens and dozens of other islands. There's traces of frog occupation all over the Pacific.'

'This watch say 1798,' Juvita said stubbornly.

'That does put the watch in a similar time bracket,' Arthur said. 'I mean 1769, pearl found, 1815 pearl disappears. Watch dated 1798, so it was what? Seventeen years old when someone went to all the trouble of engraving it.'

Bourke made a face, looking at Juvita. 'What else does it say?'

Juvita frowned in concentration. 'Bok.'

'Bok?'

'That what I say.'

'Bok,' Bourke reiterated. 'As in B-O-K?'

'Yes.'

'What does Bok mean?'

Juvita grew irritable. 'I don't know this word.'

Arthur spoke. 'Bok is a village on the island, I've heard of it before. And the savages there are just that, savages.'

'What are you saying?'

'Head-hunters!'

Bourke scoffed a laugh. 'It's 1924 Arthur. There's no such thing as a head-hunter anymore.'

'Oh, would you like a small wager on that?'

Juvita took a final scrutiny of the watch engraving. 'More writing. But French words.' She slid the watch along the table to Bourke. 'You speak French.'

'Hardly,' the captain took up the challenge. 'I can read a little bit. The first word was, 'Bok.'

'We got that bit,' Arthur said, not intending to sound discourteous.

'*Interieur nord-ouest.* That's inland north-west. *400 metres.* Same. *35 rouge.* 35 red. Le *gagnant prend tout.* Something takes all … ah winner, yes … winner takes all.'

'Sounds like roulette.'

'Interesting. Tahitian and French. French watch.'

'And mentioning *Tear of the Eclipse.* Very interesting. And your captain …'

'Cosgrove.'

'Yes, Cosgrove, was insistent you get this to his son. I think it's worth paying a visit to Kanantui on the way home.

Arthur weighed up the situation. One, he was in no position to argue, two, Cosgrove was dead, in fact as far as anyone knew, *he* was also dead. Three, Cosgrove's fifteen-year-old boy was a *spoiled shit.* Finally, and most importantly, the *Tear of the Eclipse* was worth a fortune and his share would be substantial. He would see to that.

• • •

'My my Captain Bourke sir. How you change that mind of yours,' Arsala listened to the change of plan. 'I tell you true, you are never a boring man.'

Bourke spread a map for the Coral Sea on the bridge chart table. 'Here are the co-ordinates. 9°6' degrees South by 160°9' degrees East. We need coal first. So, head directly for Tulagi village on Tulagi.' He spoke of the town with the same name as the island, and the capital of the British Solomon Islands Protectorate since 1896.

'Then New Guinea looking for treasure,' the Arsala said, tongue in cheek. 'If it is not lost gold, it is rare black pearl. What next, the Czar's diamond?'

Bourke grinned.

'I am thinking yes, your daddy would be very very proud of you,' Arsala said.

• • •

Days later. 4AM. Drifter
Harry enjoyed his pipe, alone on the dark bridge, looking ahead over a calm sea. Another perfect day for steaming across the ocean was preparing to dawn. Strong man Ivan Toussaint tapped on the door frame of the bridge, the door latched open to accommodate the balmy night.

'Permission to join you boss,' Ivan asked as a formality, stepping over the bulkhead before Harry had a chance to answer. Harry liked the tall, heavy-set man. He might appear a lumbering thug, but deep down he was a gentle man who played strategic chess. Harry was yet to beat him.

'I could use the company,' Harry stifled a yawn. 'Couldn't sleep eh?'

'It's hot below. I like the fresh air.'

'Yer, me too.' Harry tapped his spent tobacco into a large glass ashtray already overflowing with ash.

'Tell me,' Ivan said. 'Capitaine Bourke has an arch enemy with Monsieur Du Bellay, does he not?'

'Bloody oath. You could say that again.'

'Why? If I can ask?'

Harry twisted to face Ivan, his large square-jawed face lit by light spilling from the compass binnacle. 'Let's just say the captain bought the consul's wife one drink too many.'

'Huh,' Ivan laughed. 'So, the rumours are true?'

'What rumours?'

'Well, some of the crew joked about the captain having to leave Papeete in a big hurry. Madame Du Bellay's name came up in conversation.'

'Yes, well,' Harry grew defensive. 'Cap'n Bourke is a good man, right.'

'Of course.'

'But sometimes he gets led astray.'

'Don't we all,' Ivan agreed. 'That's what got me incarcerated.'

'Oh?'

Ivan went on to explain that he had a dalliance with another man's wife also, a wayward woman free with her sexual favours. But when he was attacked by the angry husband with a machete, he beat the attacker senseless. This man had many contacts in high places and Ivan was sentenced to ten years.

'Ten years,' Harry whistled. 'Jesus, that was a bit rich.'

'Yes. But the reason I ask you about this Monsieur Du Bellay, Harry, is that this man has a cocaine addiction and I think you should know he too is a smuggler.'

Harry's bottom jaw dropped. 'He's what?'

Ivan sighed. 'Look I cannot prove this, but when you hear from different sources the same information, these sources being drug runners and others who have connections with gangsters in America, there must be some truth in it. What do they say in English ... where there's smoke there's fire?' Ivan studied Harry a long moment. 'Harry, I like you, I respect your captain. I think he should know. One day this information might help him, because I know for a fact Du Bellay has connections in high places, in parliament and government and I believe he deals with the Chinese in Melbourne. His diplomatic status, you see, gives him immunity against being questioned by the department of trade and customs.'

'Well, I'll be stuffed. What's he smuggle? Opium?'

'No, cocaine.'

· · ·

Captain Bourke was interested, very interested indeed.

'What's cocaine anyway?' Harry asked the captain. 'I mean, I know what it is but where's it come from?'

'It's a narcotic made from the coca plant.'

'How?'

'By soaking the leaf of the coca plant, then drying it. The resulting powder gets mixed with solvents, then pressed and heated into a cake. It became popular fifty odd years ago, especially in America, although it's been around since the ancient times.'

'Oh?'

'Yeh. Indigenous South American Indians have used the stuff for centuries. But it was medicinal originally.'

'Like what?'

'Like curing ailments. Crook gut, nausea. The leaf's full of nutrients I believe, like calories and vitamins, minerals and stuff. And it gives the user energy.'

'How come you know so much about it?' Harry said.

'I read a lot.'

'Fair enough. So, why's it illegal?'

'Well, it's been abused and people get addicted to it. The Americans once sold it in cigarettes, cordials like Coca Cola, they even put it in wine I've been told, some drink called *Vin Mariani*. It's only become illegal a few years back, beginning of the war in about 1914, I think. So now it's illegal it's more valuable.' Bourke's thoughts returned to Du Bellay. 'That hypocrite.'

'Did you know he is due to talk in Parliament in Melbourne soon?'

'So, you said. You know Harry, I don't think we've seen the last of him.'

CHAPTER TEN

Tulagi. Eight days after leaving New Caledonia.
Steaming into the tranquil bay Bourke panned his binoculars across the water, searching for a safe passage through the reef. 'Not much here cap'n,' Harry said, hand shading his eyes.

'Not really. It's only three and a half miles long and just over half a mile wide,' Bourke said, steadying the glasses as best he could against the gentle swell.

'Why did the Limeys settle on this pissant island and not one o' the bigger ones?'

'Health reasons,' Bourke said. 'Less chance of catching diseases I believe.'

Tulagi settlement, same name as the island, Bourke knew, was under jurisdiction of the British Protectorate. A pod of dolphins gambolled nearby.

'I hope the natives are as friendly as them,' Flash said, joining them at the bow.

No sooner had he said this when the settlement came into view. White timber European style buildings were outnumbered by the simple, yet sturdy, grass huts of the natives.

'Not much here skipper.'

'No. But we need to refuel, and this is our only chance between here and New Guinea.'

Drifter anchored in the relatively deep water out in the bay. They were instantly surrounded by canoes with the locals selling fresh produce. The coal, Bourke knew, would have to be carted out on colliers followed by the gruelling task of lifting it on board in sixteen-pound bucketsful, where it was eventually dumped down a chute to the bunkers. Bourke would pay experienced natives to do the work, including the trimmers who levelled the piles of coal. It was a thankless and dangerous employment, some men choking on coal dust, or breathing foul air. Many trimmers fell ill, spitting blood and having difficulty breathing. Meanwhile Bourke was invited to the Resident Commissioner's home overlooking the bay.

· · ·

The Resident Commissioner made his way awkwardly down the sweeping front stairs of his official tropical residence, hobbling on a makeshift crutch. He had twisted his angle rather badly, but with visitors so scarce he was keen for the social interaction. Jonathon Bourke, Arsala, Juvita and Harry beached their replacement tender and climbed the steep embankment leading through a copse of palms and jungle growth and into a clearing before the stately abode. Stately that is, for a remote tropical island outpost. Harry carried a crate of tinned mullet – the genuine product – on his shoulder as a gift for the commissioner.

'Hello, hello,' the commissioner called out, heading in their direction, swaying left to right on his crutch, reminding Bourke of Long John Silver in Robert Louis Stevenson's novel, *Treasure Island* – except the unshaven uncouth pirate was replaced by a toffy Englishman. 'Marmaduke Algernon Taplow,' he introduced himself in his *terribly* English accent.

'I'm guessing that steamer of yours requires coal, what?'

'Yes sir,' Bourke met the man halfway, offering his hand. 'Jonathon Bourke, captain of *Drifter* and some of my crew, Arsala, Juvita and Harry.'

The Englishman's hand was limp as a pancake. 'Jolly nice to meet you all. Welcome to Tulagi.' Marmaduke read the mullet label aloud. 'Lighthouse Brand Mullet, Cooktown … is that for me?'

'Yes sir,' Bourke said. 'It's our own product, we have a cannery in Queensland.'

'That's awfully generous my dear chap. Mullet eh. My favourite.' His face spoke differently.

'Let's get out of the sun. Come up to the house for refreshments.'

'Thank you. Most kind,' Bourke wore his gentleman's cap. Here in the shelter of tropical vegetation it was certainly humid, the air still and the cicadas made enough racket to disturb the spirits of the dead. Marmaduke opened the fly wire, propping the door with his stick. The crew stepped into the relative coolness of the shaded dwelling. A cat appeared, cutting in front of the commissioner, who nearly tripped over the animal.

'Fucking cat!' he spat, taking a swipe with his crutch. Harry laughed. A spontaneous guffaw at the Englishman's language. A second's awkwardness. Harry busied himself putting the carton of mullet on a side table. The cat jumped onto the box and sniffed.

'Fucking thing will be the death of me.'

'Now now Marmaduke,' the commissioner's wife appeared, holding a large tumbler. She was clearly drunk. 'You are not using that foul language in front of our guests are you?'

'It's that fucking cat of yours. That's how I twisted my fucking ankle.'

The wife, dressed smartly yet quickly for their guests, sauntered across the large living room, her steps calculated to accommodate her inebriation. 'Sorry about that,' she slurred, referring to her husband. 'Mrs Taplow,' she introduced herself. 'Lady of the house.'

'Lady! Huh?' Marmaduke coughed a laugh. 'Fucking news to me.'

'Drink?' Lady Taplow offered Bourke.

Clearly their hosts were well on the way and the sun was nowhere near the yardarm.

'Why not,' Bourke said.

Lady Taplow drained her tumbler before hefting the gin decanter with both hands, pouring herself a stiff four fingers. A splash of tonic followed with half a lime.

'If you don't mind, would you please pour your own?' She sat heavily into a wicker armchair covered in embroidery and cushions, fiddling with her pearl necklace. Being positioned where the sun shone through the shutters Bourke noticed her makeup. The ruby lipstick was skewwhiff, and her mascara smudged.

'These gentlemen are here for coal,' Marmaduke told his wife, eyeing the decanter. Bourke poured for Harry and himself and held the decanter high in offering the commissioner a top-up. The man nodded, involuntarily licking his lip.

'Coal eh?' the wife said, her eye lids heavy. 'Everyone wants coal.'

'Well steamers need fucking coal to chuff along, dearest.'

Bourke made his and Harry's gin a long refreshing drink rather than a belt around the ears. 'How long have you been stationed here?' he asked.

'Too fucking long old chap.'

The wife said. 'Three years.'

'Three fucking years apparently.'

'It can't be that bad,' Harry spoke. 'I mean, tropical island ... paradise ain't it?'

'Fucking paradise, not likely lovey.'

Harry stiffened.

'Fucking head-hunters, snakes, spiders, fucking diseases and savages. It's a fucking prison sentence.'

'So where are you off to from here?' the wife asked.

'Kanantui,' Harry said without thinking.

'Kanantui?'

'Back to Australia,' Bourke said smartly before Harry put his foot in it further.

'Well, where is it, Australia or fucking Kanantui?'

'Where's Kanantui in Australia?' Mrs Taplow asked.

'What Harry meant to say,' Bourke corrected, 'is we are headed for Cooktown, north Queensland.'

'Aye,' Harry nodded. 'In Australia.'

•   •   •

Salty stopped Herr Kohl at the Jacob's ladder. He descended into one of the empty coal colliers returning ashore. 'Hey there, Herr *Cabbage*, where yer think yer off to?' he said, the smirk on his face busting to laugh.

'Vot you call me?'

'Herr *Cabbage* ... ain't that yer name, translated into the King's English that is.'

'Nein. Ees Herr Kohl, ja?'

'Yer but ain't kohl the kraut word for cabbage?'

'Ja, but you have names in English same.'

'Like what?'

Kohl thought a moment. 'Ah ... like Catt, ja. Mister Catt. Eet does not mean cat, *miaou*, ja?'

Salty, put back in his box, continued on regardless. 'Yer well ... so where are yer off to any'ow?'

'My ribs give me much pain,' he said of his cracked ribs. 'I am going to island infirmary for something to stop the pain.'

Salty shrugged and spat into the bay. He didn't like the Hun, never had done since the day he met him.

•   •   •

Late afternoon.

Tulagi Island morphed into a mirage before vanishing over the horizon. Harry Pickles stood legs apart, his size twelve boots planted firmly on the deck enjoying a pipe of rum infused tobacco whilst keeping *Drifter* steady nor-west for New Guinea. Flash, Salty and Hank joined him on the bridge for a smoke. Flash tapped cigarettes loose from his packet of Capstans and offered them around. Salty and Hank dampened the ends of their smokes with wet tongues, looking at Flash expectantly.

'I s'pose yer want me to light the bloody things for yer too, huh?' Flash chaffed. Both men nodded. Flash patted his pockets. 'Where's me lighter?' Suddenly Flash looked serious. 'Me lighter?' He emptied his pockets. All crew knew how much Flash treasured his lighter with its novel erotic image decorating the silver casing. He forked out a half week's pay for it in Singapore.

'Jesus Christ!' Flash cried. 'Where's Herr *Cabbage*? I lent it to him to light a fag an' he never returned it.' Flash wedged his Capstan behind his ear and went looking for the German.

Fifteen minutes later.

'Any sign?' Bourke asked, now on the bridge where the others had assembled.

'There's not a bloody sign o' him,' Flash was angry. 'Me bloody lighter!'

'Bill.' Bourke looked to the engineer stoker. 'You and Hank searched everywhere; I mean he hasn't had an accident …unconscious somewhere down in the engine room?' Cap'n Bourke fished for answers.

'He's jumped ship,' Harry said. 'That's what the bastard's done.'

'Salty,' Bourke said. 'You saw him last apparently.'

'Yer, he were catchin' a ride on a collier. Said his ribs were killin' him and he needed pain relief. Said he was goin' to the infirmary on Tulagi. Sorry cap'n, I should 'ave ...'

'Don't blame yourself.' Bourke bit a thumbnail in thought. He stepped out onto the bridge wing searching their wake. Tulagi was barely a speck. 'Why would he want to jump ship?'

'Let's go back an' ask the bastard,' Bill said.

Clearly that wasn't an option.

Arsala and Juvita finally joined the crew. 'Nothing Captain Bourke sir,' Arsala said. Juvita nodded her confirmation. 'We search everywhere. There is no where he could hide.'

'Why hide? From what?' Harry said.

Bourke agreed. 'Exactly.' But what plagued Bourke now was the thought Herr Kohl had not been telling the truth about the German gold on board the SS *Prinzessin*.

· · ·

Days later. Tulagi Island

La Grenouille steamed into Tulagi Island. Monsieur Felix Du Bellay was not a happy man. After three days searching Manning Strait at the western tip of tip of Borora Island, north of Santa Isabel Island and part of the Solomon Island group, there was no sign of *Drifter*. The French had lost hope, though Du Bellay was convinced that he would find the Australians searching for the SS *Prinzessin* gold. Now he had to concede defeat. It appeared the *bastard Australian philanderer* had made his escape to Queensland. And to top off his bad day he now suffered chronic indigestion from the rich foie gras he just consumed with toasted rye bread as a snack. He shouldn't have eaten the entire 300-gram tin.

La Grenouille would refuel at Tulagi Island coal station before sailing on to Melbourne where he was expected to speak at a diplomatic conference to the Australian Federal Parliament in Melbourne.

Du Bellay looked out the stateroom window of his shipboard quarters. *Sacré bleu*, he blasphemed. Coconut palms and blue water, heat, and diseases. He was over it, desperate for a windfall so he could retire to the village of Cernobbio on Lake Como in Northern Italy where his wife Vignetta had family.

She might have picked up bad habits while he was stationed in Tahiti, but he would claim his entitlement over her bricks and mortar inheritance, that was for certain. Might even take a lover of my own, he thought. But in reality, food and wine was his mistress ... and cocaine.

Du Bellay took a silver cigarette case from his pocket and tapped cocaine onto a dinner plate. Dividing it into two neat lines he rolled a fifty-franc note into a tight straw and snorted, one line up each nostril. Being a large man and a regular user of the narcotic, he was generous with his portions. The effect was an instant euphoria. The indigestion subsided. He felt invincible. Checking his cabin door was locked, the diplomat lifted the bottom drawer of his clothes chest free and took a parcel of cocaine from its hiding place. Stacked neatly were ten one-pound parcels stored in greaseproof paper, sealed with cheesecloth. Value when delivered to Huang Ying in Melbourne's Chinatown ... five hundred pounds each.

The white gold from South America, smuggled into New Orleans and shipped to San Diego where Du Bellay picked it up, was in endless supply. This would be the consul's third delivery in as many years. *Five thousand pounds,* Du Bellay whispered reverently before replacing the drawer and locking it. He smiled at the thought of diplomatic immunity. The arrogance. He would sail through customs, literally. Did he give a consideration to the young girls kidnapped, forced into a world of drug dependency to be used as prostitutes? No. Or any other of the degradations accompanying drug addiction. Definitely not. It was all about Monsieur Felix Du Bellay.

The heavy anchor chain clanking through the stern hawsehole disturbed Du Bellay's reverie. It was time for officialdom. Another quick snort should see him tolerate the boredom of meeting his British counterpart on this *pissy island,* the Resident Commissioner Marmaduke Algernon Taplow and his drunken wife, once a pretty young woman, turned into a scrawny mannequin with a blotched red face, tropical sores and yellow eyes. But like all steamers cruising the seven seas, *La Grenouille* needed fuel.

· · ·

Herr Adolf Kohl watched the French ship moor in the bay. All he wanted was to return to Germany. He hadn't seen his fatherland since 1914. 1914! A whole decade. He jumped ship here on Tulagi in the hope of a German, Dutch, Spanish or maybe Norwegian ship calling for fuel. To work his passage back to Europe where he would walk to Germany if need be. All he wanted was to go home. The thought of being recaptured by the French and returned to the Isle of Pine terrified him. So, what is the first ship to call on this tiny island since *Drifter*? A damned French ship.

As he watched on, hidden amongst the rocks of the western shore, Kohl was certain he recognised Monsieur Du Bellay standing at the bow of his tender looking like Jules Dumont d' Urville or an obese version of Captain Cook. Du Bellay, the man he knew was responsible for his prolonged incarceration, the man searching for the *Prinzessin* gold.

'Bah! The *Prinzessin* gold!' Kohl cursed. 'Don't they realise it is lost forever?'

'Hot day what?' Commissioner Taplow greeted the French party on his veranda, a little unsteady on his feet. He slopped gin down the front of his shirt. 'Ah!' Marmaduke apologised for his untidiness. 'Got a dodgy ankle. Tripped over the wife's fucking cat.'

'Bonjour Monsieur Taplow,' Du Bellay smiled at the drunken Englishman. 'I see you have brought cocktail hour forward a few hours.'

'Few?' Marmaduke laughed out loud. 'A friend once told me, Marmaduke he said, you can't say you've been drinking all day unless you start first thing in the morning.'

Capitaine Claude de Forbin allowed his monocle drop to his palm where he proceeded to clean it with his handkerchief. Immediately an overweight ginger cat miaowed at his feet, tail erect, rubbing itself against him. The captain hated cats and jerked his boot. He was busy dusting cat fur from his trousers when *Lady* Taplow swanned through the flywire and onto the deck.

'Monsieur Du Bellay, how nice to see you again. Here for coal?'

Marmaduke stiffened. 'Of course he's here for fucking coal.'

'Now now Marmaduke. No need to curse.' Mrs Taplow used her long cadaverous finger with its extra-long nail to swivel her recently freshened gin and tonic.

'Yes madame,' Du Bellay had seen it all before. 'Here for coal. And may I say you look ravishing this morning.'

'Thank you monsieur, I can assure you flattery will get you everywhere,' she flirted back. Marmaduke rolled his eyes and took a long drink. 'Refreshments, gentlemen?'

Grateful to be in the shade Du Bellay was feeling his last hit of cocaine petering out. Maybe a gin would pep him up. He accepted the offer. Meanwhile the cat annoyingly pushed an empty can around the bare floorboards whilst licking the insides of the tin. Du Bellay watched with interest when he recognised the yellow can with the red lighthouse label. He leant over to read it clearly.

'Lighthouse Brand,' he said. 'Where did you get this from?'

'A lovely young man by the name of Captain Jonathon Bourke left us a carton of mullet,' the wife said. 'Audrey loves it.'

'Audrey?'

'The fucking cat,' Marmaduke said.

Du Bellay grew serious. 'When was this, ah, Captain Bourke here?'

'Yesterday wasn't it dear?'

'The day before I think my love.'

Du Bellay's anger had sobered him completely. He snatched the tin from the cat to read the label clearly. *Lighthouse Brand Mullet – Cooktown - Fresh from the sea.* 'I need my ship refuelled. Quickly Commissioner.'

'Commissioner?'

'Yes monsieur. We need to sail as soon as possible.'

'What's the hurry old chap? Has this Bourke fellow done anything I should know about?'

'All I can say is he is a dangerous man. Please monsieur, order the loading of my coal immediately.'

'Would this have anything to do with the sneaky German?'

'The who?'

'There's a German chappy, jumped Captain Bourke's ship. He's been hiding on the northern shore here. Silly bugger doesn't think I know about him … me for Christ's sake, the Resident Commissioner.' He puffed out his cheeks. 'God knows what he's up to.'

'A German on the *Drifter*?'

'That's what I said.'

'German?'

'Christ, is there a parrot here somewhere? Yes, fucking German.'

Du Bellay looked at Captain de Forbin. 'Are you thinking what I am thinking?' he asked the captain in their mother tongue.

'Oui.'

'I need to see this German. Now!'

The commissioner looked at the consul. He *was* serious. 'Wouldn't you like a little refreshment first?'

'No!' Du Bellay caught Marmaduke's facial twitch. 'Look, I don't mean to be rude, but this is of the highest priority. Now monsieur, your domain is tiny, yes. So where can I find this … this Hun?'

Within the hour Herr Kohl was coaxed out of hiding in a small cave on the north coast, a mere half mile from the official residence, by six armed French crewmen. Prised from his hidey-hole like an escargot from its shell, he was bedraggled, scared and dragged screaming and shouting back to the bay where he was immediately ferried out to Du Bellay.

'Well, well, well,' Du Bellay said in English, a language they shared outside their respective mother tongues. Kohl was chained at the ankles and wrists. 'What a small world we have here.'

Du Bellay had before him a large salver of sandwiches. He plucked one bursting with cold meat and pickles, stuffing it into his mouth.

Kohl's stomach growled. 'I will die before I let you take me back to prison,' he said, his voice breaking.

'That can be arranged, don't you worry. And I will see you die nice and slow.' Du Bellay wiped sauce off his chin and lit a cigar, puffing until the end glowed red like lava. He savoured the smoke on his palate, finally discharging the vapour with a satisfying sigh. The Frenchman stood face to face with the German, barely inches separating them. He expelled another cloud of smoke in the prisoner's face before holding the smouldering ash just beneath Kohl's left eye.

'I might start with burning one eye. How would you like that?'

Kohl whimpered. He struggled. But two marines held him securely.

'I asked you a question Hun, how would you ...'

'I know where Bourke is headed,' Kohl's words spewed without hesitation. 'You are looking for him, ja?'

Du Bellay smelt victory. 'Where? To the reef, yes. Looking for the *Prinzessin*, yes?'

'No monsieur. The *Prinzessin* shifted off the reef many years ago, it sank into deep water where no man can go.'

Du Bellay held the burning cigar so close to the man's cheek he scorched skin.

'The *Tear of the Eclipse*!' Kohl cried out. 'It is a rare black pearl stolen from the Tahitians a long time ago and now Bourke knows where to look for it.'

Monsieur Felix Du Bellay knew of the pearl. It was often talked about at the dining tables of officials entertaining in Papeete. A pearl so large, so rare, and worth an emperor's ransom.

'The *Tear of the Eclipse* is a myth, a legend,' Du Bellay answered, greed seeping from the pores of his sweating skin.

Kohl sensed he had a bargaining chip. 'That's where you are wrong Herr Du Bellay. Capitaine Bourke discovered a map. He found clues.'

'What clues? Where?'

Herr Kohl looked at the sandwiches and involuntarily dribbled.

'I said what clues? Where?'

Kohl proceeded to tell Du Bellay everything he knew between mouthfuls.

CHAPTER ELEVEN

One day out from Kanantui

All aboard *Drifter* saw the smoke. And it smelt sulphuric.

Captain Bourke raised his chin, sniffing the air as if the elevated position would improve his analysis. 'That's volcanic,' he told those around him. 'And you can see the haze is from the nor-west.'

'New Guinea,' Harry said.

'Without a doubt.'

The experienced Coral Sea travellers knew there were many volcanoes dotted along the thousand-mile Bismarck arc, as geologists called it, and most were active. 'I hope it's not Kanantui,' Bourke said.

They approached Kanantui at night. Even from ten miles out at sea the sight was daunting. Red, yellow, and orange lava snaked slowly, purposely, down the steep slopes of the island, spilling into the sea creating monstrous clouds of steam. All on board, watched in awe and silence.

Jonathon Bourke levelled his binoculars on the closest peak, where molten rock spewed steadily from earth's exit, the oozing flow interrupted occasionally by explosive geysers of *fire and brimstone*.

'There are actually two volcanoes on Kanantui,' Bourke told those closest. 'Stratovolcanoes it says in the Britannica.' He had read about them only an hour earlier. 'Wewakhui and Tekahui. The Encyclopedia says the main volcano itself collapsed in three major eruptions over the past 16,000 years. These explosions left a huge caldera ...'

'A what?'

'Caldera. That's the mouth of a volcano. This one's about five miles by seven and is now a freshwater lake.'

'With so much smoke and steam it's difficult to say where we can land,' Harry said. 'What do you think cap'n?'

'That eruption is at Wewakhui about fifteen miles north. We can anchor off the village of Bok safely, it's on the south-east side of the island.

Arsala appeared on the bridge with Juvita. 'Word if you please Captain Bourke sir.'

A word.

This could mean only one thing. The crew have sent their representative and Bourke half guessed what was coming. 'Shoot, my friend.'

'The crew, that is me and Juvita, Bill, Hank, Flash and Salty ...'

'And Salty?' Bourke feigned surprise.

'Yes, yes,' Arsala frowned. 'Salty is included. We are all worried sick Captain Bourke sir. Worried sick we are. Landing on this ... this ... island of fire and devils.'

'Fire and devils huh?'

'Yes, captain Bourke sir.'

'But the danger is miles north. Here.' Bourke passed the binoculars. 'See for yourself.' At ten miles out they had a clear view of the island's entirety, even though it was a black shape on the horizon, silhouetted by the fire.

Arsala ignored the gesture. 'To what end Captain Bourke sir? You look for fairy tale pearl. It is a half-cocked idea. I tell you true, I think you agree with Arsala and Juvita. Much danger here.'

Juvita nodded the affirmative in rapid jerks.

'I appreciate your concern Arsala, Juvita. But I will kick myself if I don't investigate. We have come this far, and at the least I can do a preliminary exploration. See if there is any truth in this, fairy tale, as you call it. If need be, we come back another day.'

The moonless light was immediately flooded with the most magnificent fiery light reflected across the water although the volcano was so far away. Arthur poked his head through the companion way to the bridge. 'Permission to enter captain,' he said more out of politeness than duty. Bourke nodded. 'Magnificent, what?' Arthur said, joining the others on the darkened bridge. 'How far away is that do you think?'

'Ten miles at least.'

Arsala persisted. 'Captain Bourke sir ...'

'I'm taking a small search party ashore Arsala and that's the end of it. You will stand by here at the helm. Savvy?'

Arsala raised one eyebrow. 'Very well. But don't say you weren't warned.'

Harry winked at Bourke through the dark of night. 'Looks like it's just you and me huh?'

'And me,' Arthur said.

'Very well.' Bourke looked at Arsala. 'I believe it's your watch at four bells. I suggest you and Juvita get some sleep. You too Arthur. But on Arsala's watch I want you to rouse Ivan and call for two volunteers, preferably Salty and Hank. Bill's to stay with the boilers. We may have to leave in a hurry. We'll leave for shore at first light. Harry, get some shut eye, I'll take the helm 'til two. Then I want you prepare the tender and stow firearms.'

'So, you are afraid of head-hunters,' Arthur grinned.

'No. There's no such thing anymore. But there are many nasties in the jungle.'

'Nasties?'

'Aye, deadly poisonous taipans, death adders, saltwater crocs, cassowaries, giant tarantulas.'

And if they don't get you a monitor lizard might see you as a likely dinner, or there's poisonous birds and giant centipedes and cockroaches the size of your hand. No Arthur, the jungle here is not family friendly.'

Bourke cut the speed back to five knots and coasted slowly across a calm sea that was glowing like a scene from Dante's *Inferno*. At fifteen miles to the south of the erupting Wewakhui, Bourke felt safe enough. At four bells *Drifter* came alive. At 5AM they dropped anchor three hundred yards offshore from the native village of Bok and waited for the canoes to investigate the rare arrival of Europeans on the island. It was well known there was little of interest for the whitefella on Kanantui. Visitors were scarce. Yet no canoes rowed out.

'In fact, I can't see any life in the village,' Bourke said, sweeping his binoculars across the small village of grass and bamboo huts on stilts, spread amongst the coconut palms. Under normal circumstances, without the drifting smoke and apprehension, the scene was idyllic. Postcard perfect.

Captain Bourke stroked the week's growth bristling his chin. *Maybe this wasn't such a grand plan,* he thought. *Too late now, in for a penny in for a pound,* as his mother would have said.

Now they were anchored, the still bay seemed breathless. Almost oppressive. Humidity enveloped the ship, and Bourke felt his body sweat, particularly as he had to wear jeans, heavy boots and full sleeve shirt in preparation for the jungle. The only sounds were gentle waves lapping at the shore, washing over the steeply rising beach before drawing back into the bay. A rooster crowed somewhere, and several pigs ran along the sand nosing their snouts here and there, looking for food, and occasionally turning heads out at *Drifter* with modest curiosity.

'I can't say I exactly like the look of this Cap'n,' Harry ran a hand through his greasy hair. The water looked inviting but there was no way he was going for a swim, but, he thought, scouring the island, a waterfall would be pleasant right now.

The tender was lowered from its davits with Ivan and an apprehensive Salty steadying the boat, standing on the thwart. Hank, Arthur and Bourke climbed down the Jacob's ladder and Harry passed down a rifle for each man; war surplus Lee-Enfields, with a bandolier of fifty .303 cartridges each. Tucked under his belt Harry secured a military Luger, 1915, souvenired from a dead German in a trench during the war. Bourke was comfortable with his 1910 Browning, bought in the bar at the White Horse in Cooktown for two quid, holstered at his hip. Nursing unease, they cast off, rowing for the beach.

•   •   •

Salty volunteered for anchor duty, jumping off the bow to secure the tender, when he disappeared up to his neck in water, drawing applause and laughter from the others.

'Christ!' he spluttered and coughed, struggling with the anchor, the anchor rope and a steep incline to the water's edge. 'It's deeper than I thought.' He pulled the tender ashore and the others helped secure it well above the tide line.

Only stray pigs and a dozen scrawny chickens greeted them, from a distance. 'Where the hell is everyone?' Harry muttered. Here on the sand the air was still, accentuating the din from the cicadas.

'Don't know,' Bourke said. 'Look lively lads.' Bourke checked his pistol for the third time. Harry loaded a bullet into the breach of his Luger and the others did likewise with their rifles.

'Are you certain this is a good idea cap'n?' Hank asked.

'Dunno.' Bourke kept a sharp eye. Someone had to lead this mob. 'Let's go find out, shall we?'

Little planning had gone into the village layout. It seemed they built wherever they fancied; after all, everyone, it appeared to Bourke, had a water view. The grass huts had 'A' framed roofs with openings at each apex to allow smoke to escape. The village communal meeting hut was an elongated barn-looking structure some fifty feet long by twenty feet wide. Other smaller huts were circular. An old woman appeared in the doorway of the communal hut. She was bare from the waist up, her elongated wrinkled breasts hanging to her navel. Bourke thought she looked slightly different from most islanders they encountered. With high cheekbones, a more pointed nose and hair cropped short she would have been attractive in her youth. She held back a bunch of small children, all anxious, tugging at the woman's grass skirt and said a few words in an authoritative tone. Other old women joined her. They stood at the bamboo porch, some five feet off the ground, and stared.

'Lower the guns boys,' Bourke ordered. He gestured to the woman that they were friendly. Smiling soothing words that meant nothing to these Stone Age people.

'They're on their own' Harry said.

'Looks like the men and boys have buggered off and left the women to hold the fort,' Salty said.

'It could be an ambush,' Arthur was more pessimistic.

Suddenly the old lady started ranting. She pointed to the sky which was becoming more ominous by the minute. The sky had darkened, and the early morning sun appeared blood orange. A breeze had picked up and sulphur pollution was growing stronger. The old lady waved, pointing towards the source of the smoke and gloom. The other women joined her, all animated, pointing north.

'I wonder if she's trying to tell us the men folk have gone to investigate the volcano,' Hank offered.

'You know Hank,' Harry said. 'I reckon yer right on the money lad.'

Hank smiled. Someone was listening. 'Well as me mum would say, Hank, yer not just a pretty face.'

'Don't get too carried away yer ugly bastard,' Salty grinned.

Bourke was satisfied the women and children were alone. He could make out a dozen women or more now, and twice as many children. 'Okay, this shouldn't be too difficult. *Interieur nord-ouest* the writing in the watch read,' Bourke said. 'That means inland north-west. *400 metres*. Let's do this.' Bourke consulted his compass.

'Look there boss,' Ivan Toussaint pointed with his rifle to an opening in the jungle. 'There is pathway, yes?' Thirty yards away where the village clearing backed onto the jungle, they could see an opening.

Bourke looked back to the compass. 'Spot on. Nor-west.'

Harry said. 'Well, that was easy.' They gathered at the jungle entrance. 'Or maybe not.'

Now, stepping into the dense vegetation they realised the lay of the land. And it was steep. 'It might only be 400 meters mates,' Salty muttered. 'But it's all up hill and bloody steep.'

As they entered the entanglement of this primeval land no one noticed a small group of older boys, six to eight-year-olds, run off urgently in the direction of the volcano. It appeared the whitefella explorers were heading into sacred territory.

•　•　•

Bourke led his expedition. With the sky growing darker, the impenetrable jungle either side of the path and the heavy canopy of foliage overhead, visibility was greatly reduced. In many places the path turned into a mountain track where several rocks were fitted neatly together to provide steps, often on a forty-five-degree angle. It was arduous and slow. Sweat drenched their clothing. Arthur let out a pathetic squeal – he was the first to see a tarantula. The huge, hairy arachnid was larger than Harry's fist. He brushed against it on a low branch where it waited patiently, stalking a nearby lizard.

Bourke sighed, shaking his head. 'That's nothing Arthur. If you look about carefully, you'll see many more and plenty of other nasties as well. Just focus on the path ahead. Make a bit of noise and you'll scare the snakes.'

'Snakes!'

'Yep, and big bastards too.'

After three hundred metres the path levelled, before continuing at an even more frightening angle. But the pathway ended, and the vegetation thinned slightly. A sudden movement of colour caught Arthur's eye first.

'Jesus! What's that?'

'What?'

'That!'

The cassowary rushed out of the undergrowth darting towards Salty, last in the line.

'Don't move!' Bourke shouted.

Salty made a stance to punch the giant bird. Fists up, like a prize pugilist. The cassowary stopped dead. Bourke knew only too well the dangers of the cassowary, and it wasn't information gleaned from his precious encyclopedias, it was personal experience. It wasn't known as the world's most dangerous bird for nothing. The six-foot female studied Salty with its prehistoric brain. Salty had seen plenty of cassowaries in the rainforests around Cooktown, he knew the hazards, but had never been confronted by such a large, aggressive individual, and so close up.

'No one move,' Bourke said softly. 'No one. Got it? Salty, don't provoke it.'

'Provoke it! What if I just give it a hard slap?'

'Listen-to-me, Salty. Listen-carefully,' Bourke said, his words urgently articulated. 'I've seen one of these kill a wild boar with those feet. Those claws can rip your guts out in a flash.'

'Jesus!' Salty said, not taking his eye of the giant flightless bird. 'Now yer worryin' me cap'n.'

'Now, lower your head, don't look the thing in the eye. It will see it as a challenge.'

'Okay,' Salty lowered his eyes, wary to keep his eye on the large bird's huge, wickedly armed feet. 'Now back away, real slow.'

Salty backed off.

The cassowary stepped closer.

Salty moved further back. The bird took quick steps after him. Salty turned to run but tripped and fell. The cassowary attacked. Ivan pulled the trigger of his .303. The deadly war souvenir from the Western Front kicked into his shoulder like a mule. The bullet sizzled over the bird's back. Feathers scattered ... and so did the cassowary. Frightened off by the gunshot and a searing wound along its back.

'Jesus Christ!' Salty felt his manhood challenged. The group cheered.

'What kinda marksman are you?' Harry roared with laughter at Ivan. 'The bloody bird was the size of a house and a coupla inches away and yer still missed the bastard. No wonder you frogs needed us diggers to fight yer war.'

Heads turned to follow the fleeing bird, their eyes wide with excitement, when the most bizarre sight caught everyone's attention. Fifty, sixty metres up the mountain twenty or more figures stared back down the slopes towards them.

'What the hell?'

'Are they what I think they are?'

'If you mean, are they dead people, well yes,' Bourke said.

Where the vegetation of this part of the mountain ended, an earthen embankment of ochre coloured earth, rose for several hundred metres. At the top, held in position by a log and twine corral, were the mummified bodies of many natives. Some were partially dressed, their heads adorned with shell jewellery. Many had their limbs bandaged so the skeletal remains held their shape. For Europeans seeing this sight for the first time, it was a most macabre experience.

The group climbed on, finally standing before the remains of the village dead, an accumulation dating from the early 19th century to the present. All figures were poised in sitting or crouching positions with heads high and proud, gazing out across the jungle. Bourke had seen similar resting places for the dead in the past and knew a little about them. 'The natives feel that if they bury their loved ones underground, then they soon forget them. This way they can visit them and talk to their spirits. Occasionally they are carried back into the village for cultural celebrations.'

'Why are they orange?'

'They are smoked for a month or more first. You'll find them all over New Guinea, this lot here are just from the one village.'

The more macabre were the skeletons with faces moulded with red clay to resemble the deceased loved ones. 'Because the natives believe if they aren't recognisable, their spirits, unable to recognise their own bodies, roam the jungle causing havoc like diseases and crop failures.'

Somewhere, not too distant, they heard the unmistakable crackling of fire. The increasing breeze brought thickening smoke and the unmistakable acrid gases of an erupting volcano. 'It's getting worse cap'n,' Harry said.

For the first time Jonathon Bourke looked anxious. 'We better move it.' Bourke started back up the steep incline to what he guessed was their goal all this time; a cathedral sized cave another fifty metres up the mountain. Bourke arrived first, turning to watch the others struggling to keep up. From here he could see the top of the village buildings. Out on the bay, *Drifter* rose and dipped on a gentle swell. Behind them in the cave the grisly island custom continued, well into the cave.

'It's a regular mausoleum.'

'Like catacombs in Paris, oui,' Ivan said.

'I'll take your word for it,' Arthur agreed.

'So,' Harry asked Bourke. 'Now what?'

'*35 rouge* … 35 red. Le *gagnant prend tout*. Winner takes all.'

'All of what?'

'My understanding is that that is the final clue to the discovery of the *Tear of the Eclipse*.'

'Yes, and I said it sounds like roulette.'

'Red, yes? Red and black are the colours of roulette. And over there you have skulls painted red and black.'

'Well spotted!' Bourke climbed gingerly over loose tibias, fibulas, broken ribs, pelvis bones and craniums, apologising to the dead en route. One large wall of the cave was decorated with skulls. Bourke made his way directly to the skull-coloured red with ochre. As respectfully as possible he lifted the skull, but the loose mandible fell away. Instantly a giant centipede slithered out the eye socket. Bourke instinctively dropped the artefact. It shattered.

'That was bit heavy-handed,' Harry said, not seeing the centipede and assuming the captain deliberately smashed it.

'I dropped it.'

'Right.'

'Anyway, it's empty. Nothing.' Bourke checked the one next to it, stained black with soot. He studied it a moment, finally giving it a respectful shake. 'Empty.' Reverently, he sat the skull back where here found it. Bourke glanced at the shards of red painted skull at his feet. It lay in a dozen pieces …

Best leave it be.

'In all respect cap'n,' what did yer expect to find?'

'I don't know Harry.'

But Harry *did* know. It was Bourke's adventurousness that brought them here. Harry was twenty years Jonathon's senior. The youthful wild skipper kept Harry young. Kept arthritis at bay. Kept him alive. This impetuous dreamer could be his own son. Harry would follow him anywhere.

'Look it's been some time, eh?' Salty offered. 'I reckon it was found years ago.'

'I reckon yer on the money.'

Hank climbed awkwardly into the cave entrance to join them, trying his darndest not to desecrate remains by treading all over them. 'Cap'n Bourke sar. The smoke. It ain't gettin' any clearer out there. If I didn't know any better sar, I'd say that fire is coming this-aways.'

Immediately the foghorn on board *Drifter* echoed off the bay. Once, twice and then urgently repeated. Arsala was clearly nervous. Bourke mounted a boulder at the cave's entrance where he had a clear view down to the roof tops of the village dwellings. Out on the water he could make out Arsala and Juvita pacing the deck.

The foghorn groaned its mournful cry again.

Instantly a flock of plumed ducks flew from the north escaping the worsening fires. Bourke identified other panicked birds; the blue billed, yellow crown and green throat of a bird of paradise followed, while on the ground, wild boar, brush turkeys, red jungle fowl, quail and finally more cassowaries raced away from the fire.

'Time to move out,' Bourke yelled as he jumped with ease from a rock as high as he was tall. He led them off, tripping down the steep slopes at three times the speed it took to ascend. Minutes later they burst from the jungle into a terrified community.

The islander men had returned, fifty, sixty strong and many more women and children had appeared. It was mayhem.

They looked splendid, dressed in elaborate headpieces of coloured feathers and shell, with their bodies painted with various dyes. Most were naked except for codpieces made from animal skins and bark to protect their genitals. Many had pierced ears and noses adorned with boar tusks and bones. But, Bourke noted, like the old woman they met earlier, these people, seemed more Polynesian than Melanesian, with their smaller noses and high cheekbones. The women in particular were attractive to the eyes of these white men, with their straight hair, not the curly, tight, matted hair of the people from the neighbouring islands.

The men, armed with bows and arrows, spears and gnarly clubs were animated, frightened. It was now that Bourke noticed their canoes pulled up onto the beach. When *Drifter* arrived, the men had been along the coast towards the northern volcano.

Their chief singled out Bourke as the whitefella leader.

Waving his hands like a crazy man he stabbed a finger towards *Drifter*, yelling at Bourke in a language he could not possibly understand.

'I think he's asking for help,' Harry said. 'They would never get far in those canoes.'

Bourke was about to answer Harry when ...

'Are you serious?' Arthur was fixated, his gaze southwest. Bourke wheeled about, as did the others. Only a few miles southwest of the village, Kanantui's second volcano, Tekahui, was erupting and the lava flow now threatened the village. As they watched on, a plume of volcanic ash and gas exploded towards the clouds, thousands of feet into the sky.

The ground shook.

'This ain't good cap'n,' Salty said.

Bourke rounded on the chief. He poked the savage in the chest and pointed towards *Drifter* before swinging his arm in a wide arc, pointing at the villagers and trying to sign ...

All of you. On the ship.

The other crew read the urgency of the situation. 'What can we do capitaine?' Ivan asked. 'We have to help these people out to sea,' Bourke yelled over the building urgency. 'We've got to get them on board and fast. Salty, Ivan,'

'Aye.'

'Women and children into those canoes. Quickly now and see that each canoe is full. Salty, you go coxswain on the first canoe, and the others'll follow.'

'Got yer.'

. . .

The pyroclastic flow roared down the mountain side ploughing through the jungle towards the village – a tsunami of molten ash. Every living thing in its path died a horrific and immediate death. The volcano itself sounded like the Battle of the Somme, with explosions reminiscent of giant artillery. The pyroclastic avalanche of volcanic ash and searing hot gases headed towards the village … crashing towards them at over three hundred miles an hour.

Less than a mile distant an earthquake breached a section of the elevated lake's southern wall. Water cascaded down the hillside into the path of the pyroclastic flow. The resulting slurry bulldozed on – a boiling fast-moving rush of red-hot ash and mud.

. . .

Salty and a dozen natives launched the largest canoe. A war outrigger built to hold thirty warriors. Most of the older women and youngest children squeezed aboard. Ten native rowers manoeuvred the vessel. Other villagers shoved the canoe into the waves whilst Salty stood tall in the bow yelling encouragement.

On board *Drifter* Arsala and Juvita threw rope ladders over the side. They cleared the main deck. Down in the boiler room Bill Brown fed the furnace and coal glowed the colour of hot lava.

Three more canoes followed suit. The last spare spaces filled with pigs and chickens. The preliminary wind preceding the mudslide whipped across the beach. Steaming hot gases – over a thousand degrees centigrade – followed. The noise intensified. The ground shook constantly. On the bay waves chopped the surface. The sun disappeared behind black clouds and ever thickening ash rained from the sky.

It was terrifying.

Cap'n Bourke watched the last canoe head for *Drifter*. On board the first arrivals were hauled aboard. Not very far inland eighty-foot palms could be heard snapping and crashing to the ground like straw skittles.

The heat seared their skins. Hair singed. Eyes burned. Red hot sand whipped up by mini tornadoes lashed their legs. Clothes caught alight.

Bourke screamed at his crew. 'Move it move!'

Harry heaved the anchor into the ship's boat, pushing, dragging the craft into the water. Bourke, Ivan, Arthur and Hank put their shoulders to the stern. It was every man for himself. Somersaulting, rolling, falling into the ship's tender. Ivan and Hank snatched an oar each.

'Row! For Christ's sake, row!'

The pyroclastic cloud reached the shoreline. Grass huts exploded in flame; palms lit up like giant torches. A split second behind the scorching gases was the boiling mud flow. Ten … fifteen-foot thick, rushing at the water's edge.

A wave of death.

Bourke was closest to the catastrophe, standing in the stern sheets, one leg up on the gunwale, defying the elemental forces around him, challenging nature. It was the finest line between survival and death that anyone present had ever experienced. The bubbling, angry slurry hit the water's edge sending steam clouds into the sky. Fortunately, the water dropped away deeply at the beach and the assailing tsunami of seething mud sank harmlessly in the sea. As the escapees rowed well out into the bay, they had a moment to watch the devastation. The village was destroyed. But the most incredible sight was watching the beach boil. The surf bubbled and blistered as surge after surge of turbulent hot mud poured into the water.

Bourke was last on board *Drifter* to a cheer from his crew. Arsala hugging him like a lost son.

'Huzzah! Huzzah! Huzzah!'

The islanders danced on the deck cheering in their own way, mimicking their whitefella saviours. But once the adrenalin subsided the realisation, they had lost everything cast a gloom over the villagers.

Once the canoes were secured in tow, Arsala resumed the helm and they pushed away from the bay into deep water a mile or so out to sea. From here it appeared the entire island had succumbed to the volcano's wrath. Fifteen miles north the first volcano still spewed lava. Bourke joined Arsala on the bridge where they watched the natives on the main deck. They had grown solemn.

'Now what do you suggest, Captain Bourke sir? What will we do with all these, these people?'

'We'll have to relocate them, somewhere safe on this island. It's their home after all.'

Harry joined them at the helm. 'The cap'n's right,' Harry told Arsala. 'This island's their home.'

'Yes, yes, I agree. But I tell you true. Where we locate them?'

'We sail north, there are other villages, maybe they will take them.'

'I dunno cap'n,' Harry said. 'You ever caught a possum in a cage, hiding in the roof o' yer house, and yer relocate the bastard away from its territory. They fight like mongrel dogs. Fight to the death they do.' Bourke looked at Harry, somewhat beguiled. Harry recognised the look on his captain's face. 'What?' Harry asked, frowning.

'Since when did you catch a possum in a cage? I thought you'd shoot the poor bastard, not relocate it.'

'Well, there you go, Jonathon … cap'n. You don't know me at all, do yer?'

'You reckon?'

Harry's face widened into a huge grin. 'Okay, so I might have shot a few possums in me time, but me cousin Allan has relocated them, an' he said they fight like a bastard.'

'Shooting possums or not Captain Bourke sir,' Arsala said, 'what are your orders if you please.'

'North up the coast.' Bourke took another searching glance across the deck. 'These people were displaced certainly, but they are resilient, every one of them by all accounts. Just sail up the coast Arsala and I'll try to communicate with their chief.'

•   •   •

Chief Moimango and daughter Kimtasu.

To the male crew on board the *Drifter*, the semi-naked women did not go unnoticed. All the women were bare breasted, but it was the younger adult women that had the men restless. In particular, one young woman who it appeared was the chieftain's daughter. With some effort and mime, Bourke was able to share his name with the chief. He poked himself in the chest and spoke clearly, articulating his name. 'Jon-a-thon.'

After several attempts the chief caught on. The chief reciprocated, his own name sounding like Moimango. 'Moimango,' Bourke repeated. The chief seemed to approve, chattering excitedly to the natives closest to him. 'Jon-a-thon,' the chief said over and over.

'Moimango.'

'Jon-a-thon.'

Bourke felt a level of progress. The chief grabbed his daughter by the arm, pulling her close. 'Kimtasu,' he said, pushing his daughter close to Bourke. He said a few short words and the daughter managed a curt smile and made what could be taken as a short bow.

'Kimtasu,' Bourke said and the villagers within ear-shot spoke excitedly amongst themselves.

'Kimtasu.'

'Jon-a-thon.'

The young woman had caught Bourke's eye earlier. She was by far the most attractive female on his ship, with rich chocolate-coloured eyes three shades darker than her soft firm skin. Her un-covered breasts were pert, yet fully rounded with areola the diameter of an English silver crown and nipples the size of peanuts. Kimtasu's full lips would be the envy of many white women. When she smiled she displayed perfect white teeth. Her hair had been cut short. Kimtasu wore several lengths of a vine necklace threaded with tiny shells. Boar tusks hung near her exposed belly. For modesty, or maybe fashion, her midriff was dressed in a skirt of dried grass threaded horizontally with green and reds to make an attractive costume. She wore a yellow hibiscus behind one ear and her high cheekbones, pointed chin and forehead were tattooed in a geometric design. Bourke guessed this meant something of importance to her people.

But what really attracted Bourke was her headband, with mother of pearl and plumed with the multi-coloured feathers of small parrots. In the centre of the headband was a large black pearl, tear-shaped, the size of a quail's egg.

Bourke looked closer at the pearl, a gesture that was taken as a compliment. Moimango could not be happier. This white chieftain, with the big metal canoe, was taken with his daughter. The chief muttered something and his minions now gathered about to witness this unexpected union, chatted back, moved by the moment. Clearly, something was afoot. Bourke however, mesmerized by the pearl, made gestures of his own.

Could I see the pearl?

Confused faces.

He reached out. Kimtasu pulled back.

'What is it?' Harry said, watching his skipper with some interest.

'The headband. Look carefully at that headband.'

'Jesus! Is that what I think it is?'

'Easy Harry let's not draw attention to it. Not yet anyhow.'

'You're right. Bloody oath cap'n, *the tear of the eclipse* was here all the time.'

'I don't know Harry. It might not be *the tear*, but mate, that has got to be worth a few bob.'

The chieftain looked bemused. He spoke with his daughter, and she touched the pearl in the centre of her head band, also bemused. But Bourke knew it was paramount he unload these people, and soon. He didn't have enough drinking water to last and certainly not enough food.

'Where's Juvita?' Bourke asked Flash.

'In the saloon cap'n, she's fetched the medical cabinet.'

'Tell her to meet me on the bridge.'

'Aye.'

•   •   •

Bourke coaxed the chieftain to the bridge where the man was like a child in a patisserie for the first time. Bourke gave the man a moment. He was touching equipment, mesmerised by all the modern technology. Arsala was less impressed. Finally, a map of New Guinea was unfurled onto the chart table. Moimango took a moment. He studied it carefully, with some interest.

'I think he's seen charts before,' Salty said.

Moimango finally grew animated. Grinning, his eyes darted to all on the bridge before Bourke got his attention. 'Kanantui,' the captain said, pointing to the native's home island. Naturally the words meant nothing to Moimango until Bourke offered the man a magnifying glass, hovering it over the island on the map. It took a minute and Bourke thought he had lost the chieftain when suddenly Moimango jabbed his gnarly finger into the map before pointing out the bridge window towards land.

'There yer go,' Harry said in a somewhat condescending tone. 'He's got the hang of it.'

The images of the two volcanoes, drawn by the cartographer for aesthetics only, were readily identifiable and Moimango nodded profusely at the lake on the map.

'Ah! So, you do understand.'

Apparently, yes.

'Maybe he see map before,' Arsala said.

'Maybe.' Bourke located two other villages marked on his map. One, Koep, was less than twelve miles north of Bok and should come into view shortly. The other was the coastal village of Malala on the north-east coast, another about thirty miles past Koep. He pointed them both out to Moimango and articulated their names. Moimango looked none the wiser. In fact, he looked vague, when Arsala had an idea. Putting his hands together in prayer Arsala placed them on his own right cheek, tilted his head as if horizontal and pretended to snore, before pointing at the island.

Juvita appeared on the bridge and said a few words in Tok Pisin, a pidgin dialect used in New Guinea. A language she had only started to learn. Moimango became animated once more. It appeared he understood. He looked back at the chart. 'Malala,' he said to Juvita pointing to another village marked on the chart. He then copied Arsala's sleep mime and laughed. 'Malala ... Malala ...'

Bourke looked at Juvita. 'Good work. Now we're getting somewhere.'

Juvita persevered, a few words managed, and a communication finally bonded the two. 'He say Malala his brothers. Take them to Malala.'

Bourke felt a weight lift from his shoulders. 'Arsala.'

'Yes, Captain Bourke sir.'

'You heard the man. Malala.

•　•　•

Both the villages of Koep and Malala were barely damaged by the disaster, but Moimango had made it clear he did not want to be taken to the village marked Koep on the map. All Harry had to say was, *bloody possums*. It must be a territorial thing.

The two extreme worlds, whitefella and blackfella, had only been in each other's company less than eight hours, but a bond had been formed. *Drifter's* crew traded personal items for native trinkets and artefacts. Hank opened a tin of mullet for one pretty young woman who smelt the contents and horrified, she heaved the can overboard, much to everyone's amusement.

Bourke felt a rare friendship with Moimango. The old man had an openness about him, an honesty that Bourke hoped was genuine. But more unsettling was the fact he couldn't take his eyes off the beautiful native woman Kimtasu. She was not as young as she looked. In her early twenties, Bourke imagined. Surely, she had a husband amongst the tribesmen.

•　•　•

It was early evening when they moored off Malala village. In the distance, Wewakhui continued to spew lava, but it was nowhere as volatile as its southern cousin, Tekahui. The natives of Bok were only too keen to file into their canoes and paddle ashore, where the entire Malala community waited to greet them on the beach. It seemed they were expected.

Moimango prepared to descend the Jacob's ladder into his own outrigger. He took Bourke's hand in both of his, cupping his calloused hands tightly around Bourke's and smiled warmly, a heartfelt thank you. Words were not necessary. Suddenly he clicked his tongue, his face grew serious and immediately he was joined by two young warriors and three of the younger women, Kimtasu amongst them. He spoke rapidly to Bourke, still holding the captain's hands tight in his. Juvita hurried over.

'What's he saying?' Bourke asked.

Juvita told the man to speak slowly. He said a few words. Juvita asked him to repeat himself. The body language was serious. Juvita managed as best she could while Bourke waited patiently. Arsala wasn't so forbearing.

'What is now, for goodness' sake? What does …'

Juvita's hand shot into the air, stopping Arsala in his tracks. She looked to Bourke and sighed.

'He say,' Juvita said in her own accented English. 'He say you must take these five peoples west towards your lands.'

Bourke frowned. 'Must!'

Juvita was trying to analyse the request in pidgin, to translate into English, which was not her first language either. 'I think he say life on Kanantui is finish for Tamesi peoples. He say you take his daughter and these warriors to look for new home for Tamesi peoples.'

'I can't do that!'

Moimango read Bourke's face. The whitefella's reaction was universal. No dialogue was necessary. Neither was the plea that followed. If anything, it was downright embarrassing. Moimango dropped to the deck on bare knees and with hands before, pleading, him he rattled on in his native tongue. He snatched Bourke's hands once more and held them tight. Eventually Juvita settled the old man. They spoke again at length. Many words repeated over and over until Juvita thought she understood enough.

'Moimango,' Juvita started and Moimango tugged at Bourke's hands once more on hearing his name. 'Moimango, he say Tamesi are finished here. The gods of fire mountains have spoken. Kanantui is finish. The gods will destroy all.'

Well that's a possibility, Bourke thought.

'Moimango say we must take warriors in search of new land. New island. He means west where the sun sleeps. Moimango say there is much land for them. He has heard from ancestors, the great fishermen.'

Salty. 'He means New Guinea cap'n.' Salty had his arm on the shoulder of one of the young native women and to Bourke they seemed ... familiar.

'I know that, but ... Jesus!'

'There's islands all over the place 'round 'ere,' Salty argued. 'Surely we could ...'

Bourke held up his hand demanding silence. 'Let me think.' He motioned for Moimango to stand. Bourke caught Kimtasu looking at him with her large dark eyes. He sighed. 'We have commitments back in Cooktown, we've already been delayed six weeks thanks to the bloody frogs.'

'So, we head back to Cooktown first,' Salty persisted. His arm had dropped to the woman's backside. 'Get the factory sorted, then find these people an island on our next trip to Honolulu in a month or so. What's the hurry?'

'Salty's right Captain, there's no great hurry, eh?'

Bourke recognised the lust in Salty's eyes. This wasn't the first time the crew had taken advantage of native women. He was hardly a saint himself. 'Since when did you two become good Samaritans?' Bourke tried to avoid Kimtasu's eye. Her beauty took his breath away. And she appeared to be attracted to *him*. So close. So desirable, yet worlds apart.

Or were they?

Kimtasu stepped forward, her face inches from his. Her firm breasts pushing against his tightened chest. With her breath perfumed like the hibiscus behind her ear, Kimtasu rubbed noses in that unique Polynesian custom of greeting. Maybe she was more worldly than Bourke realised. The captain was speechless, not that *he* could communicate with her through a common language anyhow. He held her by the waist. He hadn't meant to, but he did. Kimtasu pulled back.

The chief's outrigger was almost fully loaded. 'What I tell Moimango,' Juvita wanted to know.

'Yes, skip,' Harry asked. 'What's it to be?'

Bourke's confusion could be miscued as angst. He was frowning, mystified. But Bourke felt his heart thumping in his chest. 'Explain to Moimango we might be several months,' Bourke said. Salty slapped his skipper on the back grinning like *that* child in a lolly shop. 'How do you tell these people,' Bourke went on, 'we will be some time, some months ... you say moons maybe?'

Juvita bantered in pidgin. For the first time Moimango listened without interrupting. He appeared to understand. He spoke with the two warriors and then to the three women. All nodded heads in what could only be interpreted as positive. Moimango turned back to Bourke and took him by the wrists. The chief spoke pidgin. Juvita translated as best she could. 'He say he and all his peoples are grateful. He want his daughter and son to accompany us as an offer of goodwill. The gods insist ...'

'Wait a second,' Bourke said. 'Did you say son?'

Juvita spoke briefly to Moimango. 'He say first born here is warrior. At least that what I hear.' Juvita seemed satisfied. Moimango held an open hand against his heart and placed his other hand on Bourke's. The natives remaining all smiled. It had been a success. They exchanged farewells, Moimango climbed into his rigger and was paddled ashore. He never looked back.

Kimtasu smiled afresh, her face bursting with enthusiasm. She looked to Bourke warmly, as he convinced himself he was doing the right thing. Together they watched the canoes land safely on the beach. Back at the helm Arsala stared down from the port bridge wing where Bourke read the Arsala's lips, clear as any book ...

Captain Bourke sir. What are you doing?

• • •

They were ten days steaming from Cooktown. With a fair sea and maintaining fifteen knots, maybe nine days. One part of Bourke said, *do the humanitarian thing man, get these people resettled. It'll only take you a few weeks.*

But another side, the romantic, tested Bourke. He had been tempted by Cupid's arrow. As the volcanic island of Kanantui disappeared over the horizon, he studied Kimtasu's reaction. She seemed apprehensive, yet happy enough. Now he studied the warriors. The taller, stockier man, Kimtasu's brother, had some similarities to Kimtasu. *Brother huh?* But there appeared no regrets of their decision to journey with the whitefella. They were on an adventure, a pilgrimage. Kimtasu lingered at the stern with her fellow islanders, watching her home island vanish. *Had they ever been this far away before*, Bourke wondered.

Once *Drifter* was on her homeward heading, Bourke approached the five Tamesi. At first, they were aware, but Kimtasu made the first move. She placed her right hand on the skipper's heart and said a few words in her native tongue. Juvita joined them, seeing Bourke would need help. 'She say to you, thank you.'

Bourke smiled warmly. 'Tell them I welcome them.'

Being unable to converse presented an awkwardness. But there was one question Bourke wanted to ask. A confirmation.

He pointed to the taller warrior. 'Ask if this man is Kimtasu's brother?'

Juvita exchanged names, including her own. 'Yes, Jon-a-thon. His name Gemtasu. You happy now?' Juvita asked, spilling a cheeky grin.

'Happy?'

'Yes. Happy. Happy man is brother of Kimtasu, and not husband.'

· · ·

The days passed. The islanders kept together, squatting on deck day and night. That is except for Awateng, the woman Salty had fallen for, who now spent most of her time in his cabin.

The two warriors were travelling well-armed, with several spears, bows and arrows, shields and clubs. All which Bourke insisted be stored below.

Occasionally Bourke questioned his decision to accept these islanders. But as he promised himself, if things did not work out, if they couldn't find an island or land for them to find a fresh start, then he would see these people back with their kin.

The captain spent more and more time with Kimtasu, who flirted with his emotions. From what he could ascertain, with Juvita's assistance, she was around twenty-four. She had had a warrior husband who lost his life in a skirmish with enemy islanders two years prior. Bourke tried to hold back but he had to admit to himself that he was smitten.

On the third night Kimtasu dined with Bourke in his cabin, both grinning and chatting in their own languages like they were communicating. Kimtasu, wary at first, took to Juvita's cooking, with relish. She particularly enjoyed the spiced fish and Juvita lent her traditional Malaysian clothing. She looked stunning. When possible Juvita translated a sentence here, a request there. There were so many questions. But they would have to wait for answers. Back at Cooktown Bourke had a cousin who worked with missionaries in New Guinea. Cousin Sandy knew the language, and although the island of Kanantui's dialect would be different, there would be similarities. Kimtasu was young and intelligent. She would learn English quickly he thought. For most of the journey to Cooktown the two were left alone; although Bourke slept in a smaller crew bunk cabin, forward, insisting Kimtasu spend the night in his cabin.

Cap'n Jonathon Bourke, it seemed, was falling in love.

•   •   •

On the fourth night Bourke broached the subject of the mother of pearl headband, notably the large black pearl itself, secured to the centre like a crown jewel. Kimtasu had worn the headband all this time, and, combined with her Malaysian attire she looked quite the princess. Juvita was on hand for the occasion. Bourke reached out to touch the magnificent pearl, but Kimtasu reeled back, defensive. She cupped a hand protectively over it. Now was not the time, it seemed.

•   •   •

One day out of Cooktown
Harry cornered the captain for an audience. 'I've known yer a long time Jonathon. You're like a son to me.'

'I agree.' Bourke knew where this was headed.

'So, I feel I can talk to yer, man to man.'

'Of course, Harry, what's on your mind?'

Harry's face tightened. 'What's on my mind? What the fuck are you doin'? Shaggin' a diplomat's wife in Papeete was one thing, and Christ knows you've done plenty worse. But takin' a native girl hostage, Jesus …'

'H-hold it right there Harry. She's not a hostage.'

'Well, what the hell is she then. She's locked away in yer cabin?'

Suddenly Jonathon felt foolish. Had he been the compulsive? 'I … Harry I …ah.'

'Well? Spit it out cap'n?'

'I think I'm in love,' Bourke expelled a heavy sigh. 'There I said it. I've fallen in love.'

'Love huh. Jesus yer've only known her a minute.'

'I don't know Harry. I can't explain it. She, we … it was love at first sight.'

'Love at first sight. Jesus cap'n. I hope yer know what yer doin'.'

'Well thanks for your concern Harry, very noble of you.'

'Your concern! I'm concerned for the young lass. You can't even speak the same language.'

'Love is blind,' Bourke persisted. 'As they say.'

'Fuckin' blind alright.'

CHAPTER TWELVE

At sea aboard La Grenouille

Monsieur Felix Du Bellay caught the draught about his legs as Capitaine Claude de Forbin entered the stateroom, the heavy cabin door closing tightly behind him. 'Blowing a gale out there this evening Felix,' the capitaine said, joining Du Bellay at the dinner table squeezing his own rounded belly under the tabletop. He poured himself a Burgundy from a cut glass decanter with a wide base, designed for use at sea. He offered the consul a refill. Du Bellay nodded.

'Is this weather going to get worse?' Du Bellay asked.

'I don't think so.'

Du Bellay was not a great seaman. Travelling on the high seas he could do without. Claude de Forbin removed his braided capitaine's cap, brushing it off affectionately, placing it on the table. He routinely combed his coiffed moustache and matching beard before wetting his fingers to tidy his generous eyebrows. This preening like a damned cat irritated Du Bellay, but he said nothing. The steward appeared and took the man's heavy woollen coat with its brass buttons and white collar.

'Would you like the fish this evening or the duck?' the steward asked the captain.

'I had the fish,' Du Bellay commented. 'It was actually quite nice,'

'Duck,' Claude de Forbin said. 'Extra potatoes.' The capitaine waited for the steward to leave for the galley when he fixed Du Bellay with a stare, his eyes magnified through wire rimmed glasses. 'This man Bourke,' he started. 'He's become an obsession to you.'

Du Bellay held the capitaine's eye. 'We have had this discussion over and over Claude, I will not be swayed. The man must be reprimanded.'

'Reprimanded! Is that what you call it?'

'Well punished then.'

'Maybe,' the capitaine sighed. 'But sailing to Cooktown in Australia under Australian jurisdiction, what possibly do you hope to achieve?'

'Jonathon Bourke has a fish cannery north of Cooktown. Some months back I managed to get my hands on a carton of his Lighthouse Brand Mullet.' Du Bellay held both hands high and mimed inverted commas to the words … *Lighthouse Brand Mullet.*

'The carton was confiscated by port authorities in Papeete. And when opened the cans contained rum. Jonathon Bourke's home distilled gut rot by all accounts. Illegal rum that he has been smuggling into Honolulu where America has a prohibition on alcohol. He's been at it for some time I believe, a year at least.'

'I know this, Felix.' Claude de Forbin looked over his shoulder to the galley door to be certain they weren't being overheard. 'What we ship to Australia is far worse.'

'So be it. But that is our business. No Claude. I want the bastard to suffer. And suffer he will.' Du Bellay gulped his wine and looked about. 'I need a brandy.'

Far worse huh? Bloody hypocrite, Du Bellay thought. *Claude doesn't mind when each pay day comes along.*

'I'm not a fool Felix,' the capitaine said.

'Never said you were Claude.'

'I know it's this accursed black pearl you chase, what's it called, the *Tear of the Eclipse*?'

Du Bellay grew serious. He plucked the brandy decanter from a spirit cruet set on the bar, pouring himself a generous serve. 'Maybe, capitaine, maybe.'

A moment's silence followed. 'We'll be in Melbourne by next Friday,' the capitaine finally said.

'Good. I will meet with Ying in Chinatown on Saturday. I'm expected in parliament on the Monday. I am certain the debate about the Australian Embassies in Papeete and Noumea, which is really just a formality, will spill into Tuesday. But it's a great excuse to travel to Melbourne as you well know. Then we should be en route for Cooktown by Thursday at the latest.' Du Bellay considered those last words. 'So, if we have smooth sailing we should be in North Queensland by when, two weeks hence?'

* * *

Kanantui Island

La Grenouille sailed the east coast of Kanantui from Bok north to Malala Bay. It had been a sobering experience. Never in all their years sailing the Pacific had the Frenchmen seen such devastation; where the lava had poured into the sea it had solidified like burnt honeycomb. To their south-west Tekahui had blown her cap looking like pictures Du Bellay had seen of Vesuvius in Italy, which had last erupted back in '06. To their north-west Wewakhui still smoked, but apparently, they had missed the worst of it.

'Never been ashore here before?' Capitaine Claude de Forbin asked Du Bellay.

'Why would I?' Du Bellay muttered, sour-faced, disappointed there was no sign of *Drifter*. The two men stood side by side, hands behind backs, staring at the passing coastline from five-hundred-yards offshore, reminding Chevalier the helmsman of Lewis Carol's creations, Tweedledum and Tweedledee.

'Why on earth would anyone want to visit this godforsaken island?' Du Bellay grumbled.

'For the *Tear of the Eclipse* possibly,' the capitaine answered.

'Besides that.' This comment put a semblance of enthusiasm back into the diplomat's frame of mind. For the past two days and nights all Du Bellay had talked about was the *Tear of the Eclipse*. 'A pearl so rare, so unique – an opaque iridescent black pearl as large as an egg.'

'Bird's egg?'

'Chicken my friend, as large as a chicken's egg I have heard!' the Frenchman gloated. 'Worth a queen's ransom Claude. It's been talked about at the dinner tables of the rich and famous since the 18th century, a prized gem that would fetch hundreds of thousands of pounds. No Claude, we *must* find Captain Jonathon Bourke to make him lead us to this pearl.'

'First *Prinzessin* gold, now you chase an accursed pearl,' the capitaine tutted.

'Who said it was cursed?'

'I was speaking figuratively. But who knows,' the capitaine said meaningfully. 'It probably *is* cursed. How do you know it even exists?'

'Jesus Claude. Do you not listen? I said it is legendary, spoken about for generations.' Du Bellay took a deep breath in, pushing his chest out, only to make his belly look three times its size. 'It was a French merchant ship, in 1815 I seem to remember, named *Africain*, anchored off what now is now Papeete. They were welcomed by the Tahitians who were having some kind of ceremony for the chieftain's daughter, a most beautiful young lady who just happened to be wearing the pearl in a headband. The story goes that the crew kidnapped the princess and sailed away. Weeks later they went ashore on an island. An island we now know was Kanantui.' Du Bellay turned to face de Forbin. 'Kanantui, Claude. Right here!'

'Why this island?'

'To fill water kegs and gather fruit. Well, they were attacked by head-hunters. All were taken prisoner, but the princess was revered for her beauty. The pearl of course became a sacred relic. Over the weeks all the crew were murdered and as is the custom, eaten. One man however lived to tell the tale. He stole a canoe, escaped the cannibals, and eventually made it to Batavia, where he worked his passage back to France. This is where the legend of the pearl gets interesting.'

'And it isn't so far?'

'Ha! He recorded his story and even found investors to take him back to Papua New Guinea. But his story also attracted a bad element. He refused to say where the island was and went into hiding. The search did not eventuate. Now, the story goes on that he died of yellow fever in Normandy. Later it appears this Frenchman's son married an English woman and as the generations came and went so did a silver pocket watch – engraved with the clues about the island apparently – ended up in the hands of an English sea captain through marriage. Captain Bourke it appears …'

•   •   •

Du Bellay spoke to the steward who had brought them coffee. 'Fetch Teiki.' Teiki had on occasion joined Du Bellay's diplomatic visits to various Pacific islands. He was fluent in many Polynesian languages and some Melanesian and could converse in pidgin English. His French was passable.

A longboat was lowered and Du Bellay, Teiki and ten armed seamen rowed ashore. They were welcomed warmly, although curiously. The whitefella rarely landed on these shores. They were immediately surrounded by the villagers. An officer of the guard nervously kept them back with rifle and bayonet. Teiki managed communication in a variation of a Papua New Guinea dialect. Enough to learn that the islanders here revered a whitefella and his ship for saving the lives of the villagers from Bok, the destroyed village to the south.

'Mountain … fire,' Teiki explained, throwing his arms in the air to mimic an explosion.

'He's speaking of the volcanic eruption I would say, monsieur,' the officer said, pleased with his communication skills. The consul shook his head.

'Good mans they say. He save many peoples,' Teiki told Du Bellay in broken French.

Du Bellay slapped at a large flying insect, determined to land on his face. He grew impatient. 'Spare me the sentiment,' he snapped at Teiki.' Teiki shrugged. Du Bellay grew even more impatient. 'When was this?'

'Two night, two day … gone.'

There was no reason to stay on this beach a moment longer. Clearly Bourke was ahead of the game. If Bourke had the information that Du Bellay had and had now departed, he had clearly been successful and had the *Tear of the Eclipse* in his possession or … Du Bellay allowed the slightest smile. Or Bourke could have left empty-handed. Either way, *this damned smuggling pirate bastard Australian was really getting up Du Bellay's nose.* The heat was catching up with the overweight Frenchman. He leaned against the tender, wiping down his sweating brow, trying to clear his thoughts. What to do next?

So close yet so far.

Du Bellay looked at the officer standing with the launch and jerked his head towards their anchored ship. 'Let's go.' They were about to depart when Teiki said, 'This man Moimango,' he said of the older native at his side. 'He say his last born, mans, and womans, they go with whitefella.'

'He what?'

'He say, whitefella take his daughter. His son, he go too.'

'Where?'

Teiki pointed back towards the late afternoon sun low in the sky.

'Over the mountain?' the officer said.

'No mountain,' Teiki said. 'On big ship.'

'West!' Du Bellay cried out loud. 'Could only be Australia?'

Kimtasu's father, chief Moimango chatted away in his native tongue, nodding his head furiously. He seemed happy and proud.

'His last born?' Du Bellay reiterated to Teiki. 'Son *and* daughter huh?'

'Yes, yes, womans. Name Kimtasu.'

'Interesting. Ask him if he knows anything about a black pearl.'

Immediately Moimango was animated. He frowned and looked guarded.

'What did he say?' Du Bellay asked impatiently.

'Moimango, he say daughter and pearl with whitefella. The pearl sacred to Kimtasu. Pearl is Kimtasu star in sky.' Teiki stabbed a finger skywards.

'Guiding star!' the officer offered.

Du Bellay looked at the officer. For once the dullard was right. The pearl was the chief's daughter's talisman. Her lucky charm. Her guiding star. *But why would she sail away with a strange whitefella?*

•   •   •

While ashore *La Grenouilles* galley crew had been busy and had caught several large reef fish, which they dutifully baked with tarragon and lemon and creamed yams for the captain's table that evening while they steamed west from Kanantui Island. Du Bellay's commitment to be in Melbourne to speak on behalf of

France in the Australian Parliament, regarding an Embassy in Noumea, frustrated Du Bellay. Du Bellay and Capitaine de Forbin had other interests to deal with in Australia's great southern city.

'Our greatest advantage against this Capitaine Bourke fellow will be surprise, Claude,' Du Bellay told the capitaine as he tucked into a large portion of coral trout. The two men dined alone in the stateroom, where they were assured privacy. 'I asked many questions around Papeete about this Bourke fellow, and I found evidence in Noumea from his past visits before I had him imprisoned.'

'What evidence?'

'I told you before Claude, do you not listen? He sold illegal spirits to Americans in Honolulu.'

'Oh yes'

'Hooch they call it.'

'In cans of fish you said.'

'Yes. Illegal rum he smuggles in the canned mullet he sells all over the Pacific.'

The capitaine nodded sagely. 'Clever, really.'

'Yes. The rum,' Du Bellay poised with a loaded fork hovering before his buttery lips, 'is very high in alcohol. I actually managed to acquire a can and, I hate to confess, it is quite a good product. As I said before he distils the rum himself.'

'Well now, isn't he the entrepreneur?' Claude resumed eating his coral trout. 'But he sells legitimate mullet, does he not, Felix?'

'Yes, from his Cooktown cannery,' Du Bellay said. 'You read the labels on the cans. *Lighthouse Brand Mullet, Cooktown, Fresh from the sea*. Fresh from the still more like,' Du Bellay said with a grunt.

Capitaine Claude de Forbin was a keen fisherman, loving a chance to angle for fish whenever the fancy took him. Fish were a kind of hobby. 'Yes Felix, I *have* read the labels, but mullet is caught in southern Queensland, I've caught it myself on occasion over the years and I've seen the commercial fishers catch them in ring nets in shallow coastal water like bays and estuaries. They can inhabit fresh water coastal rivers also.'

'So, what are you saying?'

'Well, why wouldn't he open his cannery in that area?'

'In the south you mean?'

'Yes.'

'Well, Cooktown's a wild frontier Claude. My guess is it's remote enough for his illegal practices to go unnoticed.' Du Bellay forked in another large morsel of fish and spoke as he munched. 'He has fishing boats from Moreton Bay deliver mullet up the coast and pays a premium. That alone sounds suspicious to me. No Claude, the cannery is just a front, you mark my words. Although I hear he has a second product, canned marlin, and that is local to Cooktown.'

Capitaine de Forbin wiped up creamy mashed yam from his dish with the crust of a fresh baguette. 'So, you are still bent on travelling to Cooktown after Melbourne, are you?' the capitaine asked. 'In pursuit of the cursed black pearl,' he said condescendingly.

'Yes Claude. Yes I am. And do not patronise me monsieur.'

'But surely you don't plan on kidnapping Bourke to return to the Isle of Pines, or god forbid, Devil's Island.'

'I'll see how the mood takes me on the day. I'll tell you one thing.'

'Oh. And what's that Felix?'

'I can't wait to see the look on his face when I do catch up with him.' Du Bellay was playing with the capitaine. Truth beknown he would like to see Bourke dead. But greed was his priority, and he had a new ambition. *The Tear of the Eclipse*.

But Bourke and this precious pearl would have to wait. The round voyage to Cooktown would be a fortnight away, at least.

CHAPTER THIRTEEN

Cooktown 1924
After the gold rush of 1873 petered out in the 80s Cooktown's population dropped dramatically. The town was no longer prosperous. Originally, Cooktown had been settled at the Endeavour River Estuary in order to supply the Palmer River Goldfields 173 miles inland. If Bourke was to be asked the current population he wouldn't know, but it was several thousand shy of the 7000 of its heyday. The town was no more than a frontier village these days, with a main street of shabby, dusty weatherboard businesses presided over by its Mount Cook backdrop. Back in 1907 a cyclone caused considerable damage, and five years ago in '19, a major fire destroyed many buildings, including shops and warehouses in the main township. Many buildings remained in disrepair.

It was perfect for Bourke and his clandestine business operations.

Everyone knew everyone. Mostly. Except for transient fishermen like the bêche-de-mer fishers living on board their ten-ton luggers, where many of their vessels could be seen listing dramatically in the low tide mud.

· · ·

The cannery, Cooktown. Several weeks since sailing from Kanantui.
At the top end of the northern tributary of the Endeavour River, Captain Jonathon Bourke built his little empire. He had started

off small. Eight years earlier he won the moderate cannery property on a ten-acre grant of swamp land in a poker game at the White Horse Hotel, here in Cooktown. It was a wild, bold move but he nursed a royal flush. He was only twenty-five at the time and hasn't gambled since, figuring he had used up all his good fortune at the card table in that last lucky game.

The cannery had been a money drain for the previous owner since it was damaged in a major fire that also ravaged nearby Cooktown. Now the poker player was only too glad to rid himself of the family business.

Jonathon poured a thousand pounds into restructure, turned trade around and within a year *Lighthouse Brand Mullet* was in the black.

The factory canned giant marlin and other large Coral Sea fish, but mullet transported by sea from Moreton Bay, a four-day sail south, made up most of its product.

The cannery, fronting onto a tributary several miles inland, was an unprepossessing two storey structure of grey vertical board with a rusted iron roof, skylights and unglazed windows. Bourke's home was the upper floor with its separate deck and sweeping views across rainforest and mangroves. Crew often bunked down here as well, while Arsala and Juvita lived on board the *Drifter* moored near Cooktown. The construction stood on tall stilts to accommodate the tides. At low tide it was often surrounded by mud and frequently, crocodiles. Inside, the main factory was filled with bench tables, sorting benches, washing tanks, rows of scales for weighing and wood-fired steamers. At the rear was the main store where the finished product was stockpiled. But this was a front for the real money spinner, the hidden distillery in the mangroves.

'Sugar's cheap in North Queensland,' the oldies kept saying. 'And there's more money in rum than lollies, eh lad?'

All it took, other than sugar, was fresh water – and there was plenty of that in the rainforest and wetlands.

A large brewing pot, raw sugar, blackstrap molasses, yeast, fire, a thermometer, a long spoon and a still. The copper upright stills – there were two – came all the way from Kentucky and were over a hundred years old when Jonathon installed them. Used for whisky originally, they made a fine dark overproof rum.

The distillery was well hidden, fifty yards further back from the cannery, amongst mangroves bordering on dense forest. It was not a place to venture after dark, not with at least two male saltwater crocodiles watching over their females with several nests nearby. The biggest croc they called Charlie, not that they were friendly with the one-ton brute, because Charlie wouldn't hesitate to take any inattentive stray human in a death roll and stuff his or her corpse under a log to rot. His full length was guessed at eighteen feet, some reckoned twenty.

'They're the perfect guards,' Bourke would say when people asked why he didn't exterminate the monstrous reptiles. On the contrary, he fed them chicken carcasses to keep them around. 'Did you know they have 64 teeth?'

'You counted them?'

'Not personally,' Bourke answered without pause. 'These teeth are constantly being replaced. They have jaws four times more powerful than a lion. They can hold their breath underwater for six hours. The females, who are fiercely territorial, lay sixty to seventy eggs in their nests.'

'That's plain scary.'

'Yes, well, the survival rate of the eggs is less than one per cent.'

'Where'd yer learn all this Bourkie?'

'Encyclopedia Britannica.'

Bourke employed Aboriginal women from nearby Jack River to work the cannery and distillery, building them a small camp downriver on high ground. They were good honest folk and, he had to admit, they were cheap labour. His biggest problem was keeping them away from the rum.

Kimtasu was wary of the black women, and they were suspicious of her motives. But *if the boss want blackfella womans, then good for him. He wasn't the first whitefella to take a concubine.*

•   •   •

Weeks flashed by quickly. Everyone was busy. It was all work and no play. Bourke's missionary cousin, Sandy, was only too happy to take the three Kanantui women under her wing and give them lessons in English. They were slow learners at first, but Kimtasu took it upon herself to learn, so desperate was she to communicate with *Jon-a-thon* without Juvita.

The bush telegraph notified Jonathon Bourke that his latest delivery of mullet was only hours away, off the coast. Accompanied by Salty, Harry, Arsala, Hank and Flash, the crew waited with the cannery transport on Cooktown's docks. The cannery, well upriver, had its own jetty and loading wharf. *Drifter* remained moored at Cooktown while Bourke operated a crank-started motorboat and a single masted sloop – both flat bottomed with a shallow draught – to transport his stock and the finished product up and down river. In addition, he owned two long canoe-hulled river boats powered by the latest Evinrude twin outboard motors for faster passenger-only transport.

Harry filled his pipe, propping himself on an empty hogshead on the jetty. 'How much cap'n?' Harry referred to the weight of fish en route.

Bourke had received a wired message three days ago. 'Sixteen tons all up.'

'Nice.' Unloading and transporting sixteen tons of fish was going to be hard work, but the thought of cold beer at the White Horse once the fish was off loaded at the cannery, kept the men keen.

Moreton Bay fishing boats *Betsy* and *Maori Pride* arrived within hours of each other after three and a half days steaming up the coast from Brisbane. Both boats had large holding tanks full of live mullet. Bourke was a happy man. This delivery helped secure the legitimacy of his cannery business. Without it he would not be able to operate the distillery. All the while, the local authorities, that is the police sergeant Andy Tucker, his offsider constable Timmy Moore and the harbour master Sam Fry, all enjoyed many home comforts given them by Cooktown's young entrepreneur, and looked the other way.

•　•　•

Kimtasu burst through the door leading to *Drifter's* stateroom and into Jonathon's arms. She was in high spirits. *God damn it, she was always in high spirits*, and she looked more beautiful than ever. Maybe it was the frangipani thread into her hair. Jonathon looked up from his bookwork, where he was alone in the crew mess while the fish was being loaded onto his river craft.

'Hello Jon-a-thon,' she said with the widest of smiles. 'My name Kimtasu. I like you much.'

'Like?'

Kimtasu thought a moment. What had she learnt at the mission recently? She giggled, then corrected herself. 'I lo … love you much.' This put a huge smile on Jonathon's face, but he doubted she knew the true meaning of the English word, *love*. Certainly, they had not slept together. As much as the captain had genuine feelings for Kimtasu and wanted her in his bed, her enthusiasm had been waning. The adventurous Australian seaman was not accustomed to rejection and for the first time in his life, he had a challenge. But is that what this was really all about? *A challenge?*

Bourke's years of sowing his wild oats, as his old man would have said, were well behind him. Bourke watched Salty with Dua. They seemed happy, really happy. Bourke had never seen the man so cheerful. There was love in the air. Kimtasu teased

Bourke endlessly with hugs and kisses, although the kisses were more a daughter-father peck on the cheek. This was not the affection Bourke craved.

'I lo-ove you much,' Kimtasu repeated her statement.

Jonathon hugged Kimtasu tightly. He didn't want to loosen his grip. Her English was coming along better than he had anticipated and Jonathon made a mental note to visit Sandy at the mission to thank her personally for her progress in teaching Kimtasu and her two friends. The warriors, one being Kimtasu's brother Gemtasu, were less enthusiastic at first, but now they too were keen to learn the language of the whitefella.

• • •

Over evenings of practising the language, Bourke learnt that Kimtasu's village tribe were called the Tamesi. They were proud people ostracized for being different. Their skin was a shade lighter than neighbouring islanders and for many, their hair was more Polynesian. Somewhere in the past, Bourke guessed, there had been cross-breeding. The people of Koep, that is the village north of Kimtasu's village of Bok, were tolerant of their southern brothers. Other villages on the island were less forgiving, not trusting their lighter-skinned neighbours. Tribes had gone to war. Many warriors had been killed.

'You wear the pearl,' Bourke said as Kimtasu stood at his side in the stateroom. He was slightly annoyed as he had warned her about wearing it every day in public.

'I must wear Jon-a-thon. Is my … ah …'

'Lucky charm.'

'Luck-ee charm.'

Bourke tried to explain the meaning but gave up. But the pearl was clearly Kimtasu's talisman. 'I am afraid it will attract attention.'

Kimtasu looked vague.

'I am afraid bad whitefella take from Kimtasu.'

The black pearl was the most magnificent pearl anyone had ever seen. Jonathon had the oversized jewel of the sea set into a new mother of pearl headband – the original being damaged in the evacuation – by a local Chinese craftsman, and restored the treasure to Kimtasu. 'You must keep this forever,' he explained. 'And give to your children.'

Children.

Kimtasu threw her arms tighter about Bourke. He pushed his chair back to stand, but she shoved him back into the seat before saddling him, kissing him on the lips for the first time. *Had the word children motivated her?* They kissed, this time passionately. Kimtasu put her hands to Bourke's face, a hand on each cheek. She pulled her lips away and stared intensely into his eyes, before kissing him a second time. Playfully she nibbled his nose. Now she felt her captain's arousal. They were alone in the stateroom. Bourke wanted her here and now. But Juvita was right next door in the galley.

Did Kimtasu know this? Was this yet another tease?

It was futile. Bourke knew his place. He forced her back but instead of a rebuke Kimtasu gave a reassuring smile.

Later?

Juvita appeared from the galley and cleared her throat, loudly. Kimtasu unsaddled from her man and stood. The cook held a large platter of cooked fish and steamed rice.

'Ah, you're just in time for lunch,' Bourke told Kimtasu, his face flushed. 'Time to eat.' Bourke made a suitable mime. Juvita had cooked some of the fresh mullet destined for the cannery.

'What a fine job you have made of it too,' Bourke told her. The large plump, silvery, oily mullet had great flavour and was perfect in a Malaysian curry.

Juvita looked at Kimtasu. The two women had become friends, however Juvita was fiercely protective of her captain.

'Eat!' she told Kimtasu, without even slightly revealing her hidden smile.

•   •   •

Kanantui Island

Kimtasu's father Moimango made certain he wasn't seen. It was breaking dawn. A cockerel crowed the new day. He watched as the last of the women waded into the shallows to conduct their morning toilet. Wearing only a loin type cloth to protect his genitals against harsh vegetation, he collected up a clutch of long thin spears twice his height. Then, certain he was alone, Moimango slipped into the dense jungle which bordered his village. Armed with a whitefella machete, traded for pearls years earlier, he cut a path in the direction of the northern Volcano. The volcano the whitefella called Wewakhui.

He would be away for the entire day, but had left instructions he was on a sacred mission and must not be followed. He would return when the sun disappeared over the island.

CHAPTER FOURTEEN

Huang Ying Chinatown, Melbourne

Huang Ying's grandfather had come to the Victorian goldfields from Guangxi, near Canton in 1853. He worked hard, found gold, invested wisely. Huang's father proved a wastrel and a gambler. He lost his inheritance. Huang had no choice but to fend for himself. There was no inheritance for Huang or his seven siblings. Huang was sharp, savvy. At twenty he opened a small restaurant in Chinatown in Melbourne and soon progressed to selling opium. In 1901 the *Immigration Restriction Act* affected the people of Chinatown; however, Huang had established a clientele of white Australians who enjoyed opium, and then the new drug on the block since 1918, cocaine.

The recent war, now being referred to as the Great War, was beneficial for the Chinese businessman. Thousands of young men had died on the battlefields and life in the following decade was tough. Although rent was cheap, as were the brothels, and there was a huge market for 'sly grog', illegal gambling and ... drugs. There was a lot of money to be made if one took some risks.

And Huang Ying was a risk taker.

Opium had been made illegal in Australia nine years earlier. Now cocaine was king. Ying soon learnt that cocaine, used as a dental anaesthetic, could be purchased from the chemist for 22 shillings an ounce. Adulterated with boric acid an ounce could be used to make 250 packets for sale on the street at five shillings a packet. The law soon tightened its distribution through the pharmacies, and the smuggling trade boomed. In the state of Victoria, bars shut by law at 6PM. The law was designed to curb alcohol consumption and like prohibition in America it had exactly the opposite effect. Sly grog sales soared as did the popularity of cocaine, which steadily increased in price on the hard streets of Melbourne. And Monsieur Du Bellay was keenly aware of these developments.

•   •   •

Williamstown, Port Melbourne

Du Bellay strutted down the gangway of *La Grenouille* like he was Napoleon himself, his gelatinous paunch wobbling as his thin legs carried him onto the Melbourne wharf. He hired a waterfront porter to trolley his luggage, one carry bag the size of a carpet bag, and two Louis Vuitton trunks . With diplomatic immunity, immigration and customs were but a formality. A government car waited. Chauffeur Marcus Billiard met the French Consul on the docks. 'It's nice to see you again Monsieur Du Bellay.'

The Frenchman was less than subtle, insisting his driver drop him off near Chinatown. 'Have the porters at The Windsor take my trunks to my room. But I will keep the carry bag. I am meeting associates for lunch and have diplomatic documents.'

Du Bellay would have cut a fine figure in his three-piece pinstripe suit, fat belly rolling side to side as he hurried up Bourke Street. He was headed for Little Lon as the red-light district of Chinatown was named; being the city block incorporating Lonsdale, Spring, La Trobe and Exhibition Streets.

He'd been here before of course. Du Bellay skipped over the shiny cobbles of Lonsdale St, finally stopping outside number 68. He craned his stumpy neck, peering up at the four-storey redbrick building. Even out here on the street he could smell the sweet aroma of smouldering opium.

The *flower of joy*, some called it.

Wrapping both arms tightly around his carry bag, hugging it to his chest, Du Bellay moved quickly, stepping into the dark entrance hallway. All windows were blacked out. He stopped briefly, adjusting to the light, before taking to the stairs. The first two floors were given over to prostitutes, both white and Oriental. Most of the girls were hooked on opium, some on cocaine, and were kept as sex slaves, always under the power and influence of drug lord Huang Ying. Yet Huang Ying maintained a clean environment, the girls were clean, young and attractive. Du Bellay caught the scent of Oriental incense and perfumes. He could hear copulating. Upmarket businessmen enjoying a midday dalliance, and the thought aroused the fat Frenchman.

Du Bellay reached the third floor. He was unfit, breathing heavily. He pressed on down a narrow corridor where only curtains hung over the open doorways. He avoided looking into the rooms. He had seen it all before. Opium addicts lying on communal beds. This horizontal position was the most convenient to light each pipe bowl, and also the most sensible posture to be in when the smoker *chased the dragon* ...

Du Bellay was apprehended by Chinese bodyguards at the bottom of the stairs leading to the fourth, and top floor. He was touched down – searched – for weapons. Being familiar with this procedure, Du Bellay tolerated the humiliation and proceeded to Ying's office apartment where an attractive middle-aged woman dressed in traditional clothing, and most pleasing to the eye, ushered him to the roof.

Huang Ying watered orchards in his rooftop conservatory. He kept Du Bellay waiting a moment as he sang softly to one of his flowers. Finally, he turned calmly to face the diplomat. At first Du Bellay had thought the man was high on his own drugs, but soon learned Ying practised a form of yoga. Ying was forty-nine but looked twenty-nine. His boyish face was clean shaven, his short-cropped, raven black hair oiled flat. He loved nothing more than wearing western clothes, always immaculate, in tailor-made suits with a silk bowtie. He wore wire rim glasses. But under all that apparent innocence was a vicious and ruthless man, not to be crossed.

'I like to sing to my babies,' Ying said in their common language, English. His voice was soft. 'It makes them happy. They grow into the most beautiful things.'

'That's nice,' Du Bellay panted, hinting at impatience.

'Look at this one for instance,' Ying said, waving the Frenchman closer. 'I call it the lion's head orchid. Can you see why?'

'If one used their imagination, I'm guessing you can see the face of a lion, yes.'

'Imagination! Look more carefully,' he said with indignation. 'There's the eyes, the whiskers, the yellow mane.'

'Look Ying, I'm in a bit of a hurry. I've sailed halfway around the world and I'm due at Parliament.'

'A hurry!' Ying's calm vanished, replaced by a frown. 'Parliament, that's right, you are a diplomat, a man of importance. A government representative of trust. A consul and ambassador for your country of birth, France. Yes, I almost forgot. So, you have brought me more cocaine I see. Wonderful.'

If Ying was trying to humiliate Du Bellay he was succeeding.

•   •   •

Insisting Du Bellay partake of green tea, Ying prolonged the procedure even longer. The plate of cold coconut dumplings, however, softened Du Bellay's impatience. The fact that his host insisted on enjoying his tea on the rooftop, in the orchid conservatory, did not raise any suspicions in the Frenchman.

Ying finally demanded the transaction take place here on the roof. Du Bellay stacked the ten one-pound bags on the table. Ying took a small oyster shucking knife and, piercing one of the bags, he extracted a small amount of the off-white, pinkish powder. He smelt it and approved the floral sweetness with that hint of metal left by solvents. Finally, he placed a small amount on his finger, rubbing it on the inside of his gum. The resulting numbness of the skin told him it was pure.

There would be no bartering. A price had been pre-set. With a nod from Ying, the Chinese assistant counted out 250 twenty-pound notes which Du Bellay folded, secured into a leather satchel and stuffed into his pocket, before sitting expectantly, smiling awkwardly at the Chinaman. Huang Ying let the diplomat sit a moment. *Keep the man in suspense.* Finally, he stood, clapping his hands.

'Your bonus Monsieur Felix,' Huang said, his face unsmiling.

Du Bellay watched the Chinese girl enter the conservatory and swallowed hard. She was a doll. A porcelain white figurine, a child's toy. She was Felix Du Bellay's plaything ...

For now.

Huang Ying clapped his hands once more. The tea tray was removed, and he followed the waiter to the door.

'Enjoy,' Huang Ying said, before closing the door.

Sex in a conservatory on a discrete rooftop was the highlight of Du Bellay's Melbourne trip. Ah, the life of a diplomat he thought, as the girl satisfied his wildest fantasies.

Du Bellay had no idea ... all the while the French diplomat had been secretly photographed and he was none the wiser. This was Huang Ying's insurance.

Two days later *La Grenouille* set sail up the eastern seaboard of Australia, headed for Cooktown.

•   •   •

Snakeskin Coen. Cooktown

With sixteen tons of fresh mullet transferred safely to the cannery, tradition dictated that Bourke shout the skippers and their crews from Brisbane drinks at the White Horse.

The White Horse Hotel *was* a Cooktown survivor. The white painted timber, iron roofed pub was already half a century old. It had been a pioneer watering hole since 1879, so the older locals crowed. And Jonathon Bourke had heard his old man speak highly of the pub years earlier, when the cosmopolitan community thrived. For Bourke and his crew, the *Horse* was home from home, their pub when in town. It had been since Jonathon moved to Cooktown nearly thirteen years ago.

Kimtasu's brother Awateng and the other three Kanantui Islanders were happy to sit in the shade outside. Only Salty's native companion, Dua, had acquired a recent taste for grog. Juvita purchased a stone crock of ginger beer and joined the natives, whose tattooed bodies had become somewhat of an attraction around town.

Occasionally, like this day, *Drifter's* crew shared the bar with some rough and ready labourers and seamen, some of whom couldn't hold their grog. Snakeskin Coen was one of these men, a scar-faced trouble maker, his mother a Torres Strait Islander, and daddy a Dutch seaman. Pale-skinned Coen had the build of a Torres Strait Islander with the indigenous flat nose, but with the white hair and red eyes of an Albino. And the scar? That nasty cut from his left eye, down his cheek and across his neck was from the lash of a crocodile's tail. An occupational hazard when one catches and skins snakes and crocodiles for a living.

Snakeskin Coen sold many of his skins to the Chinese in Cooktown, who traded them on to Hong Kong to be crafted into handbags and other fashion accessories. Snakeskin worked Cape York mostly, only sailing south in his lugger, *Torres Girl*, every few months to sell his skins. The *Torres Girl*, built in Fremantle, Western Australia, in '03, was a thirty-six-foot, twelve-ton lugger. Her beam was 12 feet and she had a shallow draft. A strengthened hull allowed the ex-pearler to withstand the frequent beachings – the tidal ranges in this part of the world were enormous.

Trade in skins was lucrative, but not as lucrative as *Lighthouse Brand Mullet*, and for this reason Coen had a chip on his shoulder. But Bourke had also been the successful rival on more than one occasion for the affections of women Coen had set his own sights on. After all Cooktown was a small place and available female company not exactly a plague of mice.

·   ·   ·

Coen sat in his favourite corner drinking from a longneck of Castlemaine XXXX Sparkling Prize Ale. Had been for two hours. With him were his mates, a young wannabe who called himself Bullet, Jack Lawson his right-hand man, and an alcoholic Aboriginal tracker, known only as Wally.

Bourke, Kimtasu, Harry, Salty, Dua, Hank, Flash and both crews off the two Brisbane fishing boats stepped off the busy street and into the bar where newly installed, electrically powered ceiling fans spun lazily, offering some downward draft. After ten weeks with Jonathon, Kimtasu was adjusting to the ways of the whitefella, but turned her nose up at beer or rum, preferring lemonade.

'I wonder where he got the darky?' Snakeskin Coen said loud enough for the entire bar to hear. Jack and Bullet sniggered; Wally grinned behind hooded eyes. Kimtasu didn't so much understand the terminology but read enough body language to know she was being talked about in a derogatory sense. Kimtasu was used to this by now and strong-willed enough not to let it bother her. Even though the streets of Cooktown were filled with mixed race people, this tattooed-faced native woman was a novelty. Bourke ignored the remark. He smiled a greeting at Bertha the barmaid.

'A crate of beers and a lemonade please Berth.'

The fishermen took seats in a corner, while Harry and Salty waited to give their cap'n a hand.

Coen shifted on his bar stool. 'Lemonade for the darky or yer goin' soft Bourke?'

Harry turned to face Coen, balling his fists in anger. Salty put a hand on Harry's shoulder. 'He's drunk, ignore the bastard.' Truth beknown, Harry and Salty had been itching to give the loudmouth a hiding for some time.

'That's right, do what your girlfriend says,' Coen said, blowing Harry a kiss. Harry moved forward. Salty pulled him back. Bourke slapped a five-pound note on the bar and Bertha peeled it away from the sticky counter. 'I'll see there's more in the fridge,' the barmaid said. 'Cos it looks like yer thirsty.'

'Thanks.' Bourke passed longnecks, four at a time, down the line and headed to join his guests, as far from Snakeskin Coen and his cohorts as possible.

'So, Bourke,' Coen baited. 'Blackbirding now, are we?' Coen was speaking of the abhorrent trade in virtual slave labour that had been commonplace over the years, where Pacific Islanders were brought to Australia as cheap labour, mainly to be used in the sugar cane plantations. Bourke sighed, kept walking. 'What, cat got yer tongue? Or has yer darky whore made yer soft?'

Bourke rounded on the mouth. 'Listen to yourself snowball ...'

Snowball. If there was anything that ruffled the Albino's feathers it was being called snowball.

'Have you forgotten who *your* mother was?' Bourke spat back. 'And Christ knows, you certainly don't know who yer father was.'

The fishermen crews laughed.

Snakeskin pounced. His stool went skittling. Agile as a monkey and full of grog he came at Bourke. Salty swung a right hook smacking the Islander in the right jaw in passing. Coen's head spun. 'Fuck!' he cried out spitting blood.

'Leave it Salty,' Bourke said putting his own longneck back on the bar. 'This is my fight.'

'Now yer wanna fight huh,' Coen ripped his shirt off, throwing it to Wally.

Wearing only three-quarter britches and bare feet, he took a pugilist stance with closed fists and white knuckles. For a large Islander he was nimble on his feet, dancing about.

'Fight! Fight!' some drunk in the bar chanted. Others joined in.

Salty was raring to brawl. 'Let me finish this.'

'No. I said this is my fight,' Bourke said, feeling his adrenalin boil. Bourke removed his own shirt showing off rippling muscles. He was in his early thirties and he was lean and fit.

He faced off Coen.

Both men poised for the first blow. Coen danced forward, but Harry intervened.

'Wait!' he snatched Coen's hunting knife from its sheath on his belt and turned to his skipper with his hand out. 'Cap'n.' Bourke handed over his own knife.

'Fair fight!' Harry said, knowing very well it would be dirty.

Harry stepped back. Coen charged. Alcohol-fuelled adrenalin bulldozed Bourke to the floor. He managed a rapid backflip landing on his feet. Holding fists high, Bourke too danced. Some of Bourke's fishermen mates reared up, but Salty ordered them back. Coen threw a right hook. Bourke pivoted. Coen's fist brushed his cheek. Bourke stood tall, back straight, feet shoulder width apart, skipping foot to foot. Coen struck out again. Bourke ducked his head, stretched onto his toes, and delivered a two shot. One hit the chin, the other Coen's left jaw.

Spectators cheered.

Coen's anger raged. His fists tightened. Bourke didn't expect the sudden jab. It smashed into his jaw. The second missed. Bourke pirouetted a few feet left. Coen faced off, and Bourke delivered a powerful right hook. Hands, feet and hips moving as one. He managed another jab. Coen's head flipped backwards. Bourke slammed his fist into his adversary's throat. Coen dropped to one knee, stunned. Bourke moved in for the kill, but the big Islander bounced back, running at Bourke, head down, throwing wild punches. Bourke was taken off guard. He tripped backwards, crashing against the bar. Coen repositioned, but this gave Bourke that precious second to resume his stance. He bounced on both feet. Coen rushed again. Bourke held his position. The punch came. He jerked his head left. The fist whistled by. Bourke had a clear shot. His back heel lifted, placing his weight on his front foot, and with knees bent he pivoted on the ball of his other foot to deliver a perfect uppercut. He crushed Coen's lower jaw.

Coen cursed. He rushed the bar, snatched the longneck, smashed the bottle against the brass rail and came at Bourke with the jagged glass. Salty and Harry stepped in, but they were no match for Kimtasu, who leapt onto Coen's back, the second he stabbed out with the bottle. Bourke twisted aside. Kimtasu bit down on Coen's ear, clamping hard she shook her head violently.

The crowd shouted. Never had they seen such entertainment. With Coen screaming in pain Bourke kicked the bottle free. Kimtasu slid from the huge Islander's back, her mouth bloodied. Coen turned to face his attacker, giving Kimtasu the chance she wanted. She didn't hesitate. Her hand shot out clutching the man's testicles. She squeezed with one mighty grip. Coen squealed. The crowd hooted with laughter.

Snakeskin Coen had lost face and the woman from New Guinea had earned a new respect. Coen snatched his shirt from Wally and stormed from the bar onto the street where he turned to glare at Bourke and his exotic woman. He pointed two fingers at his own eyes before pointing them at Bourke. 'Your time'll come Bourke. Mark my words.'

'Bring it on Snowball,' Bourke spat back.

Coen's crew followed. Kimtasu, Bourke and the others watched the hunters leave. But Bourke had a strong sense they would meet again, sooner than later.

• • •

Kanantui Island

Kimtasu's father Moimango stood at the entrance to the sacred cave downwind of the nearer of the erupting volcanoes. Although the fire mountain had calmed down – for the moment – the jungle all about was permeated by the smell of its smoke with a stink like rotting eggs. The climb had taken him a large portion of the daylight hours, hiking through gorges, crossing rivers and negotiating waterfalls. Moimango paused a moment, exhausted. From this high and wild vantage point he watched as hundreds of cockatoos swooped over the treetops.

He was apprehensive. He had never been here alone before, only ever with his elders, and for sacred ceremonies. For the entire climb he had wondered how he would feel at this moment. Now he was here, standing before the home of the spirit people, fearful of what his presence might bring.

The whitefella called this volcano Wewakhui. But the indigenous owners of this island, Moimango's people the Tamesi, called the fire mountain *Matowot* and the spirit cave

Lokoko, meaning *whispering spirits*. For it was in this cave Moimango's ancestors' physical remains were preserved. Their spirits lived on for eternity.

It was also the sacred resting place of the *Tear of the Eclipse*. A black pearl, the largest black pearl ever seen by man, brought fortuitously to the island several generations ago and revered by the Tamesi. Revered so much that it was said, should the *Tear of the Eclipse* leave this place the island would be cursed. Until now, the artefact had brought prosperity. But lately the fire mountains had spoken. The gods were angry. On behalf of the Tamesi, Moimango made preparations for a new life. A new beginning on a new island far from the current dangers.

Moimango stepped into the cool of the cave. The ceiling was as high as a mature palm tree, but it tapered considerably a stone's throw in. There in the distant darkness, whispers from the ghosts spoke to the living. Why even now Moimango could feel the cool breath, the breeze, emanating from the spirit world, drawing him to enter. On either side of the cave were the mummified and skeletal remains of the island's dead. Many decayed skulls, their faces built up with red clay to resemble the living, stared back at the chief.

Although Moimango was from the village of Bok, recently destroyed, he had ancestors here from the village of Koep. High up the cave wall he looked to his father's father Moiangi, a fierce and respected warrior from the days when it was customary to eat your enemy. Moimango had memories as a child of this custom, but the whitefella who speak of a chief whitefella called Jesus, said it was wrong to eat your enemies.

Carefully, respectfully, anxiously, Moimango crept further into the cave …

•   •   •

Six days since sailing from Williamstown
On board La Grenouille. South of Cooktown

Du Bellay stepped onto the bridge, joining Capitaine Claude de Forbin studying local maps. 'Quarantine Bay,' de Forbin told the consul. 'I've noticed this place on the charts before, it's perfect, a remote place to anchor and easy to get ashore.'

It had been agreed that a French ex-Navy ship docking in Cooktown would draw immediate attention in the small community and possibly send Bourke into hiding. The steward followed Du Bellay with a tray laden with a coffee pot, sugar lumps, two cups and a colourful selection of petite fours.

Du Bellay hooked his thumbs behind elasticized braces, straightening his back, pushing his belly out. 'How far to Cooktown from there?'

'Three miles.' The capitaine noticed white powder under the consul's nose. 'You can travel overland,' he said, reaching out with a serviette to dust away the cocaine. Du Bellay slapped his hand away. 'You can follow the shoreline and walk into Cooktown from Finch Bay around the first headland.'

'Walk?' Du Bellay repeated the word as if it was the key word to some spell attracting the wrath of evil spirits. 'What's wrong with the launch?'

'Nothing,' Capitaine de Forbin said. *How stupid of me*, he wanted to say. *As if a fat lazy bastard like you would want to walk.* 'Of course, Felix, I'll have the launch launched.'

The two men sipped hot black coffee, staring at the foreshore, alone with their separate thoughts a moment, as *La Grenouille* lay at anchor in deep water. At low tide here it was possible to walk out to the reef. 'So, Felix, what are your plans?'

'Plans?'

'Yes, plans.'

Du Bellay was quite looking forward to this. 'I shall dress down and go ashore masquerading as Monsieur Pierre ...' he thought a moment. 'Monsieur Pierre Bourdain, yes, that's it. I am an exotic leather merchant from Marseilles, no … Paris, purchasing crocodile skins for the European market. Once I have established contact with the locals, I will broach the subject of pearls also. When I have their confidence, I will deliver my coup de grâce.'

'And what might that be Felix?'

'The black pearl you silly man. I will return with Bourke as my prisoner and his native woman and the *Tear of the Eclipse*, of which everyone speaks.'

•   •   •

Capitaine de Forbin mulled over the comment, *you silly man*, and chuckled, watching Du Bellay being helped into the launch via the stern. The bow rose markedly. *Who looks silly now, Felix?* de Forbin thought to himself. Du Bellay, of course, believed he looked the bee's knees as the Americans would say, dressed in safari jacket, jodhpurs belted high around the belly, wide-flared cuffed gloves, pith helmet with smoked glass goggles and knee-high boots.

•   •   •

Four French Navy matelots, discreetly armed, accompanied the launch and would remain with the boat while Du Bellay made his initial enquiries around the township, accompanied by Antonio Bourvil, a consulate staff member who often travelled with Du Bellay. The motor launch approached the shore before cruising parallel to the pebbly beach of Finch Bay, just over half a mile long and backing onto unexplored rainforest with Mount Cook as a backdrop. Occasionally, on hearing the motor, what appeared at first to be logs slithered into the water. Du Bellay looked apprehensive. He had heard stories of crocodiles attacking motorboats, even biting the propellers off outboard motors. He removed his hand from the gunwale and shuffled his large derriere to the middle of his bench seat.

* * *

Bullet was a wiry little runt with missing front teeth, from brawling mostly, some from wrestling crocs. He never washed and drank only beer. 'Me, drink water?' he yelled at a fellow drinker in the pub one night. 'Now why would I wanna do that, fish shit in it.'

He sat in a shady corner of the Joss House Bar with Wally the Aborigine.

The Joss House – real name The Crow – was so nicknamed by locals because the Chinese frequented the place regularly after Li Yin took over the lease in '19. Both Bullet and Wally were *topping up* from the night before when Bullet overheard the two foreigners enquiring to Li Yin at the bar, in regard to purchasing crocodile skins. Bullet could hardly misunderstand the conversation when the Chinaman and the foreigner conversed slowly in their shared language, English.

'Why you wan' this skins?' Li Yin asked.

'I – am – a – merchant – from – Paris,' Du Bellay said clearly.

'Crocodile. Yes?'

'Yes.'

'Plenty crocodile here.'

'I – know – that. That – is – why – I – am – here.'

'You wan' drink? What you wan'? Wice wine werry good. Chinese wice wine.'

Du Bellay was about to say, *I am right thank you,* when he understood he had no choice. He looked at Antonio Bourvil who pinched his face, not too keen to partake of the rice wine either, but not in any position to refuse. Du Bellay nodded to Li Yin, who poured two small wines into grubby glasses from a pear-shaped pottery bottle with a flanged lip, labelled entirely in Hanzi script. 'Ten shilling,' Li Yin demanded.

Du Bellay's jaw dropped. 'Ten shilling … s!'

'That what I say. Ten shilling.'

Du Bellay looked to his companion. 'Pay the man, Antonio.' Du Bellay lifted his glass to his nose and sniffed. It smelt a bit like dirty socks. Li Yin watched on. His sloe eyes narrowed and he twisted his long black moustache at the ends below his chin. 'Dwink.'

Du Bellay tipped it back in one mouthful. It was as warm as the day outside but really wasn't that bad. Antonio followed.

'One more. You like, yes?'

'No!' Du Bellay said louder than he intended when a rather shifty character stood at his side. Bullet held a half empty longneck of XXXX with what appeared more a dirty claw than a hand. 'You lookin' for skins huh?'

Du Bellay stepped back. The man's breath was like Roquefort cheese. 'Ah … yes.'

'Well, you've come ter the right place mate. Bullet!' he said, and his hand shot out as fast as his namesake. Du Bellay was caught between a rock and a hard place. Uncomfortably, he accepted the calloused paw. And as if that wasn't enough Wally shouldered in, also gripping his longneck like it was some treasured trophy. 'I'm Wally,' the Aboriginal grinned, taking the Frenchman's hand, shaking it like he had a wasp on his finger.

'Me and Wally work for Mr Coen,' Bullet said proudly. ''You 'eard o' him? Nar, o' course yer ain't. Well Mr Coen, Snakeskin Coen they call 'im, well 'e's a crocodile an' snake 'unter. Best in all Queensland, an' 'e'll get yer all the skin's yer want.'

Du Bellay thought this was exactly the contact he'd hoped for. 'Monsieur Pierre Bourdain,' he introduced himself. 'And this is my associate, Monsieur Antonio Bourvil.'

'Frogs, eh?'

Du Bellay accepted the comment gracefully. Behind the counter Li Yin was vying for more sales. 'Is there somewhere we can talk in private?' Du Bellay asked.

'Sure mate. We'll go meet Mr Coen at his office right this minute.'

•   •   •

The 'office' was at the end of a finger jetty secured atop tall pylons driven into the mudflats of Cooktown's waterfront. Built onto the end of the pier was a small outhouse, a garderobe lavatory, and built off this was a tin shelter offering some shade. This was the *office*. Home, however, was a lugger tied loosely to a pier. She sat on her keel in the mud, listing sharply to starboard where the retreating tide had deserted her temporarily. Du Bellay read the name on the bow, *Torres Girl*. The large Torres Strait Islander half-caste or whatever he was, Du Bellay now knew was known as Snakeskin Coen. He watched the strangers approach with caution. He was barbequing meat on an Asian style charcoal grill. Bullet made introductions, explaining the situation, immediately gaining Coen's attention.

'How many are yer lookin' for?' Coen asked about the skins.

'I'll take everything you can sell me.'

'Music to me ears, friend,' Coen wiped sweat off his forehead and rubbed smoke from his eyes. 'Why is it the bloody smoke always follows yer around when yer barbeque?' Coen said.

'It keeps the bloody flies away boss,' Walter laughed.

'Yer.' Coen poked the meat. 'Bloody beautiful ... it's cooked. Youse hungry?'

It smelt delicious. 'What is it?' Du Bellay asked. 'Chicken?'

'Crocodile.'

The fourth member of the hunting crew, Jack Lawson, walked towards them along the jetty with a loaf of bread under one arm and a carry bag of longnecks in the other.

'About bloody time,' Bullet called out, acting tough in front of their guests.

Over barbequed crocodile sandwiches with hot English mustard the six men dined alfresco. Coen was amused by this snobby fat Frenchman, dressed like an elephant hunter on safari. He seemed to be enjoying himself. Du Bellay even drank a Castlemaine longneck straight from the bottle. It must have been the weather.

After lunch the tide slowly meandered inland. The lugger righted itself slowly. Two longnecks later, Du Bellay pulled his hip flask from his safari jacket and passed around Armagnac. He was starting to feel relaxed in the company of these uncouth barbarians.

'Pearls,' Du Bellay said, casual as you like as if studying the clouds and suggesting it was about to rain.

Coen stirred. 'What about 'em?'

'I … I just have a thing about them.'

'Me too,' said Bullet. 'Especially around a sheila's neck.'

'I particularly fancy black pearls,' the consul said in a most casual manner. 'Do you ever come across those in your travels?'

'Sometimes,' Coen said. 'Black pearls are rare.'

'So, I believe,' Du Bellay took his flask from Wally, wiped the mouthpiece on his sleeve and took a long tug. 'I heard a story once about a black pearl as big as a quail's egg.'

Snakeskin Coen became wary. He was an expert judge of character. Especially bad character. He was beginning to smell a rat.

Is that what this toffy bastard was really after? Surely it was no coincidence that Cap'n Jonathon Bourke turned up with his tattooed blackbird wearing a black pearl the size of a quail's egg and now this bloke dressed like a character out of a Kipling novel, shows up asking about the said pearl.

'You're talkin' about Bourke's new woman,' Jack Lawson said before Coen had a chance to quell his offsider's enthusiasm to be of assistance. 'She's an islander from somewhere near the Solomons I think an' I seen her once with a huge black pearl in a headband.'

'Bourke,' the Frenchman feigned lack of interest. 'Who is he?'

'Cap'n Jonathon bloody Bourke,' Jack Lawson said. Coen shot his cohorts a silencing look, but it was misread somewhere in the translation.

'He give our skipper 'ere a beatin',' Wally slurred.

'I was attacked by that wild native woman,' Coen spat in his own defence. 'Jumped from behind when I wasn't lookin'.'

'That's 'ow the boss 'ere got that chewed ear.'

Du Bellay sat forward. 'What woman? What are you talking about?'

Begrudgingly Coen told his version of the story, how he was forced into a corner at the White Horse and how it took Bourke and the woman to floor him. 'And yes, the bitch even chewed me ear,' Coen said, showing off the scabby skin under his white, albino hair.

'And you said this native woman happened to be in possession of a large black pearl?'

'Yeh, in a headband it is.'

'So, you *do* know about the pearl,' Coen scowled.

'I must confess, monsieur, I have heard stories, yes. Where can we find this man Bourke and his native woman?'

Snakeskin Coen shot each of his crew a threatening scowl, man to man. The jetty fell quiet.

'I'll pay,' Du Bellay shook his wallet free and held up the beaver skin pouch like a punter's paddle at an auction.

'How much?' Bullet asked and received an extra scowl from the boss.

Coen interrupted. 'What this eager little runt is tryin' to say is, what's it worth to yer?'

This was all falling into place easier than Du Bellay could ever have imagined. 'Let me get this straight,' Du Bellay continued mindfully. He looked directly at Jack Lawson. 'Are you saying you have definitely seen this large pearl, set in a headband?'

'Aye.'

Coen sighed. *I give up.*

Du Bellay opened his wallet, retrieving a ten-pound note. 'So where can I find this native woman?'

Coen jumped to his feet rounding on Jack Lawson who had his hand out.

'Wait! Jack,' he said aloud, before continuing in a calm voice. 'Just …. just wait a mo, alright?' Coen had seen several banknotes before this *frog toff* closed his wallet. He turned to Du Bellay and Antonio who was looking restless. 'It'll cost yer fifty quid, not a penny less.'

'F-fifty!'

'You 'eard. Fifty pounds. Take it or leave it.'

Du Bellay studied the large half-breed Islander. He might be slightly dim-witted, but for the sake of a few extra pounds he decided not to negotiate. He peeled another twenty-pound note from his wallet. 'That's thirty pounds, you get the other twenty when we see this native woman. Savvy?'

Savvy. The Frenchman loved this English word he understood meant exactly that.

Understand.

'Savvy,' Snakeskin pocketed the notes before spitting into the palm of his hand and offering a gentleman's agreement. Du Bellay did likewise. Coen gripped his hand tightly and locked eyes. 'Don't fuck with me mon-sewer. Alright?' He turned to the Aborigine. 'Wally, you stay with the *Girl*,' he spoke of the lugger. 'Bullet.'

'Aye boss.'

'Fetch *Sally*.'

Bullet leapt onto the righting deck of the *Torres Girl*, crossing to the starboard side where Du Bellay now noticed their shallow draft river boat, *Sally*, tied alongside. The fifteen-foot shallow-draft wooden runabout, with its Evinrude outboard, was built for speed in flat water, although it was in need of fresh varnish. Bullet checked the fuel tank before starting the motor and manoeuvring alongside the *office*, where the five men climbed on board.

'Where are we going?' Antonio Bourvil asked. There was a hint of trepidation in his voice.

'Upriver mate,' Jack Lawson said, enjoying the moment. 'That's where this Bourke bloke has a fish cannery. And that's where he lives above the factory.'

'Yer, with his native sheila,' Bullet added.

'How do we know he will be there, now?'

'Me and Wally was up there earlier,' Bullet looked all serious. ''e's there alright.'

•   •   •

Kanantui Island

Kimtasu's father Moimango stood alone in the sacred cave and studied his mummified grandfather Moiangi, carefully. The old warrior was perched with fellow tribesmen on a rock ledge, arranged on bamboo scaffolding, high up the cave wall, placed there so as to watch down over those entering and leaving. The mummified bodies were positioned foetus-like. Moiangi peered down at his grandson through empty eye sockets – who was now almost as old as he had been when he passed into the spirit world – and Moimango was transported back to the time he and the elders preserved his grandfather's body. This ritual took place in a purpose-built smokehouse in the village, before being carried to this most sacred place. Moimango had been instrumental in many mummifications, where the deceased body was suspended over a fire for three months. As the body bloated from decomposition Moimango had penetrated the skin with sharpened sticks to allow the fluids drain. From beginning to end Moimango and the other mummifiers had always remained with the body to be certain no part ever touched the ground. This would bring bad luck to the deceased. By mummifying the dead, they could always be remembered, whereas those who buried their dead, it was believed, often forgot them.

Moimango was proud of his people. They were a spiritual community who took great care of their ancestors. Rituals were an important part of their life. Like the dance of the mud men, when warriors of the tribe made fearsome masks from river mud to frighten their foe. They would circle their enemy very slowly and in silence, except for a clicking sound made with their long claws. Bamboo flutes played haunting sounds believed to be the voices of ancestral spirits.

Moimango acknowledged the altar with skulls and wood carvings at the entrance, requesting permission from the ancestors to enter the sacred cave. Confident he had been accepted, Moimango climbed the steep incline to the rear of the cave. Here he prepared a fire, the way of his ancestors had for generations. Using the dried branch of a hibiscus tree he prepared a fire plough, by rubbing another dry branch in the furrow of the split hibiscus. Once kindled with dried bamboo leaves, Moimango lit a bamboo torch before crawling through a narrow space on his hands and knees. Now he entered a hidden cavern known only to his people. Finally, after a low entrance, Moimango stood erect. He held the torch high. He had reached the most sacred of scared places for the Tamesi, when underfoot he felt the slightest of tremors. The gods were angry.

He was being warned. That he knew. The queen of pearls belongs to the gods and it must never be taken from this place of worship.

CHAPTER FIFTEEN

Cooktown

The night of the fight in the White Horse Hotel, when Kimtasu proved her mettle defending her captain in a bar brawl, the young woman surrendered herself to Bourke. The captain may have fancied himself the seducer, Don Juan, the irresistible lover, but it was Kimtasu who was in control. The passion was heated. Sometime later, Kimtasu returned to her fellow islanders where they shared the night under the stars on a rear deck at the cannery. It was late, the night hot and still. Between the half-moon in the clear sky and the illumination from one lone lantern, Bourke enjoyed semi-darkness. He rarely smoked but this night he tapped a cigarette from a packet left on the table and stood at the rail overlooking the Endeavour Estuary, its crocodile-infested water meandering slothfully by the cannery, down river and out to sea a few miles away. Bourke drew on the tobacco, stifling a cough. He had never been a committed smoker. Behind him, where Salty had built his small bungalow off the west deck, with its louvres angled to catch any breeze on offer, Bourke heard the soft whimpers, the rhythmic groans, of love making. *Salty was at it again*, Bourke thought. *Lucky bastard, he'd found true love.*

Captain Bourke flicked the half-smoked cigarette into the blackness of night where sparks exploded on impact before it was doused by the muddy river. This brief disturbance caused a ripple on the surface nearby. The irony, Bourke thought. The voyeur was being watched. Now his thoughts quickly returned to Kimtasu.

• • •

The weeks had gone by swiftly. Kimtasu was young. She was also smart, learning English at an alarming rate, and it was not uncommon for Bourke to catch her sitting in a bay window, knees up around her chin, attempting to read excerpts from newspapers or magazines and constantly asking questions. She struggled to understand the recent war in Europe but told Bourke how, when she was a little girl, some other whitefella came to her island on a ship similar to *Drifter*, but much larger. She explained they spoke a different language to the English she was learning. Bourke guessed this to be a German gunboat, staking the German Protectorate in Papua New Guinea before the war. Bourke explained, as best he could, how Germany was then at war with his English-speaking country and how the Germans lost that war, and in so doing Germany lost grip on the territories they had claimed.

Kimtasu told Bourke how she was nearly taken as a prize wife for the man who killed her warrior husband, but her father Moimango and his warriors fought off these waring intruders from another island.

When Bourke thought their language barrier was broken down enough for her to understand, he broached the subject of the black pearl fastened into her headband. This is one of five Kimtasu said, counting one to five on her fingers like she had been taught.

'Five!' Bourke was shocked.

They are worn by each chief's oldest daughter from five different tribes.

'Did they arrive by whitefella ship to your island?' he asked.

'No Jon-a-thon, pearls from my island. From sea. Found over many many years.'

'All black?'

'All like this, big,' Kimtasu said fingering the pearl on her headband. 'Not same ... ah ...' She made a circle with her fingers.

'Not same shape?' Bourke suggested. Kimtasu nodded but he wasn't certain she really understood. Bourke was confused. Five black pearls the size of a quail's egg. All worth a small fortune ... each. Wasn't this the *Tear of the Eclipse?* Bourke questioned Kimtasu, the best he could. She laughed.

'The queen pearl,' she said referring to what Bourke called the *Tear of the Eclipse*.

As best as Bourke could ascertain, with some help from Juvita, he learnt that this pearl belonged to the gods. It was a sacred talisman for her tribe. Should it be stolen or removed it would bring death and pestilence to the five tribes. 'Is one, two, three bigger.'

'Three times the size of yours?' Bourke stared at the headband. Kimtasu nodded. 'It come to island from far away, on whitefella ship.'

'Tahiti,' Bourke whispered to himself reverently. There had been rumours the *Tear of the Eclipse* was cursed, now Bourke thought it possible.

'Where is this pearl, the queen pearl?' he asked.

Kimtasu understood the greed of the whitefella well. She shrugged. 'I see queen pearl once in my life.' Kimtasu explained the best she could, that it is in a sacred cave but she would not say where. Bourke listened respectfully. He would have to be patient. For now.

•   •   •

Lance Pepper was twenty-three, a wiry, tough little mongrel who loved a fight and loved Aboriginal women, and not necessarily in that order. At the age of fourteen and a half he looked old enough to convince the recruiting officers he was eighteen. He fought in France in 1916 and '17, and though many of his mates returned from the war with shellshock he came home with a hankering for a good scrap and a hatred for the Hun. But growing up in New Norfolk, Tasmania, as the youngest in a family of eleven, eight of them boys, he was a tough nuggetty bastard. Lance was one of those lucky people, if that's the way to look at it, who could eat Cadburys Dairy Milk Chocolate bars weeks on end and not gain weight. Not an ounce. When he was angry or annoyed, he had the habit of sucking his cheeks in, rather resembling a fish swimming towards you, hence the nickname Mullet. Now Lance Pepper didn't mind the sobriquet Mullet for two reasons. He didn't like his christened name Lancelot and he was the head supervisor over all the Aboriginal women working a mullet canning factory. And with thirty-three women to choose from under his authority he went at it like a bush rabbit. Harassment for sexual favours in the workplace was not an issue to Mullet, because he was great at his job, fiercely loyal to Bourke and … well … occupational bonuses were there for the taking.

The lads guessed it was the thrill of the illicit still, the dangers of being caught, that turned Lance into such a Lothario. 'He'd root a rat with a harelip,' Harry would laugh.

Either way the women loved him. He treated them all like queens and in return the factory was productive. Another of Lance's responsibilities was to feed the crocs thriving around the swampy marshland and mangroves surrounding the distillery. Usually chickens, but when it was canning time there were fish heads and scraps aplenty and the crocs lingered like blowflies around a barbie.

· · ·

Eighteen-foot, one ton saltwater crocodile Charlie rose from the low tide mud like a submarine surfacing. Charlie knew it was snack time. He heard the chickens being butchered earlier up on the deck of the stilted cannery and he could smell the fish guts and bones in the sun waiting in bins outside the factory. Charlie raised his huge armour-plated head, his mouth wide open displaying lethal teeth, and hissed. He was growing impatient. Mullet, holding four chickens by their feet, was joined by two women carrying a drum of fish scraps between them. Using the concealed doorway built behind moveable shelves, they descended the wooden treads through thick mangroves growing against the rear wall of the cannery, to the lower deck. Normally this deck would be surrounded by water at high tide. They stepped onto duckboards leading across mangrove roots and through wild swampland to the distillery, which could only be approached during low tide. Although the duckboards were covered in mud, reminding Mullet of the battlefields in France, they were secure. The three moved swiftly towards the distillery, best not to linger with so many hungry crocs lurking.

Charlie waited, wallowing in muck where a raised platform gave those in transit, some semblance of safety. Charlie was joined by three twelve-foot females while Mullet noted another male he hadn't noticed earlier, a new kid on the block, prowling beneath the surface in deeper water.

'Chuck it then,' Mullet ordered the women. 'Don't mess about.' The women emptied the drum of fish scraps onto the mud and the giant reptiles came forward, warily at first, before attacking their lunch.

Charlie knew he was special.

He held back, jaws wide, making his usual throaty growl and hiss until Mullet tossed him a chicken. With three crushing bites the bird disappeared down the huge beast's orange-brown gullet. Mullet tossed another to Charlie, before dropping the remaining carcasses into the mud.

•   •   •

The distillery was a simple set up. The thirty-foot by twenty foot building itself was all corrugated iron; walls and roof, with timber floor over ten-foot stilts. The boiler was built over bricks, like the galley of a sailing ship, for fire was a real danger. The windows were unglazed with gunport shutters to allow any breeze flow through from the stifling hot mangroves. One area was set aside for preparing the mash from molasses, raw sugar and yeast and another for the antique copper stills themselves. In one corner a low Japanese style bed called a futon was covered with pillows for women staying the night. There were always two on night duty.

All going well, they could distil five gallons of rum per day. This was stored in stoneware jars and carried to the cannery where it could be canned and labelled, as Lighthouse Brand Mullet, before being ferried down river to *Drifter*. At a sale price of two dollars US a can, it was a financial winner.

Bourke waited for Mullet at the mash table. Kimtasu was by his side. Ship's cook and rescued castaway Arthur J. Money stood at a bench, grading various desiccated coconut flakes. He had taken to the distillery business like an ant to jam and had been experimenting, quite successfully.

'Sir Lancelot,' Bourke called out as Mullet entered. 'How were the guardians of the gate today?' he said, speaking of the crocodiles.

'Charlie's gettin' crankier every day,' Lance said.

'Yeh, well. He's getting old.' Bourke held a brandy balloon in his hand, enjoying a snifter, with a measure from the currently being distilled product. 'Arthur's coconut rum is going to be a winner, Lance. You lot have all done well.'

'Yer reckon. Bit fancy for my taste.' Mullet clearly wasn't so keen. He looked serious. 'Say boss, can I ask yer somethin'?'

'Shoot.'

'The lads was sayin' you've made an enemy o' Snakeskin.'

'Nothing out of the ordinary. You know what he's like when he's full o' grog.'

'Yeh, but, well ...' Mullet looked at Kimtasu. 'They was sayin' Kim 'ere chewed his ear off.'

'Only a taster Lance,' Bourke said with a cheeky smile, putting an arm around Kimtasu. 'Do you know what he called Kimtasu?'

'I can guess.' Mullet knew only too well. With his penchant for Aboriginal women, he was often subject to racial abuse, even in such a mixed-race frontier port as Cooktown.

'I'm just worried if 'e poked around enough 'e might find this distillery. We've managed to keep it quiet a year now and Tommy was sayin' 'e seen Snakeskin's boys Bullet and Walter sniffin' about.'

'When?'

'This mornin'.'

'Sniffing about? Where?'

'On the river here. They was in their motor launch.'

'Interesting, we never saw them,' he said looking at Kimtasu.

'That's cos they was sneakin' about, quiet like. That's what bothered me and I thought you should know cap'n.'

Harry and Arthur appeared with three women at the distillery entrance. 'Tide's turnin' cap'n,' Harry said.

With the change of tide, they would have to return to the cannery otherwise they would be trapped in the distillery until the tide withdrew again. Old Charlie would see to that.

'Snakeskin's been spying on us,' Bourke told Harry. Mullet reiterated what Tommy had seen.

'I'll fetch the gun.' Harry spoke of the German Maschinengewehr 08 he'd purchased in Noumea. Bourke agreed. It would be best kept at the cannery anyway, as local authorities might not approve of him carrying a German machinegun on board *Drifter*.

All the same, firearms were a way of life here in the wilderness of north Queensland and it was not unheard of for disputes to be settled looking down the barrel of a loaded gun.

Like clockwork the tide reclaimed the land. Those not staying the night hurried back through the mangroves to the cannery.

On their approach the salties that had been basking in the sun earlier slid back into the water before twisting about to watch the disturbance pass by. Only eyes showed above the surface.

'Jesus!' Harry jumped.

'What's up?'

'Bloody bird scared the hell outa me.'

The others laughed as the cassowary ran across the path before them and disappeared into the thick mangroves. 'Bloody thing's lost again,' Harry said. Although it was unusual to find a cassowary in the mangroves here, it wasn't the first time.

'Sneaky bastard,' Mullet grinned. 'I wish they'd make more noise, give a bloke some warning like.'

• • •

It was the late afternoon when Du Bellay met Snakeskin Coen ...

If nothing else their cruise upriver was pleasant enough with plenty of wildlife to entertain the visitors. Du Bellay enjoyed observing the wildlife. Either side of the river, where the tangled mangrove roots kept the banks together, the Frenchman saw kingfishers, sugar gliders and even a wallaby. Dark elongated shapes crawled on their bellies into the water as they passed by. His assistant Antonio Bourvil sat with him, amidships, while Coen helmed the motorboat. Bullet and Jack Lawson sat raised at the bow, keeping an eye on the path ahead. The Endeavour River was not an ideal place in which to strike a log and sink.

• • •

Harry was back in the trenches. He loved his work, and he loved his Cap'n Bourke. Harry ran an oily rag along the barrel of the machinegun. He adored this weapon. There was something erotic–about its long hard barrel that was capable of spitting hundreds of bullets a minute into the enemy.

And Harry should know. He had mowed down the Hun invaders in France by the hundreds as a gunner handling the British Lewis machinegun. But he had to admit, the German Maschinengewehr 08 had the edge.

'You've done well Harry,' Bourke said, joining Harry on the patio, one floor above the cannery.

'Thanks, cap'n.' Harry checked the sweep of the gun from this position. It was perfect, covering a wide arc of the river to the opposite shore. He spotted a large croc on the riverbank a hundred yards away. 'Demonstration, cap'n?' Harry grinned.

'Why not?'

Kimtasu brought a tray of tea and Harry smiled at how she had taken to the *whitefellas'* way of life, like the proverbial duck to water. Harry thought Kimtasu looked stunning. She wore a purple and gold Batik silk wrap around and shawl accompanied by her black pearl headband. She looked like royalty. Kimtasu sat the tray on one of the wooden barrels, positioned to hide the machinegun and stepped back.

'Okay Cap'n,' Harry nodded to the bandolier of bullets. 'Feed me.'

As Bourke fed the bullets into the breach Harry aimed the machinegun. He squeezed off a short burst, ten, maybe twelve .292's scattering mud only feet from the croc that hissed as it slid back into the river. Kimtasu had covered her ears. But out here in the wilderness no one would hear them.

Bourke cheered, slapping Harry on the back. 'Well done, had the bugger on the run just like those frogs on the beach on the Isle of Pines.'

Harry threw a tarp over the gun. 'No one will be any the wiser.'

• • •

Dusk was upon them when Bourke and Kimtasu heard the motor slowly approaching from downriver. The undeniable sound echoing off the heavy vegetation either side of the river was distinctive, even over the high-pitched chirps of thousands of bats filling the evening sky. Travellers this far up the river were scarce. Kimtasu had closed all the gunport shutters as the mosquitoes were coming to life, but Bourke prised one shutter open slightly, just enough to see who approached. Downstairs, production in the cannery had ceased for the day and Bourke's crew ferried the women back downriver, a mile or so, to where they lived in the purpose-built huts Bourke had constructed for them on high ground.

Only Harry and Salty and his new friend Dua decided to stay behind for the night. Salty, in the open galley, had volunteered to cook dinner. Steak and onions stewed in a pan, and if they were lucky the smoke took flight through gaps in the tin roof.

'Anyone we know?' Salty asked, armed with tongs, watching the others.

'It's Coen.'

'No!'

'See for yourself.'

Salty and Harry padded across the decking and peered out. 'What the ...'

'He's got a cheek. What's that bastard up to?'

'No bloody good, you can bet on that.'

• • •

'Captain Bourke,' Coen called up when he caught Bourke's face in the opening. He cut the motor to his runabout and drifted beneath the cannery. Bullet and Jack Lawson grappled with the pylons, steadying the motor launch. 'Captain Jonathon Bourke,' Coen called out. 'Can we parley?'

Bourke's tone was sour. 'What do you want Coen?'

'Parley ... can we talk?'

'I've got nothing to say to you Coen.'

'Maybe. But *I* have a proposition for you.'

Two other men sat in the stern, one a large man wearing what could only be described as a safari suit, his fat head hidden beneath a pith helmet and another stiff looking character who appeared official. Bourke was wary.

'Proposition? What proposition?'

'Permission to come aboard cap'n?'

'Who's the explorer?' Bourke called down to the safari suit. 'Not Livingstone I presume?'

'Ha. You was always a funny bastard Bourke,' Coen laughed nervously. Bourke didn't so much as crack a smile.

'We have met before,' the fat man said with a strong French accent. 'Under less salubrious circumstances.' Du Bellay slowly raised his chin to look up at Bourke. 'Remember me?'

Bourke was flabbergasted. 'You! What in god's name are you doing here?'

'Who is it?' Harry hissed over Bourke's shoulder.

'Monsieur Felix Du Bellay.'

'No. What? Here?' Salty and Harry opened the neighbouring shutter, peering down. It *was* the French consul alright.

'Yes gentlemen, it's me,' Du Bellay wore that same smug smile he had in Tahiti when Bourke was arrested. The Frenchman also saw for the first time, the most attractive native woman with Bourke, and she wore what appeared to be a large black pearl on a headband.

Bourke steadied his voice. 'You've got a bloody nerve showing your face here. I've got a mind to cut your throat and feed you to the crocs.'

The reminder that they were indeed in crocodile territory made the consul stiffen. He looked about the river warily. 'Yes … well … maybe I was a little impulsive.'

'Impulsive! You had me sent to prison. No, you can bugger off, you too Coen.'

'Hear the man out Bourke,' Coen pleaded.

'Why should he?' Harry yelled down. 'You heard the man, piss off or we'll feed you to the crocs.'

'I have a proposition for you,' Du Bellay said. 'Something lucrative for both of us.'

'I don't know what your game is Bellay, but this is Australia, you have no jurisdiction here.'

'Oh, fear not Jonathon … may I call you Jonathon?'

'Bourke will do fine.'

'Very well, Monsieur Bourke. Fear not, I am here as a businessman, let bygones be bygones, as you English like to say. I wish to discuss buying product from you.'

Snakeskin Coen had heard enough. 'So you knew this bloke already?' he said in a loud whisper. 'Product? What are you on about? You wanna buy canned mullet?'

Du Bellay ignored Coen. 'I think you know what I am speaking about,' he called up to Bourke. 'Let us talk in private. As you and Monsieur Coen seem to have had a falling out, he can wait here.'

'Oh, can I now,' Coen grew angry.

Du Bellay was prepared for this and passed five twenty-pound notes folded discreetly in a bundle to Coen. 'You're to take Monsieur Bourvil back to Cooktown and return for me. There's another hundred in it for you when you get me back to Cooktown.'

Coen counted the notes. His anger subsided. 'I'll be one hour,' he said, stuffing the money in his pocket. 'It'll be dark by then. You be ready or I'll leave yer here.'

'Fine.' The consul looked up at Bourke. 'So, Monsieur Bourke, you heard my conversation with Monsieur Coen. What's it to be? I have a proposition that will make you a rich man.'

If nothing else, Bourke was curious. What harm could he do? He looked at Harry who said, 'One false move and yer goin' in the drink.'

Bourke looked down, jerking his head towards a landing platform on the west side of the cannery. 'Excellent,' the Frenchman said. 'You won't regret this.'

· · ·

Bourke and Du Bellay stood before each other, enemies in a bizarre situation. The weeks in solitary confinement flooded back. *This mongrel had a lot to answer for.*

'Give me one excuse Bellay, one false move and I'll kill you, so help me.'

'My dear fellow,' Du Bellay said in fluent English, making Bourke envious that he had not learnt another language. 'You are the ...' Du Bellay looked to Kimtasu with whom he had not been introduced. 'Ah, you are the man who forced himself upon my wife.'

'I did not force myself. Vignetta ...'

'Yes, yes, whatever. It is irrelevant now.'

'Look Bellay, what do you want?'

'Straight to the point. I like that. You know ...'

'The cap'n said what – do – you – want?' Harry spat, growing irritated.

Du Bellay paused. 'Very well. Where do you distil the rum, you have been smuggling to Honolulu, amongst other places?'

'What?'

'The rum. You have a still somewhere?'

'Don't know what you're talking about.'

'Come now Monsieur Bourke, your rum is the toast of the South Pacific ... and America too, now I believe, since you cracked the prohibition market in the United States. Most fortuitous monsieur. You are quite the entrepreneur.'

'You are misinformed.' Deep down Bourke wanted to learn more. How much did this bloke know? Should he be worried? 'I don't know where you got this information, but ...'

'Let's stop the games. I have tasted the product myself in your own brand of mullet cans. Clever monsieur. Very clever indeed. And quite tasty also, that is if you drink rum. So, tell me, where is your distillery?'

Harry grabbed Du Bellay's arm. 'Time to leave, frog,' he growled. 'You goin' quietly down them steps or do yer wanna swim?' Harry frogmarched the diplomat a few steps when Bourke interfered. 'Harry! One second.'

Harry allowed Du Bellay a moment to face his cap'n, but he held his arm tight.

'For argument's sake, let's say you're right,' Bourke said. 'What do you want?'

'That's more like it,' Du Bellay shook his arm free. 'We need to talk in private, you and me.'

'We talk right here, right now, or you can forget it.'

Du Bellay looked about. Salty remembered his steaks smoking away and returned with Dua to salvage dinner. Harry stood close by, fists bunched and Kimtasu stood by Bourke, looking ravishing, especially with that large black pearl set into her mother of pear head band. Du Bellay sighed.

'I know someone who has a product to … move, for use of a better word. Like your rum hidden in the canned fish.'

'What sort of product?'

'Well, it's not exactly legal …'

'What product?'

'Cocaine.'

'Forget it.'

'Come now monsieur …'

'I said forget it. Even if I was a smuggler …'

'Which you are!'

Bourke chose to ignore this comment. 'Even if I was a smuggler, I wouldn't smuggle drugs.'

'Why?'

'It's morally wrong for starters.'

'Huh! You speak to me of morals, and you bed my wife.'

'It was a mutual agreement, Monsieur Felix Du Bellay. And you know it.'

'I'll not take no for an answer.'

Bourke fumed. He turned to Harry. 'Escort this man out of here.'

'I have proof of your illegal practices,' Du Bellay said smartly. 'I have made arrangements for information to be leaked to your authorities,' he lied, calling Bourke's bluff. 'I have contacts in high places in your Parliament. If you do not co-operate you will be arrested and gaoled for a long time. Then, before you are released, I will see you are extradited for crimes conducted on French soil. Extradited to a French prison, namely Devil's Island.'

Devil's Island. The very name sent a chill down Bourke's spine.

Bourke was no murderer, but at this moment he had the powerful urge to strangle this overweight mongrel with his bare hands. He needed a plan. He didn't know what. But he knew he couldn't allow Du Bellay to leave the cannery until he had made some kind of deal to appease the fat bastard.

'You're talking of filling the mullet cans with cocaine?' Bourke said so softly, so calmly he surprised even himself.

'You catch on quick Jonathon.'

Jonathon!

Bourke would have to live with it.

Jonathon.

Bourke didn't know what? When? Or how? But something would come to him. He just knew it. 'Then we'll start with a tour of the distillery,' he said.

'Ah, now you're thinking rationally, Jonathon.'

'Cap'n?' Harry was transfixed. Now he took Bourke by the arm. 'What are yer doin' cap'n?' But Bourke managed to turn his back on the Frenchman as Harry whispered 'I hope yer know what yer doin''. Bourke answered with a wink.

But Bourke, for once, *didn't* have a clue what he was doing. 'Come,' Bourke ordered. 'Follow me.'

The Frenchman's tone changed. 'Are you going to introduce me to your beautiful companion?' he asked of Kimtasu.

Bourke stopped, turned. 'Kimtasu … Monsieur Du Bellay.' Kimtasu forced a smile and Du Bellay tried to snatch a close look at the pearl.

'Enchanté mademoiselle, or is it madame?'

'Kimtasu'll do just fine,' Harry scowled, pushing the Frenchman towards the secret entrance behind store shelves leading out onto the swampland, against his better judgement.

'You are making a wise decision here,' Du Bellay said, treading warily down creaking wooden steps straining under his excess weight.

'You give me no choice.'

'Together we will make a fine team.' Du Bellay stepped from the bottom tread to the platform leading to the duckboard path to the Distillery. The air was still and the atmosphere uncomfortably humid, like a sauna. Du Bellay was already short of breath, fanning himself with his pith helmet as his ill-chosen costume moistened with sweat. 'I must commend you on your enterprise Jonathon. Who would ever have guessed? A distillery out here.'

The tide was out, the smell horrendous. 'What is that awful stink?' Du Bellay asked, slapping at mosquitoes which were more prevalent the deeper they travelled into the mangroves.

'Rotting vegetation,' Bourke said, leading the way.

'And rotting animal carcasses and fish,' Harry said with a grin.

•   •   •

Lance Pepper was not expecting visitors. He lay on the futon, smoking a cheroot and enjoying his latest brew. Coconut rum. Lying with him were two of the younger women who helped at the distillery. Both were in a state of semi-dress.

'Cap'n!' Lance jumped to his feet and wished he hadn't. Clearly, he wasn't on his first rum, probably his sixth. Lance wore tight shorts more like underwear and he was topless. 'I wasn't expectin' yer this evening.'

'No,' Bourke tried not to grin. 'No, you weren't, were yer Sir Lancelot.' Bourke grew immediately serious. 'Leave us a minute will you. We have some business to discuss.'

With the sun below the horizon a magnificent golden hue foreshadowed the rising moon. Lance tweaked the kerosene lamps and searched for his shirt before leading his companions back to the cannery.

Ten minutes later: 'Commendable,' Du Bellay was impressed with the set up. 'Most commendable. And I must congratulate you on this coconut rum,' he said, enjoying his second glass. 'It is far superior to that dark rum you've been selling to the Americans.'

•   •   •

Although Mullet had lit several kerosene lanterns designed to smoke out the mosquitoes the little beggars worsened. The jungle outside came alive with crawling creatures of the night. Du Bellay had seen enough. He had this escaped prisoner Bourke right where he wanted him. He looked at his watch, the hour was almost up. 'Time to go,' he said making his way down the distillery steps back onto the duckboard. Bourke noted also that the tide was turning. Once it flooded back, it happened quickly. He unhooked one of the lamps. Although a full moon appeared, it was dark along the jungle pathway. Harry led the way. 'Go ahead Harry, tell Lance he can return.'

Kimtasu followed Du Bellay with Bourke at the rear holding the lamp high. With the three of them alone Du Bellay suddenly stopped, he turned to face Kimtasu. 'One more thing,' he said as Kimtasu stood before him. 'That pearl, I want that as security, to keep your end of the bargain until our enterprise is up and running.'

He reached out and snatched the headband. Kimtasu fought back.

Bourke straightened. 'What the hell are you playing at?' he shouted.

'I'm keeping this pearl for security.'

'What on earth are you talking about?'

'We have a deal, have we not? For my part I will keep you out of prison. For your part, I am going to see you receive your first delivery of cocaine in a month's time. In the meanwhile, I will be hanging onto this pearl.'

Kimtasu reached out, but Du Bellay slapped her hand away. He held the headband behind his back, slipping a Derringer pistol from his coat. 'Tell your crazy woman to back away Bourke, or I'll have to shoot some sense into her.'

'Wait! Jesus.'

Kimtasu spun around to Bourke. 'No Jon-a-thon … what happen?'

'Oh, she speaks English, how noble.'

'Hand the pearl back Du Bellay. It's *not* a part of the deal.'

'Oh, but that's where you are wrong. As I said, I'm keeping this for security. You'll get it back once the first shipment is under way.' Of course, this was a lie.

'Jon-a-thon?'

Bourke looked defeated. Kimtasu spun back to Du Bellay, but he jammed the pistol into her forehead. The hammer was cocked, the threat real.

'No!' Bourke shouted. 'You win, take the damned thing.' Du Bellay's fat face grew into a malevolent smile, taunting Kimtasu, dangling the treasured pearl high in one hand while pressing the muzzle deeper into her brow.

No one heard the cassowary.

The six-foot flightless bird charged from the mangrove with the speed of a racing emu and snatched the dangling pearl in its beak. Du Bellay jumped backwards, slipping off the duckboards into the mud. He cursed in French, turning the pistol on the bird as it swallowed the pearl and a portion of the headband with it. Du Bellay fired. But his shot was wide, and the cassowary fled back into the jungle, disappearing as fast as it appeared.

All three were speechless.

At that moment Du Bellay heard his name called across the water. Snakeskin Coen had returned. Du Bellay stood awkwardly, rubbing sludge from his arms and face. The consul had the hide of a buffalo. 'I'll be back in one month Bourke,' he said. No remorse. No feeling. No guilt. 'One month. Do the right thing or you are a dead man rotting on Devil's Island. You hear me?'

And with that he fled back along the duckboard to the platform and was soon motored away in the launch.

· · ·

If there was nothing else guaranteed in Bourke's world, sunrise was. At first light the tropical gold of a new steamy dawn replaced night's dark shadows. The frogs ceased croaking and the cicadas began their incessant drone-like mating calls. Kimtasu lay on the seagrass matting of their bed chamber at the cannery. She hadn't slept all night. She was devastated. Nothing Bourke said would console her. The pearl was sacred, and that was the end of it.

Harry was angry. He smoked a pipe out on the deck and polished his metal *friend*, the Maschinengewehr 08, propped on its tripod and ready to sink Coen's motorboat if the bastard dared show his face. Bourke joined him.

'He held a gun to Kimtasu's head,' Bourke had said over and over the night before. 'A loaded gun, Harry. The bastard.'

'We'll make the mongrel pay,' was all Harry could answer. 'Mark my words cap'n, he'll pay.'

Finally Salty arrived with mugs of steaming black coffee, three sugars in each. Dua padded along barefoot and topless behind him. They stood in silence a moment. Leaning on the rail, starring across the river with their mugs, each with their own thoughts. The tide was doing its thing again. Going out. Over on the opposite river bank a fifteen-foot crocodile basked in the early morning sun.

'How is she cap'n?' Salty asked of Kimtasu.

'She's upset, how do you think she feels?' Bourke didn't mean to sound offensive, but he did. He was too angry.

Salty was more pragmatic. 'We could try and catch the bastard.'

'Who?' Harry grimaced. 'Du Bellay?'

'No, the bloody cassowary.'

'It's worth a try,' Bourke agreed. 'I don't know what the damned thing's doing in the mangroves anyway, they prefer the rainforest.'

'Maybe the bastard's lost.'

Then a flash of colour blinked behind the monotonous mud coloured vegetation of the mangrove running alongside the cannery. With the tide going out again, it seemed the cassowary had returned to the foreshore. 'Speak of the devil!' Salty said in a loud whisper. 'Look! There.' The three men froze. 'Shoot the bastard, Harry.'

Immediately outboard motors buzzed on the river, their hum travelling ahead of them on the water. The three men watched as the cannery motorboats rounded a bend down river. The women were on their way to start a new day at work. The cassowary stood erect. Listening. He too heard the motors.

'Harry,' Bourke said. 'This is our only chance.'

Harry dropped to the deck, pivoting the machine gun on its stand, aiming for the cassowary. Spreading his legs either side of the tripod he sighted the enormous bird. It approached the cannery landing platform. It was thirsty. It took a drink. 'Harry! Hurry.'

Harry hissed at Salty through the corner of his mouth, 'Feed me.' Salty raised a bandolier of ammunition into the gun. Harry cranked the first shells into the breach. He held the machinegun tight with two hands by the gunner's grip, when …

Charlie leapt from the muddy shallows of the water's edge rising on his powerful legs to take the cassowary by the neck as it drank. The bird hadn't a chance. It was no match for the hungry eighteen-foot croc. The bird kicked out with its taloned feet but the claws that could shred a human's belly were no match for the armoured hide of the crocodile. Dragging the cassowary back into the water Charlie made a death roll to drown the bird while another, smaller croc fought for what he considered his share. The bird tore apart. But Charlie tossed his head back managing the majority of the cassowary's carcass until the wretched bird dropped, piece by piece down his massive gullet.

The three men froze. Crocodiles were a way of life up here. But this was totally unexpected. Kimtasu heard the commotion, running onto the deck, when Harry reacted spontaneously. He compressed the trigger. A short burst at first … twenty, thirty rounds. The lead perforated the huge crocodile's throat as it devoured the cassowary. The reptile twisted bodily, and Harry let fly with another, longer burst … at least a hundred bullets.

The monster's side shredded. Its guts exposed and it fell dead, half on, half off the platform, where the tide had retreated, leaving the croc's carcass in shallow mud.

'Jesus Harry!' Bourke was stunned. 'That was amazing.'

Salty was first down the steps, yelling. 'We need to get that bird out before the other crocs get here.' On cue, disturbances in the swampland all about them heralded the approach of another half a dozen large crocodiles. Harry and Bourke followed Salty.

Kimtasu joined them, all armed with shovels, brooms, anything available to ward off the other reptiles until they could pull the cassowary's remains free. Bourke didn't hesitate. Leaping into the mud he sank to his waist. Armed with a huge hunter's knife he widened the wound leading into the creature's stomach and was sprayed with decomposing filth for his efforts. Fighting nausea, Bourke floundered about in the crocodile's gut. He felt feathers, a gnarly leg, a claw, and wrenched a chunk of the large bird's carcass free. 'Here!' he swung the heavy cassowary onto the deck. It landed heavily at Harry's feet. The head, a leg, its neck, and lower torso were missing. But they had the bird's stomach.

By now the motorboats arrived. At the bow of one, Arsala hitched a ride from the township. He saw the commotion, clambered onto the platform and, armed with an oar, he joined the fray.

'Jon-o-thon!' Kimtasu screamed.

'Watch out!'

Another male as large as Charlie swam at Bourke. Its massive tail propelled it through the watery mud at speed.

Bourke dived aside. He sank into the mud.

The croc thrashed about barking and hissing, hunting its kill. Submerged, Bourke was easy prey. Salty leapt from the platform landing on the reptile's back. His weight pushed it to the riverbed. The croc rose on legs, snapping wildly at anything in range. Salty was thrown aside. Harry and Kimtasu jumped feet first either side while Arsala repeatedly pounded the oar into the croc's head. Bourke rose tall, waist deep. He gasped a breath. The croc turned to the captain. They faced off, Bourke staring into the croc's yellow eyes with their black slit shaped pupils. Kimtasu didn't hesitate. She leapt onto the croc's back. She wrapped arms under its lower jaw and locked them. As the mud boiled, Kimtasu rode the monster like a rodeo mount. Bourke recovered his knife the moment the croc rose on its hind legs plunging the twelve-inch blade into the animal's throat, penetrating to the brain.

Salty was first onto the platform, reaching for Kimtasu he wrenched her to safety. Only a dozen feet away two, three, four more crocs moved to attack. 'Harry!' Salty screamed out, his hand thrust forward. Harry took his hand and was hauled aboard. Arsala swung the oar. 'Captain Bourke sir … quickly!' Bourke was weighted with mud and muck from the bog, he pushed forward, waist deep …

But it was like quicksand.

Salty's hand appeared, Harry's was next. Kimtasu snatched Bourke's collar. The lead croc leapt from the mud …

'Heave!' Salty shouted.

Arsala hit out. He struck the croc so hard the oar splintered at the blade and Arsala slipped on the muddy deck. He fell feet first and the nearest croc clamped down on his leg.

'No!' someone shouted.

Bourke was hoisted from the marsh, hauled unceremoniously onto the deck. He twisted to Arsala, being dragged into the swamp. The croc was relentless. Another croc mounted the platform and Kimtasu struck it a blow with a shovel. Hissing, the huge reptile slid back into the mud but the croc who had Arsala by the leg thrashed in a feeding frenzy. Arsala's leg was torn from his body. Bourke grabbed his friend under the arms hauling him to safety.

The two men fell to the deck. 'Jesus Christ Arsala!' Bourke yelled. That was close.

Close?

Kimtasu was speechless. The man had just lost a leg. Bourke started to laugh. All the men laughed as they watched the croc manage a death roll in the mud with the Ghurkha's artificial leg.

•   •   •

All the while, Lance and the work crew were tied up at the end of the cannery pier. They watched on in silence, totally shocked at what they had witnessed. The crocs were excited, most disappearing below the surface in deeper water, where they watched and waited. There would be no landing on the platform. Not today anyway. Harry and Salty threw down Jacob's ladders to the riverboats and one at a time the women climbed to the upper deck.

'Yer almost missed the action,' Salty told Lance, last on the upper deck. More to the point, Lance couldn't believe their luck with the cassowary showing itself so close after last night. 'Maybe it came back for another trinket,' Lance said, and was serious. 'Cassowaries are like that, stealin' anything shiny.'

The crocs made short work of Charlie. Bourke gutted the cassowary while they all stood around watching, hoping all the danger had not been in vain. 'Got it.' He held up the black pearl and what remained of the mother of pearl headband, before washing it in a bucket of water.

'Truly remarkable,' Lance muttered. Bourke threw the bird's remains into the river and it wasn't long before it too was snatched by the crocs.

• • •

On board La Grenouille.
Heading east on the Coral Sea
Du Bellay was not in the mood to converse. He was morose, angry. He could not believe he had been duped by a cassowary. He had the *Tear of the Eclipse* in his hand (so he thought) and he lost it. *How on earth could that happen?*

He looked at the breakfast platter of croissants with its porcelain bowls of freshly whipped butter and strawberry jam. He had lost his appetite and only managed to eat three. He pushed the platter aside and refilled his coffee cup. Locked in his cabin safe was the five thousand pounds in twenty-pound notes from Huang Ying, and while it was enough to by a large home in, say Melbourne, it was not nearly enough for his dream mansion on Lake Como in Italy. Certainly, Monsieur Felix Du

Bellay had made three previous trips and had twenty-four thousand pounds in a Swiss bank account, but he needed to ramp up sales. It was such a lucrative business with such massive profits, and he was in the ideal position to move the product. *Yes*, the diplomat thought to himself, *I must go all out with a one-thousand-pound weight transaction.*

•   •   •

Ten days later. Noumea. Home of the consul.
Noumea was still hurting from the cyclone, in particular the natives whose flimsy bamboo and grass huts were no match for god's wrath.

Monsieur Felix Du Bellay couldn't give a damn about the natives' plight. He chased the boiled quail's egg around his Creil et Montereau creamware dinner plate, with a silver fork but the slippery delight skidded over the plate, slipping around the caviar with the stealth of a thief in the night. His belly rumbled. Du Bellay attacked, spearing the egg, almost chipping the dinnerware. It shot across the table. Du Bellay cursed ...

Damn it, I'll use my fingers.

He plucked the egg up between forefinger and thumb, squashed it onto a canape of sturgeon's eggs and crammed it into his mouth, before it could escape a second time. This evening he dined alone. His hosts, the aging high commissioner Monsieur Olivier Martinez and his wife Catherine had excused themselves, explaining, rather lamely, that they had another dinner appointment. After Du Bellay's behaviour on his last visit, they were only too keen to avoid his company.

Du Bellay sniffed loudly, crudely. *Was he coming down with something?* He flattened another egg onto another canape and greedily stuffed into his insatiable gob, when the door opened. It was the house secretary, Monsieur Pierre Brassens. 'Ah, there you are monsieur. Enjoying your dinner, I trust?'

'I was until the door opened. What do you want?'

'You have mail monsieur. There are six pieces of personal correspondence since your journey to Australia. Here.' Brassens put the envelopes on the table within reach. Du Bellay grunted. Brassens bowed his head slightly, as he reversed out of the room.

A large envelope post marked *Melbourne, Victoria*, caught the diplomat's curiosity first up. The brown package was ten inches by eight, thereabouts. Du Bellay stuffed in another mouthful, wiped his hands on a serviette and tore open the envelope … and almost choked.

He coughed up the mouthful. He spat, slurping his tumbler of wine greedily. With eyes red and watery from coughing, Du Bellay took a long look at the sepia photo in the envelope. He was sickened. The girl looked so young! Surely, she was of legal age!

But regardless, it was clear who the obese man was, in the graphic photo. Even for a Chinese blackmailer, Huang Ying had a sense of humour.

Caught with your pants down, was written across the lower border. *Do not betray me.*

Du Bellay flew into a rage. He panicked. Igniting the photo with the dining table candelabra, Du Bellay made certain it had been totally destroyed before discarding the remains in the fireplace.

Sitting heavily back at the dinner table he snorted two lines of cocaine, one immediately after the other. The effect was instant. He gulped his glass of wine and refilled it to the top. Shaking involuntarily, he slurped down the wine and filled it again. His mind racing, what to do? If such a photo was distributed, he was a ruined.

With his thoughts scrambling Du Bellay couldn't seem to get drunk or really stoned. There could be only one answer. Sail to Mexico, collect a motherlode of cocaine Huang Ying wanted and make the delivery, collect payment and have Ying assassinated.

It was the only resolution.

Assassination ...

The thought gave Du Bellay the merest of satisfaction. He snorted a third line of pure Columbian and this time it worked.

• • •

Kanantui Island

Moimango's pilgrimage to the sacred cave had been a success. The chieftain felt energised, spiritually empowered after his ritual in the inner sanctum of the sacred cave, where he meditated before the *Tear of the Eclipse* to appease the ancestors.

If the Tamesi were to leave this island of fire and death, and resettle on safer shores, Moimango and his fellow islanders would rely heavily on his daughter Kimtasu and her new knowledge of the whitefellas. Moimango knew enough about the whitefellas to learn of their greed. For Moimango there were only three important factors in his life. Three items of value: land, women and pigs. And in that order. So Moimango relied on whitefella greed, their lust for the *Tear of the Eclipse*, to return his daughter to him, with the opportunity the islanders so desperately needed.

On the night of Moimango's return to the village, the other elders emerged from their isolation in the spirit hut to dance and celebrate. Their bodies were painted with bright coloured plant oils, their mouths red from betel nut, with breastplates and penis gourds, and with boar tusks in their noses. They were chanting, making war cries, pounding drums, blowing conch shells and dancing while holding bamboo torches. Others wore dresses of billowing leaves and two-tiered masks, or tall headdresses made from the black feathers of the cassowary with plumes of parrots' feathers. They carried spears and waved palm fronds, mimicking the high-stepping gait of a crocodile, the water spirit they worshipped, along with the other spirits they believed inhabited the rivers, mountains and trees. All the while, the women danced around them, wailing, and throwing themselves at the feet of the men.

CHAPTER SIXTEEN

Three months later, thereabouts

Captain Jonathon Bourke hurried along the duck boards resting precariously on top of the low tide mud. Dense mangroves either side joining overhead to create a gloomy passage. Old Charlie may have been annihilated by Harry's machine-gun, but other big crocs had moved in. After all it was a rich area for a hungry crocodile, with their regular rations of chickens or fish carcasses and guts being thrown into the swamp almost daily. Bourke had returned from the distillery with good news. Their order for fifty thousand cans of mullet, aka rum, was nearing completion. It would shortly be time to sail for Honolulu, and not too soon Bourke thought. He missed the open sea.

Salty straightened his back and stretched. He wasn't as young as he used to be, although his lover Dua was keeping him trim. Salty heard his captain approach and cleared the duckboards closest to the landing deck where he had been building a safety fence around the lower platforms, albeit slowly. This seemed a necessity after Charlie's performance with the cassowary three months earlier.

'Nearly there?' Salty asked of the rum order.

'Be finished at the end of the day.'

'Brilliant.'

Dua descended the steep wooden steps from the upper deck. She had seen the captain approaching and carried two long necks of Gooley's Boar Stout shipped up from Brisbane. She also carried Salty's unborn child. 'Careful love!' Salty fussed over her so, the lads were concerned he was becoming a big soft Teddy bear. Dua was at least twelve weeks and Salty joked that he must have planted his seed at his first attempt. Bourke took the bottle and drank half in one breath. 'Thanks, Dua, I was thirsty.' It might be warm, but it was wet. Dua smiled.

'Capt'n was just sayin' we'll be ready to sail soon,' Salty told Dua. Her reaction was instant and this surprised Bourke. 'Sail? *Drifter* sail soon?' She was certainly excited.

'You sound pleased,' Bourke said.

Dua frowned. 'Pleased?'

'Ah,' Bourke thought to explain. 'Dua is happy … *Drifter* sail.'

Dua nodded her head. She was more than pleased.

'Dua is excited to return home to Kanantui and her people,' Salty said of her home island. 'We have unfinished business with these people.'

'But we must move our order to Honolulu first Salty.'

'It's on the way cap'n,' Salty argued.

'Maybe, but if we are to move an entire tribe, relocate them to another island, we need to sell this rum first. Clear the hold.' Salty was clearly distracted. 'What is it Salty? What's on your mind?'

Salty put his arm around Dua. 'Well, cap'n, you know Dua's with child.'

'Yes.'

Salty gave the woman a squeeze, pulling her close. 'And Salty here's about to be a father.'

Was that a tear welling in the tough bastard's eye? Bourke wondered. 'Yes, yes,' he said impatiently. 'You're about to become a dad, and I congratulate you.'

'Well, me and Dua are stayin' together.'

Bourke sighed. 'Is that all!'

'All?'

'I mean, of course you're staying together. You're family, Dua's family now, you can set up your own joint in Cooktown.'

'No Cap'n.'

'No?'

'Me and Dua are goin' ter live together with her people.'

'Oh.'

'That's why I'm tellin' yer cap'n. We have unfinished business with the Tamesi people.'

Bourke hadn't seen this coming. He assumed they would settle together in Australia, somewhere.

Bourke leant back on the new fence and necked the remaining stout. He considered the position they were in. It had always been his intention to look after these islanders. He had even made enquiries through a friend of a friend in government. Now, since losing the war, Germany had been forced to relinquish its protectorate in east New Guinea. Papua New Guinea as it was now known, had suitable free coastal lands and islands only a day's sail from the doomed Kanantui Islands. Bourke was only too pleased to assist, but …

· · ·

Four days later …

The crew had worked hard. Harder than usual. Fifty thousand cans of rum, disguised as mullet, had been stowed in the hold, with a further five thousand cans of the real thing – *Lighthouse Brand Fresh Sea Mullet* – stowed to conceal the contraband.

It was late afternoon. Bourke watched Lance and Flash motor off back up-river after unloading the last of the cartons. Juvita was busy below deck delegating, speaking rapid pidgin to half a dozen native women from the factory. They were busy stocking the galley with dry goods, fresh produce and two butchered pigs, boned and portioned for the freezer on board.

Twenty chickens were also boarded in coops, destined for the dining table en route.

Kimtasu's brother Gemtasu and his fellow islander were only too happy to help Bill Brown the fireman, shovelling coal into bunkers, a thankless job they didn't seem to mind. For their part, they were at last doing what they had set out to do, organise the relocating of their people to safer shores.

Arsala stood stiffly on the bridge, finding his new prosthetic leg a little challenging. But he'd been forced to use a crutch the past few months and now his new limb was taking a little getting used to. Arsala handed Bourke the manifest. 'Here Captain Bourke sir. All present and correct as they say in the army, true?'

'True Arsala.' Bourke ran a sharp eye over the list. 'You happy?' he asked Arsala regarding their contraband.

'Arsala happy.'

'Then I'm happy too my friend.' Bourke heard the bridge door open and looked over his shoulder. Harry, Ivan Toussaint and Salty had gathered. 'All done skip,' Harry said. 'When do yer reckon we'll be weighing anchor? I'll organise the troops.'

'We'll sail first thing Thursday.'

'Sparrow's fart Thursdee it is then.'

Salty slapped a hand on Harry's shoulder. 'An' yer know what that means right now capt'n?'

'Beer o'clock,' Bourke grinned.

Arsala watched the drinkers head down the gangway for the White Horse. He would stay on board tonight, along with Juvita and Salty who would return with Dua and the other islanders, Kimtasu amongst them. Like Juvita, Arsala had grown fond of Kimtasu, she was truly a princess. But as the days for departure approached, Arsala had noticed the islander grow apart from Bourke. It appeared the chemistry the skipper sensed between them in those first weeks, had evaporated.

It was wet season. The skies blackened. The clouds burst open. Beneath the tin roof of the White Horse the rain sounded like ten thousand cheering fans at an Aussie Rules Grand Final. The packed bar didn't help. Maybe everyone came in before the rain hit. Bourke bought a crate of Castlemaine XXXX longnecks and passed them around his crew. Leaning his back to the bar he drank his beer. A few patrons were locals, but there were a lot of new faces also. The crowded harbour attested to the several vessels of varying sizes taking shelter in the harbour. A storm was on its way.

'Bourkie yer mad bastard!' Bourke twisted to the voice to be greeted by an old cobber he hadn't seen in a year or so.

'Murry Jones yer skinny prick. I didn't know you were back in town,' he had to yell to be heard. The two men embraced with macho slaps on the back.

'I got in this arvo.'

'I didn't notice.' They clinked longnecks. 'Cheers.' Bourke eyed his mate. 'You gone an' lost more weight?'

'Nar, don't be crazy.' Murry patted his belly. It was round and tight, like he had a balloon stuffed under his shirt. Otherwise, the man was a rake.

'I heard yer sailin' soon huh?' Murry said.

'Aye. Got a big order from the yanks, fifty thousand cans.'

'Bloody oath mate,' Murry whistled. 'Nice one.' He took a long drink and wiped froth from around his mouth with his sleeve. 'It ain't the best weather, can't yer hang about a few days?'

'We're not sailing until Thursday.'

'Fair enough.'

'And I have a commitment to five islanders I promised to help.'

'Oh?'

Bourke explained his unusual predicament.

'Kanantui yer say!' Murry asked.

'Yes. You been there?'

'No mate. And I doubt anyone will after this week.'

'What?'

'The volcanoes are erupting Bourkie.'

'Yes, I know that, I was there when Tekahui blew its top a few months back.'

'No mate. It's eruptin' right now. We just sailed from the Solomons and met up with fishermen from Port Moresby who saw it for themselves. They reckon she's really goin' to blow this time, probably wipe out the island.'

'Jesus!'

'Yes, Jesus.'

The two old mates shouting to be heard over the din in the pub, unfortunately, were eavesdropped upon by Snakeskin Coen's deckie, Bullet. On seeing Bourke enter the bar he positioned himself as close as he dared, where he stood and listened with his back to Bourke and his crew. Twenty minutes later he'd heard enough. It was time to tell the boss.

•   •   •

Torres Girl moored in deep water off Cooktown docks. She was taking a drenching with raindrops warm and wet, the size of marbles. But skipper Snakeskin Coen was confident the storm would blow over shortly. Bullet and Jack Lawson tied their tender to the stern of the sixty-seven-foot, gaff-rigged schooner. They slipped down the companionway into the saloon like two drowned rats.

'Boss,' Bullet acknowledged Coen. The two men stank of grog, but nothing could match the stink of the crocodile and snake skins stored in the hold and destined for Thursday Island. Coen had had a more lucrative offer of late and once his hold was full, he was taking his skins to a Malayan dealer on Thursday Island who he'd made contact with over the telegraph.

Coen looked up from the table where he was patiently attempting, for the first time, to put a model ship in a bottle. But the cheap whiskey he drank, to wash down his smoked crocodile and pickles, had befuddled his movements somewhat.

'Boss. You'll never guess what we just gone an' 'eard.'

'Oh,' Coen speared his fork into a pickled onion and pressed a piece of orange-yellow croc meat onto its tines. He took the lot in one bite. 'And what might that be?' he asked, barely coherent.

Jack Lawson watched Coen's whiskery chin twitch as he spilt Bourke's name before his mate Bullet had a chance.

'Bourke!' Vinegar and saliva dribbled from the corner of Coen's mouth. He coughed. Nearly choking, he barely managed to swallow what was in his gob without chewing. 'Bourke! What of him?' he bristled, his eyes watering.

''e were in the pub.'

'So?'

Bullet explained everything, with Jack Lawson filling in gaps when he thought Bullet had missed something …

The islanders, the volcanos, Kanantui Island to be devastated, Bourke the good Samaritan …

'Good Samaritan my arse,' Coen flared. ''e's after that *Tear of the Eclipse*. 'e must have finally found out from that darkie whore where it is an' he's going for it.' Coen looked at the food. He'd lost his appetite and shoved the plate aside. 'I bloody knew it. When they sailin'?'

'Thursdee. Sparrow's fart.'

'Then we're goin' tonight.'

'Tonight boss?'

'We sail, they steam. We need a head start. Bullet, chase up the lads,' he said referring to their Aboriginal deckhands. Coen scratched down a list of provisions. 'That should do it,' he passed it to Jack Lawson.

Jack ran an eye over the list. 'Dynamite boss?'

'Aye, can never be too careful. Here's an advance note.'

'Grocer's closed boss.'

Coen took a leather purse from his pocket, unfolding the creases from a ten-pound note that had been waiting such an occasion. 'Give Chung this. Bloody Chinese love money more than you like your grog. Now move it.'

•   •   •

Next day, early morning

Police Sergeant Andy Tucker stepped from the police launch and onto the loading platform on the eastern side of the cannery. He adjusted his crotch, pinched by his tight fitting pants, and made a mental note to get the wife to undo some of the stitching in his britches. Remaining behind at the tiller was a somewhat nervous Police constable Timmy Moore and three uniformed blacks Bourke hadn't seen before.

Something moved in the murky waters only a dozen feet away and Tucker moved quickly to the wooden steps elevating him away from this terrifying place.

'Andy,' Bourke called down a greeting as the lawman climbed. 'What a pleasant surprise,' he lied.

'I don't know how you live like this,' Tucker said, stepping onto the deck before glancing back over his shoulder to his launch where *whatever-it-was* had submerged completely.

'Treat the crocs with respect, Andy, and they'll leave you alone.'

'Yeah ... right,' Tucker said. But he wasn't convinced.

Bourke eyed the policeman with a wary eye. Whilst these frontier lawmen were in his pocket, so to speak, any attempt to genuinely befriend them had failed. They were happy to take handouts but were guarded. Kimtasu, dressed in Juvita's Malaysian attire, joined them on the deck, playing her part as she had been pre-trained by Jon-a-thon. Her warm smile melted the heart of the sergeant, who floundered.

'Good morning miss. I … I ah … Kim, isn't it?'

'Kimtasu. Good morning, Sar-gant Tucker,' she greeted in perfect English.

'Please, call me Andy,' Tucker said and immediately reminded himself to keep this meeting formal.

'Coffee?' Bourke smiled, although he was sensing a negative vibe. Harry and Salty stepped out onto the deck – trained decoys – as Lance slipped through the secret store shelves to make his way to the distillery. On the lower level the women were already busy in the cannery. Although the last shipment of *canned mullet* had been transported to *Drifter*, the women had much cleaning to complete, as the cannery would be closed until further notice. Sergeant Tucker took a moment to watch the women from his elevated vantage point where he could see into part of the factory. They were a happy bunch, chatting away in their native dialect.

Bourke asked. 'Was that a yes, or no?'

'Sorry, what?'

'Coffee?'

'Coffee, ah … no thanks Mr Bourke.'

'Mr Bourke?' Bourke repeated. 'Sounds formal Andy.'

'Well …' The sergeant took a deep breath and sighed, 'I'm here on formal business.'

'Don't like the sound of that,' Bourke forced a smile.

The policeman looked uncomfortable. 'Look, Captain Bourke …'

'Jonathon, please.'

'Jonathon. I … I, ah, I'm just doing my job, alright?'

'Sure Andy. What's up?'

'Well, I've orders to … orders to search the cannery.'

'Search the cannery! Andy, Andy, what the hell's this all about?'

'Orders from Brisbane. It seems like there have been some complaints. The brass sent orders to search this cannery for anything untoward.'

'Complaints? Untoward? Like what exactly?'

'Come on Bourke, don't make this anymore unpleasant that it already is … please.'

Bourke was feeling confident. Cheeky even. All the contraband was on board *Drifter*. As long as they didn't find the distillery, although Lance was already in action with some of the women, hiding or destroying evidence and surrounding the stills themselves with a custom-built covering that looked like storage cover for thousands of empty cans. 'Fill yer boots sergeant.'

Tucker looked relieved. 'You don't mind then?'

'No. As you said, you're just doing your job. Go for it.'

A weight lifted from Tucker's shoulders. He whistled and the other lawmen joined him.

Salty had heard enough. He fetched Dua from their bungalow on the balcony and he excused himself, exchanging a discreet wink with his cap'n. It was time for *plan B*.

Plan B …

Plan B had been in place sometime specifically for this situation. Harry would take one of the river boats and head directly to *Drifter* where he and Arsala would see the ship moved south to the Annon River Estuary, south of Cooktown. Out of sight out of mind, until they sailed. Which now would be sooner than later.

• • •

Bourke sat back lazily in a cane chair, legs wide apart, allowing the morning sun to wash over his body. He took a long satisfying gulp of hot black coffee. 'This brass … back in Brisbane,' Bourke asked the policeman, fishing for answers. 'Who exactly are we talking about?'

'Can't say.'

'Come on Andy. Can't say or won't say?'

'All I know is it came from well up the ladder. Someone in a high position has an eye on your operation.'

'Cripes. Typical. A man makes a few quid working his guts out and the brass want a piece of the pie.' Bourke had an immediate thought Du Bellay may be involved. He had threatened him after all. 'Wouldn't be a foreigner would it, a frog maybe?'

Tucker blushed, taking the steps back down into the cannery.

• • •

Later that afternoon

Bourke stepped into the ANZ Bank in the heart of Cooktown, where it felt a good ten degrees hotter. The single teller, a scrawny middle-aged man with a red face lathered in sweat standing behind a narrow grill, sorted banknotes into their various denominations.

'Mornin' Mr Bourke,' he greeted Bourke in what Bourke had always surmised was an Irish accent, but could never really put a finger on it.

'Owen,' Bourke acknowledged the greeting, adding, 'Hot enough for you?'

Owen gave the standard reply. 'My wife Audrey says I should grow tomatoes in here.'

Laughs.

Bourke hefted a bag of mixed coins onto the counter, takings from local sales which was never a real money spinner. 'Thirty-three quid, six shillings and fourpence-halfpenny there Owen. Or there should be. And here's another forty-seven quid in notes and five hundred francs in notes.'

'Francs?'

'They're Harry's, he had them left from our last trip to Tahiti and asked me to get them changed for pounds.'

'Francs, eh?' Owen eyed the well-travelled, well worn, *Banque de France* banknotes. 'Been a few of these in lately.'

'Oh, how's that?'

'Well Andy Tucker deposited a thousand francs here two days ago in notes, just like these, and Timmy Moore his constable, do you know him?'

'I know Timmy, sure.'

'Well, he deposited three hundred francs the same day.'

'Did you ask where they got them?'

'No Mr Bourke. It's not my place to ask questions.'

• • •

Bourke stepped onto Charlotte Street. Anger temped him to go drag Sergeant Tucker out of the police station and horsewhip the two-faced mongrel. Common sense prevailed. Tucker would have to wait. The dirty copper might have placed his bets on *even money* for a win, but at least Sam Fry, the Cooktown harbour master looked after his interests. Bourke had confirmation, Harry and Arsala were safely anchored five miles down the coast.

Sam Fry was forty-eight, a good-looking rooster with a trickle of the Orient in his veins somewhere back in the family tree. Subtle sloe eyes and olive skin gave that away. 'Jonathon!' he called out, catching Bourke on Charlotte Street, looking serious.

'Sam.'

'Glad I found yer. When are yer sailing?'

Bourke trusted the man, he slipped him backsheesh regularly to close a blind eye on port duties and brought the man fine Parisienne dresses, hats and cosmetics for Mrs Fry, whenever he had the opportunity. But sometimes it was necessary to lie. 'When am I sailing? Not certain Sam, why's that?'

Sam looked up and down Charlotte Street. It was busier than usual this morning. He took Bourke's arm, ushering him into a shady alley. 'I've been getting some pressure from Brisbane lately.'

'Oh?'

You too?

'Someone in government is asking a lot of questions. I've been ordered to keep an eye on you.'

'Who?'

'Barry Turner.'

'Minister for Foreign Affairs?'

Sam nodded. 'You know him?'

'Heard of him.'

'Well, word is you have a price on your head.'

'What?'

'In Noumea.' Sam Fry leant in close, lowering his voice. 'Said you escaped prison.'

Bourke puffed out his cheeks. 'I ... I, ah, don't know what to say Sam.'

'Well, did you?'

'Did I what?'

'Escape prison, Isle of Pines to be exact.'

'Don't know what you're talking about Sammy. You'll be the first to know when I find out,' Bourke shot a cheeky grin Sam's way. 'But I'll be out of your hair soon, anyways.'

• • •

On board La Belle Dame.

Papeete Harbour. Tahiti

The signs of withdrawal were evident, had been to Capitaine Claude Forbin for some time. His lifelong friend Felix Du Bellay was dependent on cocaine. He had grown increasingly sensitive, morose and negative, more interested in that next hit rather than that next delicious meal the gourmand once cherished. Which was a pity, for it was something the two friends had in common. Du Bellay's growing tolerance to the drug demanded higher doses, searching for that degree of pleasure he originally enjoyed.

• • •

Capitaine Forbin opened the stateroom door ajar and peeped in warily. He was a passenger aboard the 120-foot luxury motor yacht, a guest of Du Bellay's while *La Grenouille* was on the slips being repainted. Increasingly, lately, he feared the mood of his colleague and friend. Du Bellay sat in an armchair; his plump hand wrapped around a balloon of Armagnac. He stared straight ahead, fixedly, apparently gazing into a *fleur de lis* embroidered into the lush woollen carpet. Forbin pushed the door wide open and stepped over the bulkhead. He cleared his throat.

'Felix … Felix … have you seen the latest *L'Intransigeant?*' he said waving the Paris newspaper. It had been sent aboard with mail and other paperwork as they prepared to sail west. Du Bellay turned his head only slightly, his mouth open and his eyes hooded and bloodshot. 'What is it, Claude?'

'Here, read this,' Claude waved the paper in his face.

'For Christ's sake read it to me will you.'

The capitaine looked at his friend a moment and sighed. Claude knew the man had increased his cocaine habit of late, leading to irritability and restlessness. At the moment he was down.

'You should lay off that … that … powder, Felix. Look at you.'

'Just read the paper will you.'

Claude shook the paper to straighten the creases. '*Kanantui Island Threatened with Annihilation,*' he read the headline. Felix shuffled in his chair, trying to sit up. *'The island off the east coast of Papua New Guinea and its native inhabitants, the Tamesi, are under serious threat as both the island's volcanoes erupt for the third time in as many months ...'*

'The Tear of the Eclipse?' Felix said, his voice hoarse. The diplomat blew his nose loudly. *'The Tear of the Eclipse* Claude, what's it say about it?'

Claude knew only too well how his friend had become obsessed by the black pearl. 'Nothing Felix. Why on earth should the paper mention the pearl?'

'Yes, yes, you're right. Of course.'

'This is the Papeete supplement for *L'Intransigeant*, it comes with the Paris paper which is six weeks old.'

'So, its recent news then, about the eruptions that is?'

'Exactly.'

Felix slipped his silver cigarette holder open, skilfully pouring two fine lines of powder on the cover before snorting quickly.

'Jesus Felix ...'

'Don't start Claude.' Suddenly Felix Du Bellay was thinking clearly, for the moment. 'Send a telegram to Monsieur Balvenie,' Felix spoke of *La Belle Dame's* owner and good friend of his, still in Paris, the wealthy businessman who gave Du Bellay carte blanche to use his motor yacht in the Pacific. Political favours were expected in return, however chasing a legendary pearl might not have been what Balvenie would approve. 'Let him know we are sailing west. And fetch the Capitaine.'

La Belle Dame's Capitaine Marcel Badeaux was as honest as the days were long. He certainly wasn't in Du Bellay's pocket; why should he be, as he was paid handsomely by his wealthy employer in Paris. Badeaux was certainly not aware of the hundred kilos of cocaine smuggled aboard his charge; the parcels being disguised as vanilla extract and stored in Du Bellay's cabin.

Badeaux did not like Monsieur Du Bellay. Not the slightest. The overweight diplomat was a parasite in his eyes, using his employer's state-of-the-art luxury art-deco yacht like it was his own plaything. Monsieur Balvenie, the owner, however, would not hear a word against the diplomat and the capitaine was under orders to take the man and his friends wherever he wished to go.

'I have further meetings in Melbourne,' Du Bellay told Capitaine Badeaux. 'I am expected in Parliament in six weeks. Meanwhile I wish to conduct a humanitarian mission to Kanantui.'

'Kanantui?' the capitaine coughed. 'New Guinea?'

Du Bellay forced the newspaper *L'Intransigeant* upon the unsuspecting capitaine. 'Read this. People are going to die; an entire race might be annihilated. They need our assistance.' Capitaine Marcel Badeaux speed read the article. 'This is sad news, sad news indeed monsieur. But what can we do?'

'We can sail to the island immediately and we'll see when we get there.'

This was the most unprepared answer one could imagine. 'But monsieur …'

'But nothing. How long will it take you to ready the ship?'

'Twenty-four-hours monsieur, at least.'

'You have twelve.' Du Bellay looked at the stateroom clock. 'We leave at dawn.'

CHAPTER SEVENTEEN

The Island of Kanantui
Seven days later...
Arsala eased *Drifter* around the headland, immediately telegraphing Bill Brown in the engine room ... *Slow ahead. Stand by to stop.*

'This look bad Captain Bourke sir,' the Ghurkha told his captain. 'I tell you true. Very, very, very bad.'

With engines stopped, they drifted slowly towards the mayhem while Bourke's brilliant strategic mind kicked into action. For days under *full steam* they had seen the distant smoke, like an insidious dragon meandering over the ocean when the winds changed direction. For the past twelve hours they had been able to see the erupting volcano from well out to sea. Now they recognised the urgency. But nothing prepared them for this.

Bourke, Salty, Harry and Juvita gaped through the ever-thickening smoke obstructing their view across the bay ahead to Kanantui Island and specifically the village of Koep. Towering above was the blazing volcano, Wewakhui. Overhead the pewter sky cast gloom and doom.

To Bourke, first impressions of the harbour was one of a regatta, turned to chaos. Several large vessels had already anchored offshore. He counted eleven, recognising the flags of at least five nations. Native canoes were being paddled frantically out to the larger vessels, where the islanders were hauled on board like livestock. On the shore hordes of islanders gathered from many villages. As Bourke panned the binoculars down the coast to the south and further north he could make out lines of refugees hurrying with their meagre belongings, scrambling along the shoreline towards Koep. He guessed them to be in their thousands. In Koep itself Bourke noted several huts already in flames while soccer-ball-sized pieces of pumice, fireball red, bombarded the village, dropping indiscriminately from the sky.

It was a free-for-all panic.

'Jesus Christ! Have you ever seen anything like this?' Salty took Dua under his wing, as terrified, she searched the shore for family. Arsala passed her the binoculars and, pressing them hard to her eyes, Dua scoured the shoreline. Kimtasu joined them on the bridge.

'I go to Moimango,' Kimtasu was desperate. Within sight people could be seen dying. Already some drowned souls floated on the tide. As they watched a large tiger shark appeared, mouth wide, it turned on its side to take a pig's carcass in its gaping jaws. A moment later and Bourke was certain he recognised the shape of a large saltwater crocodile cruising the bottom. It must have been the size of Charlie back home and Bourke surmised it had swum down from the river estuary to their north. *Where there's one, there more.*

They heard screaming from the beach. On shore some villagers were being burnt alive. Even out here in the bay burning cinders were raining like fiery confetti. Others fought for a place in the canoes or landing craft sent ashore. Rescuers themselves were panicking, striking natives with whatever they had at hand. Going ashore was madness. Bourke ordered the crew to be vigilant.

Without warning Kimtasu rushed the davits. She tore into the safely lines securing the tender.

Bourke held her back before she harmed herself. 'No Kimtasu!'

'I go. Kimtasu go.' The woman fought like a warrior. Bourke pinned her to the post. 'It is dangerous. We must think this through.'

They were still half a mile from shore.

Harry's face was taut with stress. His brow furrowed. 'Capt'n.'

'Not now Harry.'

'But Capt'n.'

'What?'

'There's something you should know.'

'We haven't time for …'

'It's urgent.'

'Jesus Harry, what?'

'Kimtasu has a six-year-old daughter, Tasui!'

Bourke thought he was hearing things. 'She what?'

'Tasui. Kimtasu has a daughter here, she is six and lives with the grandfather.'

For the briefest of moments, it was as if time stood still. All around them seemed void of sound, like a deaf man might perceive the world. Bourke looked incredulous. 'H-how do you know this?'

'Dua told me.'

'Jesus Harry, why didn't you tell me sooner?'

'Because I was sworn to secrecy, but hell …' Harry waved an arm at the chaos all around them. 'Now this.'

Kimtasu stood frozen. She heard Harry say the name Tasui. 'You have daughter,' Bourke said. 'Ah … you have small girl?'

Kimtasu nodded. Tears wet her cheeks. 'Why did you not tell me? Why you not say to Bourke?' he grabbed the woman's arm.

'Kimtasu go to Kanantui,' is all Kimtasu could say. She stabbed a finger at the mayhem. 'Kimtasu go to Moimango. Go to Tasui.'

There was no time for arguing. They heard gunfire from one of the ships. The rescuers were fearing for their own lives. A volume of thick smoke cleared briefly. 'Is that *La Belle Dame?*' Harry recognised the sleek 120-foot luxury motor yacht from Noumea. The Art Deco style rich man's toy had been blocked from view by the Dutch Merchant ship *MS Alcinous* on its port side. The *Alcinous* being one of four large ships that had answered the Mayday call radioed by the first European vessel on site, the American ex-whaler *Seattle*.

La Belle Dame! Monsieur Du Bellay!

Bourke knew only too well that was Du Bellay's transport in the Coral Sea. He stared through the smoke. 'You have got to be joking.'

Kimtasu broke free. She tugged at the slip knot and the stern of the tender dropped from the davit. Harry leapt forward slashing the bow rope with his knife before the tender was lost. The craft settled obediently on the surface. Kimtasu was instantly over the side.

'Shit!' Bourke had no choice. 'Hold her,' he yelled at Harry. 'I'll be right back.'

Bourke unlocked his gun cupboard, taking two Lee Enfield.303 rifles. He rammed a magazine into each and slung a bandolier over his shoulder. Hefting a huge coil of rope over the other arm he managed to juggle two carbide lanterns. With khakis tucked into boots, a ten-inch Bowie knife sheathed on his belt and his favourite Akubra rakishly positioned on his head, Bourke slipped over the side and into the tender. Harry had read his skipper's mind. In that brief moment he fetched his Luger, Flash bolted an outboard onto the tender.

'We're coming too cap'n,' Salty said, lowing Dua over the side before Bourke had a chance to protest. Flash started the motor.

'Wait!' Ivan and Hank dropped over the side. 'You'll need all the help yer can get.'

Flash pushed away with an oar, throttled the engine and steered for shore. Immediately they heard a splash nearby. Kimtasu's brother Gemtasu and the other warrior dived overboard and swam to friends approaching in a canoe. A fin broke the surface only yards away. But the natives were fearless. In a matter of seconds, they were hauled into the outrigger and paddled ashore without delay.

•   •   •

A few hours earlier, before sunrise ...
The *Torres Girl*, beat around the headland of Kanantui Island's Koep Bay, hurried along by a south-westerly, and into hell. As handsome a sailboat under full sail as she was, no one noticed another vessel arrive in the bay.

Snakeskin Coen had arrived late on the scene. He'd had a three-day head start from Cooktown with strong winds, but as he expected *Drifter* had beaten him. But *Drifter* was only a part of the scene. Coen stood at the helm, legs spread, arms holding her steady, with his mouth wide open in bewilderment. The bay was still full of craft, even though he had passed many that had already sailed, their decks crowded with refugees. The call had gone out to surrounding islands. *Torres Girl* had sailed into a major civilian rescue operation. The vista was terrifying. Certainly, Coen and his crew had seen the volcanoes from well out to sea, but here in the bay it was a war zone. With the sun yet to rise and the sky soot black, fires lit the bay like the torches of an advancing army. They clearly saw the path of molten lava oozing down the slopes. An unstoppable slow-moving avalanche of liquefied rock. So deadly, boiling and toxic, yet it was beautiful to behold.

'Furl in the sails,' Coen yelled at the deckhands. 'Move it, move it.'

'What's the plan boss?' Bullet grovelled about the helm.

'Get the sails in, I'm goin' to get closer to *Drifter*, but I don't want them to see us. Not yet any'ow. Get ready to drop anchor.'

• • •

High in the mountains ...

Du Bellay positioned himself atop a pillar of stone, uncapped his flask of brandy and took a generous swig. The spirit burnt his throat, but it settled the nagging pain in his chest. The Frenchman had snorted two generous lines of cocaine at the beach. He had been invigorated. He had the strength of a lion. He was so close to finally snatching the *Tear of the Eclipse* for himself. He was invincible. He was about to become a very wealthy man. Du Bellay allowed a moment of pleasurable thoughts. *Ah ... Paris, Sturgeon caviar, Lake Como, champagne fountains, Belgium chocolate, diamonds, white truffles, beautiful women, foie gras ...*

His beady eyes darted to his accomplice. 'We must be close,' he said to Claude de Forbin standing next to him. Forbin racked his brain – *why on earth he had let Du Bellay talk him into this madness. They were going to die. He just knew it.*

They were on the windward side of the volcano, well away from the eruption causing havoc on the eastern side, destroying the village, and threatening the entire island. Beneath them the earth tremors had become more frequent. They had been climbing for well over an hour now and from this vantage point the view was stunning ... under normal circumstances.

Du Bellay pulled the child by a leather strap. He tugged her long black hair until she squealed. It had the right effect. Moimango had no choice but to cooperate. He continued up the goat track not understanding what this *hog like whitefella* was saying, but he knew only too well *what* the fat man wanted.

• • •

On the bay ...

A pod of dolphins gambolled below the surface. Two or three enthusiastically circled in the shallows as *Drifter's* tender bottomed on the sand of the beach. To seafarers they were a beacon of hope. The dolphins sensed the danger. They wanted to help. In all the crew's haste it seemed Harry had forgotten how steep the shore dropped away in this bay. Once again, he leapt over the bow to secure the craft only to drop up to his chin in water. But this day, it was no laughing matter. To Harry this beach looked more desperate than the day he landed at Anzac Cove on the 25th of April 1915, a date etched in his memory.

People crammed the shoreline. Many were weighed down with possessions, livestock, chickens, pigs. Disturbingly some men demanded to take the place of women in the boats hurrying back and forth from the rescue ships. The steep incline into the mountains behind them was ablaze. Cinders filled the air. Spot fires exploded to life. Women hugged babies while men tried to shelter their women. Along the coastline coconut palms flared like gigantic torches while fireballs of pumice landed like artillery along the foreshore and into the sea. Bourke saw one woman hit by a fiery missile. Her arms flayed and she collapsed into the sand. Dead.

Many bodies lay where they fell. Some trampled. Some bludgeoned. It appeared rival villages still existed on Kanantui. However, they had one common goal right now. Survival.

The deep throaty blast of a ship's horn echoed about the bay. The Dutch Merchant ship *MS Alcinous* was fully laden, her decks precariously overloaded. Thick smoke expelled from her smokestack and the huge ship started for the open sea. Bourke snatched a look at the inland vista. If the last eruption was anything to go by, it was likely this volcano would release a pyroclastic blast very soon.

Salty hoisted Dua free of the craft. 'We're going to find Dua's family,' he called out to Bourke through a nimbus of black choking smoke. Immediately the tender was rushed by desperate natives.

There was no time to argue.

Bourke looked at his long-time friend. 'Take care.'

Salty was instantly felled by an aggressive warrior clutching spears and a club. Salty lost his footing. The tall native dragged a mother and child back and made to take her place in the tender. Salty straightened, rose from the sand like Titan himself and hauled the fighting islander back to shore. A scuffle broke out. Salty pounced, punching the man with a left hook to the jaw. The warrior staggered back, lifted a spear and lurched forward. Salty stepped aside, snatched the spear, snapped it over his knee and attacked. The native swung his club but Salty disarmed him once more. Salty hefted the club like a juggler, caught it by the handle and brought the weapon down on the native's shoulder. Bones shattered. Salty heaved the club into the bay. Another warrior came to his friend's aid. He wielded a machete and flew at an unarmed Salty. Bourke caught the man out of the corner of his eye. His foot shot forward. The native tripped. Bourke pounced, slamming the man's face into the sand. He struggled. Bourke only grew angrier. He pushed even harder. The native battled to breath. 'What's it to be mate?' he yelled in the man's ear. The warrior didn't understand the words but there was no mistaking Bourke's intention. Bourke disarmed the man of his machete and gave the native a kick up the beach.

Bourke turned to Flash, who was manning the tender. 'Women and children only. Take as many of these poor beggars as you deem safe, back to *Drifter*. Hank, Ivan, you stay with Flash.'

Bourke was pushed aside by another panicked native. Wheeling around he dropped the man to the sand with one powerful punch. 'Women and children only,' Bourke spat, standing one boot on the man's back. 'For Christ's sake Flash, look after this tender. Meet us back here in two hours.' He looked at his watch.

'Sure capt'n. What about you?'

Bourke helped Kimtasu onto the beach. 'We've got someone precious to find.'

Ivan stepped forward. Bourke shoved the spare rifle into his chest. 'Stay here, they need you.'

'But what about you cap'n?'

'I'll be right. Just get women and children onto *Drifter*.' Bourke had a fair idea about the sacred cave. He imagined he would need a two-hour window to get there and back. He looked to Harry as he shouldered a particularly large warrior aside. The warrior challenged him. Harry balled his fist pummelling the man in the belly. He doubled over. Harry planted his boot on the man's backside and shoved him aside. The native was no match for this big angry whitefella. He ran. Flash passed Harry the spare rifle and rope. Harry picked up the machete for good measure. 'Wish us luck,' he said with an inspiring confidence.

Flash managed to yell out, 'If I didn't know any better Harry, I'd say yer enjoying yerself.'

Harry winked, elbowed another islander aside and hurried after Bourke and Kimtasu, already striding through the sand towards the community longhouse. Inside was bedlam. Kimtasu found a cousin, a woman younger than her, she bundled items into a woven cloth. They exchanged dialogue. Rapid words in a tongue Bourke would never understand.

'What did she say?' Bourke asked. Kimtasu fought back tears.

'She say Tasui and Moimango taken by big whitefella.'

This was no surprise. 'Where? Where whitefella take Tasui and Moimango?' But Bourke knew the answer.

'To the sacred cave. To *The Tear of the Eclipse.*'

Bourke turned to Harry who had heard everything. A tremor shot through the earth at their feet and the rear of the longhouse collapsed. Outside a burning palm crashed to earth scattering sparks in a huge arc. The hall roof caught fire.

'How far?' Harry asked.

'An hour if we hurry.'

'What are we waitin' for?'

• • •

Little Tasui kicked and scratched her torturer. The six-year-old native girl, heir to the *Tear of the Eclipse,* was a fighter. 'Stop struggling you little bitch,' Du Bellay said in French and then English, neither of which she understood. He tugged her hair harder, pushing her in front of him, but she turned and bit down hard on his wrist.

'Bah!' the fat man cursed. He slapped her face. Moimango turned, yelling in his native tongue. But Du Bellay rammed his pistol harder into the child's back and Moimango knew only too well what that small metal tool was capable of. The *hog-like whitefella* had already spat fire from it on the beach extinguishing the life of one of his warriors. Now he was terrified the evil man would send his granddaughter to the *land of spirits.*

'Move it!' Du Bellay shouted. Tasui skipped over the rocks with childhood ease, only to have the *fat whitefella* pull her back by the strap he had used to harness her. Twenty minutes later they stepped from the canopy of the rainforest to a steep incline of tumbled rock, loosened by earth tremors over many years.

'Oh goodness!' Claude de Forbin was the first of the two men to notice the bamboo cradles high in the cliff face, each housing eight or ten skeletons, some macabre – with moulded faces of clay – the others just all bone. They had arrived at the sacred cave.

On entering the underground chamber system Bourke recognised what was so special to the Tamesi people. The main limestone cave was a cathedral of stalactites and stalagmites. The floor was carpeted with human bones, most predominantly skulls, and he noted many had been here so long the mineral deposits, although seeping slowly from above, had encased many of the skulls. Kimtasu forged ahead. Bourke lit the carbides, handing one to Kimtasu. Harry followed close behind, guarding the rear. Outside winds had changed direction as the fires drew on air currents. The cave systems were filling with smoke, toxic, breathtaking, sulphurous smoke. Bourke found pools of water filled with recent rainwater. He soaked bandanas, passing one to Kimtasu, to tie about their mouths. Kimtasu beckoned Bourke to follow. 'Come. This is the way. There is no other.'

Bourke had learnt from Kimtasu back in Cooktown that the most hallowed chamber, the most sacred home to the spirits of this island, was up this steep passageway – a long narrow gallery six storeys high, yet barely wide enough to crawl through, a fissure left by an ancient eruption.

The ground shook. A minor quake, but with enough strength to loosen rocks from above. Bourke suddenly felt vulnerable. If a boulder rolled into this space, they would be trapped hundreds of yards into the guts of the mountain.

There would be no rescue.

After fifty yards the passage widened slightly. Enough for ancient islanders to have decorated the walls with cave art. As primitive as it was, Bourke thought there was something spiritual about it. They finally entered a cavernous opening. Bourke felt bones underfoot. He trod on ceremonial pottery, the low-temperature fired ceramics crushing under foot. If he felt sacrilegious, Kimtasu wasn't bothered. He led on …

When they heard voices. A man's voice. He spoke French.

'Du Bellay!' Bourke hissed softly. Harry caught up. 'Du Bellay's here.'

Bourke lowered his lamp and signalled for Kimtasu to do likewise. But Kimtasu heard the voice of a small child.

'Tasui!' she said in a loud whisper.

Bourke slapped a hand over her mouth. He tweaked their lamps until they barely shone in the blackness. They waited, listening. More scowls in a foreign voice. Then a second voice.

Another man.

Finally, Kimtasu recognised the high-pitched voice of her father, Moimango. He sounded upset, angry, desperate. Kimtasu took a step forward. Bourke blocked her path. 'Wait,' he whispered. Bourke crept to the edge of the house-sized boulder obstructing their view. Through the blackness of a cavern the size of a train station he saw figures, thirty yards away.

Maybe forty.

They were surrounded by a ring of light. Bourke identified Du Bellay immediately, but there was another large man silhouetted at his side. Both seemed to be holding handguns. He saw a struggle and realised Du Bellay was restraining a small child, a native girl.

It was Tasui.

Now Bourke saw Moimango, his wiry old body, slim yet muscular, standing on a rockslide and facing his captors. Then, in the faintest of light from Moimango's burning bamboo torch, Bourke made out the holy of holies. The altar of the gods. A cabin-sized structure built up from thousands of skulls. Bourke knew that cannibals of the past prized their enemy's heads as trophies and that the practice was more prevalent on the coastal areas of New Guinea. But this collection astounded him. At the apex of the pinnacle was one particular skull, painted red and embedded within the eye sockets were cowrie shells staring out into the darkness. As macabre as the entire structure appeared, there was something mesmerising about its entirety. Bourke felt a respect he had never felt before. An awe. A spiritual moment. As he watched on in silence, Moimango retrieved the cowrie skull and climbed down off the *altar*. He passed the artefact to Du Bellay who removed something from the skull that Bourke thought could only be the *Tear of the Eclipse*.

No! Surely not.

Du Bellay looked pleased with himself. He threw the skull aside. It shattered into shards of bone. Moimango cried out in horror. The sacrilege. Such *whitefella* contempt. *The gods will be angry,* he wailed in the Tamesi language. Du Bellay held the artefact, *The Tear of the Eclipse* before him. 'Light!' he demanded.

Bourke watched on as the accomplice reached over with his burning torch. Bourke could make out their devilish features, greedily inspecting the mother of all pearls.

Bourke planned his best move. He had the rifle, but they had pistols and Tasui as hostage. In his moment of indecision Kimtasu pressed forward. Moimango caught movement in the darkness. He recognised his daughter.

'Kimtasu!' he called out.

Tasui twisted about. 'Mother!' she cried in their native language.

Du Bellay turned best he could, his overweight body balanced on the rock pile. Claude de Forbin's position was equally precarious. Du Bellay was spooked.

'Who's there? Show yourselves,' he spoke French before changing to English. 'Show yourselves now I say.'

Bourke rushed forward, snatching Kimtasu by the arm, but the woman wrenched herself free and ran towards her daughter, screaming her name over and over.

'Capitaine Bourke,' Du Bellay yelled. 'Well, is this not a surprise?'

He tugged at Tasui's restraint, and the child squealed as the rope tightened about her neck.

'Stop where you are,' Du Bellay shouted at Kimtasu, now a dozen yards from him.

Harry shouldered his rifle and aimed. Bourke lowered the barrel. 'No Harry. The girl.'

'Back away,' Du Bellay yelled pointing the gun at Tasui. 'Or so help me the little bitch will die.'

'No!'

Du Bellay waved the gun about recklessly. 'Tell her to back off Capitaine Bourke.'

'Kimtasu. Stop.'

Du Bellay fired a warning shot into the air. The bullet ricocheting around the cave. Beneath them the cavern floor quaked, this time more violently.

Somewhere nearby a rockslide echoed around the chamber. Immediately fissures opened up while sporadic cracks appeared in the ground.

Du Bellay stuffed the chicken-egg-sized pearl into his pocket. His bloated face now fearful, he started back, awkwardly tripping on the uneven ground and pulling the child behind him like a dog. Claude de Forbin followed, equally panicked. Neither said a word. They approached Bourke who blocked their path. Du Bellay had the loaded pistol aimed at Tasui. This time his words were cold. Quieter. Calculated. 'Out of my way Capitaine.'

'Leave the girl.'

Du Bellay was arrogant and stubborn. The earth quaked, this time the stalactites around the altar loosened. Mammoth tusk-sized stalactites speared into the ground all about them.

'Take the wretched child,' Du Bellay shrieked, shoving Tasui so she fell to her knees. He threw the rope after her and brought his pistol to bear on Bourke. 'Now move.'

Bourke didn't argue. He stepped aside as Kimtasu ran to her daughter. They embraced. Harry raised the rifle once more, but Bourke's face warned of dire consequences.

We have the girl, let them pass.

The Frenchmen squeezed into the passage and were soon swallowed by darkness. Kimtasu wanted revenge. She made to chase the two men into the narrow passageway, their only exit out when another, more violent tremor, shook the entire cave. More fissures opened. Kimtasu pushed towards the passage.

'Wait!' Bourke took her arm, hauling her back. Overhead several thousands of tons of rock were dislodged from high above. The rumble was deafening. Moimango appeared, snatching Tasui he threw her under a stone ledge. Harry joined them. The avalanche of rubble seemed slow in motion. It broke away in segments first, before the cavern cliff face collapsed completely, blocking off their exit. It was thirty seconds, maybe even a minute before the dust settled enough for them to see they were trapped.

It was eerily quiet.

While Du Bellay had taken the two burning torches, the carbide lamps were intact. Bourke climbed all over the rubble blocking the exit passageway. He could make out slivers of light through gaps in the rubble, but even a rat would have difficulty climbing through. The faint shafts of light shifted, and Bourke realised, to his utmost horror, it was the light from Du Bellay's torches.

The bastards had made it out.

Bourke turned, shining his lamp under the ledge where Moimango had put Tasui. Kimtasu was with them. Harry crawled free, his face smothered with dust. Everyone was in shock. The old scrawny native was first to speak, he held

Kimtasu's carbide lamp, chatting to it with rapid speech. Clicking his tongue, he tried to understand how the gods made this tool of light he held in his hand. To Bourke, Moimango seemed unfazed that they were trapped inside a volcano that would soon become their tomb. Yet he was determined to keep face.

Bourke took Kimtasu by both her hands. 'I am sorry,' he said slowly.

'Sorry? But this is not your doing Jon-o-thon.'

'I have failed you.' Bourke looked at Moimango who had finally worked out how to aim the torch. He pointed it back up the collapsed rubble towards the *altar*. 'I failed your father,' Bourke continued. 'I failed your village. I …'

Moimango interrupted Bourke's speech. He looked impatient. Waving his torch about he rattled off a sentence or two.

'What's he saying?' Bourke asked Kimtasu.

'Moimango, he say Why *whitefella* still here talking. Come. We must leave. The gods are angry.'

'Leave!' Harry said. 'But we are trapped.'

'No, Harry, no Jon-o-thon. Moimango, he say, come. We must climb mountain before climb down mountain.'

'That makes sense,' Bourke said with an air of sarcasm. He was about to query the chieftain's wisdom when the squealing of thousands of bats filled the cavern. As they watched on, the cloud of bats gathered momentum, flying in order, one after the other, into a dark passage not noticed earlier.

Moimango led on.

More fissures tested their passage, opening beneath them. Bourke took Tasui under his arm. 'Where are we going?'

'Come Jon-o-thon. Moimango know way.'

• • •

Monsieur Du Bellay was hauled on board *La Belle Dame* and made his way instantly to his cabin. His increased use of cocaine had now lead to smell loss, nosebleeds, difficulty swallowing, hoarseness of voice, runny nose and heart palpitations. He had become irritable, restless and was experiencing panic attacks. It was suspected he was even experiencing full-on psychosis where he lost touch with reality. Du Bellay was hearing voices.

He snorted two generous lines and wiped powder from his nose, licking his fingers, massaging his gums with the residue. Claude de Forbin caught up with him five minutes later. 'Felix, I've never been so terrified in my life.'

'Nonsense,' Du Bellay's heart was pinging. His red eyes bulged. He was on an extreme high. 'Nothing like a little adventure Claude. Tell Capitaine Badeaux we are to leave this instant.'

'Ah,' de Forbin looked sheepish. 'But that's why I have come to you, to pass on a message from the capitaine that we are to be taking on refugees once the *Acorrazado Espagna* is filled to capacity.'

'What?'

The Spanish ship is taking on refugees …'

'I know that.'

'So Capitaine Badeaux has ordered we are next once the Spanish ship leaves the bay.'

'No!'

'I'm sorry Felix, we have a humanitarian responsibility here.'

'Damned if I'm letting that stop us. Claude, look out the window. People are dying here. We will die here. No I won't have a bar of it. Tell the capitaine we …'

'You tell him Felix.'

'What? How dare you speak to me like that.' Du Bellay shoved Capitaine de Forbin so hard he fell backwards over a chair.

Du Bellay felt the mother of all pearls in his safari jacket pocket. In his other pocket, he felt the comforting cold steel of his Saint Etienne double action revolver. He slammed the cabin door open and stormed the bridge.

The exit from the sacred cave system had been perilous. The route they had used to climb to the caves was a steep narrow valley. It was now a conduit for lava, channelling the molten rock down towards the coast. Moimango indicated another path. Kimtasu, Harry and Bourke hurried after the old man', Tasui had a high vantage point, carried on Bourke's shoulders. The descent was precipitous. Earth tremors threatened rockslides. More fissures opened like old wounds, spitting boiling mud and steam – Nature's vitriol stalking their every move.

Jesus, are we ever going to get away? Harry thought, slashing the jungle with a machete. But he dared not speak the words. Suddenly the jungle opened up. The vista across the bay was so bittersweet – the magnificent view, spoiled by devastation of the coastline, showed they were still a thousand feet above sea-level and a mile from the shoreline.

Then they realised there was a sheer cliff between them and the sea.

Harry stood at the edge and looked down. 'Couple o' hundred feet at least.'

'There's only eighty-foot o' rope in that coil.'

'Hmm,' Harry took a second look over the drop. Moimango joined him, scratching his head. 'There's a ledge two thirds the way down,' Harry said.

'Sure, but we are a hundred foot of rope short.'

Instantly the ground shook.

A huge crack opened at the cliff edge.

'Jesus Harry. That doesn't sound too good.'

Kimtasu called a warning. Twenty feet behind them palms were being pulled into the earth, into fresh crevices like a giant hand tugging at weeds.

'You've gotta be kidding me!' Bourke lifted Tasui from his shoulders to the ground. Holding her firmly by the hand he hurried to the far end of the ledge where a massive rock blocked their path. 'There's gotta be another way.'

A narrow ledge shelf, like the sill circling the outside of a high-rise building, edged around a shed-sized boulder. It was not much wider than Bourke's boots, but it was navigable.

Just.

Bourke called to the others. They rushed over. Harry's jaw dropped. Bourke yelled, 'It's our only chance.'

'Christ cap'n,' Harry puffed out his cheeks. The war veteran suffered from vertigo. 'I dunno 'bout that.'

'Got a better plan?'

The drop was sheer. Hundreds of feet. The ledge was narrow, precarious and damned frightening. But … if they could reach the other side of the huge boulder via the sill, there appeared a natural rock slide that they could negotiate to the jungle below. Bourke turned to Kimtasu.

'This is our only hope.' Kimtasu knew Bourke was right. 'Tell Tasui she must trust me. Do you understand?'

Kimtasu swallowed hard. She dropped to her knees taking her daughter with both hands. The little girl was terrified. Kimtasu said the words over and over in the only language the child understood.

'You must trust my friend,' Kimtasu said. 'He is good a man. He is a brave warrior. You must trust him. I love you. Hold tight.' Tasui nodded, holding back tears. 'Go,' Kimtasu told Bourke. 'Hold her tight.'

Bourke had a dozen feet of restricted shelf to pass. Taking Tasui by the hand, he squeezed hard and pushed his back against the rock. He looked to the young girl and managed a smile. 'Ready?' Tasui guessed what he was asking. 'Ready Tasui?' Tasui nodded, the fear in her eyes evident. Bourke edged along the ledge, tiny shuffles, one shuffle at a time. Slow as she goes. He looked out across the landscape; eyes fixed on the horizon. One slip in his confidence, one slip of the foot, and the two would plunge hundreds of feet to certain death.

Kimtasu, Harry and Moimango watched, terrified for Bourke and the child. Terrified that they were next. No one breathed.

Bourke sensed he was close. He managed to twist his head. Safety was only feet away when he felt a tremor. The boulder at his back vibrated. It appeared to shift slightly. He made hurried last steps, finally jumping the last few feet. Tasui slipped off the ledge, but Bourke held her hand firmly, swinging her wide over the sheer drop and onto terra firma where the child crawled well away from the edge. They had made it.

The others let out a relieved cheer.

Once Tasui was safe Bourke made a quick reconnaissance. A recent rockslide here made it possible to climb down to the jungle. It was steep but negotiable. Kimtasu was next, followed by her father.

Harry, burdened by the heavy rope, called to Bourke, 'Do we need this?'

'No. Leave it.' Bourke was concerned about his mate. Harry was a big man. Bold and bulky. 'Take it easy Harry. Take it real slow.'

Harry stepped unsteadily onto the sill, disturbing loose pebbles. They rolled off the ledge. Harry looked down and wished he hadn't. The rocks scattered out of control, following gravity, plunging hundreds of feet. Harry felt nausea, a little lightheaded. The captain sensed his angst.

'Deep breath in,' Bourke coaxed from the far end. 'Just take it nice and slow.'

Harry shuffled his heavy boots one up against the other, then another shuffle and another, the right foot met the left. Over and over. Harry could feel his heart thumping. His brow dripped sweat. He could taste the salt. He could taste his own fear. Harry had been to war and survived, but heights terrified him far more. Bourke reached out, snatching Harry by the shoulder. He had made it. He pulled his mate towards him the last two feet and Harry fell onto the captain.

'Jesus Christ, I don't wanna do that again,' Harry wheezed. 'Ever.'

· · ·

The rockslide saw them to the jungle, but with the continuous tremors the very rocks that saved them now threatened to crush them. 'We need to get away from here, fast!'

Moimango beckoned the others follow. He knew a path, a route through the jungle used throughout time by his ancestors.

Thousands of feet overhead, the volcano's emissions of toxic smoke and gasses accumulated, blocking out the sun. Day turned to night and the horizon was scarlet.

The shoreline evacuation had been relatively successful, with most craft packed to the gunwales with refugees sailing to safety.

Bourke and Harry had seen this before. The mushroom cloud of smoke and steam pouring out of the volcano was like an industrial chimney about to collapse in on itself. It could only be a matter of time before a pyroclastic blast wiped out the eastern side of Kanantui Island.

· · ·

On board *La Belle Dame*, Capitaine Marcel Badeaux refused to be intimidated by this tiresome, arrogant, self-indulgent, greedy diplomat. From the bridge of *La Belle Dame*, the world looked like a scene of eternal damnation. Molten lava was bulldozing its path of destruction to the beaches. Thousands of islanders had been evacuated but there were still hundreds to save, and the fiercely patriotic sea capitaine was so proud he could help. *In fact*, he thought to himself, *I am one of the last vessels here. My name will go down in the history books.*

'We sail immediately,' Du Bellay squealed. 'At this very minute. You hear me Capitaine Badeaux.'

'Not until we have rescued the remaining islanders.'

'Are you deaf man? I said ...'

'I know what you said, monsieur. Even if I wanted to leave at this minute, we have crew ashore. We leave when I say.'

'Why you insubordinate bastard,' Du Bellay yelled and screamed, rubbing white powder from his face. He pulled his pistol from his pocket, cocked the hammer and pointed the barrel at the capitaine's head. Badeaux flinched. His eye twitched.

Was this man serious?

'I'm deadly serious.'

•　•　•

Only a handful now remained on the beach by the time Bourke and his group found Flash anxiously waiting. With another dozen stragglers, their livestock and the possessions they had with them, the tender sat dangerously low in the water. They motored out towards *Drifter*.

'Du Bellay's still here!' Bourke's face grew dark.

'Are you thinking what I'm thinking cap'n?' Harry's face was lined with anger.

'We'll unload this lot first.'

Harry couldn't agree more. 'And I'll fetch the gun.' The thought of putting the Maschinengewehr 08 back into service curled the corners of Harry's mouth.

•   •   •

It was at this moment Snakeskin Coen summoned the courage to approach *La Belle Dame*. He had been following the fat Frenchman through his spyglass since he arrived, and a shore party had confirmed the man's eagerness to leave the island. By all accounts he had what he had come for. And that could only be *The Tear of the Eclipse*. Using his headsail only, Coen drew alongside the French luxury yacht. In all the mayhem they were hardly noticed until they were only a dozen feet off *La Belle Dame's* starboard side.

Capitaine Marcel Badeaux smelt a rat. He had kept an eye on this gaff-rigged schooner – an unkempt ship that had seen better days – since they appeared in the bay before sunrise. But they had made no effort to evacuate any islanders. In fact, if he didn't know any better he would say they were spying on his yacht. And now he knew all about this cursed pearl Du Bellay was obsessed with, he guessed that is what they were after. He read their stern plate, *Torres Girl*.

'Ahoy there *Torres Girl*,' Badeaux called out through his megaphone in English. 'State your business.'

The rat Badeaux thought he could smell showed his face. 'Permission to come aboard, cap'n.'

'What do you want?'

'Permission to come on board.'

'So you said. And I repeat, what do you want?'

Du Bellay, planning his next move on the insubordinate capitaine, caught the conversation. He made his way from port to starboard. 'Coen!' he scowled through his cocaine fug.

'Ah there you are. Monsieur Du Bellay, ain't it? Felix if I recall correctly.'

Du Bellay flinched. What was this rodent doing here? He patted the pearl in his pocket and the hen's-egg-sized jewel felt even bigger than before. 'What are you doing here Coen?'

'Permission to come on board monsieur.'

'Permission denied.' Capitaine Badeaux said. 'Now cast away if you please.'

'Oh, don't be like that captain,' Coen said. 'Just cos yer got a pretty yacht. Yer don't have to get all snooty with us poor travellers less fortunate than yourselves.'

Du Bellay called up to Badeaux on the bridge wing. 'We need to leave. Now.'

'And I told you monsieur, we will leave after we take on the remaining evacuees.' He twisted back to Coen. 'You there, cast away. That's an order.'

Coen cut to the chase.

He drew a stick of dynamite from his coat pocket, held it high and waved a cigarette lighter about. 'I want the pearl monsieur. And I ain't leaving without it.'

The last thing on Snakeskin Coen's mind was that the French diplomat would be armed. Du Bellay answered by raising the revolver and squeezing the trigger. The bullet buried itself in the hatch. Coen was taken completely by surprise. The second shot had him dive for cover. Coen lit the fuse and the black powder wick sparkled in his hand like a huge firecracker. Du Bellay's drugged senses registered danger. He fired another shot, hopelessly missing.

The wick burnt down.

Coen raised his arm, planning to lob the explosive onto *La Belle Dame*'s amidships, before storming the yacht with Bullet and Jack Lawson. Du Bellay took more careful aim. He fired. This bullet ripped through Coen's hand. Squealing in shock and pain, he dropped the dynamite, which skittled along the deck before disappearing down the companionway. Bullet, Jack Lawson and the deckhands leapt aside.

The resulting explosion blew a great hole in the bottom of *Torres Girl*, which took on water immediately. Within seconds she was sinking in thirty foot of water. The hold opened and Coen's precious cargo of skins destined for Hong Kong escaped back into the sea from whence they had come. Bullet managed to launch their tender. They climbed on board, pulling their wounded skipper in after them.

•   •   •

Du Bellay couldn't believe what had happened in such a short time. But his dark side would be his downfall. Jeering at his adversary, he laughed until he coughed. Suddenly purple-faced, he choked, slipped on the deck and slammed heavily into the gunwale. The unsecured gate flew open, and the Frenchman dropped into the bay. He sank deep. His eyes bulged in fear. Fear of the water. Fear of creatures beyond his control. He kicked frantically for the surface. Movement to his left had him twist about. A shape the size of a horse cruised towards him … a tiger shark.

Initially curious to see what else had fallen into the sea, the shark circled cautiously. Overhead a brief ray of sunshine escaped the blackened sky. A shaft of light highlighted the massive fish's body, like a marbling effect, making the creature look even more threatening. Du Bellay caught sight of other blurred shapes lurking further off, circling. Panicked, he thrashed his arms and legs, kicking for the surface. His small round chubby face gasped air greedily. But his clothes threatened to drag him under. Floundering in panic he managed to jettison his safari jacket. The coat sank immediately, taking with it the mother of all pearls. Those on board *La Belle Dame* were slow to act. But finally, one, then two lifebuoys hit the water near the drowning man. Du Bellay clawed at the life-rings. He was buoyant. He would survive.

He made strokes towards the ship now twenty feet away. Without warning something rubbed by his leg. Another creature swam in front of him. Instantly Du Bellay was surrounded by crocodiles. Ten, twelve, maybe fifteen of the twelve-foot beasts. They circled him. Death was imminent. Du Bellay thrashed and screamed but before the crocodiles attacked the Frenchman suffered a heart attack. He drowned before an audience, dying pathetically, fitting for a man whose life had been devoted to greed.

By now several crew members were watching from the ship. Amongst them Claude de Forbin, watched on as *La Belle Dame's* crew used grappling hooks to hoist aboard the floating crocodile skins from Coen's hold.

* * *

If it wasn't so serious it would have been funny. Bourke and his crew saw everything. As they coasted alongside *La Belle Dame*, they watched Felix Du Bellay's body retrieved from the bay. He was clearly dead.

Capitaine Marcel Badeaux was dumbfounded. The interest in this cursed black pearl was disturbing. Bourke singled out Capitaine Claude de Forbin. The man made no attempt to hide.

'The pearl,' Bourke called over the mayhem still unfolding all about them. 'That pearl belongs to the people of this island. Where is it?'

'It was in his coat monsieur, he discarded it. It is gone.'

'Gone!'

'Where?'

'To the bottom.'

Bourke paced the deck, peering into the crystal-clear waters of the tropical cove. It was thirty feet deep. Tops. But damned if he could see anything, although the bottom was clear and sandy. Surely …

Ripping his shirt free, Bourke snatched a deep breath and dived into the bay. He kicked off directly for the bottom. With powerful strokes he swam to two fathoms above the bottom. There was no discarded coat. Although the current was minimal there was no sign. Bourke surfaced. He floated a moment, scouring the seabed. Then he saw it. A safari jacket, weightlessly gathered around a knob of coral covered in seagrass. Once again, he descended, kicking hard for the bottom. He didn't hear the warning before he dived.

Shark!

The female tiger sensed its prey from a hundred feet away. With a powerful flick of her tail the shark propelled forward ... in for the attack. There was no reason to circle. This was easy pickings.

Bourke swam over the coat. He searched the pockets and couldn't believe his good fortune. The pearl was there in the left pocket. He was running out of breath. There was no time to admire the jewel. He pushed it into his pocket and kicked away from the sandy bottom. Instantly he caught the shark in his peripheral vision. It was headed for him ... and at speed, with open jaws.

Bourke slipped his knife from its sheath but in his urgency he dropped it. The huge tiger shark came at its prey with the speed of a torpedo. Bourke back-paddled. Aware he was shouting underwater he prepared to fend off the monster. Kicking. Punching, when ...

The first dolphin glanced off the shark, punching its nose into its underbelly. The second dolphin ploughed into its side. Blindsided, the shark veered off only feet from its target. The dolphins circled the shark. Another two, three joined the first. Never had Bourke experienced such a connection with nature. The shark also circled. But it had to admit defeat.

Bourke's lungs were bursting. He pushed off once more for the surface where Harry, Ivan and Flash dragged him on board.

Bourke sprawled on his back on the deck, laughing nervously between gasps of air. He was immediately surrounded by Kimtasu, Tasui, Moimango and his crew. Juvita was the first to speak.

'You one lucky mans, Jon-o-thon.'

Kimtasu was the only one not revelling. Bourke took the pearl from his pocket and, keeping it hidden in his closed fist, he looked Kimtasu in the eye, his expression one of failure.

'Sorry,' he shook his head.

Kimtasu's shoulders sagged. But she would not give up. Kimtasu peered over the side of the ship once more. She searched the seabed before stripping to her underclothes.

'Wait!' Bourke yelled anxiously, not having thought she would dive after the pearl. "Kimtasu. Wait.'

Bourke caught her as she mounted the gunwale. He pulled her back. 'Here.' Like a conjuror would reveal a ball, Bourke opened his hand revealing the sacred talisman. The lustre of the pearl was breathtaking, seen for the first time in the open. Bourke opened Kimtasu's hand, placing the pearl reverently in her palm. Kimtasu nursed it in both hands, before passing it onto her father. Bourke felt a kinship with these people. The gratitude they now displayed had been worth risking his life.

· · ·

Suddenly a ripple juddered across the bay. All about the coastline the earth shook. A mile overhead, into the clouds over Kanantui, the volcanic ash was cooling. As they watched on the monstrous mushroom shaped cloud was collapsing in on itself. Already fine pumice was raining down out on the bay. Bourke scanned the beaches with his binoculars. The village was deserted. The buildings were ablaze, the lava was spilling into the sea. It was time to flee.

•   •   •

It had been a harrowing escape. All vessels had maintained radio contact and rendezvoused at the Witu Islands, half a day's sail on the east coast of Papua New Guinea and north of the largest island in the territory, New Britain, recently renamed following the collapse of Germany's Protectorate in the Coral Sea.

While other tribes inhabiting the coast here, on the Witu Islands, welcomed the Tamesi, the resettlement would always be a temporary solution. The Tamesi people were a proud race who had lived with volcanos, earthquakes, and tsunamis for generations. They would return to Kanantui, Bourke just knew it. But for Bourke it had been heart-warming to see Kimtasu reunited with her daughter. That night a celebration was held, the Tamesi thanking their gods they were still in the land of the living.

The next morning the *Drifter* crew paid their respects and were seen off by the natives in grand style. Hundreds of Witu Islanders paddled alongside the whitefella steamers as they all set sail for home. Captain Jonathon Bourke was allowed one last glimpse at the *Tear of the Eclipse* and now the pieces of the puzzle all joined together. Kimtasu was a descendent of the kidnapped princess, all those generations ago in Tahiti. She was but a guardian of the mother of all pearls, and would see the responsibility passed onto her daughter, Tasui.

Tasui finally realised the whitefellas were leaving and raced into the surf as Flash started the longboat's outboard.

'Jon-a-thon!' she cried out, sounding like her mother. The child was chest deep in water. Bourke hailed Flash to hold steady and Tasui climbed into *Drifter's* tender. The little girl hugged her hero. Bourke returned the affection.

'Au revoir,' she said.

Bourke had a tear in his eye. Had her mother taught her those whitefella words? He gave Tasui a final hug before lowering her back into the water, and threw Kimtasu and Moimango a final wave. Sadly, Tamesi custom forbade their liaison.

On the bridge Arsala watched the tender raised into the davits before telegraphing Bill Brown in the engine room, *slow ahead.* Bourke joined him.

'I tell you true Captain Bourke sir. You are one lucky mans, yes.'

'Aye to that matey.'

'Where to captain? Because I must tell you we are very very low on coal.'

'I guessed as much. Then we better head to Port Moresby my friend, and then home to Cooktown.'

Honolulu would have to wait.

CHAPTER EIGHTEEN

Port Moresby Harbour

Port Moresby's coaling station was busy this day. At least seven vessels waited to fill their coal bunkers before continuing their various journeys. Arsala and Juvita joined Bourke, Harry, Ivan and Flash on the bridge. Here the playful screams of children splashing about at the water's edge or playing in the fishermen's beached canoes could be heard travelling across the water as clear as if they were on board.

The crew watched in silence a while, each alone, no doubt, with their own childhood memories, and stared with interest at the village of Hanuabada. Here the native huts with flimsy grass roofs sat precariously on tall thin stilts. They looked as though the gentlest breeze would knock them over. There wasn't a great deal else to attract visitors to Papua New Guinea's largest port.

'Back in the 1880s this was called British New Guinea,' Bourke said. 'Until we got our Federation in Australia twenty odd years ago.'

'Now its Australian territory?'

'Technically, well, yes.'

Harry lit his pipe, passing it to Ivan for a puff, when Bourke noticed Flash had changed his shirt for a clean one.

'Going somewhere?' Bourke asked with a cheeky grin.

'Cap'n?'

'I said are you going somewhere Flash? You've changed your shirt I notice.'

If the semi-naked native women waving to the vessels from the beach had caught Flash's attention, he wasn't letting on. 'Oh, I … ah …. I thought it's about time I changed it cap'n, been wearing the other one a week now.'

'Fair enough. Cos if you were thinking of going ashore, there's no pub.'

'No pub?'

'Don't be daft,' Harry said. 'They didn't even have a grocery shop here until a few years back and only now I hear there's talk of finally getting electricity to the port.'

'No pub?' Flash repeated, his shoulders stooping within his clean shirt.

Ivan blew a perfect smoke ring. 'There's not much of anything there by the look of it.'

'There is a gentlemen's club for government officials and their well-dressed visitors,' Bourke said, nodding to neat white timber and iron roofed government buildings up on the hill. 'But I'm not certain the common seaman would be welcomed, Flash.'

'Yes Flash, clean shirt or not.'

'Thanks.' Flash smiled. 'That's a real vote o' confidence. How long are we stuck here then?'

Bourke called down to fireman and stoker Bill Brown on the main deck. 'Bill? What's the latest?'

'We've got the Hun *Kormoran* to load up before us then it's our turn,' Bill pointed to the German yacht moored only twenty yards away.

'Good.' Bourke looked at the steamer *Kormoran*, a 230-foot, 800-ton yacht. Built in 1920, Bourke knew of the luxury passenger yacht cruising the Pacific the past six months and wondered what attracted the wealthy owner to this part of the seven seas. Laughter drew their attention to the stern where drinks were liberally passed about.

•   •   •

The loud German host, Herr Jonas Kaulitz was gloating. Schnapps always made the rich forty-year-old adventurer gloat. 'Prost!' the man saluted, holding his shot glass of schnapps high before sculling it. His entourage of mixed crew and passengers did likewise. He slammed his empty glass on the table for the steward to refill when Bourke saw it …

It was a glint reflected in the sun. Just a flash before someone stepped to the table blocking Bourke's view.

'Arsala!'

'Yes, yes, captain sir. What is it now?'

'Pass me the binoculars.'

All heads on *Drifter's* bridge followed Captain Jonathon Bourke's eye as he focussed the field glasses on the rowdy Germans.

Harry said, 'What is it Cap'n?'

They watched Bourke, his tongue slipping from the corner of his mouth involuntarily, concentrating on the table of refreshments. He salivated. Bodies shifted before the lens. 'Move it, move,' Bourke whispered to the Germans blocking his view. At twenty yards he was certainly close enough. 'Jesus Christ, get outa the way!'

Immediately he had a clear view.

'Mother of Jesus!'

'What is it cap'n?'

'Here,' Bourke passed the binoculars to Arsala. 'Tell me I'm not seeing things.'

Arsala focussed. 'Where captain sir?'

'On the table man.'

'No!'

'So, I'm not seeing things?'

Harry shifted, impatiently. 'What are yer on about fer Christ's sake?'

'Gold!' Arsala said. 'It is a gold bar is it not?'

'Certainly is,' Bourke snatched back the glasses. 'And what is a bloody great gold bar doing being toasted on board a German ship in the Coral Sea I ask you?'

'I tell you true, captain sir,' Arsala said. 'Arsala is not possible to answer this question,'

Instantly the gathering on the bridge of the old steamer flying the Federation flag of Australia, captured the German revellers' attention.

'You there,' the strong German accented voice carried clearly across the water. 'You like to join our party, ja?'

It was the host.

Bourke's face reddened. He didn't realise he was so obvious. He lowered the glasses. 'Ah … good day to you sir,' he called back.

'Come, come,' the German beckoned. 'Ve have schnapps from Bavaria, das ist gut, ja? Come join your Deutschland friends.'

Friends?

Bourke passed the glasses to Harry who hissed out the corner of his mouth. 'Bloody Krauts cap'n.'

'Yes Harry. But the war ended six years ago. Besides I want a closer look at that gold bar.'

Jonathon and Harry both had to concede that they did not like Germans. Not since the war. And they had killed a few between them mind you. But to be fair, they had never sat down and had a conversation with one. So, to Bourke, Herr Jonas Kaulitz seemed the typical loud and arrogant Hun he knew from France, but that gold bar had him intrigued.

•   •   •

'Gut, gut,' the German host welcomed Bourke, Harry, Ivan, Arsala and Juvita aboard. The man had long athletic legs and a spring of enthusiasm in his step. 'Willkommen … ah … *wel-come* you say in Eeng-leesh. Wel-come aboard my yacht *Kormoran*. Herr Jonas Kaulitz at your pleasure.'

Another older man in a brass-buttoned uniform joined them as they stepped onto the deck. 'And thees ist my kapitan, Kapitan Dieter Klum.'

Bourke did the honours, introducing the others. He thought the German pallid, pale skinned for a man travelling the tropics. Clearly, he avoided direct sunlight. His symmetrically oval shaped head bore a high forehead with well-oiled hair, neatly combed back. Eyebrows were trimmed to follow the brow, with the most perfect trimmed moustache, Kaiser Wilhelm II style – thick, and covering the upper lip to the nose, with tapered ends pointing skywards, rather looking like a large hairy 'W', Bourke fancied. There were no sideburns. The hair disappeared behind his white ears in an orderly fashion. But the eyes …

Bourke found the black eyes unsettling.

The man seemed unable to smile, his glare intense. He appeared to analyse his company.

'We drink schnapps, ja?' Kaulitz clicked his fingers. The steward appeared promptly with a tray of shot glasses full of clear liquid. At Kaulitz's insistence they met the others, an incongruous mix of passengers Bourke judged as hangers-on.

'Prost,' Kaulitz clicked his heels and drank in one gulp. The *Drifter* crew followed suit. The white spirit was actually good quality and put an immediate fire in the belly.

Bourke drew attention to the gold ingot on the table as subtly as possible. 'Is that what I think it is?' he asked.

'Ah, ja, ja,' Kaulitz's stern demeanour relaxed ever so slightly. 'That is vot drew your attention to our small gathering, isn't it?'

'Sorry! What was that?'

'I said that is why you were … how you say …ah, spying on us, ja.'

Bourke was about to defend himself when he realised there was no point. 'Was it that obvious?'

'Vell ja … lookeen at us with your glasses from close up.' Kaulitz pointed with his chin to the table. 'You are welcome to look at it if you vont.'

As a child Jonathon had seen a sketch made by his father back in the late '90s. It was a drawing of a gold bar exactly the same as this one. A fist-sized ingot smelted into a crude clay mould and stamped with Chinese chop marks. His father, Captain Jonathon Bourke told him stories as a child, of his role in sinking the German gunboat SS *Prinzessin* on a reef off the Solomons, and how the ship sank in deep water with a large quantity of gold bullion on board. Bourke weighted the gold in his hand.

'Where did you get it?' he asked as nonchalantly as was possible, trying his hardest to feign disinterest.

'You like?'

'It's gold right?'

'Ja, gut, gut.'

'It has Chinese assayer markings.'

'Ja. You know these.' Kaulitz studied Bourke carefully. 'But I am thinking you already know these things.'

'No,' Bourke tore his eyes off the gold bar, passing it to Arsala for inspection. 'No, you are mistaken Herr Kaulitz.'

'Please … Jonas.'

'Jonas. Where *did* it come from? I am curious.'

'I will wager a bet that you *are* curious, friend.' Kaulitz reached out and took the ingot from Arsala, passing it to the steward nearby with orders in German. 'Put this back in my locker.'

'All I am at liberty to say is that it is from a lost ship, a German ship, sunk twenty-eight years ago off the Solomon Islands.'

Bourke had had enough *fishing*. It was time to plant the seed. 'The SS *Prinzessin*?'

'Ah. So, you *do* know.'

'I've heard stories.'

'Stories huh?'

'Yes. And the bullion was lost in deep water off a reef, so deep in fact it can't be retrieved.'

'Oh, that story. Ja. I hear these things as well Jon-a-thon. But *so deep in fact it can't be retrieved* ... I think not.'

'So ...' Bourke started, but was cut short.

'Ah Victoria,' Kaulitz beamed as a most attractive women appeared on the quarterdeck. 'She has finally surfaced from her cabin,' he said aloud for all present to hear. 'Come my love, we have guests.'

Bourke was lost for words. A most attractive woman of medium height, a strawberry blonde with the softest blue eyes and kind face held the seaman's gaze. Bourke didn't mean to be rude, maybe he simply didn't think, but he gaped at the approaching beauty like Howard Carter must have gaped when he opened Pharaoh Tut-Ankh-Amun's sarcophagus a few years earlier. Arsala gave his captain a subtle nudge.

Victoria gave the others a cursory glance but was instantly drawn to the tall sea captain before her. A most handsome man in his early thirties, chiselled jaw, shoulder-length hazel hair tied back in a ponytail, dark striking eyes, and a fashionable pencil thin moustache. He reminded the young German woman of Clark Gable, the Hollywood heart throb. Bourke was unexpectedly lost for words.

Harry, standing at his captain's side whispered, 'Yer drooling cap'n.'

Bourke snapped from his distraction.

'This is Victoria,' Kaulitz said. 'I'd like you to meet Harry, ah ... Salty, Arsala and Juvita from off *Drifter* alongside us.'

'Guten Morgen, es ist mir eine Freude dich kennenzulernen.'

'In English my dear. These people are Australian.'

'Very good. It is a pleasure to meet you.' Victoria turned to face Bourke with a smile that would sink ships. 'And you must be the kapitan?'

'Y-yes. Jonathon ...' Bourke cleared his throat. 'Jonathon Bourke.' Suddenly Bourke was aware his Australian twang sounded coarse after the poetry of this most beautiful woman's accented English.

Jonathon Bourke was immediately smitten. The Australian captain was floundering on board a foreign vessel. The man with the gift of the gab, as his mates often told him, was drowning in self-doubt.

'Australian?' Victoria studied *Drifter* a moment. 'What part?'

'Part?'

'Yes, what part of Australia are you from?'

'Uh, Cooktown.'

'Is that near Darwin?'

'Not really, Darwin's way up north. Cooktown's a small town in north Queensland.'

Kaulitz called for more drinks and Victoria shot a schnapps with the ease of any man on board. 'You must stay for lunch,' she told Bourke.

'Oh ... ah ... we can't, we are ...'

'Nonsense,' Kaulitz interrupted. 'You are our guests. Cook has prepared my favourite food, Rouladen and freshly baked brot, German rye bread to soak up the sauce.'

'And,' Victoria took Bourke's arm, 'Cook always prepares for extra diners.'

Bourke looked at the expectant entourage already nibbling on platters of cold sausage and pickles being handed around and felt his stomach rumble. Those in earshot agreed ...

Cook always prepares for extra diners.

Bourke looked to his crew. Juvita for one was keen to try German food. 'Very well, thank you.'

The table was set for twenty on the quarterdeck, complete with tablecloth, monogrammed crockery and silverware. The roulade of pickles and bacon wrapped in thin slices of veal braised in a rich gravy and served with dumplings, mashed potato and cabbage was superb. The wine flowed freely. Bourke relaxed. Victoria, at Bourke's side, was keen to learn all she could about Australia, while Bourke took care not to show too much interest in Victoria, not with Herr Jonas Kaulitz sitting opposite. This of course, only made Victoria more determined.

'So,' Victoria asked Bourke while her wine glass was being replenished and Kaulitz was deep in conversation with the man sitting next to him. 'What do you think of my uncle?'

'Uncle?'

'Uncle Jonas.'

'He's your uncle?'

'Yes!' Victoria turned bodily to face Jonathon with a look that could only be described as incredulous. 'Who did you think he was? My father? My husband?' Bourke's face said it all. 'You thought Jonas was my husband, didn't you?' Bourke flushed. Victoria laughed out loud.

'He is an old man, forty something. I am only twenty-eight, I am attracted to older men, certainly, like thirty-three, thirty-four maybe,' Victoria had placed her hand on Jonathon's arm. 'But forty? No.'

Jonathon Bourke's confidence rushed back. Suddenly the rooster in him surfaced. 'How stupid of me,' he drained his glass and poured them both refills from the wine jug on the table. 'As if such a beautiful woman as yourself would marry an old man.'

Sitting opposite Kaulitz noted Bourke's renewed interest. 'Did you ask kapitan Bourke already my dear,' he asked Victoria across the table.

'Ask me what?'

'Well, my niece is desperate to return to Germany. She came on this journey, my quest to find the *Prinzessin*, but she has since changed her mind. You sitting here at my table, Kapitan Bourke, is not entirely a coincidence.'

'Oh?'

'No sir. I have asked about. I have made enquiries around the harbour and you have a reputation as a valiant man, although an entrepreneur with some less than legal trade. But hey, who am I to judge. The bottom line is you are a gentleman, mostly.'

'What are you getting at, Jonas?'

'I can't return to Germany until I fulfill my mission. My niece needs to travel to Darwin where she can voyage to Singapore and then onto Europe through the Suez Canal. We, I, would appreciate you taking my niece safely to Darwin. I will pay you handsomely kapitan.'

'Pay? But I'm not sailing anywhere near Darwin.'

'As I said. I will reimburse you handsomely.'

'With gold?'

'I will present you with the *Prinzessin* ingot.'

Victoria pretended to be affronted. 'So, is that all I am worth, a gold bar?' Embarrassed, Bourke had to concede he was falling for this woman. 'Then in that case, let us drink to gold.'

'To gold,' Bourke saluted.

Victoria finished her wine and placed her hand on Jonathon's arm once more. 'My uncle calls me Victoria,' she smiled. Such a smile the likes of which Jonathon Bourke could not possibly resist. 'But I prefer, just Vicky.'

THE END

EPILOGUE

Of course, Vicky wasn't going to make it back to Germany. Not in a hurry anyhow. She didn't even make it to Darwin. Captain Jonathon Bourke would see to that. They married the following year. But Vicky found the tropics exhausting, and Bourke agreed life was tough as a pioneer in North Queensland. Craving a cooler climate they moved to Tasmania, as far south as possible, and invested in apple orchards, doing very nicely indeed. Here their family grew along with generations of descendants.

Salty married his native sweetheart Dua, eventually assisting the Tamesi people to return to Kanantui. But Dua had had a taste of whitefella's Australia. They eventually moved to Cooktown where Bourke gave over half the cannery to Salty, who, along with Dua, made a continued success of it. After the American prohibition ended on the 5th of December 1933, the distillery was dismantled.

Harry Pickles settled in Sydney where he lived with his brother for a short spell. However, he was forced onto the wrong side of the law when his brother's wife was killed by a member of a razor gang in Woolloomooloo. Harry became a vigilante, he hunted down those responsible, only to be arrested by police for carrying a concealed pistol. At fifty-five years of age in 1927

Harry was incarcerated at Long Bay. Although he was a model prisoner, he learnt the art of crime and when he was released he disappeared underground in 1928. It was rumoured he was responsible for several high-profile bank robberies. But he was never convicted.

Du Bellay's reluctant partner in crime, Capitaine Claude de Forbin, finally arrived in Melbourne with the hundred one-pound bags of cocaine, only to be arrested by federal police. Huang Ying, it appeared, had become an informer to the law, after his own arrest not long after Du Bellay had sailed for Cooktown a year earlier. Forbin became a long serving guest of the Australian Government in Pentridge Prison.

Jonathon Bourke felt a heavy bond with the crude gold ingot given him by Vicky's uncle. It was a direct connection with his father's misadventure sinking the SS *Prinzessin* in 1898. He happily paid all his crew a bonus and kept the lump of gold with his other trophies.

When the cannery passed to Salty and Dua. Arsala and Juvita moved to Singapore and opened a food stall in a hawker centre in Bugis Village, specialising in seafood.

As for Monsieur Felix Du Bellay: Natives returning to Kanantui Island some weeks later found his mauled body washed up half a mile from the bay. He was identified as the evil whitefella, the whitefella who tried to steal the *Tear of the Eclipse*. For this reason, he was seen as the perfect vessel to guard the cursed pearl for future generations. His skull was picked clean by the birds, painted with red ochre. Cowrie shells were glued into his eye sockets and he was placed deep within the sacred cave, atop a cairn of other victim's skulls, where for eternity, he wears the pearl upon his head in a shell tiara.

Madame Vignetta Du Bellay never found out what happened to her husband but it was said she enjoyed a long life as a socialite at Lake Como in Italy. Kimtasu returned to her home island, united in tribal wedlock, and bore Tasui several siblings.

ACKNOWLEDGEMENTS

Arthur J Money's castaway misfortune was inspired by the writings of true castaway Daniel Foss in 1810-15. Isle of Pines colonial prison and Devil's Island both existed.

The 'Tamesi' people are fictional, although I have drawn on South-West Pacific islander history for this novel. Kanantui Island is based on Long Island, named by Dampier in 1770. For the sake of a novel, the fictitious name Kanantui sounds better I believe. However, there are two volcanoes on Long Island: Cerisy Peak and Mount Reaumur. As they were not indigenous names, I called them Tekahui and Wewakhui.

ABOUT THE AUTHOR

Craig Godfrey was born in Hobart in 1952 and traveled extensively giving him the experiences and escapades he so enjoys putting into print. This includes working as a chef for a restaurant owned by Sydney underbelly figures in the early 70's and cooking in Darwin when Cyclone Tracy destroyed the city in 1974.

In the 90's, Craig independently shot two feature films, a murder mystery set in Southern Tasmania sold to the Nine Network and a splatter comedy, *Back from the Dead*, available online.

A major interest of Craig's is history and, in particular, the stories behind the Transportation of Convicts, the backbone of Australia's population today. Using Tasmania as a blank canvas, Craig loves nothing more than weaving fiction and adventure through archival facts.

NOTE FROM THE AUTHOR

Word-of-mouth is crucial for any author to succeed. If you enjoyed *Cap'n Jonathon Bourke*, please leave a review online — anywhere you are able. Even if it's just a sentence or two. It would make all the difference and would be very much appreciated.

Thanks!
Craig Godfrey

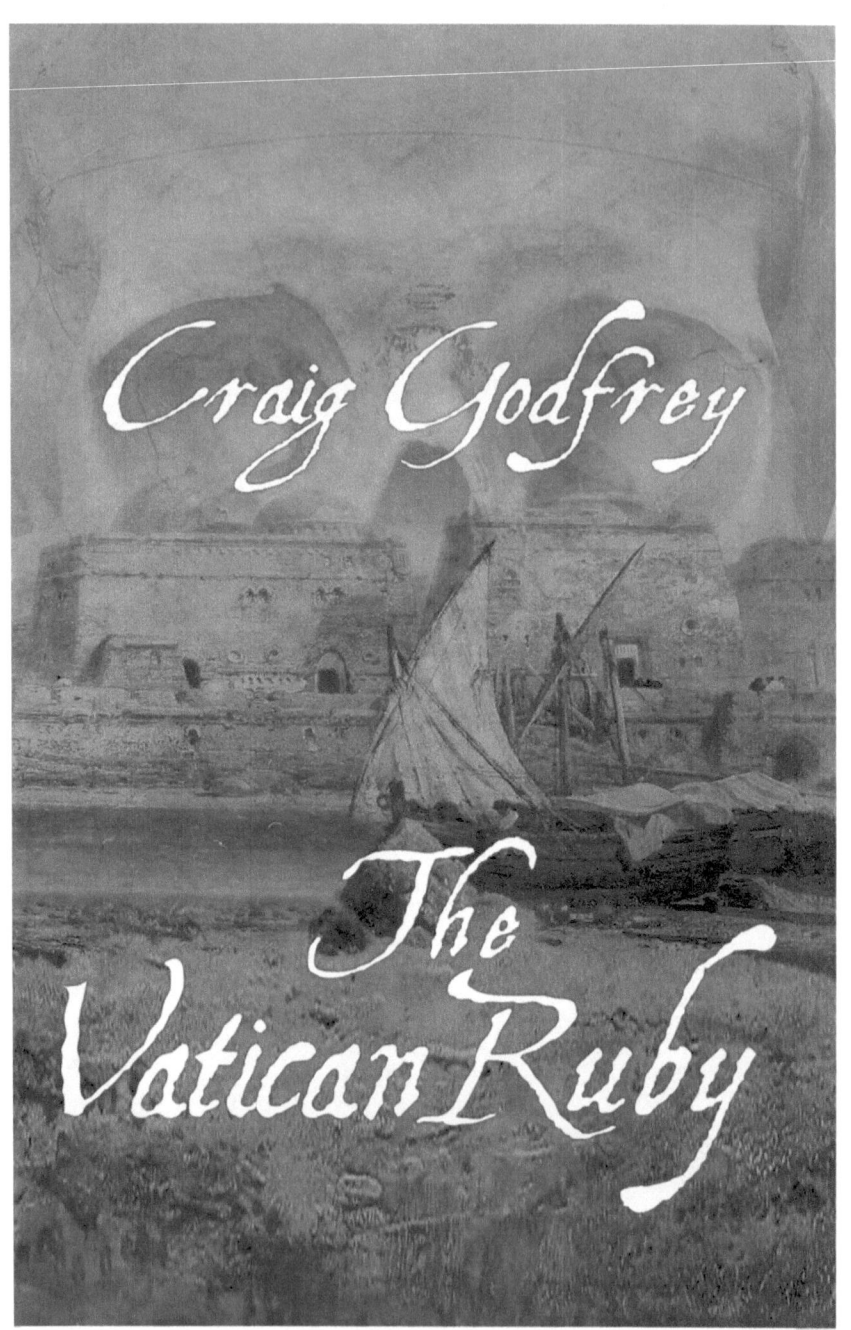

We hope you enjoyed reading this title from:

BLACK🌹ROSE
writing™

www.blackrosewriting.com

Subscribe to our mailing list – *The Rosevine* – and receive **FREE** books, daily deals, and stay current with news about upcoming releases and our hottest authors.
Scan the QR code below to sign up.

Already a subscriber? Please accept a sincere thank you for being a fan of Black Rose Writing authors.

View other Black Rose Writing titles at
www.blackrosewriting.com/books and use promo code
PRINT to receive a **20% discount** when purchasing.